Tarnished Heroes

By David Kessler

First published in Great Britain in 1998 by Hodder and Stoughton

First published in paperback in 1999 by Coronet
A division of Hodder Headline PLC

This edition published by House of Solomon 2014

ISBN: 978-1-904037-42-2

Chapter 1

Rose Crowne was aware of the man's eyes upon her. She didn't need to pull the old stunt of taking out a powder compact and looking in the mirror. She felt the danger in the proverbial tingling at the back of the neck. It might be a cliché, she thought, but it's real.

She had felt the claw of his stare gripping the back of her neck even before she had stepped out into the slightly chilly night air from Jack Straw's Castle, a pub on the border of Hampstead Heath. She had been sure that he would follow her from the moment she had caught his eye in the mirror beside the bar. It was one of those old-fashioned advertising mirrors, with the name of a long-established brewery emblazoned across it. A few minutes earlier she had paused in front of it to check out her appearance and had noticed him staring at her.

He was just above average height, and his build seemed fuller than when he had last been in the news. His face was also rounder, but not to the extent that she could have failed to recognize him. It was only about five years since the whole thing had started and he must be about thirty-three now. He had that same stooping posture when he walked, though it escaped attention as long as he stood still. His trousers were beige and his shirt white, like a flag of surrender. Not that surrender was a word that she associated with a man like him.

She had studiously avoided eye contact with him after that single moment with the mirror, turning her back on him and looking down as she finished her drink, a lemon bitter shandy. The pub had an old-fashioned feeling about it, an ambience created by the dark brown wood of the furniture. There was an awkward kind of "almost matching" quality about the different shades and grains of wood, marked by variation between the tables, chairs and floorboards. The pub was large, but reduced to warm, cosy sections by pillars, beams and partitions of the same dark wood that slashed their way across it. It was a place where people could enjoy the feeling of being out of their homes and yet still be sheltered from others, a place where privacy shook hands with freedom.

But it was hard to admire the decor when she was so alert to the danger posed by the man who had been watching her. From his reactions, if nothing else, she knew that she had set in motion a chain of events over which she had, at best, very limited control.

As she stepped out of the pub into the darkness, she saw across the road, the great stone monument rising up majestically, dedicated to "the men and women of Hampstead who gave their lives for their country in two great wars. "

She had intended to turn right and walk towards Hampstead station. That was nearer than Golders Green. But there might be fewer people around when she got there. If she turned left, on the other hand, she could go to Golders Green with its bus terminal and brightly-lit late-night bakery where the Jewish teenagers hung out on almost every night except Friday when the Jewish Sabbath commenced at sunset. But she would have to walk through a dark lonely stretch of road to get there.

In an instant of sudden awakening to the situation, she became aware of the fact that she was out of her depth – though it was hard to say what had brought this awareness upon her. The silence seemed like the obvious candidate for blame. But it couldn't have been the silence alone, for it was far from complete. It was permeated by the occasional rumble of a car engine in the background. It was the absence of other people, she realized. She had expected people to be spilling out of the pubs after closing time. But tonight was a Monday, when people went home, exhausted from the first day of work after the fun and games of the weekend.

Monday was a quiet day for places of entertainment and Rose Crowne realised now that the scarcity of people in the pub itself wasn't just an odd coincidence. But, if she was to conquer her demons from the past, she would have to go this way, not in spite of, but *because* of the danger.

The prospect of turning right and walking past the Pond to Hampstead tube station, offered itself to her as a tempting proposition. But it also seemed to mock her. It was as if it was telling her that she lacked the courage of the men and women whose memorial stood there opposite – a subtle form of critical contempt of her for the dilemma over which she was agonizing. Then her fear gave way to ire.

I'm not a frightened little girl, she told herself. *I'm a grown woman. I don't have to fear the darkness - or a man who's probably more frightened of me than I am of him.*

The decision was made neither by reason nor by fear. It was made by anger.

She turned left, sharply, determined to go through with it, gripping the CS spray canister in her handbag as she started the long trek. She carried herself forward with brisk strides. The anger had drowned out the fear, like a wave sweeping over a rock. But when the wave passed, the rock was still there – likewise the fear.

She continued hurriedly on her way.

To her right, across the road, was a brick wall, the demarcation line of some stretch of private land. To her left was the dark, shapeless void of Golders Hill Park, the western part of Hampstead Heath, a wilderness at night, where beauty merged with uncertainty like a cold sea. On a summer's day its green carpet was as warm and inviting as any tropical paradise, but at night it was a desolate expanse of bleak emptiness as inhospitable as a minefield in a war-torn country.

And yet it held Rose Crowne's attention. As fearful a sight as it was in the thick darkness, it was also a sight that aroused her curiosity. Its trees – dark, spreading silhouettes of giants – stood there almost as an impudent challenge, daring her to face their silent menace, if not to enter their hostile domain.

She had read somewhere that beneath this area, the Northern Line of the London Underground reached its lowest point below the surface, probably in the area of the Pond to the right of Jack Straw's Castle. Yet here, on the surface, with only the open night sky overhead, she felt as vulnerable as if she were locked up in the bowels of the earth.

She didn't understand why now, of all times, she remembered the fishing trip.

It was when she was thirteen, when her father had come back into her life. Her parents were still together, but there had been a period when for several years she had barely seen her father. He was working for an oil company in a far-off country "called Abba Dabba" her mother had said and couldn't see her often. She

4

resented his absence, but her mother had always spoken well of him. It was only when he came back home, looking bitter and broken, that she really got to know him and feel sorry for him. That was when she had learned words like "redundancy" and "downsizing".

It was ironic that the father who had had so little time for her in her childhood had so much time to share with her now, in her adolescence, when she wanted to join in with a new crowd of friends and do her own thing. But she was never very good at socializing anyway and her selfishness towards her father melted away, along with her resentment for his past absence. He seemed to be trying to atone for his own selfishness of the past, to obtain absolution for an act of abandonment. Also, she never really was one for blending in with a group. And in any case, at least he wasn't trying to run her life or restrict her freedom the way some of her peers' parents did. The only thing he was demanding of her was time, and even then he knew not to push too hard.

But the fishing trip was something special. It was during the summer holidays, when for once she had the time to share his free time. He had taken her to the Lake District, where for five days they shared the pleasure of living close to nature.

*　　*

Martin Roebuck felt a pang of excitement when he saw the woman. It was so unexpected and welcome. The glance in the mirror, the smile that slipped away to be replaced by a frown when she caught his reflection. She was in her mid-twenties and she was afraid – he could see that. She was not his perfect type, but certainly a good approximation. She was blonde and the eyes were blue. The cheekbones were not as high as he would have liked, but the hips were wide. Her arms and shoulders, in contrast, were thin. Most significantly, she did not look strong.

She was wearing a short skirt, displaying bare thighs that were ample, but not over-ample, at least not to Roebuck's taste. The open display of flesh and the flimsiness of the white fabric gave her a look of vulnerability but he sensed that this was deliberate, in a manner of speaking. Monday was not the most likely night for going 'on the pull', yet here she was, all tarted up like she was putting herself in a showcase if not on the market. 'Prostitute' was the first word that came to mind when he caught sight of her in the pub, with her back to him. Not 'slag' or 'slapper', but 'prostitute'.

It was so unexpected, so frightening… and so thrilling. He had thought that he would never again get a chance like this. Yet here it was presenting itself to him – if indeed it *was* a chance. Past experience had taught him to be suspicious.

But when he saw her walking towards the door, he decided to follow her.

* *

'I don't know how you can say that the moon landing never took place, Beth,' an irritated man's voice came through the radio. 'The broadcasts from Apollo were picked up all over the place.'

'You know, Robert,' a confident sounding woman with an American accent cut back. Some people can be very naive. All those so-called moon walks were filmed on a studio back lot in Hollywood. The Americans didn't have the technology to send a man to the moon in 1969. They were just trying to frighten the Russians, like when they bombed Hiroshima.'

'Yet you're saying they had the technology to *fake* the landing and fool the Russians?'

'That's right. Scientists have analyzed the pictures from the moon landing and found that they were fake. Let's go to John on line three.'

In a police car a few miles away, the voices were coming over through the radio.

'Why do you listen to that crap?' asked PC Douglas, naturedly, flicking a strand of dark hair out of his eyes.

His patience was fraying a little at yet another example of what passed for intelligent discussion on talk radio these days.

'Who, Beth Porter?' asked PC Lloyd. 'I like her. She's kind of sexy.'

'You've seen her?' asked Neil.

'No, but her voice is kind of sexy.'

The frown on Neil's round boyish face gave way to a grin.

They were driving down Finchley Road, an affluent high street of mixed commercial and residential properties in an area with a large Jewish population, both orthodox and secular It was, like many parts of North London, an area with a relatively low crime rate, though not so pacific as to absolve them of the need to remain alert. But here, at least, they could relax, listening to the radio as they cruised along in comfort.

'Sir Bernard Lovell said that the broadcasts came from the moon,' argued a man's voice over the radio.

'But Bernard Lovell had his own axe to grind,' said Beth, smugly. 'He knew that funding for his Jodrell Bank radio telescope came from the public coffers and he needed to play along with the conspiracy to generate public excitement about the so called moon landing. Mary in Islington is on Line 12.'

It was the Bitching Hour and Beth Porter was at her most bitchy.

A turn of the steering wheel took Nick Lloyd and Neil Douglas into Ravenscroft Avenue, a quiet street of expensive houses where a Mercedes or even a Jaguar in the driveway was not an uncommon sight. They didn't expect to find any crime there, but it was a short cut to Golders Green Road. Neil Douglas was varying his pattern. Instead of going all the way to Golders Green tube station and turning right up Golders Green Road, he would turn left at the end of Ravenscroft and go down Golders Green Road towards Hampstead.

A vice like grip of tension still clutched firmly at Rose Crowne as she trudged on through the darkness, past the thick, untended foliage to her left and the wooden bollards just beyond them. She was still holding the fear of her pursuer at bay, remembering her father and the fishing trip.

'You have to be careful that the fish doesn't turn on you,' her father had said in jest. Somehow the present danger seemed to intrude on her thoughts even when her mind managed to wander from it.

There was an eerie stillness in the mixture of trees, some with thick trunks, others thin, interspersed with the undergrowth. But Rose Crowne didn't slow down to dwell on it. She strode on steadily, past a dirt track on her left that was blocked to motor vehicles by an iron gate. She could have left the street and fled that way on foot, but the path sloped down into a black void rather less inviting than the threat from which she was fleeing. A few yards further on, the scenery switched to almost a mirror image of what it had been before, with the wall to her left this time and the vegetation to her right.

7

By now the man's footsteps had fallen behind. But she knew that he was still there, feeling his presence in the silence. Neither slowing down nor looking back to locate him, she continued past the construction work on the wall to the left, looking ahead at the road as it dipped into a steep decline. But the pedestrian footpath did not go down with it. The road ahead, in effect, split into different levels between the asphalt footpath, that stayed substantially on a constant level, and the road that continued in steady decline.

As she approached it she slowed down, wrestling with indecision. Should she walk on the road, where she could be seen in the headlights of cars but risked getting hit by one, if the driver failed to see her past a bend in the road? Or should she keep to the deserted footpath where she would be safe from the fast-driven cars, but where she couldn't be seen from the road and from where her screams might go unheard and unheeded?

Realizing that to walk in the road would be to create a new danger, when the danger behind her might not even be real, she opted for the footpath, prepared, if necessary, to leap over the iron railings into the road. But as the road dropped away and its descent steepened, this option became less and less practical, even in the direst circumstances. But by the time this dawned on her, it was too late to turn back.

Martin Roebuck had kept her in his sights at first, but once her route became clear, it was obvious that she had only one direction to go in, and he could afford to drop back. He didn't want to frighten her - not yet anyway. He just wanted to indulge his curiosity. So he slowed his pace and let her disappear past the curve of the road. She was just beyond his view, but Roebuck could hear her heels clicking against the asphalt.

Nick Lloyd was in his forties and still a constable. He had drifted into the job in his early thirties when he was made redundant from a private security firm, and had failed the first part of OSPRE, the promotion exam. Because he had got less than 45 per cent he had to wait a full year to retake it. A year later he managed to get 60 per cent, but it wasn't until six months later that he was able to clear the 75 percent pass mark. But then he failed the second part twice and had to go back to square one and retake Part 1. He had tried again several times, and eventually cleared the second hurdle but couldn't convince the review board that he was sergeant material. To some extent it suited him to remain on the beat. He could shake down the pushers and the ticket touts who picked up used tickets at the underground station and resold them to dishonest customers. But if he tried to shake down criminals of the kind that an Inspector came up against, he'd have found himself out of his depth.

He was even smart enough to keep his extracurricular activity beyond the knowledge of his partner. Neil Douglas was too much of a greenhorn to be able to keep it under his hat, and too fresh and starry eyed to realize that a copper- even a good one - had to supplement his income in the face of hopelessly inadequate pay from a government that bowed to the meanness of the electorate.

Rose Crowne continued on her way in the darkness. To her left, the grassy hill sloped above her, again thick with coarse vegetation that would cut her flesh if she tried to walk there. In the heavy silence she heard the advancing steps of her pursuer. As their pace quickened and the sound increased in the distance, the nagging fear that she thought she had shaken off welled up again within her, as she desperately looked around for the comfort of another human being, even an anonymous stranger.

And then the footpath she trod began to descend, as if to meet the road below from which she had only recently taken her leave.

Slightly ahead was a break in the hill; vegetation. Through it there ran a dirt path, leading into that disconsolate black void that was Hampstead Heath at night. She had almost reached the end where the road and footpath drew level with one another. Ahead of her, to the left just across the road, she saw the Old Bull and Bush, the public house immortalized in a celebrated old music hall sing-along. The Old Bull and Bush, or North End, the street that ran by it, were the alternative names of an old underground station on the Northern Line between Hampstead and Golders Green that had been excavated at platform level in 1907 but never opened. The thought of an unused hole in the ground made her wince. It was like a grave, waiting for some one to be buried. But then again, she realized, maybe it was just her fears that needed to be laid to rest - the fears that had haunted since the day she had looked at the

9

pictures of a helpless young woman who lay bloodstained and dead on Hampstead Heath.

In any case, she was getting close to Golders Green now. The road ahead was rising up to meet the falling footpath and soon there would be people about and the signs of life would welcome her back from the solitude.

And then the silhouette emerged from the Heath, clad in black, round-shouldered and short-haired. Rose Crowne had caught the movement out of the corner of her left eye and turned to see who it was. But there was something strange and unexpected in what she saw, in no way reassuring. It wasn't the man who had followed her from the pub. This one looked like a skinhead, or a US Marine - his face was even blackened with camouflage grease but there was no doubt that he was white. The gaps between patches of grease clearly showed that. His build was thin but not lithe, more like someone who had under-eaten of late than a fit athlete or combat soldier. There was a kind of awkwardness in his movements, as if he had once been wounded and was still suffering from the after-effects. He was advancing towards her, wielding a knife.

A heart-rending scream rang out from Rose Crowne's open mouth. It sounded like 'murder!' But a second later it died in her throat as the slashing blade ripped open her windpipe. She staggered backwards, trying to get away with her last remaining trace of strength as he advanced towards her. But her attacker wasn't finished yet. He brandished the knife menacingly, prodding her with its sharp tip a few times to force her onto the Heath.

By now people were watching the events from their windows. Rose Crowne's cry for help, though brief, had been loud enough to attract attention on this otherwise quiet night. Some of them were switching off their lights to get a better view of the outside. Others just stood there watching as the attacker slashed and stabbed and drove her out of their sight, disappearing himself a few seconds later. None of them reached for the telephone to call the police. Each assumed that others were already doing so.

As she staggered backwards onto Hampstead Heath, the attacker followed her, forcing her into the cover of the trees.

Martin Roebuck heard the scream and froze as it hit his ears. Was she summoning help because of him? That made no sense.

Why now? He had been closer to her before. Now she was not even in his field of vision. Perhaps it was because she had finally seen people to whom she could call for help. But the scream had cut out abruptly, as if stifled by some unknown force.

He recovered his wits and realized that whatever had caused her to scream, it had nothing to do with him. He sprinted forward, past the curve that concealed her from him. As he rounded the bend, he caught sight of her and a black-clad figure driving her back, but in seconds the pair had vanished as the attacker forced her back into Golders Hill Park.

Roebuck froze again, not sure of what he intended to do, nor even what he should do. He knew that she was being assaulted, but he felt powerless to respond. If he went after them, what was he facing out there? Was the attacker armed? If so, with what? If he went to her aid could he necessarily help her, or would he merely add himself to the casualties? Would he be risking his life? If he succeeded in helping her, would anyone believe that he was just an innocent bystander? Did she even deserve his help?

He remembered how he had spent thirteen months on remand while awaiting trial; how others had conspired to fit him up. He remembered how even after his acquittal, people still vilified him in the press and shouted 'murderer' at him on the streets. Even his neighbours were divided, although many remained loyal. Worst of all, strangers who had never known him presumed to judge him on the strength of a few second-hand and, for the most part, grossly misleading statements about him in the press.

That was 'society' for you! Was he now to serve the standards of that society by going to the aid of this woman?Did this woman deserve his help after what he had been through?

Still, she was a human being, and his religion taught him that all life is sacred. He could not ignore her plight and still be true to his faith. Human life was sacred and therefore something to be preserved by human beings who loved their environment and who treasured the great whole that was the universe.

In a few seconds his mind was made up. He sprinted onto the Western Heath.

Rose Crowne was now lying on the ground. The knife blows had ended, but the attacker was shifting the attack from the

11

infliction of pain and death to personal violation as he pulled down her underwear and forced the hilt of the knife into her anus. By now the last breath of consciousness had almost ebbed away but the pain lingered, as if it were destined to accompany her to the grave. And then the pain stopped. She had heard a shout somewhere in the distance, a faint cry of anger or warning, before all fell silent and the darkness descended forever, conveying her into a realm beyond pain.

'Leave her alone, you bastard!' shouted Roebuck.

The attacker looked up to see Martin Roebuck standing there holding what looked like a branch of a tree. It wasn't a big branch, but the way he held it and the snarl on his face as he eye balled the attacker made it look as menacing as a long-handled baton in the hands of a police officer in the riot squad.

'Get away from her,' Roebuck growled as he took a couple of steps towards the attacker. There was nothing tentative in these steps. He held back and refrained from charging. The attacker still held a sharp knife by the blade in a gloved hand, the handle inserted into the woman. He withdrew it and held it by the handle. For a few seconds they stood eyeball to eyeball, Roebuck trying to stare the attacker down without antagonizing him. When that failed, he took another step forward. The attacker tightened his grip upon the knife and waved it in the air.

Then they were struck by a pair of headlights through the trees and Roebuck, from his vantage point closer to the road, saw that it was a police car. This would be interesting, he thought. But when he looked back, the attacker was already sprinting for the cover of the night into the thicker concentration of trees further in the Heath, having dropped the knife.

Evidently no stomach for a fight, was Roebuck's contemptuous conclusion.

The two policemen from the car had leapt out and were now racing across the road towards Roebuck. Common sense told him that he should drop the branch immediately. But an instinct for survival told him that he should hold onto it until they had been given the chance to see that he was not the attacker. 'OK, drop that right now!' said Nick Lloyd in his most aggressive manner as he sprinted up the grass hill and reached for his CS spray canister. He looked at the two of them: the tall athletic one who looked angry and the short, squat, bull-shouldered one who looked menacing.

'I didn't touch her,' said Roebuck, looking back and forth between Lloyd and Neil Douglas, who had taken out his three stage, collapsible baton and flicked it open.

Neil was by now looking at the girl lying helpless and bleeding on the ground. He didn't know about Roebuck's past, but he could tell a victim when he saw one. It didn't seem possible that the flimsy branch in the man's hands could have inflicted this much damage on the girl. But then he saw the knife lying on the grass and he had to assume that this man was still a threat. In the past it had always been Nick who had taken the lead in dealing with troublemakers on the streets. Neil Douglas was the less experienced of the two - by far the less experienced - and he was content to let his more streetwise colleague call the shots, while he stood close by, facing the same danger and ready to make a move when necessary to back up his partner in any way required.

'You can tell us your side at the station,' said Neil, taking another step forward angrily.

For a second Roebuck froze with fear. Once again, the police had assessed the situation all wrong. Then he realised that there was only one way to straighten things out and that was to make it clear that he wasn't a threat to them. He allowed his grip on the branch to soften and let it slip out of his hands towards the grass.

In truth, Neil Douglas had already made a decision. The sight of the young women lying there in a pool of blood had been too much for him. Consequently as the branch fell from Roebuck's hands he lashed out, with his baton, at the side of Roebuck's head, making contact with a degree of force that spoke of the depth of his anger and the intensity of his sympathy with the victim. Neil Douglas and Nick Lloyd heard an almighty cracking sound that reverberated into the night, and less than half a second later Martin Roebuck crumpled onto the grass in a lifeless heap. Some yards from where they were standing, an engine roared to life and a car sped away into the distance. Neither Neil Douglas nor Nick Lloyd thought anything of it. They were still transfixed by the unmoving body of Martin Roebuck and the woman whom they still thought had been his victim.

However, one other person was taking an interest in the speeding car. A woman walking further up the road saw it speed off and had the presence of mind to whip out a pen and a scrap of paper to make a note of its registration number. Because of its speed and the dim street light, she wasn't able to get the whole number. She noted only that it was a blue Ford and that the registration number began with M244. The rest was lost in the haze and confusion.

Chapter 2

'It wasn't your fault. It really looked like he was about to hit you.'

Neil Douglas and Nick Lloyd were now back at the office in Golders Green police station. They were supposed to be writing up their reports, but Neil was still in a state of shock and couldn't get his mind off what he had done. His discomfort was contagious and while Neil was now sitting, it was his partner who had taken to pacing up and down.

'I should have waited. If I'd just held back instead of lashing out.'

Nick put a comforting hand on his shoulder.

'They said at the hospital that he's not even on the critical list,' he added with an encouraging smile. 'His chances of making a full recovery are excellent.'

Neil Douglas managed to return the smile and took a sip of coffee from the polystyrene cup that Nick had brought him. It was the dark granulated blend, the one that he didn't like, and it tasted more bitter than usual. They had run out of the lighter brown powdered blend. He screwed up his face and took another sip. At least it had cooled down somewhat and no longer burned his tongue. He stared down at the cup, lost in thought, or at least, trying to get lost in thought, but Nick Lloyd wasn't letting him.

'He wasn't so innocent, you know,' said Nick. 'You remember what that bastard did to Leah Irons? And he got away with it!'

'It was never proved,' Neil mumbled in a muted tone.

'The fuck it wasn't! If it hadn't been for that arse hole of a judge it would have gone for trial.'

Neil was tired, and in a state of confusion over what had happened on the Heath. But in some ways he was thinking more clearly than Nick and in his torment he felt the irresistible urge to argue.

'The judge didn't throw the charges out. He just ruled against the Annie Jacobs evidence.'

'That's what I mean,' said Nick. 'Even if he didn't allow the psychology and character evidence from Peter Eckland, he could have allowed the Annie Jacobs evidence about what Roebuck said about the position and state of the body. That would have been enough to nail the bastard!'

'The Crown Prosecution Service didn't think so. They were the ones who decided not to go ahead with the case.'

'The CPS were also pretty spineless! If they'd had the bollocks to go ahead with it they could have nailed that piece of shit. And then all of this wouldn't have happened.'

Nick Lloyd was raging now and wasn't thinking rationally. Even in his depression Neil could see that.

'What are you talking about? He was innocent this time.'

'What's that got to do with it?'

'Well, you can't say it wouldn't have happened this time. It was someone else who attacked Rose Crowne.'

'Maybe, but if Roebuck had been banged up in chokey where he belongs, then he wouldn't have been there to get hurt and then you wouldn't have hit him.'

'You just don't understand, do you?' Neil whined in a pleading tone. 'He went to help her! Half a dozen witnesses saw that! That's why he was holding that branch from a tree and not the knife. That's why his prints weren't on the knife even though he wasn't wearing gloves. He went to help her, for Christ's sake! He risked his life for her!r'

'Maybe because he felt guilty about what he did to Leah Irons,' said Nick Lloyd smirking cynically.

'Or maybe because he's not the animal that everyone seems to think he is.'

It was all too much for Neil. He broke down in tears, sobbing into his forearm on the table. Nick just didn't understand He wasn't looking for reassurance that he was innocent He wanted Nick to empathize with the guilt that he felt, and it wasn't happening. Nick was trying to be a friend but Neil couldn't accept Nick's detached view that 'the other guy' was to blame, or that the other guy 'deserved it.'

He had read about the Leah Irons/Martin Roebuck case, both at the time of the murder and during the débâcle in court. Like most people on his side of the fence he assumed that Martin Roebuck had been guilty and that he had getaway with it through lack of evidence and the obstructive approach of a bleeding-heart liberal judge. But on this occasion witnesses had come forward immediately, telling how the man in light trousers had rushed onto the Heath after the woman had been forced there at knife point. He tried to rationalize it. These were the same witnesses, he told himself, who had stood at their windows gaping and done nothing themselves to help the woman as she was savagely attacked in their presence. But they had no reason to lie about this. It was not as if saying that a man had gone to the woman's aid would have been a valid reason for not calling the police. No, he realized, it could not just be a lie to salve their consciences. And besides, too many of them had come up with the same story for it to be anything other than true.

His sobbing continued. It was impossible to avoid the inevitable conclusion that Martin Roebuck had not only not been the attacker but had actually been the only person with enough courage and concern for a fellow human being to go to the woman's aid, and to do so even at risk to his life.

And now he lay unconscious at the Royal Free Hospital in Hampstead, with possible brain damage, his health if not his life hanging in the balance. Whatever Nick said, Neil Douglas knew that he was responsible for whatever happened to Roebuck. If he had held back just a moment longer to assess the situation, if he had hesitated for only a split-second more, he would have realized that Roebuck was innocent. But when Roebuck released the branch to show that he wasn't resisting, Neil had seen his window of opportunity for revenge slipping away and lashed out while there was still time to feign justification. Even Nick was fooled - or at least had chosen to let himself be fooled

'Look Neil I don't know what to say.'

Nick Lloyd trailed off, embarrassed at the sight of his partner's tears. He didn't know how to handle situations like this. He knew how to act tough on the streets and when to look the other way. But he didn't know how to be gentle. His father had known only the belt and the back of the hand and if his ex-wife hadn't effectively taken his son away he would be passing on the philosophy of violence to the next generation to continue the cycle. As it was all he could do was hope that Neil would get over it. A partner who was haunted by guilt was useless on the streets and a poor comrade in arms to guard one's back.

17

He slipped out of the room into the corridor.

'Oh Nick, there you are,' said the station sergeant.

'Yes,' said Nick. 'What is it?'

'A witness has come forward.'

'Another one?'

'This one saw something the others didn't.'

'What?' asked Nick nervously. The incident with Martin Roebuck had occurred on the Heath itself, or rather in Golders Hill Park, the Western Heath, and Nick Lloyd assumed that it had taken place out of sight of those who had watched the beginning of the attack from the windows of houses nearby. But a witness who saw Neil striking the blow against Roebuck was like a joker in the pack - it could lead to unexpected results. Nick wanted to protect his partner in any way he could. It wasn't Neil's fault that some idiot had taken it upon himself to play the Good Samaritan. It wasn't Neil's fault that Martin Roebuck had picked up a stick and held it even after the attacker ran off. But it wouldn't be easy to protect him from a witness who could contradict their testimony with an alternative account - especially an independent witness who had no reason to lie.

'It was dark,' said Nick. 'We couldn't see anything clearly.' He realized after he said it that it was a mistake. Arguing with the unknown witness before he had been told what the witness had said was a sign of guilt, or at least a sign that he was trying to hide something I know,' said the station sergeant. 'But she saw part of it'

'She?' echoed Nick, relieved that the station sergeant didn't appear to have noticed the implications of his last remark.

'A woman, Meredith de Mur. She was going for a late night stroll when she heard the screams.'

'Another late night stroller? Has everyone got a death wish or what?'

'It used to be a good area. I mean, it still is. There's no reason why a woman should be afraid to go for a late night stroll there. I mean, there are usually plenty of people about at that time. In any case, she wasn't actually on the Heath, just near it, in North End Road.'

'And what did she see?'

'She saw a car speeding away afterwards.'

'A car?' Nick Lloyd hoped that the relief in his voice had sounded more like curiosity.

'It started just after the attack.'

'What do you mean, "started"?'

'Well, it didn't just drive past. The car was actually right there nearby. The engine started just after the attack.'

'How does she know?' asked Nick. 'Did she see the attack?'

'No, but she saw the police car arrive. She saw you guys arrive and race onto the Heath when the other people started pointing and shouting from their windows. She slowed down to see what was going on and that's when it happened. The engine came to life out of the blue and the car sped away.'

'And you think it might have been the attacker?'

'That's the most likely explanation.'

'Did she get the number?'

'Only part of it,' the station sergeant sounded disappointed. 'Like you said, it was dark.'

'What about the type? Colour?'

'A blue Ford. M reg.'

'What about the driver?'

'She didn't see. She thinks it was one occupant, but she couldn't swear even to that. She said she had a feeling it might be important and was concentrating on getting the number.'

'Do you think we can narrow it down from those details?' asked Nick.

'If she's right about the colour we should. She got the number, the make and the colour. Between those three we should be able to limit it considerably.'

'What if she's wrong about the colour?'

'That shouldn't open it up all that much. But the problem is, if it comes to trial and we have to depend on her, it could undermine her cred with the jury.'

'Hopefully, we'll have other evidence by then.'

'Hopefully,' the station sergeant echoed.

'I don't suppose I could speak to her?' asked Nick, nervously.

'It wouldn't be appropriate at this stage. There may be a disciplinary hearing,' said the station sergeant. 'Besides, we've given her a lift home. She was trying to put a brave face on it, but I think she was in shock too. Lara asked if she wanted someone to stay over, but she said she was OK.'

Lara was PC Lara Woodward, a policewoman determined to get into the Criminal Investigations Department as soon as she completed her two years beat duty.

'Well, I'd better get back in there with Neil. I think he needs a friend right now.'

'OK, but don't spend too long with him. We don't want the tabloids saying you were cooking up a story together.'

'That wouldn't be the tabloids,' said Nick with a smile. 'That would be the guardian'

A few miles away, the door to a flat in Camden Town was being opened cautiously and quietly. Technically it was not yet a burglary because it was not a forced entry, merely a trespass. But there was deliberate caution in the act, as if the person doing it was well aware of the danger Not that there was likely to be anyone in the flat The woman who had once lived there, had lived alone Still, there was always the possibility that the police were already there. So, the burglar entered with caution, using a torch instead of switching on the lights, and keeping it low to avoid giving any tell-tale signs that might be spotted from beyond the window. The first port of call was the bedroom. That was where the letters would be kept. Apart from having the key, one of the advantages that the intruder had over a conventional burglar was that, being a close confidante of the victim, no searching was required. Everything was in its proper place and it was a simple matter of going to where things were supposed to be and taking them.

The letters were in the lower drawer of the dressing table. One of the strange things about Good Samaritans is that in many cases they like to keep a record of their generosity and kindness for posterity, something they can show to future generations to win kudos in this world as well as brownie points in the next.

Maybe I'm being cynical, thought the burglar. But then again, maybe there is no such thing as real idealism in the world. Maybe human generosity is just a myth and maybe human generosity is an expression of guilt for past cruelty. or past indifference.

After the letters had been put into a large canvas shoulder bag, the next room requiring a search was the living room. There were two framed pictures, but there could be any number of unframed ones as well, not to mention negatives. The framed pictures were easy. They sat majestically in heavy imitation gilt frames on the mantelpiece. In an instant, they were scooped up and deposited in the bag. Finding the rest took effort. It was uncomfortable crouching on the faded purple carpet and holding the torch awkwardly while going through all five photo albums, but it had to be done. Worse still, they were distributed over three of the albums. The question was whether to prise up the clear plastic and take out the pictures individually or take the entire albums. If the pictures were seen to be missing from the album that would attract attention and alert people to the motive behind the burglary. So it had to be the whole albums, all three of them. The burglar struggled to fit them all into the bag, because of their round bulging spines, turning the top one around and then sliding one out from the bottom and putting it on the top so that the reversed album was in the middle. It was a tight fit, but it worked.

So far so good, but there were still the negatives.

now where would she have put them?r the burglar wondered.

A frantic search followed. Drawers were pulled open, shelves were scanned, even the wardrobe and dressing table had to be checked out. Ten minutes of searching proved fruitless, until eventually an old shoe box under the dressing table turned up pay dirt. It contained not shoes but a collection of photographic negatives, as well as quite a few prints not mounted in the albums. A quick flip through the prints revealed a few more of the kind that had to be removed.

But the negatives were a problem. It was hard to see their contents clearly in the torchlight and there were scores of them to go through. They only occupied a small amount of space, but looking through them individually in this light would take ages.

It was better to take the lot, the burglar decided. And with that, they were shoved into the bag, by the side of the albums, and the torch switched off. It was easy getting to the door, relying on the light from the street through the window. From there it was a simple matter of out through the front door, locking the door to leave no sign of an entry and away into the night.

The job was done and the trail was erased.

It was half past one in the morning when Neil Douglas finally got home. Home for Neil was the middle flat in a converted house in a quiet street just off a main road. He was about to switch on the light, but then hesitated. He didn't really want too much light. It would make him self-conscious and aware of his surroundings. The smallish living room wasn't especially attractive, nor was it particularly tidy. On top of everything that had happened today it would be a depressing sight. And then there was also a picture of his father by the phone. He didn't want to look into his father's eyes right now. Apart from that, the living room looked out onto the street and the houses opposite. He didn't want to feel like he was in a goldfish bowl either, even if most the neighbours were asleep.

After switching on the TV, he made his way to the kitchen and opened the microwave oven door to give the room some soft, unobtrusive light. It was too late for coffee, but he would have a cup of tea. He knew that tea also had caffeine but unlike coffee it had never stopped him sleeping. From the TV he could hear the theme music for Baywatch. It was one of those old reruns that they show in the small hours. He often watched these early morning reruns when he couldn't sleep. Whenever he got home late at night, no matter how tired he had been beforehand, he couldn't get to sleep immediately. He needed half an hour or so to unwind. All the more so today after the incident on the Heath and the dreadful realization afterwards.

He wondered if it would hit the morning papers, but then realized that it almost certainly wouldn't. It was far too late for their deadlines, even for the late editions. At most it might make the stop press of the late editions. On the other hand, it would be covered by the morning news of most of the London radio stations and talked about considerably in the phone-in discussions on LBC and Talk Radio UK. He knew what this meant. People who had never met him and who had only the most cursory knowledge of the incident would dissect the events of a few hours ago in the finest detail as they passed summary judgement upon him.

He had seen it all before: the carnival of the spectators;the orgy of the voyeurs. And they would feast on his carcass until there was no more meat worth chewing. Then they would turn to other carrion to indulge their gluttony.

He brought his mug of tea into the living room and slouched down on the low black-upholstered couch to watch the displays of flesh that were tagged onto the paper thin storyline, but he didn't take in what was happening on the screen. Even the show of female pulchritude left him with a feeling of discomfort. Normally he could enjoy the pleasant view as somnolence set in and displaced the tension of patrolling the streets. But after seeing the slashed and bleeding corpse of that woman on Hampstead Heath, it was impossible to take pleasure in the sight of an attractive female body. That was the price he paid for pursuing the idealistic vision of being a protector of society.

He wondered if he had been right to follow in his father's footsteps. He had originally aspired to an academic career after getting his psychology degree. He had developed an interest in psychology in his adolescence. He wanted to know why people acted as they did. But he had never understood his own motivation and so he had stumbled headlong into police training in a desperate effort to please his father. In effect, he had abandoned his own dream in order to fulfil his father's. They had grown close after his mother died and the bond between them had grown so tight that it was perhaps only natural that he should have given up psychology for police work.

'I can use my psychology on the streets,' he had said byway of rationalization. And his father had been too happy at his son's career choice to question the logic behind it.

By two o'clock in the morning, Neil felt his eyelids drooping and could no longer focus his eyes on the TV screen. He looked down at his tea mug. It was two thirds full. He realized that he didn't really want to drink it, but he took one more sip before putting it down on the glass and chrome coffee table. The tea was almost cold, and it didn't even have the soothing effect on his sore throat that he was hoping for.

He switched off the TV with the remote control and dragged himself up from the couch. He felt himself waking up as he trudged to the bedroom. In quick succession, he switched on the halogen lamp by the bed and then the radio. He had intended to take a shower, but he felt too lethargic to try. As he flopped down onto the bed, he heard Beth Porter rounding off the Bitching Hour with her comments on the most recent news.

'And in the news, it looks like the government is getting another reprieve from public attention because we've got yet another sensational story to fill our headlines for the next few weeks. This time it isn't road rage, it's a woman being attacked in a public place and a man getting knocked senselessly an over-zealous policeman with his baton. Remember those long-handled batons that were going to bring law and order to our streets. Well, it looks like all they're bringing us is murder and mayhem.

'A few hours ago, a woman was attacked on Hampstead Heath by a madman with a knife. God knows what the silly cow was doing there. But anyway, she was attacked and stabbed several times, apparently fatally. A man walking nearby went to her aid and apparently chased off the attacker. Then the police arrived and thought that the man who chased off the attacker was the attacker. And - get this - instead of just arresting him or holding him for questioning, one of London's finest lashed out with his baton and hit the man on the head, knocking him unconscious. That's the man who went to rescue the woman please note, not the man who attacked her. And so now the man who went to help the woman who was being attacked is lying in a hospital bed and the man who attacked the woman is running around scot-free. As to what's happening to the overzealous constable, apparently the reports don't say. But I wouldn't be surprised if he getaway with it. Policemen who kill or injure innocent members of the public are seldom put on trial - and even if they are, they're seldom convicted.'

Then she added in her most vitriolic tone: 'And some people want to give them guns. Personally, I wouldn't trust them with water pistols. This is Beth Porter, your nocturnal bitch, wishing you good night and sweet dreams, including that trigger-happy copper - if you can sleep tonight.'

Beth Porter's sarcastic tone and American accent were the last thing Neil Douglas heard before an uneasy, nightmare ridden, sleep drifted over him.

Chapter 3

Nick Lloyd?' said a young uniformed policewoman.

Nick looked up from the sports section of the tabloid he had been reading.

'Yes?'

'You can go in now.'

Nick Lloyd and Neil Douglas had been sitting on a bench in the stark whitewashed corridor outside the interview room of the local divisional station. Nick stood up and turned to Neil, who was trying to hide his nervousness by keeping his nose buried in a middle-brow tabloid.

'Did Roebuck do it?' shouted the headline above an article that raised serious doubts about the prosecution case that had never actually been presented. The editors seemed refreshingly free of embarrassment over the fact that this was the same tabloid that had come dangerously close to suggesting on more than one occasion that Roebuck had done it.

'Don't worry, Neil. I've been before more of these "rubber heels" inquiries than you've had hot dinners.'

'Rubber heels' was the name the police gave to the Complaints and Discipline Department.

'Yes,' Neil replied, taking up Nick's attempt at reassurance. 'But then it was usually you in the hot seat.'

They exchanged nervous grins and then Nick Lloyd walked into the room.

The room was cool and whitewashed, more reminiscent of a hospital than a police station. There was a simple table, on which stood a cassette recorder, and four chairs: two behind the table, already occupied by two men, one in a corner and one in front of the table. The policewoman took her seat in the corner as one of the men at the desk switched on the cassette recorder.

Nick Lloyd stood in front of a desk, behind which was seated a stern-faced middle-aged officer in plain clothes, whose ample girth prevented him from pulling his chair too close to the table. PC Lloyd didn't recognize him personally, but being a veteran of these internal disciplinary inquiries, he knew from the procedural rules that this man was a Detective Chief Inspector. To his right sat a younger man, also a stranger but almost certainly from the same department.

'I'm DCI Adams,' said the rotund officer. 'I am conducting this inquiry on behalf of the Complaints and Discipline Department. I am being assisted in this investigation by Detective Sergeant Johnson. At the end of my inquiries I will prepare a report with recommendations which may be forwarded to the Crown Prosecution Service or the Police Complaints Authority. It may subsequently be passed to your Chief Constable for disciplinary decisions. I presume that you've been Reg 7'd?'

The DCI was asking if PC Lloyd had received his notice of disciplinary investigation under Regulation 7 of the Police Discipline Regulations.

'Yes sir.'

It was actually a superfluous question. Nick wouldn't have been here otherwise. But Adams did things by the book and wanted to create a record of all the formalities being duly fulfilled.

'It is my duty to remind you,' Adams continued stiffly, 'that this inquiry may result in criminal proceedings and/or internal disciplinary sanctions including fines or even dismissal from the force. It is further my duty to remind you that you have the right to remain silent and to have a friend or colleague present during your interview. Do you understand all this?'

'Yes sir.'

'Do you wish to have a colleague or friend present during your interview?'

'No sir,' said Nick confidently. He knew how the game was played. The DCI had to pretend that he knew none of the facts even though he had read the written reports and was already fully conversant with the background. He- like Nick - knew that it was Neil Douglas who was in jeopardy of disciplinary procedures or criminal charges, but he had to appear to approach the case with an open mind. Officially, it was possible that the written-up reports were wrong, incomplete or even misleading. He had a duty to explore their accuracy and veracity by questioning the parties concerned and comparing their answers to each other's answers and to the written record for consistency, or the lack of it.

'Sit down,' said the DCI.

Nick took his seat opposite the DCI and leaned back, shifting a couple of times to get himself comfortable.

'Let's begin by going back to the night of Monday the24th of May. Could you tell me about the events from when the incident on Hampstead Heath first came to your attention?'

'Well, we were on our routine patrol, driving along Golders Green Road in the direction of North End Road. We crossed over Finchley Road and past the tube station and into North End Road, in the direction of Golders Hill Park. As we got close to the Old Bull and Bush, we noticed people at their windows pointing towards Golders Hill Park. They appeared to be trying to signal us. I have to say that it was Neil -that is PC Douglas - who noticed it. I was concentrating on the road and would have probably gone straight past if Neil hadn't told me. So we stopped the car and got out and someone - an old man I think - opened a window and called out something like: "He stabbed her, on the Heath. "

'He was pointing towards Golders Hill Park, which is West Heath. And quite a few other people were pointing there too. So me and Neil - I mean PC Douglas--'

'It's all right, you can call him Neil.'

'OK, me and Neil ran across the road and up the path a short distance into Golders Hill Park, where we saw a man standing over a woman, with a tree branch in his hand.'

'Would you say it was a large branch?' asked the DCI.

'Well, large enough to hurt someone if used as a weapon. I mean, I'd say it was no less dangerous than a long-handled baton if used as a weapon. Probably more so, because of the rough surface and the sharp bits sticking out of it.'

'You saw sharp bits sticking out of it?'

'No sir. But, I mean, branches like that usually have bits sticking out here and there. I mean they're never smooth -branches of trees, I mean.'

He broke off, having lost his thread.

'Go on,' said the DCI encouragingly.

'Well, the man was standing over the woman, and he had this snarling look on his face.'

'What condition was the woman in?' asked the DCI, careful to use neutral words even as he prompted PC Lloyd for an answer.

'She was bleeding.'

'You could actually see blood flowing?' asked the DCI.

'Well, she was covered in blood. I mean, we didn't actually see blood flowing. But there was blood all over her.'

'We?' echoed the DCI.

'Pardon, sir?'

'You said "we didn't actually see blood".'

'Well, I mean me and Neil.'

'You talked about what you and Neil saw?' the DCI asked sternly.

Nick Lloyd rubbed under his collar. This wasn't going to be as easy as he'd thought. There was nothing wrong with talking about what they saw. It was just the DCI's tone. One minute Adams was prompting him and reminding him of the important details that had to be put into the record to clear his partner's name, the next minute the DCI was catching him out on a trivial point that could be made to look as if they had co-ordinated their stories - something that could be made to look bad if this matter were taken further.

'I mean I saw blood all over her. I just assumed that Neil saw what I saw because we were standing in the same place more or less.'

'Well, don't assume in the future, constable. You know the saying "Assume makes an ass out of you and me. "'

'I'm sorry, sir,' said PC Lloyd, suddenly finding himself short of breath. But he noticed, with relief, that the Detective Chief Inspector was almost smiling.

'Anyway, I noticed that she had blood all over her face and body and there was no sign of movement.'

'Could you see clearly in that light?'

'Enough to see that there was no movement.'

'No, I mean about the blood.'

'Well, there was light from the road, sir.'

'But neither of you had taken out a torch,' said the DCI.

'No sir, there wasn't enough time.'

'But there was enough light to distinguish colours.'

'I'm sorry, sir?'

'Was there enough light to recognize colours or only different shades of light and dark?'

He was beginning to see where the question was leading, but it was too late to wriggle out of it. They could test how light it was at that time and under those conditions and it was pointless to lie.

'Well, only different shades of light, I guess.'

'So how could you tell that it was blood?'

Nick Lloyd was now thoroughly confused. He was used to tough questioning from defence lawyers when they cross-examined him in court. And he usually prepared for it with the aid of other officers so as not to fall into their fairly predictable traps. But he wasn't used to it from a 'rubber heels' officer. They were not usually hostile, to their fellow officers. Analytical yes, and sometimes even downright pedantic. But not hostile. Not usually. Sometimes they came under pressure from the Home Office to satisfy public lust for a sacrificial lamb, but this officer had until now seemed reasonable and even sympathetic in a stiff, starched-collar sort of way. Now, however, he was springing the kind of trap that PC Lloyd normally expected to hear from some courtroom shyster. At least there was no jury to see him falling into it, and no journalists to write about it.

'I didn't know that it was blood. But it was sort of a dark discolouration all over her face and body and on the grass and on the asphalt path that we crossed over to get there. There were obvious cuts and lacerations on the woman and so it was reasonable to assume - I know I shouldn't assume- but at the time it seemed reasonable to assume that it was blood.'

He noticed that again the DCI was coming dangerously close to a smile.

In fact, from the DCI's point of view, this was a very reasonable answer and it was not at all an unreasonable assumption that PC Lloyd had made. Policeman are expected to use their judgement on the beat, and he couldn't fault PC Lloyd for assuming, correctly, that the dark discolouration all over the woman's face, body and clothes was blood. He merely wanted to see how PC Lloyd handled the question and the pressure. Was his answer defensive or aggressive?In fact it was somewhere in between. That suggested an element of honesty and an element of falsehood. It was up to DCI Adams to discover where the falsehood lay, if he really wanted to know.

'And what happened when you confronted this man who was holding the branch?'

'I said "OK drop that right now" or words to that effect, at the same time taking out my CS spray canister. At the same time, Neil took out his baton. At that stage we were prepared for resistance and ready to respond to it but still hoping to persuade him to drop the branch and come quietly. At that point he said - that is the suspect said - "I didn't touch her. " He seemed extremely agitated and he kept looking back between me and Neil.

'And then Neil said: "You can tell us your side at the station, " making clear that he'd get a fair hearing.'

'And how did the suspect react to that?'

'Well, he seemed to get into a bit of a panic. He took a step towards Neil, still holding the branch high in the air, and it looked like he was going to whack Neil across the face.'

'And what did you do?'

'Well, I didn't do anything. I mean I was going to but Neil was nearer and it was his call. So he hit the suspect once with his baton.'

'On the head?' 'Well, I don't think he was aiming for the head sir. I think he was aiming for the arm - the arm holding the branch that is. But because of the way Roebuck - I mean the suspect - stepped forward, he ended up hitting the suspect's head.'

They were in private and there was no one from the outside world to hear what he was saying. But it was important not to break the trained courtroom habit of humanizing one's colleagues while depersonalizing the suspect. Thus his colleague was 'Neil' and Roebuck was 'the suspect.'

'And it was only one blow?' asked Adams.

'Yes sir.'

'But you didn't think it was necessary.'

'I didn't say that!' Nick replied defensively.

'Well, you said it was his call, implying that you would have done things differently.'

'No, I meant that I was about to do something too, but Neil was quicker. I mean he was nearer and in a better position to react.'

'Is it possible that he was too quick?' asked the DCI, stony-faced.

'No, I don't think so, sir. Like I said, I was about to react myself, so I can hardly say that he reacted prematurely. He just had quicker reactions than I did. You know these young people, sir. Fit and quick.'

He said this with a smile on his face, hoping for an encouraging smile in return. All he got was the same stony-faced stare that the DCI had given him through most of the interview. Neither was there any reassurance from the sergeant, who seemed to have his lips sewn into a particular position that was not exactly a frown but definitely not a smile.

'What were you about to do?' asked the DCI.

'I'm sorry?' said Nick, confused.

'You said that at the time Neil hit Roebuck you were about to react. I was just wondering what you were about to do?'

'Well, I was about to spray him with CS.'

'Did you warn him not to come forward?'

According to the guidelines - they were not really rules of engagement - he was supposed to hold out an extended arm, hand upright with palm opened towards the suspect, and warn the suspect not to resist or come forward, while holding the CS spray canister well back in the other hand.

'Well, I'd already warned him to drop the branch and an attack on my colleague looked imminent.'

'Wasn't there a danger that if you sprayed him you might have got PC Douglas too?'

'There was that danger. That was probably why I hesitated.'

'Hesitated? So you did hold back.'

'Well, my reaction was sluggish. I think that may have been--'

'Sluggish?'

'Well, I mean I was about to move, but it just didn't seem to happen as quickly as I intended. I think I was subconsciously aware of the fact that if I sprayed the suspect I might have harmed Neil and that's probably what slowed me down.'

'But there is no doubt in your mind that Martin Roebuck was about to hit PC Douglas with the branch of the tree that he was holding?'

'Well, it certainly looked that way sir.'

'Can you think of any reason why he would do such a thing in the light of the fact - which we know - that he was innocent of this attack?'

'I don't know, sir. He might have panicked. He might just not have trusted the police. He is a violent man sir. He's attacked journalists in the past. And he was arrested once for brandishing a baseball bat. Presumably this was just one more of his outbursts.'

'But on this occasion he was actually helping the girl. He was on the side of the angels, to coin a phrase. Don't you think it's suspicious that he was so ready to lash out like that, given the fact that he was going to the aid of a victim? Especially after PC Douglas told him that he would have the chance to tell his side of the story at the police station. I mean, going to help the victim at the risk of his own life displays a somewhat noble intent, wouldn't you say? Is it likely that a man would show such noble and gallant motives one minute and then lash out for no good reason the next?'

'I can't explain it, sir. He's a bit unstable, by all accounts. And he doesn't like the police. Maybe he lashed out because he saw our uniforms and thought of us as the enemy.'

'Lashed out?' asked the DCI with raised eyebrows.

'Well, he would've done if Neil hadn't stopped him.'

He knew that the DCI didn't believe him. But that was irrelevant. As with criminal inquiries, police disciplinary charge shave to be proved beyond reasonable doubt - although that was due to change soon, thanks to woolly liberal government policy. At the moment, the main problem he faced was that disciplinary charges were broader than criminal charges.

'OK, PC Lloyd,' said the DCI, not troubling to hide the tone of scepticism. 'That'll be all.'

Nick Lloyd suppressed a sigh of relief and left the room. Neil sat up and looked at him when he came out.

'Finished already?' asked Neil, encouraged by the brevity of the interview.

'Piece of cake,' replied Nick with a puerile grin. But then he remembered that Neil was not so experienced at facing these 'rubber heels' inquiries - a complete greenhorn in fact. 'It might be a good idea if I go in with you though.'

'Do you think they'll let you?' asked Neil. 'I mean you were there with me - on the Heath, I mean. Doesn't it have to be some one neutral?'

'We can ask,' said Nick. 'It doesn't hurt to ask.'

'I think I'd rather go in alone,' said Neil, coolly. 'It isn't going to be long.'

Nick noticed a strange trace of confident promise in Neil's tone, and in his words.

'They might take longer with you than they did with me.'

'I don't think so,' said Neil ominously.

'Neil Douglas?' came a woman's voice out of the blue.

It was the policewoman, calling from down the corridor. She had half stepped out of the room and was looking at Neil encouragingly.

'That's me,' said Neil.

'We'll see you now,' she said.

Neil stood up, gave Nick a nervous smile and walked towards the door to the interview room. Nick watched him with some degree of trepidation. He considered telling Neil to be careful, but that would only make him more nervous.

The door closed behind Neil, and Nick went off to the toilet to smoke a cigarette.

There was smell of fish and chips in the flat in Camden Town. He had bought them in the fish and chip shop in the tube station nearby and was nibbling away at the last of them, much to the disgust of his colleague. A group of removal men were boxing up and removing the furniture, clothes and personal effects of Rose Crowne. They were acting under the scrutiny and supervision of the two besuited men who were here in their capacity as the executors of Rose Crowne's estate. One of them was, however, clearly superior to the other and the other, accordingly, addressed him with suitable deference.

Their names were Joe and Harold. Harold was the senior of the two. Joe was the lackey who did Harold's bidding- except when he asserted his independence by eating fish and chips in the face of his colleague's disapproval. Harold stood in one corner of the living room, watching as the removal men did their work. Joe was wandering aimlessly from room to room, keeping a cursory eye on the situation but not really sure of what he was doing there. There was no chance of these men stealing anything. And even if they did, it didn't really matter. Rose Crowne wouldn't have been so careless as to leave anything sensitive lying around.

Joe returned to the living room and decided to take a look at the books. The removal men hadn't touched the bookcase yet. Maybe he could find something to read in the meantime.

He crouched down and started to browse, but not for long.

'Sir! Take a look at this.'

Harold turned and looked but didn't move any closer.

'What is it?' he asked, uninterested.

'Take a look at these photo albums.' Harold reluctantly took a step closer, unsure of what his subordinate was going on about. He saw a couple of photo albums on the lowest shelf of the bookcase, leaning heavily to one side against a one volume encyclopaedia.

'What about it?' he asked, impatiently.

'There's a space, sir. Quite a big one.'

'So what?' said Harold. 'Where is it written that a bookcase has to be packed like a sardine tin?'

'I know, sir. But you didn't know Rose Crowne, sir. If she'd had that much space on one shelf, she wouldn't have packed the other shelves so tightly. She would have rearranged the books from the other shelves. She wouldn't have had the photo albums leaning like that sir. It wasn't her style. She had a sense of aesthetics.'

'Oh, aesthetics,' Harold mimicked. 'Have we been taking one of those correspondence courses again?'

'No, I'm serious, sir. This wasn't like her at all.'

'So what are you saying?'

'I'm saying that I think something's been taken from here?'

'What, you mean something like a book?'

'Yes sir.'

'I don't suppose it's occurred to you that she might have taken the book out to read and it might have been amongst the things they carted away from the bedroom? Or maybe she lent a book to someone else - a friend, for instance. I mean, I don't know much about her private life, but she may have had friends, you know, believe it or not.'

'Yes sir, but it would have to have been a pretty big book.'

'So what?'

'Well, I think it may have been more than one book.'

'So she lent one of her books to one of her friends!' Harold blurted out, losing patience. 'Or maybe she lent one and was reading the other.'

'Two books from adjacent places on the same shelf?'

'Ah, so now it's the old coincidences-never-happen syndrome,' said Harold spitting his usual sarcasm, so characteristic of the man when anger alone failed to do the trick. 'Besides, I don't think it was a book, sir,' said Joe, inspecting the shelf more carefully.

'But I thought you said it was!' shouted his superior, exasperated.

'I mean, I think it was photo albums, sir.'

'Photo albums,' Harold repeated, no longer sounding completely sceptical, but still a long way from believing.

'Yes sir. *Three* photo albums.'

'*Three* albums,' Harold echoed. 'How do you figure that out? I mean, how do you pin it down to three?'

'From the width of the space.'

'There might have been a slight space. Even for a woman with a sense of aesthetics?'

'And from the dust pattern. There was some slight space around all of the albums because of the extra width of spine. There must have been five of them originally. There's a dust pattern around them, and it shows the total width. I haven't got a ruler with me, but my calibrated eyeball tells me that it adds up to the width of five of them.'

'A dust pattern Joe?' His superior parroted, the sarcasm returning even more heavily than before. 'In the home of a woman with a sense of aesthetics?'

'A busy woman with a sense of aesthetics sir,' Joe corrected, this time deliberately placing undue emphasis on the term of respect after the exaggerated pause. It was the only form of defiance that he felt confident enough to getaway with.

For a second or two Harold stood there, surprised by his subordinate's display of anger. Then he realized that he had bigger things to think about. He took a step forward and crouched down to examine what Joe had been looking at.

35

'You know what, Joe?' Joe held his breath, expecting more sarcasm. 'You're right.'

Joe exhaled, audibly.

'Now,' said Harold standing up, wiping the dust from his hands, 'why would anyone want to take three photo albums from Rose Crowne?'

Joe stood up 'Perhaps for the same reason that we're taking everything else, sir?'

'Pardon.'

'To cover their tracks.'

'What we're doing, Joe, is making sure that the press don't get to see any of this in case it gives away anything that Rose was doing.'

'Well, in a roundabout way, that is covering our tracks sir.'

'All right. Fair enough,' said Harold. 'So what's your theory about this person or persons unknown who took these three albums?'

'I think someone didn't want us to see something in them.'

'Well, that's a pretty reasonable assumption when photo albums are stolen, Joe. Can we flesh it out a bit perhaps?'

Joe bit his lip with frustration. Harold had the knack of being sarcastic even when he was giving his approval.

'Well, until we find them, we won't know what was in them, sir.'

Harold was about to say something but he noticed that Joe was looking through one of the two remaining photo albums.

'What are you looking for?' he asked.

'Well, I wanted to see what sort of thing she had in the albums. As far as I can tell it's all just personal pictures of her and views of parks, places like that.'

'Including Hampstead Heath?'

'Yes sir.'

'And what does that tell us?'

'I don't know, sir.'

'Well, doesn't it tell us that she didn't know many people.'

'How d'you mean, sir?'

'Well, if she doesn't have any pictures of anyone else, doesn't that tell us that she was a bit of a loner?'

'Well, I guess so, sir. I mean, I think she was. I mean, that was one of the reasons she was--'

'I know that,' said Harold. 'But look carefully at those pictures.' Joe flicked through them again. He saw Rose Crowne's vivacious smiling face and slim body in some and the views of trees and flowers in others. But he didn't have a clue what his superior was driving at.

'Has it occurred to you that she must have known someone?'

'Well, I'm sure she knew people, sir. You said so yourself. I mean, she knew us for a start.'

'Yes, Joe,' said Harold, through his teeth. 'But she must have known someone in a personal capacity.'

'How do you make that out, sir?'

'Well, for goodness sake, Joe! someone must have taken the pictures of her.'

'I see what you mean.'

Joe flushed with embarrassment. He realized that, with all his attention to the physical detail, he had overlooked the human side. And his superior, for all his detachment and disinterest, had spotted a relevant, not to say highly intriguing, detail that he had overlooked.

'You mean, like a close friend.'

'Precisely, Joe.'

'But, in that case, sir,' Joe continued nervously. 'How come there are no pictures of the friend in either of these albums?'

'How, indeed, Joe.'

Joe thought to himself for a minute.'

'Oh--oooohhhh!'

'Having an orgasm, are we, Joe?'

'Sorry sir. I mean, I've got it.'

'Ah, so the penny has dropped.'

'Er, yes sir. Sorry it took me so long to figure out it, sir.'

'That's all right, Joe. That's why I'm the gaffer and you're the coolie.'

Neil Douglas looked around the room at the three faces. The two men looked cold and unsympathetic. Only the young uniformed policewoman looked as though she had a trace of pity. She seemed young, barely more than a schoolgirl. She had a notebook in front of her, although it couldn't be to take notes of the proceedings, as they were being recorded. Her main job appeared to be to mark the tapes as they came out of the cassette recorder. That would explain the notebook, Neil realized. She also had to log them for future reference in the inquiry.

Detective Chief Inspector Adams began by reciting the same litany of warnings and cautions that he had given to Nick Lloyd. Unlike Nick however, Neil Douglas was hearing these things for the first time.

'As with your colleague, I'd like to begin by going back to the night of Monday the 24th of May.'

Neil was sitting opposite DCI Adams and the inscrutable, ever silent Detective Sergeant Johnson in the interview room.

'Could you tell me, PC Douglas, about the events from when the incident on Hampstead Heath first came to your attention.'

There was a heavy pause. Neil took a deep breath before speaking, tensing up noticeably.

'I refuse to answer sir.'

He released his breath, the tension slipping away in time with the motion of his lungs.

DCI Adams looked like he'd just been hit in the face.

'You what?'

'Refuse to answer sir.'

'What are you talking about, constable? It's not as if the question is particularly incriminating. I could understand if you refused to answer a specific question. But all I'm asking you to do at this stage is cast your mind back to the day in question.'

'I know, sir. But I've consulted the duty solicitor for advice, and I've decided to exercise my right to remain silent.'

'Is that what he advised you to do?' asked Adams incredulously.

'I'm sorry, but I'm not at liberty to discuss any legal advice I may have been given.'

'Look, constable, you do realize that this hearing is as much for your benefit as for anyone else's. It's to give you the chance to tell your side of the story and to make sure you're given a chance to tell us what happened, from your point of view. If, for instance, we hear from other witnesses any facts or purported facts that are incriminating to you, this is your chance to pre-empt them or to answer the points they've raised. Now, I'm not saying that anyone has accused you of anything, but if any of the private citizens who we hope to question say anything against you, it won't look good if you've had the chance to give us your version of events already and refused to do so.'

'I understand that, sir, but as you said, I have the right to remain silent and at the end of the day, if the governors think I've broken any of the rules it's up to them to prove it.'

'You do realize what you're saying constable?'

'Fully, sir. I'm taking advantage of the same right to remain silent that any common criminal has.'

'Exactly. If you know the implications of that.'

'And like any common criminal sir, or any ordinary member of the public for that matter, I'm innocent until proven guilty.'

'That may be, constable, but the range of charges that you can be guilty of is somewhat wider than the range of charges that can be laid at the door of an ordinary member of the public.'

'Such as what, sir?' asked Neil trying to avoid sounding truculent but ending up sounding afraid.

'Such as Neglect of Duty.'

'I can hardly be accused of that, sir. I may have been overzealous in my performance of it.'

The DCI smiled. PC Douglas had already broken his resolve to remain silent.

'Or there's Bringing the Force into Disrepute,' the Discontinued. 'That's quite a wide one. We could probably have got Mother Teresa on that one - if she'd been a copper.'

Neil said nothing. The DCI watched him for a few seconds, wondering if his façade of resilience would crack a second time. Neil felt the clock on the wall ticking away as he glowed under the DCI's scrutiny.

'You have an academic degree don't you, Neil?' The DCI's tone had suddenly become friendly. Neil's suspicions were alerted.

'Yes sir. Psychology.'

'And I understand you've been accepted to the Accelerated Promotion Scheme.'

'Yes sir. I'm due to start in four months.'

That meant two years at the National Police College at Bramshill, returning to active duty as an Inspector.

'You do realize of course that this case could prejudice your application. I mean, you've been accepted, but Bramshill is a privilege, not a right.'

The truth of the matter was that he had thought about it. And he knew that he was playing with fire. He just didn't know what to do, and being paralysed by indecision he felt that doing nothing was the least of the choice of evils. In any case, he knew they wouldn't rush into a decision about him. They'd give him time to reconsider and maybe the problem would resolve itself without a statement from him.

After a few seconds the inquisitor broke eye contact and Neil knew that he had won.

'All right, constable, I'll tell you what I'm going to do. There's two weeks before the inquest into Rose Crowne's death and you're probably worried about that. Presumably you've been subpoenaed.'

'Yes sir.'

'And no doubt you're worried about what they're going to ask you there, and maybe you're also concerned that you may get some of the details wrong or not remember things accurately and then find you've committed yourself. So, I'll tell you what I'm going to do. I'm going to recommend to your regional Chief Superintendent that you be given two weeks' sick leave. We'll say it's to help you with the psychological stress of the incident and, if necessary, we'll get one of our more cooperative doctors to sign the papers. You go home and think about it and then we'll resume after the inquest.'

Neil realized that, taken one way, this could be read as the DCI telling him to make sure he got his story right for the inquest. But on the other hand, Neil knew he had the right to remain silent at the inquest too, and he wasn't sure whether or not to avail himself of the right.

What bothered him was that he remembered all too clearly another time when he had used the false excuse of illness to evade doing his duty. It had led to one of the most painful sequences of events in his life - one that had left scars that still hadn't fully healed. But this time he really needed to get his thoughts under control. And there was no other way he could do it.

All he could think of now was that he was glad to be getting out of this room.

'Thank you, sir,' he mumbled.

Chapter 4

'Yes folks, once again, it's that time when all the dirty laundry comes out,' Beth Porter's American accented voice rang out stridently over the strains of the final chorus of Elton John's *The Bitch is Back*. 'When the liars and the cheats get their comeuppance and when you have the chance to say what *you* think about the people who make this world such a miserable place. It's ten p.m. and that makes it *The Bitching Hour*. Four hours actually. Four hours of non-stop talk and music mix, in which I call the topic but you call the tune. I'm your host, Beth Porter, the nocturnal bitch - that means bitch of the night to you uneducated oiks out there.'

She slid the fader down quickly to fade out the music completely. She wanted to be heard now, without straining her voice. Furthermore, she knew that when the sound got too loud at this time of night people turned their radios down in order to avoid disturbing the neighbours and that made it hard for them to hear the talk afterwards. This was especially difficult for a programme like hers, a mixture of music and talk. One of the reasons that the radio industry preferred to keep discussion programmes and music separate- not just the programmes but even the stations as a whole-was because they wanted to maintain a fairly constant volume level, something that a mixture of talk and music makes very hard to achieve.

'Tonight we've got a very interesting programme lined up as always. We've got music from the seventies and, hopefully, we're going to have a lively discussion on some of the interesting things in the news lately - one in particular's been nagging away at me and I want to share my thoughts about it with you. Hopefully, you'll also share your thoughts about it with me. But I warn you in advance, as usual, if you say anything stupid, I'll tell you straight out what an idiot you are before cutting you off the air. That's right folks, once again I give you this timely reminder that tact and politeness are not my middle names. But first off let's have a taste of some vintage seventies from ABBA.'

She pressed a button on one of the two CD players and the sound of *Give me a man after midnight* blared into the homes of three and half million listeners in the London, Middlesex and Essex areas.

'Pass my coffee,' she said to Mick, the sixteen-year-old school leaver who served as one of her assistants.

He handed it over meekly, and more than a little resentfully. She always asked Mick to make her coffee rather than Jane, her eighteen-year-old female assistant, because she wanted to make sure that he didn't get the idea that women were the secretaries and coffee-makers while men did the more important work.

On the other hand, she was never vindictive towards him. On one occasion, when she overheard him telling a technician that she was a lesbian, which was at best a half-truth, she didn't report him to the producer or tick him off but merely came up behind him and said 'with men like you, can you blame me?' She had said it chidingly, but it actually made him feel good, if for no other reason than because she referred to him as a 'man', not a 'boy'.

As he put the coffee down on her left side, where she liked it, she adjusted the microphone boom and arranged her papers to make sure that everything was in order for the first hour of her programme. In addition to the various computers for advertisements, jingles and 'visual talkback' with those outside the studio, she had a laptop computer so she could quickly check things up. There were often factual queries from listeners, or things she needed to look up quickly. With a few keystrokes she could track down all manner of information from anywhere in the world. The computer was between her and Jane so that she could turn the screen on its stand and hand the keyboard over when she needed to concentrate on other callers while something was being checked up.

Jane was also a school leaver. She had arrived there with an A grade A level in Art and a C pass in Government and Politics, but nothing in the sciences. She was, by her own admission, completely computer illiterate when she first got the job, but under Beth's training and tutelage she had undergone a complete transformation and now styled herself 'the first female nerd.' This wasn't strictly true, for a number of reasons. First of all, she was neither a programmer nor a hacker in any sense of the word. She couldn't actually program a computer, merely configure one and find her way around it efficiently, learning how to use new software packages quickly and without fear or fuss. Secondly, there were plenty of girls before her who had just as much skill and some who could program, or hack into restricted access areas on the Internet, something that Jane still couldn't do - although not for lack of trying. Finally, she was too pretty to be a nerd; blonde and with a perfect, smooth complexion she was the stuff of the masturbatory fantasies of nerds, certainly not one of them herself.

Beth eyed Jane's perfect complexion, displayed in abundance by a skimpy white halter top, and let her mind run free with a fantasy of her own.

'Why can't I stay up and listen to mummy?'

'Because you're too young, Steven. You can have the radio on in bed, but quietly.'

Steven was Beth's four-year-old son. He hated not having mummy around at night, especially when he couldn't sleep. On days when he slept in the afternoon, he was full of energy at night and was wide awake. At the weekend he had mummy around to comfort him, but when he couldn't sleep in the middle of the week, he felt lonely. And although Paula was nice enough, she wasn't mummy.

Paula, a student who shared a converted flat in the house next door, genuinely loved children and hoped one day to have children of her own. But she really felt that Beth ought to spend more time with Steven, even if it meant scaling down her career.

The music came to an end just as Beth was taking a quick sip of coffee. She scowled at Mick. He had made it too hot as usual, but she didn't have time to tell him. She grabbed the microphone boom and pulled it closer to her face.

'That was ABBA with *Give Me a Man After Midnight* – and *please* don't phone in with that stupid joke about "why not before midnight?" or I'll scream. I've heard it so many times, I just wish I had a pound for every time I've heard it – in fact, even a penny would do.

'OK, now the topic I want to talk about today is the case of Martin Roebuck. Now, I mean not just this latest case where some

Wild Bill Hickok of a policeman hit him on the head with a baton and left him in a coma. I'm also talking about the original case that put Martin Roebuck in the headlines a few years ago: the murder of Leah Irons and the case against him that collapsed. I've been reading up about the case and there seem to be some interesting facts that don't get talked about. And I'd like to share some of these things with you.

'For example, another man - the one with long hair - was seen on Hampstead Heath that day. Secondly, a lot of people think that in the undercover operation with Annie Jacobs, that Martin Roebuck confessed to the murder of Leah Irons. In fact, he did nothing of the sort. He told Annie Jacobs that he didn't do it, even when she made it a condition of continuing their relationship that he confess to the murder. In other words, she said that she would only continue with him if he did it and instead he said "I'm sorry, but I didn't. " But not many people know that. You see, this is where people get mixed up. Because the Annie Jacobs evidence was excluded, and because the exclusion of the evidence led to the collapse of the case against Martin Roebuck, everyone assumes that Roebuck must have confessed to her. In fact, he didn't. The police claim that he told Annie Jacobs details of the crime that he couldn't have known from the papers or from the pictures they showed him, but we only have their word for that. The psychologist, Peter Eckland, claimed that his character profile matched Martin Roebuck perfectly; but that's just his opinion, and the question is, when did he prepare his profile and did he change it to match Roebuck? Could he really know that much about a murderer's character from a single crime. I mean, from a serial crime pattern perhaps, but a single crime?

'Well, that's my opinion anyway. But it's your opinions that make the show, when they're not too stupid, that is. So what I'd like to hear, ladies and gentlemen, are your thoughts on the two cases. I won't repeat the rest of the facts, but we'll talk about them as you raise them. The question is, how do you feel about the fact that an innocent man is lying in a hospital bed in a coma, possibly with permanent brain damage, because some gung ho cop doesn't have the degree of self-control that we've got the right to expect from our policemen?

'If you've got any thoughts on this subject, the number to ring is 020 7946 0909.'

Neil Douglas was in the kitchen, making a cup of tea. He had been planning to watch News at Ten, but he had already seen the BBC news at nine o'clock and he didn't expect to hear or see anything else of interest. A feeling of discomfort and unfamiliarity inhabited his bones. He couldn't get used to the feeling of having spent the whole day at home on a weekday. On days like this, if he spent the day at home at all, he'd be spending the night out on patrol in the streets, but he had nothing to do now except watch TV or go to bed. The Teletubbies and the afternoon soaps had become his staple diet. He was also afflicted by an impatience that rendered him unable to read more than a few pages at a time. He used to read a lot until he was twenty and then he just stopped. He had given up studying and the only things he read nowadays were police manuals. His whole mood was perpetually hyper. He just couldn't concentrate on the written word. Television was easy. One didn't have to focus on a string of words forming sentences and concepts. One just had to look at moving pictures, recognize faces and listen to spoken words which seldom added up to anything that taxed his faculty for conceptual thinking.

There had been nothing in the nine o'clock news that appealed to his curiosity. It wasn't that he was indifferent, he just hadn't seen anything about which he felt he needed further information. There wasn't really any news at all;just the latest reports of ongoing conflicts at home and abroad. Even the reporting of his own case was confined to a reference to the fact that he was on sick leave and that the coroner's inquest for Rose Crowne was two weeks away. There wasn't even any mention of the fact that Martin Roebuck was still in a coma with doctors refusing to speculate on his recovery prospects. People were beginning to forget already. People had become blasé about the suffering of others, although quick to fall back on the contemporary quackery of 'counselling' when they were the victims.

It was just that he couldn't forget. He had relived the moment over and over again when his hand had lashed out. He had dreamed about it and woken up in a cold sweat. He had tried to tell himself over and over again that his hand had been acting on its own, unconnected from his mind. That's how it was in the dream, with his mind shouting 'no!' even as the hand lashed out and struck Roebuck on the temple. But in his waking moments he knew that this was not the reality. The reality was that he had lashed out, not in cold blood but deliberately in anger. When he had looked down at the bleeding and lifeless form of Rose Crowne, he had genuinely believed that Roebuck was the man who attacked her. There seemed no room for any other interpretation of what he saw at the time. There was no one else there. Roebuck was standing over the woman holding the branch of a tree. There was blood all over the victim, and in the dim light there was no way he could have known what particular type of weapon had inflicted those wounds. It could as easily have been a blunt object as a sharp one. Only when field lights were set up around the body did it become clear that they were knife wounds.

And to top it all, the attacker had got away. Worse still, there was little chance of catching him. So many police and ambulance men had trampled over the site. Taking Roebuck to the hospital had been a priority over preserving the crime scene for the SOCO and the forensic scientists who would have to sift through and analyse the physical evidence.

No, there was nothing he wanted to see on the television. And nothing else he really wanted to do. He went to the bathroom and turned on the water in the shower. It usually took about a minute for the water from the immersion heater to run hot and then it was usually too hot and he had to fiddle with the cold tap to get it right. So he left it running while he went to the bedroom to get undressed.

'Well, I mean, like that picture of the suspect,' said a man in a South London accent, through the telephone. 'You know that police picture.'

'The photofit?' Beth prompted.

'Yeah, that one.'

'What about it?'

'Well, I mean, blimey, it looked exactly like Roebuck. And that woman who was there on 'ampstead 'eaf. She picked 'im out from a line-up.'

47

By now, as many as four million people were listening to The Bitching Hour in London and the Home Counties.

'First of all, Charlie, the hairline was completely different. Secondly, you do know that it was the same woman who gave the information that formed the basis for the photofit. So, all she was doing was picking a man who vaguely resembled her own description. Thirdly, the man in that picture was not necessarily the man who murdered Leah Irons.'

'Course 'e was.'

'Why do you say that, Charlie?'

''e must've been.'

'Why *must* he?'

'Well. . . I mean. . . they said so, didn't they?'

'Who said so, Charlie?'

'The coppers.'

'And how do they know?'

'Well, blimey. . . I mean. . . they're not stupid.'

'I never said they were stupid, Charlie. I haven't even said *you're* stupid yet. I don't want to insult my listeners' intelligence by pointing out the obvious. But how do they know that the man in the picture was the man who murdered her? And are you sure they actually said it was?'

'Well, why did they show 'is picture on *Crimewatch* if 'e didn't do it?'

'All right, Charlie. Let me see if I can get through to that peanut brain of yours.'

She had changed her style, Jane and Mick realized. Usually, she would have cut off a caller like this by now, but she was playing with him, like a cat playing with a cornered mouse, knowing that it has nowhere to run.

What they didn't know was why. But Beth did. For once in her life she really believed in what she was doing. Normally, she just stirred up controversy for the sake of it, as with her 'moon landing never took place' campaign. She knew perfectly well that the so-called evidence against the moon landing was pure unadulterated drivel. But it stirred people up and excited them. Her only disappointment was that too many people had believed her and the other revisionists and so she had been forced to drop the campaign somewhat earlier than she had intended. But now she really

48

believed what she was saying, and she was going at it hammer and tongs.

'Let me ask you again the question you didn't answer, Charlie. How did the police know that the man in the picture was the murderer?'

'Well, I dunno. I s'ppose someone *sor*rim.'

'Yes, Charlie, someone saw him. That was the barrister's wife, Bridget Anne Vanderbilt. She was on the Heath with her children. But what I wanted to know was are you saying that she - or let's say the person who gave the police the description for the picture. Are you saying that the person who gave the police the description for the picture saw the murder being committed?'

'Well, no, I'm not saying that.'

'Are you saying that the person who gave that description saw the man running away and then immediately saw the body on the spot where he had run from?'

'Well, I don't know. I mean, it might've been.'

'Might've been?'

'Yeah.'

'Charlie, will you take my word for it if I tell you that all she saw was a man who looked suspicious, three times, each time carrying a large bag, and once with a belt or strap round his shoulder that wasn't there the other two times?'

'Well yeah, I suppose so.'

'OK, then would you also accept the logical conclusion that this means that the man in the picture wasn't necessarily the murderer, just someone who one witness thought was acting suspiciously.'

'Yeah, but even so. She did pick 'im from the line up. So 'e must've been there and not at 'ome like 'e said.'

'Are you aware of the fact that her children were also given the chance to identify at the identity parade and that none of them picked him?'

'Yeah, but they was children. They might've been too young to recognize 'im. And also, she said afterwards that she was sure. When he was filmed walking out of court after 'e was convicted of something else? When she saw his stooping walk.'

'Yes, that's right, Charlie. But all that means is that she wasn't sure before. So why did she pick him?'

49

'Well you'll 'ave to ask 'er that, won't you?'

Beth smiled, but not without a tinge of disappointment. All the fight had gone out of him.

'By the way, Charlie, are you aware of the fact that serious questions have been raised about whether or not the other men in the identity parade even looked like Martin Roebuck?'

'They all say that.'

'You mean, they really did look like him?' asked Beth, dangling the bait in front of him again.'

'Well, I don't know' Charlie replied hesitantly, smelling the trap.

'No, you don't, Charlie,' she said her voice uncharacteristically gentle for delivering the customary *coup de grace* to an ignorant caller. 'But you assume. And that's the trouble Charlie, we assume too much. You don't know that the other people in the line-up didn't look like Roebuck, but you assumer they did.'

She was speaking from the heart, and for once her voice was not stinging and vitriolic but warm and embracing.

'You don't know that the man in the picture was the man who murdered Leah Irons, but you *assume* he was. People out there don't know that Roebuck never confessed to killing Leah Irons, but they *assume* he did. And that's why this man has been systematically hounded by the press and by strangers who shout abuse at him in the street. Because people assume things even when they don't know – instead of keeping open minds.'

At the end of her diatribe her voice perked up, but only slightly.

'Let's take a break and listen to some music from Don McLean. This one's very appropriate to what we've just been talking about. It's called *The Pride Parade*.'

She pushed back the microphone and took a major swig from her coffee cup.

'It's getting to you, isn't it, Beth?' said Jane comfortingly.

'You're learning to read me, honey,' Beth replied, gently stroking Jane's bare arm with the tip of her index finger.

Neil left the bathroom with a towel wrapped round his waist and another smaller one round his head. He walked into the

50

bedroom, a fairly large room by the standards of a British flat, lit by two halogen desk lamps, one on the desk itself and the other by his bed. The curtains were drawn across open windows, protecting his privacy but letting in the air to cool the room in the face of the unceasing summer heat-wave.

With a flick of a finger, he switched on the radio, flooding the room with music. He recognized the voice as that of Don McLean. He was a fan of that genre: Paul Simon, Leonard Cohen, Don McLean, Suzanne Vega – troubadours whose songs were poems set to music, not just rhythms to guide the movement of adolescent feet on a dance floor. The last verse came to an end with words asking where the listener belongs?' It had a strange haunting quality about it, but he didn't want to dwell on it.

'That was *The Pride Parade* from Don McLean. This time the voice was Beth Porter's. Neil didn't like her, but he liked her choice of music. If the rest of the show was going to be like this, then he might listen to it, at least for a while. Also, he was curious if she was going to say anything more about him. She had mentioned him a couple of times since the incident and it was usually some derogatory comment about 'that gung ho cop'.

'OK, we have Paul from Hammersmith on the line. Good evening, Paul.'

'Hello, Beth.'

'Now I understand you want to say something in defence of our baton-wielding copper.'

Neil froze, petrified, as he recognized the snide reference to himself. He had heard her talking about him in the past, but now it felt as if she was there in the room with him, taunting him with his guilt.

'Yes, that's right, and could I just say I think you're being very unfair to him.' He sounded like a retired colonel -with that almost military brand of confidence bordering on cockiness. There was no way he was going to let a woman get the better of him. 'First of all, remember that this young policeman was out there risking his life doing a difficult and dangerous job so the rest of us can sleep safely in our beds at night. He comes across a situation in which a man is standing holding the branch of a tree over a woman who's lying there bleeding. He tells the man to drop the branch. The man doesn't drop it and he hits the man's arm *once* with his baton. Now

51

I feel very sorry for Martin Roebuck, at least in this case, but he brought it on himself.'

Neil Douglas climbed into bed, not to retreat from the sounds of others discussing him but to listen from a posture in which retreat was possible if necessary. He was relieved to hear someone else defending him but the relief was shallow because he knew that this man was wrong, and Beth, for all her harshness and sarcasm, was right.

'Paul, let me ask you a question. How do you *know* that Roebuck didn't drop the branch.'

There was a split-second of hesitation. 'Well, that's what it said in the papers.'

'Paul, you sound like an intelligent man, not like that semi-literate moron I was speaking to a few minutes ago. Now, first of all, I don't need to tell you that the fact that a policeman does a difficult and dangerous job doesn't give him carte blanche to do as he pleases at the expense of an innocent member of the public.'

'Well, I could question whether Roebuck's innocent,' said the caller stiffly, 'but I take your point.'

'Paul, he was found not guilty in the Leah Irons case and even the police have conceded his innocence in this case. He's innocent in the eyes of the law.'

'Fair enough, I accept that point. But so is this PC Douglas. He's also entitled to the presumption of innocent until proven guilty.'

'He may be entitled to that presumption as an individual with regard to criminal charges but I'm raising the issue in a different context. I'm raising the issue of the police as an institution and Neil Douglas as a representative of that institution. My question is, do the police as an institution have the right to lash out at an innocent man and put him in a coma. We don't have to wait for a criminal or civil verdict to discuss this issue. We as members of the sovereign public have the right to discuss these matters *now*.'

'Maybe, but the fact remains that Roebuck could have avoided getting hit if he'd just dropped the branch.'

The retired colonel was getting flustered. He was used to giving or taking orders and not debating moral issues with equals - especially a woman.

'But by your own admission, the only reason you think that he didn't drop the baton is because the papers said so.'

'All right. If my memory serves me right, PC Nick Lloyd, the partner of PC Douglas in the patrol car, told the papers that the suspect didn't drop the branch.'

'But what does Neil Douglas say?' asked Beth.

Again the grip of fear tightened around Neil as he wondered how much the press had discovered.

'As far as I know he hasn't said anything.'

'Exactly. He's chosen to remain silent. '

'He's been granted sick leave because he's still in a state of shock' said the ex-colonel. 'That shows he's a man with a conscience.'

'Yes, but could that perhaps be a *guilty* conscience.'

'Even if it is, that doesn't mean he's guilty in law. He probably feels guilty because he found out afterwards that the man he hit was innocent. But that doesn't mean he acted wrongly at the time.'

Neil felt like a man being torn apart on the rack. On the one hand, he was grateful to hear the voice of a stranger speaking up on his behalf, amidst the chorus of criticism and vilification that was being directed at him by Beth Porter and certain sections of the mass media. On the other hand, he knew in his own mind that he was unworthy of such eloquent defence and impassioned advocacy. To hear himself defended was in some way more painful than to hear himself attacked. He had even toyed with the idea of coming clean and telling the truth at the 'rubber heels' interview, but he knew he couldn't do that because it would sink Nick. Nick had gone out on a limb for him by saying from the beginning that Roebuck had taken a menacing step towards them. Neil knew that if he now came clean and admitted that this wasn't so, then it would be Nick's career that was damaged as well as his own. He had always suspected Nick of being a bit of a bad apple, but in this case Nick's only sin had been to go out on a limb for *him*. Neil realized that if he lifted the weight off his conscience with a full confession he would not only be ruining his own career but also dragging Nick down with him. He was prepared to give up a police career, realizing now that he was not cut out for it, but he had no right to penalize Nick for the sake of his conscience -

especially when Nick had stuck his neck out to help his less experienced partner, who had made the mistake in the first place.

A few miles away in a radio studio overlooking Knightsbridge, Beth was now really getting into it with the retired colonel. She didn't usually keep callers on the line as long as she had this evening, and Paul was likely to be on the line even longer than Charlie if things carried on like this.

'Paul, have you ever stopped to wonder, isn't it strange that Roebuck should have acted this way? Risking his life for a stranger one minute and resisting the police the next. And if we're to grant the police some latitude to act and some indulgence for their mistakes because they do a difficult and dangerous job then shouldn't we also give the benefit of the doubt to a private citizen who went to the aid of a woman who was being attacked? A man who risked his life to help a stranger? Should we be so quick to believe that such a man threatened a cop with a branch of a tree just because some ageing police constable says so? Shouldn't we give *Roebuck* the benefit of the doubt at least until we've heard *his* side of the story?'

'Well, what I want to know,' said Paul stiffly, 'is what a man with his background was doing in such close proximity to a woman on a quiet road on a dark night.'

'A man with whose background?' asked Beth. Jane gave her a side long glance, noticing the hint of rising anger in her voice.

'Martin Roebuck's.'

'Let me get this straight, Paul. Are you saying that Martin Roebuck doesn't have the right to walk down a street in his own neighbourhood at night because a woman happens to be walking down it too?'

'I mean, in view of his record,' Paul repeated belligerently.

'His *record*? Paul, have you forgotten that he was acquitted?'

'Only on a technicality.'

Jane saw Beth's face contort with anger.

'Well, Paul, you weren't charged with the offence because of the same technicality.'

'What are you talking about? I was never even a suspect!

'No? And why not?'

'Because I had nothing to do with the case. There was no reason to suspect me.'

'You mean, there was no evidence?'

'Of course there was no evidence! I had nothing to do with it! I don't even live in the area!Well, there you are then. You weren't charged because of the technicality that they didn't have any evidence against you.'

'That's ridiculous! That's not a technicality!'

'Isn't it, Paul?' said Beth with the cutting, gentle tone that sliced away the last pillar beneath the platform that supported the caller's argument. 'Roebuck was acquitted because there wasn't enough evidence to prove him guilty. And yet you call that a *technicality*. If *not enough* evidence is a technicality then no evidence is also a technicality. It's just a matter of degree and so you're no different from Roebuck.'

'That's ridiculous!' snapped Paul before slamming down the phone.

This was a first for her: a caller who put the phone down before she cut them off. But then again it was also a sign of victory. It meant that he couldn't answer her point or refute her logic. It also meant that she was riling her audience, and in ratings terms that meant she was *hot*.

Neil was lying in bed, fighting consciousness as best he could, but losing the battle. He had switched off the desk lamp but left the halogen lamp on by the bed, flooding his personal space with soft light but not to the point of straining his eyes. He couldn't face the darkness: it brought back the darkness of Hampstead Heath on that awful night, and the darkness inside him that he wanted to face even less.

From the radio, the voice of Beth Porter was still taunting him. That seemed to be his lot from now on, to be taunted by the voice of Beth Porter and haunted by the face of Martin Roebuck.

But what did Beth have against him? Why was she hounding him like this. She had used her radio programme for crusades before. But they had been one or two day crusades, until something else came along. She never really meant any of it, she just used them to stir up her listeners but she had kept this up for two weeks, relentlessly. And she didn't have that usual cheeky mocking or caustically sarcastic tone in her voice when she challenged the listeners. She sounded impassioned and angry, as if she really meant it. Neil wondered, with dread, if she really did.

He felt his nose sniffling and his throat choking up and he realized he was lucky that his father wasn't here to see it.

He found himself wondering what he had done to earn such contempt. He had always thought of himself as one of the 'good guys', one of the people who served the community and protected the people from danger. If he'd followed his early ambition, he could have had a flourishing career as a clinical psychologist but instead he spent his days and some of his nights patrolling the streets, alert and ready to face and confront any criminal on his patch at a moment's notice.

Yet now, one mistake later, he found himself on the receiving end of the opprobrium and contempt of the very people he always tried to serve and protect.

Why should she hate me this much? he asked himself, his eyes welling up with tears.

He couldn't go on like this. He had never intended his life to come to this. If this was all there was to look forward to, then there was no point to it.

He reached for the phone by the bed and keyed in the number of the radio station.

'Sheila from Islington on Line 8.'

'Hello, Beth,' an enthusiastic old woman's voice boomed.

'Hello, Sheila. I understand you want to make a point about the differences between the two cases.'

'That's right. What I wanted to say was that in the Leah Irons case, the attack took place in broad daylight. But in this latest attack on her – '

'On Rose Crowne.'

'Yes, Rose Crowne. It took place late at *night*.'

'So what's your point?'

'Well, it doesn't necessarily have to be the same person. I mean it's a different – what do they call it *modus operandi*.'

'Yes, that's true, but that doesn't necessarily mean it's a different person.'

'No, but there's a good chance. Don't forget, during the day, the killer could be sure there'd be lots of people on the Heath. That means it would be more dangerous, but on the other hand he could be sure of finding a random victim. On a Monday night, at that time, he couldn't be sure of finding anyone. Unless he was looking for some one in particular.'

'So you think that someone targeted Rose Crowne in particular?'

'Yes. I mean it could be, couldn't it?'

'It certainly could. Well, thank you, Sheila. Let's go to -on second thoughts let's take a break for some music. Let's see how many of you thirty-somethings out there remember Tina Charles. I know this is one to dance to. So for those of you night birds who aren't yet in bed, let's boogie to the vintage sound of *I Love to Love*.'

She pressed the button and turned to Mick.

'OK, what is it?' He had been signalling her frantically.

'I've got Neil Douglas on the phone - at least he *claims* to be Neil Douglas.'

Beth looked down at the screen in front of her, not the computer monitor but the white visual talkback screen where they flashed up the names and details of the callers. Neil's name wasn't there.

'So why didn't you send me his details, I could have taken him next?'

She was irritable and it showed in her voice.

'He refuses to come on the air,' said Mick, apologetically. He said he wanted to talk to you privately.'

'OK, we'll do a back to back with the next track. Put him through.' Mick put the call through to Beth's headset. 'Hello.'

'Hello, is that Beth Porter?'

'That's me,' she said, making sure to inject a suitable amount of confidence into her tone. The last thing she wanted was for a caller to take control of the conversation, even off the air.

'Why are you *doing* this?'

She realized she had nothing to fear. The voice was whining. Not a real man at all, more of a man- child who need his mother to wipe his nose.

'Who is this?'

'I told that man who answered the phone. I'm Neil Douglas.'

'And you want to know why I'm discussing a case that's been in the news? Or why I'm expressing sympathy for an innocent man who got whacked on the head by a policeman?'

'I want to know why you've got it in for me.'

'Why I've got it in for *you*? If you think I've got it in for you then you haven't really been listening to me. I have nothing against you personally. I mean, I think you did wrong, but I don't hate you for it. It's the sort of mistake that any cop could make. What bothers me is that there seems to be one law for the police and another for the rest of us. What bothers me is that what you did isn't regarded as all that serious. Normally, if a man whacks another man on the head like you did, he's arrested on the spot. He maybe released later but initially he's arrested and questioned. With you, the presumption appears to be that you did nothing wrong.'

'Then why am I being hounded by the press?'

'You're not being hounded by everyone. You've got your own group of supporters in the tabloids, in case you hadn't noticed.'

There was a pause. Beth realized that perhaps he hadn't noticed. Perhaps he was more sensitive to the criticism than he was aware of the support. Or perhaps, she speculated, the support was as much of a reproach to him as the criticism.

'But why are you going on about it so much? You don't know me. You don't know about all the good things I've done. I don't mean big things, I mean little things that make a difference. "

"Like what?"

He hesitated.

"Well. . . like a few words of comfort and support to a victim. Like talking a pair of feuding neighbours into making up their differences and seeing the other's point of view. If you knew how many neighbour disputes turn ugly, you'd know that reconciling two neighbours is as much a blow for law and order as catching a burglar or a killer.'

'Neil, I'm not disputing that you've done some good things in your life. '

'Then why don't you mention them?'

'Well, I couldn't mention what I didn't know.'

'Well, now you know so maybe you-'

'No, I *don't* know.'

'But I've told you.'

'You've told me very little. Now, if you want to go on the air and tell the listeners in your own words whatever you'd like to say that isn't slanderous or obscene, you're welcome to have your say.
"

"I can't talk about it on the air. The matter if the subject of an ongoing investigation. '

'If you can't go on the air, then there's nothing I can do to help you.'

'No,' he said bitterly. 'I guess there isn't.'

The line went dead.

Chapter 5

'Nick, could you come here a minute.'

Nick Lloyd had been halfway down the corridor towards the side exit of Golders Green police station when Inspector Walker called out to him from the incident room. Walker was third in command of the Criminal Investigation Department team looking into the murder of Rose Crowne.

'Yes sir,' Nick Lloyd turned round as Walker leaned halfway out of the room. He'd had been about to go out on patrol with his new temporary partner, who was already waiting for him in the car, but if Walker called him, there had to be a reason.

He followed Walker into the incident room. It was packed with equipment and charts, but he and Walker were the only people there. It was eight in the morning and most of the other CID men would get there at nine. PC Lloyd imagined that it must be quite crowded when they were all there. He had heard rumours that the incident room was going to be transferred to the Hendon station, which was larger, and that the investigation might even be augmented by several more plain clothes officers. Like the murder of Leah Irons several years before, the murder of Rose Crowne had shocked and outraged the public. Furthermore, there was increasing public speculation that it had been done by the same man -and that meant that Martin Roebuck was in the clear, even though he was still reviled by some as the probable killer of Leah Irons.

'Yes sir,' said Lloyd, realizing that he had been daydreaming.

'We've had the reports back from the detectives checking out the cars.'

'How do you mean?' asked Nick, confused.

'We identified four blue Fords that started with M244and we checked up the owners, others who had access to their cars and the whereabouts of the cars themselves. We assigned two pairs to each car to check out their alibis and double check with friends and neighbours.'

'And?'

'They all checked out.'

'Are you sure, sir?'

'Of course I'm sure. We couldn't have been more careful.'

'Do you think the witness was mistaken?'

'Possibly. I mean, she was sure about the number and almost sure about the colour, but not absolutely sure of the make. We'll have to broaden the search to all blue cars starting with M244, and if necessary all cars with that number of any colour. I mean, the full list from DVLA has several hundred cars. We narrowed it down to save costs but we're ready to check out the whole lot if that's what it takes.'

As with Leah Irons, the pressure was on the police to crack this case, all the more so because they desperately needed to distract public attention from the injuries inflicted on Martin Roebuck and the questions that were being raised about discipline and competence in the police force. The cost of the Leah Irons investigation had topped a million pounds and at one point had over sixty officers working on it. The pressure for a result would be no less in this case -but they would have to be very careful to get it right.

It was looking all the more likely that they would shift the inquiry to larger headquarters. There was no way they could host such a mammoth investigation from this local station. They would either shift the incident room to Area HQ at Colindale or set up a joint inquiry with Scotland Yard, with duel incident rooms co-ordinating the information.

'Do you think we'll get him, sir?' asked Nick, almost pleadingly.

'Oh, we'll get him all right. It might take a long time. It might cost a lot of money. But we'll get him.'

'What if he sells the car?'

'What if he moves? I mean, I understand that the psycho⌧logical profile says he's probably a loner.'

'You've been talking to Morgan haven't you.'

C Lloyd said nothing.

'It's all right Lloyd, you don't have to confirm it. Morgan's the only blabber-mouth on the team. I'll have to have a word with him about it. I mean I don't mind *you* knowing about these things, or even PC Douglas, but we don't want these things getting around too much. It might compromise the investigation.'

61

'I'm sorry, sir.'

'Oh don't apologise. It's not your fault if Morgan can't keep his lips buttoned. And don't look so worried. I won't tell him I found out from you.'

'Thank you, sir.'

'The thing is, that the psychological profile calls for someone unemployed or someone who can't hold a job. But an M-reg car suggests an income. Not a wildly high income necessarily, but still an income. I mean it's not like it's some beat-up old banger from the early eighties.'

'Maybe the profile is wrong,' Lloyd suggested.

'Yes, that's what I'm beginning to think,' said the Inspector, looking uneasy.

'Isn't that bad, sir?'

'It's very bad. In the Leah Irons case, the profile was practically all they had to go on. There was no physical evidence, just the crime itself and a few sightings of a couple of suspicious looking men by members of the public.'

'A *couple* sir?'

'Not together. Separate sightings of two suspicious looking men, one with long hair, one with short. But in this case we have a car speeding away right afterwards and a number. If it had happened during the day it wouldn't have had much significance because there are loads of cars on that stretch of road. But at that time of night on a Monday, a car starting up suddenly and speeding off sticks out like a sore thumb.'

'So we *will* get him sir.'

'Only if he stays put - like you said. You see the thing that worries me is that if the profile is half right then it means we could be dealing with a man who had a job but who no longer has one. A loner who's gone through good periods and bad ones. Usually, a person with a regular job doesn't go out on a Monday night. Now, if he's unemployed and doesn't own his own home, he could easily sell his car, leave his home and move on. That actually happened with one of the suspects in the Leah Irons case.'

'Could I ask you a question, sir?'

'Go ahead.'

'Why are you telling me all this?'

'You're right, why am I telling you. You're close to PC Douglas. You go drinking with him. I just want you to let him know that we're on top of this case and we're going to catch this bastard. And when that happens, the pressure will be off him. I think that what really bothers him is the thought that the real attacker got away and is somewhere out there free to do it again.'

'I'll tell him, sir.'

'OK, thank you. You'd better go and join your partner. He's probably got the engine running by now.'

'Thank you, sir,' said Nick Lloyd, hurrying out of the room.

'Forty eight . . . forty six . . . forty . . . four. . .'

Beth Porter was counting the numbers of the houses as she drove slowly along the street. The houses varied enormously, one from the other in their state of repair, but they all had the same pebble-dashed cement façades, almost all of them with an off-white finish. And the area was reasonably affluent, although there were no Jaguars in this particular street and only one Merc.

'Forty two . . . forty . . . thirty eight.'

She had found the one she was looking for but there was nowhere to park in front of it. She could see cars lined up along the side of the street, right up to where it merged into a T-junction, so she stopped, looked in her rear view and gently reversed. The mirror and a backward glance suggested no parking spaces either, so she turned off into a wider street which offered a choice of several spaces.

She left the car and pressed once on the button of the electronic automatic locking device on her keyring. She heard the double beep confirming that the car was locked and walked away. It was a safe area in any case. Many of the people here were orthodox Jews. But caution, to Beth, was second nature. There was no point taking chances.

That was partly why she was here. She was worried by the way in which Neil Douglas had rung off so abruptly last night. Although she steadfastly refused to call him back at the time, for fear of embarrassing herself in front of Mick, it had troubled her throughout the programme and all night.

What no one except Jane knew was that she wasn't the person she appeared to be. Beth realized, unlike many entertainers, that it

63

was important to distinguish between one's public persona and one's private self. It was when that line became blurred that one ended up with headlines like 'Rock singer dies of drug overdose.' To Mick she was the 'Ice Lady', cool and unfazed by anything. She enjoyed, even relished, the reputation of one who could comfortably live with the suicide of a listener whom she had cut to shreds for the mere thrill of the sport. But the reality was not like that. In truth she didn't often lose sleep over listeners. But most of them deserved what they got and in any case she only teased them mildly. With Neil Douglas, however, it was different. She had systematically torn into him the whole evening as well as the past two weeks, and had carried on even after her conversation with him, knowing that he was still listening, or at least assuming he was. So now she had that nagging fear tugging at her arm and pulling her here.

She walked up to the entrance. It was a house that had been converted to three flats and Neil lived in 38B, the middle flat. She pressed the buzzer and waited.

'Who is it?' asked a cautious voice through the intercom.

'Beth Porter. Is that Neil Douglas?'

'What do you want?' he asked, ignoring her question.

She sighed with relief. He was alive and conscious, not lying dead or in a drug-induced stupor. She found it hard to believe what she felt, as if a weight had been lifted off her.

'I wanted to know if you were all right, after last night.'

'What's it to you?' he replied bitterly.

Beth thought for a moment. Until a couple of weeks ago she wouldn't have been able to answer a question like that. But then again, until a couple of weeks ago, such a question would have been irrelevant.

'I'm not as cold as I pretend to be.'

'You mean you blow hot and cold depending on whether it's day or night.'

The bitterness was still there in his voice. But she couldn't help laughing, not in mockery but by way of congratulation. Neil's cutting rejoinder was the kind of sound bite that made good radio.

'Touché. Look, Mr Douglas, I know I've been going on about you rather a lot, and I make no bones about being a bitch on the air. That's my job. But I want you to know that I'd be more than happy to present your side of the story.'

'I don't want to.'

'Well, can I at least talk to you? Face to face?'

'OK, I'll let you in.'

She was surprised at this, thinking that more persuasion would be necessary. When she heard the buzz, she pulled the door open and walked up the stairs to the first floor.

Neil Douglas was holding open for her the door to the flat when she got there.

'If you've come to invite me onto your programme, you can forget it.'

'I *was* going to invite you onto my programme,' she replied stepping into the pink painted vestibule.

'It's rented,' he said defensively, noticing her paying excessive attention to the colour scheme.

'Oh,' she mouthed, following him into the living room. She looked around there too. It was also pink, as was the carpet. The room was on the small side, with what looked like a kitchen table by the window overlooking the street on the far side of the room.

They faced each other nervously, both wanting to speak, neither able to overcome their embarrassment.

'Would you like a cup of coffee or tea?' he asked indicating a low, black upholstered armchair. He was trying to be a gentleman, trying to play the perfect host even though it was obvious that he felt uncomfortable with Beth.

'Oh, I'm fine,' she said, sitting down. He sat facing her in the other armchair. 'Perhaps you'll tell me *why* you don't want to appear on my show.'

'The matter is under investigation. I *can't* talk about it in public. "

'what about *afterwards* – when it's all over. "

'If I'm still a serving police officer, I won't be able to speak freely about it. "

'And if you're *not?*'

'Then a may not want to. '

'So really you're just hiding behind excuses. '

'I know how these things work. '

'What things?'

'Ambushes. I know about interviews where you have your prepared questions but the other party doesn't have prepared answers.'

'Isn't it like that in court?' she asked with a piercing stare and challenging smile.

'Yes, but in court both sides get the same treatment.'

She had been about to follow up, but she stopped in her tracks, her mouth hanging open, and nodded approvingly.

'Fair enough,' she said, when she finally got over the surprise at his eloquent response. But who's to be the other side in this case? Martin Roebuck's in hospital. You and your partner are the only witnesses and as far as I know your partner's backing you up. To all intents and purposes, it's your word and your partner's against no one's.'

'Then how come I don't seem to have such a strong case in the eyes of people like you.'

'Perhaps because you refuse to submit to questioning about the details. Because you're acting like a man who's afraid to answer questions - afraid to slip up. You're acting like a man who knows he can be caught out and doesn't want to chance it. In other words, a dishonest man.'

'Maybe I just don't like to talk to the press. Maybe I believe in the old principle that a man is innocent until proven guilty. Maybe I believe that an incident involving allegations of criminal wrongdoing should be investigated by the authorities before it's splashed all over the pages of the press. That's the way we do things in England you know.'

'You haven't cooperated with the authorities either.'

'What do you mean?' he asked tensing up suspiciously.

'You stood by the right to silence with the police disciplinary investigation too.'

'How do you know that?' he asked, the suspicion turning to fear.

'Because unlike you I take an interest in matters of injustice, as distinct from matters of law.'

'If I wasn't interested in justice I wouldn't have hit . . .'His face flushed. 'I wouldn't have become a cop.'

She forced herself not to smile. She didn't want to appear to gloat over his slip up. He knew that he had given himself away.

But he didn't regret it. He just wished she would go. It wasn't the threat of exposure that he feared, it was the threat of self realization.

'Perhaps,' she replied slowly, 'you should find out the facts before you start dispensing justice. That way you won't leave innocent men lying in a hospital bed fighting for their lives.'

'Do you really think you're in any position to cast the first stone?'

'What have I done?' she snapped back defensively.

'All those bogus stories you propagate: the "never was a moon landing" story, the false accusation about the Hillsborough football fans; playing along with the claim of that lying Hollywood bimbo and her ambulance chasing shyster, about her alleged engagement to that Egyptian after he found himself in the news. The story about Nancy Reagan returning the teddy bear that the child left as a Christmas present, without bothering to mention that she slipped a fifty dollar bill into the teddy bear.'

'A journalist is sometimes the victim of other people's dishonesty. We can be on our guard against it, but we can never prevent it completely.'

'Oh, come off it! You jump at those stories. You don't bother to check them out. You just tell them what sort of things to be careful about. You practically tell them what pitfalls to avoid. And you sure as hell don't look too closely if you smell a rat. You just play up whatever evidence you've got and withhold any evidence to the contrary. You call yourself a journalist and not just a Shock Jock but you've knowingly played along with other people's lies. Do you really think that's what a journalist does? It's like a politician selling his vote to a company that gives him a consultancy or a hooker selling her body at King's Cross.'

'Hey, come on now. I may have played fast and loose with the truth, but only on trivial stories where there was no danger of hurting anyone.'

'You don't think the relatives of the Hillsborough victims were hurt by those lies?'

'Now just a minute,' she said forcefully. 'We didn't know that was a lie. We believed what the police told us.'

'Without checking it out,' he hit back mockingly.

'There was no way we could check it out.'

'No?' he asked, raising his eyebrows. 'You couldn't have spoken to some of the survivors, perhaps?'

'All right!' she snapped, defeated. 'We fucked up on that one. But that doesn't mean we deliberately lied.'

'No, not deliberately. Just recklessly, without a second thought for whether it was true or not. You weren't immoral. You were amoral. You were outside the realm of truth or falsehood.'

'Now you're trying to be the one casting the stones.'

'I'm not sitting in judgement,' said Neil, his voice almost giving out as he sensed her acceptance of what he said. 'I'm just asking who are you to sit in judgement of me?' There was a break in his voice, and he realized that he had been on the verge of crying.

'I'm not judging you,' said Beth gently. 'But you can't compare my recklessness with the truth with your recklessness with a man's life - a man who went to the aid of a woman who was being attacked by a knife man. You may well have killed a man who deserved a medal! And for what? Because you misjudged the situation. Because you put your hand in gear before your brain was engaged. Because you decided to play Wyatt Earp on the frontier instead of the responsible layman that you swore to be.'

She realized now, too late for her conscience, that she had gone too far, for Neil Douglas was now turning away from her to hide his embarrassment, but unable to conceal the fact that he was sobbing into his hands.

'I'm sorry,' she said, realising that by this stage apologies would do no good. 'I think I'd better go.'

She stood up and looked at him, wondering if it was safe to leave. She had come here because she was concerned about him. But now she was about to leave him in a state that was at least as bad as the one he had been in when he broke off communications with her last time. Only this time, it was she who was about to sever the connection.

She decided to stay a minute longer, to make sure that he was all right. She couldn't leave him this way. She cursed herself for her uninhibited frankness. Once again her bigmouth had got someone else into trouble. She knew that she didn't hate him, couldn't hate him - especially not now. Whatever he had done, he was a man with a conscience. At least she had to acknowledge that much. The tragedy was, she thought, that while he had an abundance of conscience, he was totally lacking in courage. He may have relished the thought of playing the hero on the streets but in reality hews just a boy who needed a shoulder to cry on. And however much sympathy she felt for him, she had no shoulder to offer. It was just not part of her nature.

He seemed to have got himself under control. He was no longer crying and his hands had moved away from his face.

'I'll show you to the door,' he said, red-eyed, but his voice no longer choked. Again she suppressed a smile. He was trying to put a brave face on it and she could see that he was over the worst of it.

As she turned, her handbag swept against something on the low telephone table by the couch and an object fell a distance of barely more than a foot onto the pink carpet. He started to bend down but she stooped quickly to pick it up. She was about to put it back by the telephone when she noticed what it was: a framed picture of a man in police uniform, a man in his late forties.

'Who's this?' she asked.

Gently, but firmly, he prised the picture from her hands and put it carefully back by the telephone.

'My father,' he said, softly.

'He's also a policeman?' she asked, encouragingly.

'He was.'

Bite that tongue off you stupid bitch, she thought for the third time in twenty-four hours.

'Oh, I'm sorry.'

'He was on duty on a Friday night and he got himself killed after a confrontation with a gang of rowdy youths. He was trying to calm the situation down when he took a blow to the head that cracked his skull open at the side. He died a few hours later. I saw him in the coffin. He still had that serene smile that he always had: the smile of a man who was at peace with himself and the world.'

It wasn't the whole story. But it was all that he was ready to tell her.

Beth permitted herself to show some sympathy, even overt sympathy. She placed a hand gently on his shoulder.

'Is that why you decided to become a cop?'

'I decided to become a cop before that. I was already in training. I just wanted to make him proud of me.'

'You still can,' she said gently, walking to the front door.

'I have one request,' he said quietly following her to the door. 'I can't force you so I can only ask you.' She looked at him warmly.

'What is it?' she asked, keeping her voice soft, sensing how vulnerable he still was.

'Don't tell them I cried. Call me whatever names you like but please don't tell them I cried.'

'Wouldn't it be better if I *did* tell them? It'll show people your sensitive side.'

'I'd rather keep that to myself.'

She looked at him blankly and realized that somewhere in these words was the key to understanding Neil Douglas. But now was not the time.

'Maybe that's your problem.

Chapter 6

The pictures filled the bath, prints and negatives all thrown together in one big heap. In addition, the prints from the albums had been extracted and thrown into the pile. In preparation for the impending inferno, the window was open to let out the fumes from the melting negatives, but the smell would still linger in the room for a long time afterwards. A garden fire would have been a better way of destroying them but there was always a danger that one of the pictures might get caught by a breeze and carried away, ending up in a neighbour's garden. Rose Crowne's picture had been in the papers recently and would be instantly recognizable. So the pictures had to be destroyed in this manner. The towels had been removed from the bathroom and the lever was switched to pump water through the shower hose rather than the tap, so it could be targeted wherever it was needed.

Now was the time.

The contents of the bottle of barbecue lighter fluid were poured over the pictures and then a single match thrown in at one end. A small glow of fire caught hold in the fluid and began to spread outward, creeping off in different directions as it touched the photographs here and there. It didn't flare up immediately but gradually it caught on the corners of some of the prints and spread to others, reaching eventually from one end of the bath to the other. A glowing smile flickered across the burglar's face to match the crackling flames engulfing the photographs. In the glare of the flames a picture of Rose Crowne began to smoulder, then catch fire and finally curl up into a charred black scrap. There were many pictures of each of them separately, but few showing the two of them together. Occasionally they had asked a passer-by to photograph the two of them together. But most of the time they had taken turns at photographing each other.

A shaft of flame shot up into the air with a sizzling sound as a clump of pictures caught fire. For a moment it looked like it might be necessary to direct a jet of water from the shower hose onto the inferno. It wasn't clear how safe it was to use water at this stage of the combustion process. Once the lighter fluid was all consumed and the fire was being fuelled solely by the combustion of the pictures it would be safe. But at this stage it was still possible that some of the lighter fluid was still unconsumed and any water on the fire might explode like water in a frying pan with hot oil, at least the danger could not be ruled out. In any case the flare up soon subsided into an even sheet of flames. A foul smell rose up from the bath as the photographic negatives were engulfed in the flames. The burglar remembered reading or hearing somewhere that celluloid gave off toxic fumes when burned. Prudence and caution dictated that the bathroom be abandoned temporarily.

The closed door reduced the ventilation in the room and caused the smoke to accumulate. It would drift out of the window eventually, but it would take longer to disperse. Also, it would attract the attention of neighbours and might even result in the fire brigade being called in. This was the hottest summer on record, and with people being told not to use hose pipes in their gardens the danger of garden brush fires was quite high. The burglar thought with a wry smile that it was a case of out of the frying pan into the fire. In retrospect, it would probably have been better just to tear up the picture sand throw them away in another neighbourhood, in some public litter bin or dumpster, along with the negatives. No one would look at them. But it was too late now.

Realizing the secondary danger, the burglar took a huge deep breath, rushed in and turned the shower hose onto the bath, drenching the remnants of the pictures and extinguishing the flames. The plug was in and the water had accumulated. It was obvious that the larger scraps of the pictures would not go down the plug hole, and even some of the smaller ones might get lodged in the drain pipe so the scraps were pulled out, leaving only the smallest pieces and the powdered remnants. Then the plug was removed and again the shower hose was turned on the contents of the bath, flushing the charred powder and the smaller bits down the plug hole and into the sewage system where the burglar hoped they would-be carried away unhindered. After that, the bath itself would have to be cleaned and scoured to remove the soot from the fire.

Neil Douglas stood in the street, wrestling with indecision. He knew that he shouldn't be doing this. He was not part of the Rose Crowne murder investigation, except as a witness to some of the related events. He wasn't part of *any* murder inquiry. He wasn't a detective. He never had been. He was a uniformed policeman. He wasn't even on active duty at the moment - although technically a copper is a copper twenty four hours a day. He wasn't suspended. One couldn't be suspended for refusing to answer questions in a disciplinary hearing. But he was on sick leave. And if he had been on duty he wouldn't be investigating the murder or Rose Crowne. He would be out patrolling the streets with Nick Lloyd, while holding himself available for questioning by those who *were* conducting the Rose Crowne investigation.

But he couldn't forget the sight of that woman lying there covered in blood, her face and body ripped open in a vicious attack carried out by some sort of an animal that was a human being only in name. He couldn't live with the thought that the animal that had done this was still roaming the streets of the city, and threatening to turn the city into a jungle. Also, he felt responsible that the animal had escaped, even though he knew that in reality it had already escaped before he arrived on the scene.

Worse still, he was still haunted by Martin Roebuck and the sound of his skull cracking as the baton struck. Beth Porter had told him that she would continue to discuss the case on the air but would no longer target him and would concentrate instead on the original Roebuck case, the one concerning the murder of Leah Irons and the question mark that still hung over it. But that was no comfort. Neil's torment came not from without but from within. It was ironic, he thought, that he was suffering precisely because he did have a conscience. A man without a conscience could easily live with what he had done to Roebuck. Nick Lloyd, his cynical partner, certainly could.

He cut off that thought before letting it carry him any further. He knew that if he went that route he would end up languishing in the seductive arms of self-pity. And he knew he had no right to seek solace there. It was *he* who had done wrong, and much as he could hide it from others, he had no right to hide it from himself, nor to tell himself that he was a decent person for facing up to his guilt in private. He was still concealing it from others, by the dishonesty of silence if not by the dishonesty of an outright lie.

He considered going back to work, telling them that he was feeling better now. Certainly, that's what his father would tell him to do, not to lounge around at home feeling sorry for himself. But it would be a lie and a transparent lie at that. It was questionable whether he was really ill in medical terms. But he was certainly not 'better' in terms of his mood. He was still labouring under the same burden as before and even if he could hold it in abeyance for a while, he didn't know how long he could hold up.

would it be right to put a colleague in danger by letting him down at a critical time?r

He knew that, in reality, he was ill as far as the regulations went. In his present state of mind he was not fit for duty. His father would tell him that he was giving in to cowardice and turning the sick leave into a self-fulfilling prophecy. Be that as it may, he couldn't do the job up to the standards that his partner and the public had the right to expect, to use Beth Porter's words.

Therefore, it was right that he should be on sick leave. Only he was also too restless to stay at home. He wanted to know the truth. He wanted to know who was this evil animal who had slashed at Rose Crowne and left her a bloody mess. He wanted to know who could inflict such pain and suffering on a fellow human being and for what cause. He had a degree in psychology - but he had earned it in the days when he wanted to practise the science. He wanted to help those who wanted help. Now he could use it to understand a sick mind. But there were pitfalls and peril sin seeking such understanding.

Do I really want to understand the nature of a man capable of this?r he wondered.

The truth of the matter was that to understand it, he would have to becoming part of it. One can only understand someone if one can relate, at least in part, to what is going through their mind. But how far could he carry out this process without becoming corrupted by it? One could understand a bank robber because one can relate to the human desire for wealth without necessarily condoning the actions ozone who steals or robs in order to get it. One could even understand a man who groped a female colleague at the office Christmas party, even though it would technically be indecent assault, because one can understand the sex drive in its more conventional manifestations. But what sort of an animal could gain any sort of pleasure from doing to a woman what this monster had done to Leah Irons and Rose Crowne?

74

Neil felt there was a danger that if he ever got to the stage of understanding the killer, it would only be at the price of holding similar feelings. He shuddered in horror at the thought. He would prefer to go to his grave not understanding the mind of the murderer rather than being able to identify with even the tiniest fragment of his motivation.

But the dread lingered, because of another thought more terrifying than the prospect of becoming like the murderer:the possibility that, in some as yet undiscovered way, he already was.

Enough, he thought. *I'm not trying to understand the murderer. I just want to catch him and take him down . . . one way or another.*

He walked on, his new-found resolution propelling him forward with a new lease of life and a new breath of vigour. His brisk strides carried him to the front door of Meredith de Mur's house. She was the woman who had seen the car that sped away from the murder scene. As such she might hold the key to solving this mystery, even if she remembered very few details.

He rang the doorbell and waited.

'Who is it?' a tremulous voice asked from inside.

'PC Douglas. Golders Green Police Station,' he said.

The letterbox opened and a pair of timid eyes peered through it. He realized, with a sudden feeling of acute self-consciousness, that he was not in uniform. According to regulations he should not go out in uniform, representing himself as a police officer, while on sick leave. Strictly speaking he should not even be here, interfering with an ongoing investigation, but he was ready to break the rules to exorcize his inner demons, and apart from a twinge of fear it didn't really bother him to do so.

But if he was going to do it, then it paid not to be clumsy about it.

He reached into the breast pocket of his short-sleeved summer shirt and fumbled for his warrant card. Fishing it out with his index finger and thumb, he flipped it open and held it so that she could see it.

'What do you want?' she asked, the suspicion still lingering.

'Meredith de Mur?' he said.

'Yes.'

'I was wondering if I might have a word with you- regarding the investigation of the murder of Rose Crowne.'

'I told your colleagues everything I saw,' she said nervously.

'I know but I was wondering if I might have a word with you. I was the policeman who was first on the scene. I was-in uniform.'

The letterbox closed and the door opened the merest crack.

'You're the one who hit that man, aren't you?' she said, her voice losing its traces of fear and softening as if in sympathy.
'Yes,' he said, this time his own voice showing the signs of weakness and uncertainty.

The door opened fully.

'You'd better come in,' she said.

What Neil Douglas saw in that next moment was a woman who was a sight of such pity that he realized that it was the living as much as the dead who were sometimes worthy of sympathy.

This woman was thin, not like a victim of anorexia, but certainly to an extent that suggested frailty. Her hair was shorthand thin, as if growing back after chemotherapy. Through the gap on her not fully closed dressing gown, he could seethe scars of surgery on her chest. He couldn't even guess her age. It could be anything from early twenties to fifties. Such were the ravages of disease and medical treatment upon her. It didn't take a medical degree for the word 'cancer' to spring to mind.

'Well? Are you going to stand there or come in?' she barked aggressively.

Neil realized that he had been staring at her. She had probably suffered that kind of ghoulish behaviour in the past. And it probably angered her now as much as ever. Some people get used to the foolish but well-meaning behaviour of others, he knew, but victims of illness often rise to anger in the face of it. He recognized that, in view of her suffering as much as his guilt, it was not for him to judge her.

'Sorry,' he said, absent-mindedly, stepping over the threshold.

She closed the door behind him.

'Let's go into the living room.' Neil noticed, that when she wasn't being aggressive, she was quite well-spoken.

He followed her into a room with yellow flowered wallpaper and a maroon corduroy upholstered three-piece suite. She indicated the sofa for Neil and sat facing him on the armchair.

'So, what did you want to know?' she asked.

He still hadn't recovered from the feelings of disorientation that had struck him after his *faux pas* at the door. He had come here with a clear set of questions, but now they were a haze of convoluted words, dancing through his mind.

'First of all, I want to apologize for staring at you at the door like that. They didn't tell me anything about your condition.'

'That's all right,' she said, assessing the situation very quickly. 'Presumably they didn't expect you to come here, so they didn't figure there was any need to tell you any of the details.'

'That's right,' he replied, grateful for her understanding and the swiftness with which she had expressed it. 'Strictly speaking, I shouldn't be here.'

'I gathered that,' she said. 'But I won't tell anyone if you don't.'

She gave him an encouraging smile and for the first time since he had set out on this mission he was beginning to feel relaxed.

'My mother d. . .'

He trailed off, realizing that he was suffering from a bad case of foot-in-mouth disease.

'It's more common than many people think. And I didn't have children so that made me more vulnerable - I mean, higher risk.'

'I'm sorry,' said Neil gently.

'Oh don't apologize,' Meredith replied, coolly. 'I've lived longer than the prognosis gave me.'

'How long's it been?'

'Six years. Six years of radiation and then chemotherapy. Not to mention a double mastectomy.'

'Are you in remission?'

'No, they say I'm cured. If you call this being cured.'

Neil realized that, unlike him, she had really fallen into the self-pity trap. But then again, she had a lot more to self-pity about.

'So they've stopped the chemotherapy?'

'That's right. In some ways I'll be back to normal pretty soon. Not that they can reverse the mastectomy of course, but you can't have everything.

'When you say cured. . .'

'You want to know if your mother got a raw deal? There's no way anyone can know. It can go one way or it can go the other. It depends when they catch it, how they treat it and how lucky you are. Even in my case they can't say I'll be free of recurrence in the future. All they can say is that there's no trace of cancer in my body at the moment. I can only pray that it lasts and try to enjoy life as much as I can in my present condition.'

Neil almost smiled. He wished he could be as philosophical about his problems as she was about hers. For all the self-pity, she seemed at least to have settled into a pattern of bitching about it but then accepting it. He was still in a state of confusion.

Of course, his problem was different because it was psychological - and largely of his own making.

No, not largely . . . entirely.

'I was wondering about this car you saw on the night of the murder.'

'Like I said. I told your colleagues everything.'

'I know, but they didn't clue me in on the details. Nick Lloyd - that's my partner - told me a bit about it. I was wondering if you could just fill me in on the details.'

'I heard a car engine roar and then saw a blue Ford speeding towards me and past me.'

'I understand that you got part of the number.'

'M244. That was all. I thought it might be significant at the time so I wrote it down immediately.'

'How come you didn't come up to me and Nick? We were on the Heath. In Golders Hill Park, I mean.'

'Well, I was a bit afraid about going over there, in the dark and all that.'

'You didn't see the attack, did you?'

'No. The first thing I saw was your car.'

'So, if you didn't see the attack, why were you afraid?'

'Well, I saw a police car, stopped in a very strange place. I mean, you didn't even pull over properly.'

'That was Nick,' said Neil with a smile of recollection. 'He has his own way of parking.'

'I waited to see what was going on. Then other people started coming out of their homes. One of them must have seen what happened because he told me that a woman had been attacked. I saw more police arrive and then, at an opportune moment, I told one of them about the car. Then I got passed around from one police officer to another until eventually they brought me to the station, where I made my statement. After that, they thanked me rather profusely which was somewhat embarrassing, and gave me a lift home. As far as I was concerned that was the end of the matter, although they told me they might need me to testify if they caught someone.'

'Did you see who was in the car?'

'Well, it was no one that I recognized.'

'Was it a man or a woman?'

'Well, I didn't really see. I mean, I think it was a man, but it all happened so quickly.'

'Could it have been more than one person?'

'I don't think so.'

'You don't *think* so.'

'Well no, I'm sure it wasn't. It was definitely one person. That much I can be sure of.'

'One other thing, Miss de Mur. What were you doing there at that time?'

'Well, this may sound stupid in the light of what happened to that poor woman. But I was going for a walk. I mean one doesn't think of Golders Green or Hampstead as violent areas.'

'Isn't it a rather strange time to be going for a walk?'

'One of the effects of my cancer and the treatment that I've had for it is that I sleep odd hours. Sometimes I get exhausted and sleep during the day. At other times I can't sleep at night. I don't work and so my life isn't governed quite so rigidly by the clock.'

'OK. Thank you. By the way there is one other thing. It doesn't really have anything to do with the case. It's just my personal curiosity.'

'Yes?' she said, leaning forward, intrigued.

'Your name, your surname, I mean.'

'De Mur?'

'Yes.'

'What about it?'

'Well, I know there's a name de la Mer - "of the sea", but I've never heard of *de Mur*.'

'That's very perceptive of you. Literally, it means "of wall" or something like that.'

'Shouldn't it "*du* Mur - of *the* wall"?'

Meredith smiled.

'It is if you're a grammatical purist. I don't really know the linguistic origins. You're the first person who's mentioned it. I should have known that sooner or later some intellectual would ask me about it. I must confess it's a pleasant and unexpected surprise that the intellectual in question should be a policeman.'

Neil felt himself slouching on the armchair. It made him all the more aware of the extent to which he was slipping into the bad habits that his father had once warned him about. This was the trap of the unemployed. Even those who desperately wanted and sought work could end up sliding slowly into the idleness trap. Once there, it was hard to get out. Oh yes, one could get a job and resume work - if one could find a job. But inertia becomes state of mind. In the days of enforced idleness, one gets used to doing little or nothing in particular. One becomes accustomed to getting up an hour late in accordance with the body's twenty-*five* hour clock instead of getting up bright an dearly to catch that commuter train into the office or factory or shop.

And there was the complacency trap too.

He had thought about Beth's words yesterday and he knew that she was right. It was all too easy to say that he cared about justice. But what had he done about it?He had lashed out blindly, but he hadn't taken the trouble to familiarize himself with the facts - and that was the problem. Lashing out blindly had hurt the innocent, but if he really wanted to punish the guilty, he had to know who the guilty were. That was why he had spoken to Meredith de Mur. He had hoped that she might remember something, some detail however small, that might put him on the right track. Some minor recollection that might start him on the trail of the animal that he was determined to stalk until capture . . . or death.

But all she had told him was what she had told his colleagues. And because of her physical condition, he didn't want to press her to try to remember any more.

At least she had said one thing that was useful to him. She had mentioned the fragment of the number, and Nick had already told him that they were checking out the cars that matched that number. They had apparently already checked the blue Fords with that registration number, but the owner sand their families all had alibis.

But how carefully and thoroughly were they checking out the alibis?

He had heard of cases before where the police had let suspects slip through their fingers, to kill again. The Yorkshire Ripper was the most famous example, although by no means the only one.

Could it be that, with all those cars to check, they were being sloppy? Perhaps they accepted something as simple as the word of a friend or relative of the suspect as reliable evidence of alibi. There was only one way to find out. He had to talk to them himself. If nothing else, he could gain a feel for their honesty. He was sure that he could read other people's lies by their faces, if only because he had almost seen his own face in the mirror too many times since the incident on the Heath and he knew the face of dishonesty when he looked into its eyes.

Between now and the Rose Crowne inquest, he had barely a week. He resolved to use this time, not to lounge around the flat and feel sorry for himself, but to go out there and track down the man who had really murdered Rose Crowne - the man who had brought so much suffering on himself and Martin Roebuck and no doubt others as well. He would start with the owners of those blue Fords that began with the sequence that Meredith de Mur had noted down. If necessary, he would look further. But first he needed the list.

He reached for the phone and called Nick Lloyd on his mobile. Nick would get him the list.

Chapter 7

Beth looked around the Royal Free Hospital. She had parked her car quite far away and entered via a side entrance. It was a hell of a job navigating her way down a labyrinth of corridors to find the main entrance. She had to ask three times before she got there.

'Could you tell me where the pathology department is?' she asked the woman at the desk.

'I beg your pardon?' asked the woman.

Beth took out her press card from her purse and flashed it at the woman.

'I understand that the body of Rose Crowne was brought here after she was murdered. I was wondering if I could have a word with the pathologist.'

'I don't think he can speak to you directly. Have you tried administration?'

'No. Where are they?'

The woman gave directions and again Beth had to wend her way down a maze to find the administration office.

She introduced herself to a woman in her forties who claimed to be the hospital's Public Relations officer. She shook hands with Beth and asked what she could do for her.

'Well, I'm trying to find out a bit about Rose Crowne.'

'Rose Crowne? The name sounds familiar.'

Beth figured that the woman was either obtuse or being evasive.

'She was stabbed to death near Golders Hill Park a few days ago. I understand that she was brought here. I assume that the autopsy - I mean the post-mortem - was done here but we haven't heard anything about it. And we haven't heard anything about her family or friends or who she was? I was wondering if her family had issued a statement or an appeal to the public to come forward or something like that? If so I could cover it on my show. I have a radio show.'

'Yes, Ms Porter, I know who you are. I can tell you that as far as I know there has been no public statement and none is planned.'

Beth felt frustrated. It was as if this woman was being deliberately difficult, and Beth could feel the hostility emanating from every pore of the PR officer.

'Could you tell me where I can contact her family?'

'I'm sorry but we don't give out that kind of information. It's confidential.'

'All right, what could you at least pass on my address to her family?'

'I'm afraid I can't do that either. We're not a messenger service.'

By now the gloves were off.

'Is Martin Roebuck here?'

'Could you hold on a minute.'

The woman picked up the phone and keyed in a four digit number.

'Hallo, it's Admin here. We have a woman asking about Martin Roebuck . . . I think she's a reporter . . . OK, right, I'll do that.'

She put the phone down and looked up at Beth, trying to sound calm.

'Someone will be along to speak to you in a minute.'

Beth felt that at least she was getting somewhere, but couldn't understand why the woman seemed so nervous. She found out two minutes later when two men and a woman arrived and walked straight up to her, flashing their warrant cards.

'Detective Sergeant Graham. We'd like to have a word with you.'

'Yes.'

Beth felt a mixture of fear and anger.

'We understand you've been asking questions about Martin Roebuck?'

'Well, I was originally asking about Rose Crowne. When I made no headway I casually enquired about Martin Roebuck.'

'Do you have any ID on you?'

She produced her press card. The sergeant handed it over to his colleague, who started copying out the details.

'I'm afraid, madam, that we're going to have to search you.'

Beth looked horrified as the policewoman stepped forward.

'This is outrageous!'

The detective sergeant seemed unfazed by this.

'It's a necessary security procedure, madam. We have to protect Martin Roebuck. I know this might seem a bit distressing, madam, but he's a vital witness and anyone who asks about him must be properly and thoroughly investigated. Your cooperation will be most gratefully appreciated.'

'And if I refuse?' she asked truculently.

By now, she was blushing with fear and anger.

'We can do it here or at the station, madam.'

'All right,' she said, thrusting her handbag towards the sergeant.

'I'm afraid we have to search your pockets too. Could you turn them out, please?'

She emptied out her pockets onto the desk and then the policewoman walked up to her.

'Hold your arms out, please.'

The policewoman was in her early twenties and looked quite attractive. Beth hadn't realized that there were such things as attractive policewomen, except on TV. She actually felt good in her presence, although she would have preferred it if she were doing the searching. She hoped she hadn't betrayed her feelings by smiling as she held out her arms to the sides. The policewoman's hands moved over her body and she tried to look stony faced even as she writhed mildly at the woman's touch. The only thing she resented was being watched by the men. Although their faces remained as impassive as hers, she sensed that they too were getting a thrill out of the experience, and she hated them for it. The policewoman finished and half turned to her sergeant.

'She's clean.'

'OK, Ms Porter. I'm sorry to have troubled you. You can go now.'

'Wait a minute. Aren't I going to get any answers?'

'About what?'

The sergeant seemed genuinely bewildered.

'About Rose Crowne! About Martin Roebuck!'

'I'm afraid there's nothing we can tell you. They're entitled to their privacy and our only concern here is with Martin Roebuck's security. I'm sure you understand that.'

'I'm beginning to,' muttered Beth angrily, as she angrily stuffed credit cards, pens and keys into her handbag and pockets.

'What I wanted to say,' said a woman in a South London accent over the phone, 'is that Bridget Vanderbilt wasn't the only person who identified Roebuck as being on the Heath at the time when he said he was at home that morning. There was another witness too.'

'And who was that?' asked Beth. She knew already, but she wanted to let the callers lead the show. People didn't phone in if she made them feel that they had nothing useful to contribute.

'I think her name was Cathy Hampshire. She was another neighbour and I think she knew Roebuck. I mean, she knew his face. She didn't know his name. At least, that's what it said in the papers.'

It was quarter to eleven and once again *The Bitching Hour* was in full swing, with Beth and her team on something of a high, as they held a slice of South-East England spellbound.

'What exactly did this woman say?' asked Beth.

'Well . . . she said he was wearing a shoulder-holster type bag.'

'A shoulder-holster type bag?' repeated Beth, puzzled.

'Yes. She saw him between 9:25 and 9:30. Cathy Hampshire, I mean.'

'How does she know the time so accurately?' Beth probed, gently. She was anxious to get to the truth for once, not merely to score points.

'She knew what time she left home and she knew how long it took her to walk that route. I mean, the police actually reconstructed it and timed it.'

'And what does that prove? Roebuck admitted he went for a walk on the Heath in the morning. There was never any dispute about that.'

'No, but he said he had a headache and went home by 9:15. That's ten minutes before the time when Cathy Hampshire saw him on the Heath.'

'And how long did she see him for?'

'About five seconds, I think it said.'

'That's not very long is it?' asked Beth.

'No, but she knew him from before. And also she had an unobstructed view.'

'How near to him was she?'

'She said she was about twenty five to fifty yards away from him.'

'Twenty five to *fifty*? That's quite a big variation don't you think?'

'Yes, but it was in the open.'

'And yet we're asked to trust her identification of a man she only saw for five seconds.'

'But she knew him from before, Beth. It's not like she was identifying a stranger.'

'OK, good point,' said Beth. 'Well, there we have a report about a woman who saw Roebuck after he claims he got home. Bridget Vanderbilt also identified him after that time and she claims to have seen him even later. But it would be interesting to hear from these people themselves how certain they are of what they saw. Were they really sure it was Roebuck they saw? Or did they start off with doubts and did the police help them to overcome their doubts with a bit of gentle persuasion and the mention of other witnesses whose testimony would complement their own? I wonder. Ludovic Kennedy once wrote in a book about a famous British miscarriage of justice that the police are very fair at the *start* of a criminal investigation, but once they're convinced they've got the right man they're ready to go to great lengths to secure a conviction.

'But before we go on, I just want to say that we're hearing a lot about Leah Irons, but I'm wondering about Rose Crowne. We haven't heard anything about her. So if anyone knows anything at all about Rose Crowne - who she was, what she was, anything at all, would they please phone in. You all know the number by now. Let's talk to Glen on line six.'

'Hallo, Beth.'

'Hallo, Glen. Where are you calling from?'

'Hackney.'

'And what do you want to talk about.'

'Well, I also had something to say about the Leah Irons case. It said in the all papers an' on TV an all that, that someone else saw a suspicious looking man and 'e 'ad long 'air. And according to all them reports, Martin Roebuck 'ad short 'air.'

'And that's your point.'

'Basically, yeah. 'Cause, I mean, maybe 'e couldn't tell 'em much. But if he said the man 'ad short 'air the coppers an' all that would've said that it fits in wiv Martin Roebuck. So if that's the case, then it means that because 'e said the man 'ad *long* 'air, it means it don't fit Roebuck. Know what I mean?'

'Yes, I do. OK, well thank you, Glen.' Beth sensed that this was an area worth pursuing. 'That was an interesting point. But again, if anyone knows about Rose Crowne, the number to call is 020 7946 0909.

'Let's take a break to listen to a song from Suzanne Vega's first album. This one is called *The Queen and the Soldier* and I think it's the best song she ever wrote.'

While the record played, Beth's mind went back to the events of earlier in the day, after she had left the hospital.

There was something fishy about the whole thing. She knew that hospitals and the police had to respect the privacy of the victim and the victim's family. But it was strange that there had been no statements at all about the victim. Usually, after a vicious murder like this the parents or husband or boyfriend appear on TV to tell the country what a wonderful person their Rose was.

But not in this case. No distraught husband. No tearful mother or stoic father. No friends or neighbours to say how she was always quiet or fun loving or helpful. A complete wall of silence. And like all out-of-context silences, it was deafening.

She couldn't brush aside her curiosity over Rose Crowne. The total silence about her loomed over the case like a gaping black hole, begging to be investigated. And as far as she knew, no one was investigating it.

She was, she realized, a radio talk show hostess, not an investigative reporter. But the job cried out to be done and the question that blasted away her inhibitions was the old *if not me, then who?*

So, she sat at her computer, using the technology that she knew and loved so much to scratch away at the wall of mystery.

CROWNE

She typed in the letters carefully, moved the mouse until the arrow pointer was on the 'Search' button and then clicked the left mouse button. The arrow on the screen turned into an hourglass and the word 'searching' flashed in the corner of the screen. She was using the same database that she'd used to track down Neil.

But it was proving to be a bit of a problem in the case of Rose Crowne. She may well have been ex-directory. If so, then no amount of searching would help. Beth had in fact already printed out this list once and even started phoning the numbers and speaking to the various R. Crownes that she had found - even a couple of Rose Crownes. In the cases where there was no answer, she had left messages or phoned back and she had come pretty close to establishing that all the Rose Crownes listed anywhere in the country were alive - unless they were being impersonated over the phone by others for some unstated, unguessable reason.

But there was always a possibility that the software had missed some of them the first time around. It was known to be bug-ridden and as such it might throw up more names on one occasion than another - even if the same search parameters were used. She printed off the list - preferring to work with a hard copy than strain her eyes glaring at a computer screen - and checked off the names from the new list against the old. It took about ten minutes, with a quick return run just to make sure. But in the end she was satisfied that none of the Rose Crownes listed was dead.

If Rose Crowne was her real name, then she *was* ex-directory.

At times like this she wished she was a hacker, capable of logging in to a computer belonging to the phone company or one of the other utilities. It would be so easy to search for a name and get an address to go with it. But she didn't have that skill, and neither did Jane.

She considered calling Neil Douglas. As a policeman he might have access to means of tracing people that she didn't- like the full telephone database, ex-directory numbers and all. And he was the only policeman she knew - if 'knew' was the word to apply to their less than harmonious meeting yesterday. But she could hardly go running to him after the way in which she had argued with him.

Also, she didn't want him to know that she was following up on the Rose Crowne case. He probably wanted to forget about the case and wouldn't really want anyone to start raking the muck over

Rose Crowne. It was bad enough that the inquest was coming up soon.

She printed off another list. She then spent almost half an hour cross-checking one list against the other, but to no avail. There were no other Rose Crownes. She simply wasn't there.

Beth considered her options. There were two approaches she could take. The first would be to start off by taking the press reports of Rose Crowne's approximate age and looking for her birth records. She could go to the Family Records Centre in Myddleton Street near the Angel in Islington. There, she could go through the quarterly volumes for the letter C in each of the candidate years, allowing a spread of three or four years each way until she found a record of Rose Crowne's birth, along with the borough where she was born. She could then look for Rose Crowne's parents in the voting register for that constituency and the neighbouring ones on the initial assumption that they had not moved. This would have the advantage that it was actually Rose Crowne's parents that she wanted to speak to. After all, Rose Crowne was dead. On the other hand she couldn't really be sure that Rose Crowne's parents hadn't moved far in all these years.

There was another approach. She could work on the assumption that at eleven o'clock at night, Rose Crowne would not have been too far from where she lived. If she checked the voting register in that constituency, and in all the neighbouring constituencies, she was pretty sure that she could find Rose Crowne's name. That was the great irony. People can take their number out of the phone directory easily enough but unless they have no wish to vote, they have to appear on the voting register with their address. And the voting register is open to public inspection.

She drew up a list of the constituencies that she would have to check and then made off to the local library.

The Golders Green Library was extremely poorly stocked in this regard and only had the immediate two constituencies:Golders Green and Finchley, and North Hampstead. She knew that she would have to go to other libraries to cover the entire region. What was worse was that the voting register wasn't alphabetical but went by addresses. That meant she had to look at every street and every house or flat number in search of the name Crowne. And she knew that when her eyes got tired there would be a danger that she might miss it. She considered asking Jane and Mick to help her but she realized that she couldn't. This was nothing to do with her radio programme; it was a personal crusade. As such it was something she had to do alone.

Of course she could ask them if they'd like to volunteer. But that wouldn't be fair. There would always be an element of moral pressure in that. Besides, she couldn't trust them. If it would be easy for her to miss a name despite her determination to succeed, how much easier would it be for them to make such mistakes given that they had no similar dedication to the task.

So she worked her way down the list literally address by address, name by name. Alba Gardens, Ambrose Avenue, Andrew's Road. . .

. . . Woodstock Avenue, Woodstock Road. . .

Her eyes were getting tired, but she had to press on.

'Excuse me?' said an elderly woman next to her.

'Yes?' said Beth looking up.

'Are you looking for a particular name or a particular address?'

'Why?' asked Beth, puzzled.

'Well, it's just that if you wanted a particular name it's very hard to find it there, because it's based on streets.'

'I know that,' said Beth, trying to conceal her irritation. 'But I can't think of a better way.'

'There's one of these new computer products . . . a C. . . C. . .'

'CDROM?'

'Yes, that's it.'

'I know, I have it. But it doesn't have numbers that are ex-directory.'

'Oh I know that. But it has the addresses.'

'How can it have the addresses of ex-directory numbers?They got the information by scanning in the phone books.'

'Oh, I don't mean that one,' said the elderly woman. 'I mean the Irish one.'

'Irish one?'

'Yes. It's more complete and got the information from the voting registers.'

'Wait a minute. Are you telling me they've got information from all the voting registers in the country on a CD-ROM.'

'As far as I know. Names and addresses. And phone numbers where they could get them.'

'Where can I get it?'

'That was *The Queen and the Soldier* from Suzanne Vega. We have Brian from Hammersmith on the line. Hallo, Brian.'

'Hallo, Beth. I'm a first time caller . . . a bit nervous.'

'Don't be nervous. As long as what you have to say isn't racist or bigoted or anything like that I'm pretty tolerant -at least of first time callers.'

'Yeah,' he said with a nervous chuckle. 'What I wanted to say was this. We don't know much about this Rose Crowne, now do we? It seems that nobody's come forward to say they knew her. Now, this is just a theory mind, but maybe Rose Crowne was known by the killer and/or by Martin Roebuck. Maybe they're the only two people who knew her.'

'But isn't that a bit unlikely?' said Beth.

'Well, let's think a minute. Maybe she was the wife or girlœfriend of the killer. Maybe she was Roebuck's girlfriend.'

'Yes, but other people must have known her too, Brian. I mean, she must have known people. Neighbours, friends, colleagues.'

'Well, not necessarily. I mean, maybe she kept herself to herself. Maybe she didn't work. Maybe she was foreign.'

'That's an interesting idea, Brian. I mean, not the bit about being the wife or girlfriend of the killer. But maybe she was a foreign visitor. That might explain why no one's come forward in this country to claim her or speak about her. But the trouble is, the police are being very cagey.' She thought of mentioning what had happened to her at the hospital, but decided not to. 'Also, we know her name. Rose Crowne. That's all they've given out. It isn't much but it doesn't sound foreign.'

'But Rose could be a foreign name. Or an Anglicization of a Spanish or Italian name.'

'Yes, but Crowne is very English,' said Beth.

'But maybe, like I said, maybe she was married to the killer?'

'OK, that's a possibility. Or maybe she was from another English-speaking country. America, Canada, Australia, New Zealand, South Africa. Who knows.'

'Exactly,' said Brian.

'Well, if anyone does know, could they please call in? Thanks, Brian. And could I just say that today we seem to be getting a lot more intelligent callers than usual. Could it be that people have started to think about this case and realize that it isn't quite as simple as the press made it out to be? Let's go to Sharon in Essex on line four.'

'Oh, good evening, Beth,' said a woman with a deep, husky voice.

'Good evening, Sharon.'

'I just wanted to suggest another theory about Rose Crowne.'

Beth was frustrated. She wanted answers, not theories. But in the absence of the former she'd settle for the latter. At least it kept the subject of the discussion on track.

'Go ahead.'

'Well, maybe she was one of these foreign prostitutes from the former Soviet bloc and Rose Crowne was just the name she adopted on her forged papers.'

'Get out of here!' said Beth, angered at the levity, yet at the same time amused by it.

'No, seriously. That could be why the police are being so cagey They don't want to give away the fact that they're onto this foreign prostitution racket, run by the Russian mafia. So they're keeping mum.'

'All right. Maybe that's the answer. Anything else?'

'Well, apart from that, there's also the more mundane possibility that she wasn't actually a prostitute but that she was a refugee or illegal immigrant.'

'A *white* illegal immigrant?'

'Maybe from Bosnia.'

'Possibly,' said Beth, nodding with approval towards the microphone But still, all this is just speculation. What we really need are answers. Maybe someone from the Metropolitan Police could tell us why they're being so cagey about the whole thing. I mean, hell, the public has the right to know. Let's take another call. We have Clive on the line. Good evening, Clive.'

'Oh, good evening Beth. I wanted to talk about the original Leah Irons case.'

'All right,' drawled Beth, reluctantly.

'Well, I just wanted to say something about the Annie Jacobs undercover operation and some of the things Roebuck said to her at the time.'

'Yes,' prompted Beth, encouragingly.

'Well, Roebuck invented things to impress Annie Jacobs. And some of these things were quite sordid and violent.'

'But he never admitted to the murder of Leah Irons did he?' asked Beth. 'Even when she explicitly offered him sexual favours in return for such an admission.'

'No, but that could be due to his natural cunning.'

'Well, if he was cunning enough to avoid admitting guilt then why was he so reckless as to admit to things that he didn't do?'

'Because admitting to things that never happened, that he didn't commit, wouldn't endanger him. Whereas admitting to a murder that he did commit would.'

'But what purpose would be served by admitting to things that he didn't do?'

'He was trying to impress her.'

'Why would that impress her?'

'Well, she gave him to understand that she wanted a strong, domineering man.'

'Well, if he made it up to impress a woman who wanted a strong, domineering man, then what does it prove?'

'But she didn't tell him what to say. She gave him the opportunity to say all those things and describe his sick fantasies, but she didn't force him to say it.'

'Clive, you know what that reminds me of?'

'No, what?'

'It reminds me of a line in a book by James Hadley Chase. The sidekick of the hero is trying to pull some dame in a bar and she brushes him off with the words "I don't run after men". So he replies, "maybe you don't, but then again, a mousetrap doesn't run after mice. " Let's talk to Steve in Stoke Newington.'

'Oh hi, Beth. You probably remember me.' He sounded like an old country squire or horse breeder in a tweed overcoat. 'We argued before, over the Hillsborough tragedy.'

'Oh yes, Steven. Of course, I remember you.'

'And I remember you too. You were quite aggressive at the time. Aggressive and stubborn.'

'And wrong.'

'Pardon?'

'I was wrong, Steve. I goofed and didn't want to admit it But let's not go over all that now.'

'Oh well, I'm very pleased to hear you say that. Anyway, I just wanted to add something about this Cathy Hampshire character She said that Martin Roebuck waved to her when she saw him. Now that implies that he saw her and that he knew that she'd seen him. Hallo?'

'I'm still here.'

'Right, well now, what does this tell us? If Martin Roebuck knew that she'd seen him at that time, then why did he say that he was at home before that?'

'I don't get it,' said Beth. 'I mean, what's your point.'

'Well, Beth,' he said in the tone of a tolerant father talking to a not-too-bright child, 'my point is this. The police and the Crown Prosecution Service might say that Martin Roebuck was lying when he said he got home earlier. They might say that he was lying to distance himself from the Heath at the time the crime was committed. But if what Cathy Hampshire said about him waving is true, then it would have been a stupid lie, because he would have known that it could be contradicted by a witness.'

'Ah, I see what you mean.'

'And the thing is, if he knew she'd seen him, then why not just say he got home shortly after that. He could still have distanced himself from the crime. Cathy Hampshire said she saw him at 9:25 or 9:30. The murder took place at10:30. If he was the murderer and knew when the murder was committed, then he could have said that he got home some time between 9:30 and 10:30. That way he could have distanced himself from the murder without being contradicted by Cathy Hampshire. And remember, Cathy Hampshire was quite distinct about the fact that he *waved* to her.'

'That is a *very* good point, Well, thank you, Steve.'

'And there's another thing too.'

'Yes?'

'If he knew that he had been seen by someone who knew him and could identify him, then, would it have made sense for him to go ahead and commit the murder under the circumstances, especially if he hoped to deny having been there?'

'I think the police would say that the very fact that the murder was committed in broad daylight suggests that the murderer was acting irrationally and was not in control of his reason at the time.'

'But, on the other hand, they're also saying that Martin Roebuck was a cunning man who lied to distance himself from the crime in chronological terms. Also, Cathy Hampshire saw him with a shoulder-holster bag but didn't say anything about an overnight bag. Bridget Vanderbilt said he had an overnight bag but didn't say anything about a shoulder-holster bag -contrary to what one of the Sunday tabloids said.

'So we have a man who was wearing a T-shirt and a long-sleeved shirt at the same time. A man who was wearing a shoulder-holster bag but not carrying an overnight bag but who was at the same time carrying an overnight bag but not wearing a shoulder-holster bag. A man who is both very cunning and very careless. That sounds to me like two men, if not more.'

'You make out a very good case for the defence, Steve. Those are all good points and you presented them well. I'm just wondering if anyone out there still thinks Roebuck is guilty Helen on line eight.'

Neil was lying in bed listening to the programme. He was relieved that she wasn't sniping at him this time, and fascinated to learn all these new facts about the Leah Irons case and as confused as Beth about the mystery surrounding Rose Crowne. He had previously assumed that the Leah Irons case was a routine one with a suspect who was as guilty as hell but legally untouchable because of lack of evidence. But now, more and more, he was coming to realize that just as he had misjudged the situation in his spot decision on the heath, others may have misjudged Roebuck in trying to close the Leah Irons case and satisfy the public's desire to have the head of the murderer delivered to them on a plate.

As usual, Neil was doing two things at once. With a cup of tea perched beside him and the radio on quietly in the background he was also looking at the list that Nick Lloyd had got for him. It was a photocopy at an oblique angle that Nick had got by quickly lifting the list with a pile of innocent papers and slipping it into the station photocopier before anyone noticed what was coming out at the other end. Neil was amused that his friend should have been so nervous when Nick was usually such a cool customer and it was a relatively minor matter. Even if someone had seen, he could simply say it must have scooped up with the other papers. No one would have taken it any further.

But Nick was also under pressure from the Roebuck incident, he realized, and this was affecting his behaviour in these trivial but noticeable ways. This was the initial list of those whose cars matched all of Meredith de Mur's criteria and there were only four names on it. But there could be others with access to the cars he realized. He would have to find out who else had such access and check them out too.

'Oh, hallo there, Beth.'

'Hallo Helen. By the way where are you calling from?'

'Stepney.'

'And what can I do for you?'

'Well, I just wanted to say that I knew Rose Crowne a few years ago when we were sharing a flat. I mean, it was me and Rose and my boyfriend, who is now my husband incidentally.'

'Go on,' said Beth, suddenly getting excited. She wanted to shake the woman and yell 'cut to the chase!' but as she was finally getting some answers, she realized that it behoved her to be patient. At least this woman was filling in the blanks with fact and not just speculating.

'She only lived with us a few months. I guess she felt a bit uncomfortable because Jack and I were involved with each other and she must have felt like a gooseberry half the time.'

'Helen, I don't mean to sound impatient, but millions of listeners are dying to find out who Rose Crowne was.'

'Well, that's what I'm trying to tell you. Rose Crowne was-'

'Are you mad!' a man's voice shouted in the background.

Less than a second later, the line went dead. *Damn*, thought Beth. She looked over at Mick who was shaking his head. That meant: *no incoming number logged.*

Damn again, thought Beth.

She realized that they would probably never know what the woman was going to say . . . or what happened next at the other end of the line.

'Remember folks, you heard it here first. Or rather didn't. I just hope that woman is OK,' said Beth. 'Look, I'm going to do something I don't usually do. I'm going to show my emotions. I'm going to appeal to those people we just heard. I know you don't want us to hear whatever it was that the woman was going to say. But at least let us know that the woman is all right.'

Beth's voice became gentle.

'I'm speaking to the man whose voice we heard in the background now. I don't know who you are and I don't want to know. Whoever you are, you sounded angry. I don't want to stick my nose into your personal affairs, and I'm sure you've got genuine and good reasons to feel the way you feel. I just want to know that the woman who called herself Helen is all right. So can you get her to phone in just to tell me that she's all right? Can you do that?'

She pressed a button and several advertisements ran. Jane was staring at Beth with a peculiar kind of fascination. She had felt uncomfortable watching her go all soft on the callers. She liked Beth when she was tough. She got a buzz out of hearing the crack of the whip in her voice, whether it was a caller being put down or Beth telling her off for some mistake, like putting the wrong caller through.

The advertisements came to an end and Beth was back on the air. But she didn't feel like talking, or listening.

'Ladies and gentlemen, things have been getting a bit heavy around here and some of you are probably hoping that it's going to lighten up a little. So let's take a break and listen to a song from Albert Hammond. It's called *Woman of the World.*'

She pressed the button and leaned back in her chair. It was relatively early and yet she was already feeling tired. It was the departure from routine. Usually this phase of the programme involved letting the listeners talk about the events of the day, taking a position that clashed with the more common or popular position and putting down those callers who presented the other case stupidly or in any way that lent itself to an easy put-down with a slashing sound bite.

But this time she had taken a genuine position - a position that was really hers. She had read up about the Leah Irons case, not only the recent articles since the events on the Heath, but also books about the original case, and she was determined to enlighten and inform people of the truth and to encourage the more knowledgeable listeners to phone in and share their knowledge with others. At the same time, she was trying to glean some useful information about the Rose Crowne case.

Unfortunately, it was not going quite the way she intended. She was hoping that people directly involved with the case would phone in and tell their stories. Instead, all she was getting were people who had read about the case, some in more detail, others in less, who wanted to argue the case or side they supported or speculate on things they didn't know. However, there was a possibility that this programme would get more publicity than some of the others because of the intensity with which she was covering the issue. This might prompt those who were involved with the case to tune in tomorrow night and maybe phone in. She could but hope.

Chapter 8

'I already told your colleagues!' said Justice Fortescue, spitting petulance and ire to gloss of over what, to Neil Douglas, sounded like fear. 'Why do you have to hound me like this!'

He was slouching in his armchair, by the corner of the walnut coffee table. From the contours of the smoking jacket that he had changed into on his return from the County Court, it was clear that he was losing the battle against middle-age spread. He was also hot and sticky after a long day in a poorly air-conditioned courtroom, wearing heavy judicial robes. He had in fact been intending to take a shower after finishing *The Times* crossword puzzle, when Neil had turned up unexpectedly. But he was afraid and felt that he needed to deal with this intrusion first.

Neil hadn't thought of what he was doing as 'hounding'. In fact, he had barely asked a question. But he had learned enough about the dangers of prejudging to avoid equating fear with guilt.

'I'm not trying to hound you. I just want some information.'

'But I've told you, I don't remember her name,' the judge continued, to Neil's bewilderment.

The drawing room in this house in this white plaster-fronted house in Belgravia seemed quite opulent for a man who had had to part with many of his prized possessions as the price of liberation from his spouse in a no fault divorce, but he probably invested wisely and held onto the things that mattered.

Originally, Neil had intended to tackle him at the court building during a lunchtime adjournment. But when he discovered that His Lordship was divorced and would likely be alone in the evening, he decided to tackle him at home. There would be no family present and so he could speak freely, if he so chose.

If he chose not to, of course, that would be a sign that Neil needed to look further.

'Look, perhaps I should clarify who I am. I showed you my warrant card, but you may not have recognized my name. I'm PC Neil Douglas.'

A light of recognition flashed in the judge's eyes -recognition tinged with relief.

'Of course, yes. You're the young policeman who hit Martin Roebuck.'

'That's right,' said Neil, stung by the reminder and embarrassed by the persistence of his reputation in other people's memories. There was also a feeling of sudden weakness brought on by the judge's words, even though they contained no hint of accusation, let alone judgement or condemnation. Neil realised that the roles had now reversed and that the advantage no longer rested with him. His power to play the role of policeman interrogating a suspect had all but evaporated.

'But tell me,' said the judge, leaning forward keenly, 'are you supposed to be investigating this case? I mean, you're not a detective. And as I understand it, you may be the subject of some disciplinary proceedings regarding the events on Hampstead Heath.'

There was a gleam in the judge's eye, as if he sensed that the centre of gravity in this conversation had shifted decidedly in his direction.

'Well, that's precisely it,' said Neil hurriedly. 'As you say, aside from the case proper, there's also an internal inquiry into my behaviour. I'm not allowed to investigate the case as a criminal investigation, but I am allowed to seek out witnesses who may have favourable testimony to give on my behalf at the internal disciplinary inquiry and I can take voluntary witness statements from them if they're ready to give them. As far as police disciplinary rules are concerned, I have the right to approach you to ask if you'd be prepared to answer questions that might help me. Of course you're not obliged to say anything or to answer my questions, and you can tell me to go away if you like, but if you're innocent there's no reason why you should. And the purpose of these questions is to help me defend myself against possible disciplinary charges, not to incriminate you.'

'But surely if I was the man in the car that your colleagues were inquiring about - which I'm not - I'd be the last person to tell you.' He spoke with an air of intellectual superiority, as if he were consciously trying to make Neil feel small. 'I mean, whether your purpose is to incriminate anyone else or not, the killer - whoever he may be - is hardly going to tell you is he?'

'Well, that assumes that the man who drove away was the killer. That's a line of inquiry that the police are considering, but it isn't necessarily the only explanation. He could just be a witness.'

'All right,' said the judge, nodding sympathetically, 'what do you want to know?'

Beyond the window, grey clouds were gathering ominously, like bored youths on a street corner in the evening.

'What exactly did you tell my colleagues.'

'They interviewed me for half an hour. Could you be more specific?'

'Well, you can start off by telling me where you were on May the 24th.'

'I was with a-.' He took a deep breath and started again. 'I was with a call-girl. I've already told your colleagues that.'

Neil opened his mouth to speak, but nothing came out. There was nothing really shocking in what the judge had said. He was a man, well-paid, and currently with no partner and there was no reason in principle why he should be any different from politicians or businessmen. It was just unexpected. One minute he had been cagey and defensive, then friendly and sympathetic, and now open and communicative.

It was the speed and frankness of the confession rather than the content that took Neil by surprise.

'Was this anywhere near North End or Golders Hill Park?'

It was a statement. Justice Fortescue was very familiar with the significance of the question. He had almost certainly been asked it before.

'Yes,' said Neil.

'It was nowhere near there. Admittedly, it was nowhere near here either. I prefer to hold these assignations away from where I'm liable to recognized. It was in a hotel, near Warren Street.'

'Can you remember which one?'

'Yes. Look, is this really necessary? I mean I told your colleagues and I'm sure they're going to go there to check it out. I don't want a whole stream of people checking it out.'

'How come you didn't bring her back here? I mean, you're divorced. It's not as if there's anything wrong with a single man bringing a woman back home in the nineties.'

'We're not just talking about a woman though, are we?'

101

'A *married* woman?'

'No. But a hooker. And I am still a judge.'

'So what name did you check in under?' asked Neil. 'Mr and Mrs Smith?'

'I used my own name, if you must know.'

Neil was surprised at this. To go to all that trouble to avoid being seen with a prostitute and then to use one's own name.

'They check passports,' said Fortescue, as if reading Neil's mind. 'The hotels don't just let you stay in one of their rooms without some form of ID. Especially if you haven't got any luggage. The usual accepted form of ID is a passport or driver's licence. Unless you've got a forged one of those, or want to check into a seedy little B&B with fleas on the carpet, you have to show ID. So you may as well use your own.'

'And you weren't afraid that checking into this hotel with some blonde slapper on your arm might draw the same kind of unwelcome attention as bringing her back here.'

'I didn't go there with the girl on my arm. I checked in on my own and then phoned, using one of the regular numbers I use. Then I waited until she came to my room. They're based in Soho. It isn't far.'

'And she just went straight up to your room,' said Neil, getting the hang of the procedure.

'That's right,' the judge confirmed, relieved that he didn't have to spell it out any further.

'Could you tell me the name of the girl? And the phone number?'

'I can't remember. She was a new girl. I got the number from one of those stickers in a phone box.'

'Did she specialize?'

'How do you mean?'

'Well . . . you know . . . *la vice Anglais*'

'You're getting rather personal.'

'I would have thought that given your caution, you'd stick to girls you knew.'

'I did, but the last one's moved on.'

'Moved on?' asked Neil cautiously, wondering how much to read into these ominous words.'

'Moved out to suburbia,' said the judge with a smile. 'Apparently a client made an honest woman of her.'

'And the new one?'

'OK, she *did* specialize. She was a "schoolgirl" and I was the headmaster.'

'It's probably more effective than prison,' said Neil mockingly. A bond of male camaraderie had almost built up between them.

'Just don't tell that to the tabloids,' said Fortescue, trying to sound amused. 'You can rest assured that everything I've told you I also told to your colleagues. And everything I told them has been - or will be - checked out thoroughly. So there's no need to duplicate their efforts. It's bad enough for me that I had to disclose details of my private life to *anyone*. I don't need to have my nose rubbed in it by having everything checked out twice. If you want to know if what I told you checks out, could I respectfully suggest that you ask your colleagues? I just don't want the call-girl or her pimp to start getting ideas that I'm a candidate for blackmail.'

'I think your reputation could survive using the services of a call-girl. This is the nineties after all, and you *are* no longer married.'

'That may be. But with the silly season still in progress and the tabloids hungry for the flimsiest morsels, I'd rather not put it to the test.'

'You don't have to tell me about the tabloids,' said Neil, bitterly.

'So that's the story, Nick. I was just wondering if you could ask around and find out whether his story checked out.'

They were sitting in Nick's kitchen, both on their second can from the six-pack that Nick always had at the ready in his bachelorized fridge. Neil thought about the irony that both Justice Fortescue and Nick were divorcees but the judge seemed to have done so much better out of it than the police constable.

'All right, I'll have a go,' said Neil. 'But there's something familiar about that name. Something about an argument with a policeman.'

Neil was puzzled by this. Downright baffled, in fact.

'What, he threw a case out like the judge in the Leah Irons case?'

'No. No wait a minute. . .'

Nick's hand went up to his forehead as he tried to remember. 'That's it! Fortescue's in the civil court.'

'I know,' said Neil flatly. 'So how did that get him into an argument with a policeman?'

He was sure that Nick was getting confused.

'It was a civil case. The policeman was the plaintiff. I remember now. He was suing an airline.'

'About what?'

'He'd found some glass in his food and he was suing for damages. It caused a bit of a stir at the time. The airline kept getting the case delayed while they subjected the plaintiff to a campaign of harassment including false arrest by their friends in the airport police and having him beaten up by thugs and documents stolen from his home. They were trying to wear him down, but the plan failed. So they let the case go ahead after he was taken ill in another country. His lawyers tried to get the case delayed by sending the judge faxed copies of his doctor's affidavits. But Justice Fortescue refused to adjourn the case, claiming that the faxed affidavits weren't a proper medical certificate. Then, because the plaintiff wasn't there, he threw the case out and the airline's lawyers took advantage of court privilege to issue a phony statement accusing the plaintiff of being a professional claimant. They even cited his private medical insurance claims, which were paid directly to his doctors.'

What are we talking about?' asked Neil. 'Secret handshakes?'

'I don't think so. Just judicial pigheadedness.'

'So Fortescue's a bit of a bastard.'

'From what I've heard of him.'

'Then he must have a lot of enemies,' Neil speculated.

'Probably as many as a judge in the criminal courts,' said Nick. 'Only unlike an Old Bailey judge, his enemies are all out walking the streets.'

'And if one of the people he ruled against was an ex-policeman, that would explain why he was so defensive. On the other hand, I guess I'm lucky he agreed to speak tome at all.'

104

'He was probably curious,' suggested Nick. 'He might have wanted to know how much your knew.'

'How do you mean?'

'Well, if he thinks he's got enemies in the police he might have thought it better to let you into his lair and see how much he could get out of you? By answering your question she got you to ask more. So he got to know where you were coming from.'

'That's ridiculous! If he thought I was a threat to him, in the slightest, he wouldn't have answered me as openly as he did.

'You're assuming, of course, that he was telling the truth. You don't have any of it on tape, do you?'

'Of course not.'

'So, let's say it isn't true. You could go off running to the press telling them a story about a judge who's been getting up to a bit of hanky-panky with a call-girl and the next thing you know, you're being sued for slander and the paper for libel.'

'Yes,' said Neil, thinking to himself. 'I see what you mean.'

Nick appeared to be thinking too.

'I wonder if the whole thing was a set-up.'

'You've just said that.'

'No, I don't mean by the judge. I mean by Meredith de Mur. This whole business with the car number is kind of fishy. Maybe this Meredith de Mur is an old enemy of his and she's trying to set him up.'

'Then why didn't she give the whole number?' asked Neil, secretly dismissive of his partner's efforts at playing detective, although he was in no way embarrassed by his own.

'That would have been too obvious. This way it's more subtle. She doesn't run the risk of having to accuse him in court. She just sows the seeds of suspicion.'

'But if she doesn't testify and there's no other evidence against him, then what has she accomplished?' asked Neil. 'Assuming I buy this whole preposterous idea in the first place.'

'Well, for a start, she could ruin his career.'

'Come off it, Nick. How's it going to ruin his career? They won't give out the name of a suspect if he isn't charged. And on what they've got so far there isn't even enough to arrest him.'

'No, but if a judge is being investigated, word is bound to get back to the Lord Chancellor. It shouldn't, but it probably would.'

'Yes, but if he's cleared then how can it--'

'Yes, but what if he isn't, Neil? What if the case remains unsolved? What if they catch the murderer and it turns out that he arrived and left the crime scene on foot. What if they decide that the car had nothing to do with it but was merely there at the time? What if he was there at the time but had nothing to do with it? Just a witness who left the scene because he didn't want to be caught with a slapper? That would leave a stink. Not a big stink. Not the sort of stink that would make the papers. But a stink that would make the Lord Chancellor's nose turn away every time Fortescue was considered for elevation to the Court of Appeal. I mean, he's probably got ambitions. He probably wants a seat on the Court of Appeals, maybe he even hopes to be the Master of the Rolls or Lord Chancellor. But instead he gets stuck in the High Court as plain *Mister* Justice Fortescue. If Meredith de Mur has a grudge against him, that could be her plan.'

'Yes, well has anyone checked out if she has a grudge against him.'

'I don't know. You could always check it out yourself.'

'I could,' said Neil. 'If I thought it was worthwhile. But first I'm going to check out this case with the airline. I'd like to know a bit more about mister Justice Fortescue.'

'It does seem a little unusual.'

Michael Sommerville had been a hospital administrator for nine years, the chief administrator for four, but he had never seen anything like this before. It was an order from the Health Authority to transfer Martin Roebuck to University College Hospital.

'May I ask why this is being done?' asked Sommerville. 'We have excellent facilities equipped to care for someone in Roebuck's condition. And moving him, while he is on a life support system, is not without risk.' He did not sound indignant, merely hurt. The older of the two men, the one who answered to the name 'Harold', stepped forward.

'We believe that Mr Roebuck may be in danger, owing to the fact that he is the only person known to have got a good look at the killer and survived. It is possible that the killer will try to silence him.'

'But you've had guards stationed here all the time. They never complained or anything.'

'We don't operate that way. We don't whinge about problems. We deal with them. We passed this on to our superiors and there have been representations up to and including ministerial level and you can rest assured that all the parties concerned believe this to be the best thing to do under the circumstances.

It seemed pointless to spell out the details, to explain that the head of SO10 had been onto the Home Secretary who had then been onto the Minister of Health who in turn had been onto the head of the local Health Authority. The important thing was that moving him would mean a marginal increase in security and more importantly, if it was done quietly, it would mean that it would be hard for the killer to find Roebuck without alerting the authorities.

It wasn't a foolproof scheme, but it added one extra layer to the heavy police protection already in place. They would keep the uniformed police officers at the Royal Free and have only plain clothes officers from SO10 at University College Hospital. That way they would be creating a decoy situation, while keeping Roebuck protected.

'So you're convinced he was on the take.'

'Let's just say that I can't think of any other explanation,'came the cautious reply.

They were stepping gingerly between the tourists who were sitting idly on the steps that led up to the four-tiered fountain. Above them stood the statue of Eros, the winged problem child of the love goddess Aphrodite, seemingly shooting his arrows of love at the throngs of tourists who gathered there, or passed by on foot and in open topped sightseeing buses. Neil tried to close off his mind to the hustle and bustle around him and concentrate on why he had come here.

'But you can't prove it?' said Neil, focusing his mind on the issue and pulling the other man's attention back to him.

'No,' said the man, washing his hands in the fountain and splashing water over his face.

Was that an act of purification or merely to cool off, Neil wondered as he watched the man shake them dry.

The sun was beating down on them. The man - Terence Brown - had insisted on meeting in Piccadilly Circus. He had been set up too many times by the airline and he didn't fancy being beaten up by thugs again. Nor did he want to meet the caller in his own home, out of the public eye, and risk anything from an assault, to the planting of drugs, to being murdered. So he insisted on a public place, like this public intersection of major London roads, where there would always be plenty of people about. Of course, they could set him up in others ways, like having someone assault him and photograph his response. But he had taken his own precautions against that.

Neil didn't know this, but it would have made little difference if he had. All he wanted were the answers to a few questions.

'When exactly was the case?' asked Neil.

'It was about five or six months ago. At least, that part of it.'

Neil squinted against the sunlight as he turned this over in his mind. It was hard to hear what Brown was saying in the presence of so much noise, and hard to concentrate in the face of so much distraction. They were bombarded by visual stimulation, from the huge array of illuminated billboards shouting out to the world about Coca Cola and Sanyo electronics to the ornate regency façades of stone, once white now turned grey in the urban pollution. It was as if this place was a meeting point between modernity and history, a place for travellers to assemble and be awed by the grandeur of a great city. It wasn't really suitable for the serious discussion Neil intended. But perhaps it was that kind of safety that Terence Brown wanted: the safety of deniability.

Neil's mind returned to the judge.

'So, if he was getting paid off in that case, he wouldn't be getting the money now?'

'No.'

'I understand you have another case pending.'

'Yes. My harassment suit. After I filed the original suit they started a sustained campaign of harassment in the hope I'd back off. Which of course I didn't. Also, there's the appeal against Fortescue's ruling.'

'When is the harassment case?'

Brown threw his head back. He had led Neil to a booth selling tourist trinkets, almost as if he wanted to buy something or expected Neil too, but Neil was noticing other things.

'Oh, we've got a long way to go on that one,' said Brown, finally answering Neil's question. 'At least four months.'

'So it would be too early for him to be taking bribes on that one.'

'Possibly.'

'On the other hand,' said Neil. 'If he takes bribes in some cases, he could take them in others.'

'Is that a question or a statement?'

The suspicion was mounting in the tone of Brown's replies. 'They' could be trying to get him to make a libellous remark, or even one that could be construed as contempt of court. That was why he preferred to state his case by innuendo rather than explicit accusation, leaving Neil to deduce the obvious.

Neil, for his part, had told Brown the vital elements of the story, the incident on the Heath, the sick leave and his determination to get to the bottom of things. Brown, an ex-policeman, driven out of the profession by ill health, had recognized Neil's name immediately and was sympathetic. But still there was an element of caution in his responses.

'I was just wondering about the judge,' said Neil. 'Like I said. It's not directly related to this case. I just want to know about what sort of a man he is.'

'Well, I think you can draw your own conclusions based on what I've told you so far.'

'Yes,' said Neil slowly, looking around to confirm some¤thing that he had already suspected. 'I think I can.'

By now it was Neil who was leading the way, forcing Brown to follow him round in circles past Lillywhites, a five storey sports store on one of the corners, and the Criterion Theatre, one of the oldest in London, currently showing a parody of Shakespeare.

'Tell me something, Mr Brown. Do you know anyone called Meredith de Mur?'

He was watching Terence Brown carefully now, studying his face and monitoring his body language for any sign of fear, or guilt. There was none.

'Never heard of her.'

'Her?' 'Don't play games, Mr Douglas. It's a woman's name.'

If this was an act, thought Neil, it was a good one. There was no sign of fear or even concern on Terence Brown's face. Whereas before, when he had faced Neil's leading questions, the apprehension was subdued but evident.

'One last thing,' said Neil. 'Don't turn round suddenly, but there's a man who's been following us since you arrived.'

'He's mine,' said Brown. 'My business partner. He has a concealed video camera. It's just a small precaution against being stitched up. I'm sure you can understand that.'

'Is that a question or a statement?' asked Neil, with awry smile.

Chapter 9

'I've cleared out a room upstairs,' said the older man.

'OK, I'll send them in,' said Harold. He signalled Joe to send in the movers with the boxes. They proceeded to unload the boxes from the delivery van and take them into the house.

'Did you find anything about the case? Anything that might help?'

'Nothing at all, Mr Crowne. Well, almost nothing.'

'What do you mean?'

'We found that three of her photo albums were missing.'

'How do you know that?'

'From the spaces in her bookcase, and the dust pattern.'

Mr Crowne looked puzzled.

'Why would they be missing?'

'I don't know. The only thing I can think of is that someone who knew her was trying to conceal every last trace of it by taking her photographs. We also couldn't find any negatives of any of her pictures. That's why we couldn't bring the stuff here right away. We had to go through it just in case there was something we missed.'

'What do you mean, something?'

'Well, anything. Love letters, notes in a diary, anything.'

'Did you find anything?'

'Nothing. No letters. No photographs of unaccounted-for people. Nothing at all. Do you know if she was seeing anyone?'

'Not that I know. I mean, I got the impression that she might have been but she didn't tell me. She just seemed terribly preoccupied whenever we spoke.'

Harold pursed his lips.

'Did she seem happy?'

Mr Crowne hesitated.

'No . . . no she didn't.'

'You see what I'm getting it? If she was seeing someone, you'd expect her to have been happy. I mean, normally that's the effect a new relationship has.'

'Yes. I see what you mean. But I can't say that she did seem happy. If anything, she seemed rather depressed about something.'

'Did she say what?'

'No. I mean, she didn't want me to know. She tried to hide it. But I sensed it. They say that women are more sensitive than men. But I sensed it before my wife. Are you sure that someone took these photo albums?'

'Quite sure,' said Harold.

'And you're sure of the reason?'

'Well, that's the only reason I can think of. Can you think of another?'

Again, Mr Crowne hesitated.

'No. None at all.'

The delivery men continued carrying the boxes into the house as Mrs Crowne stood watching them with tears in her eyes, as all that remained of her daughter was brought back to her.

The CDROM arrived at Beth's house by motorcycle courier in the afternoon. Not bad, considering she'd only ordered it the day before. On the other hand, not good, considering that she had to prepare for her radio show tonight. But she couldn't complain. She wanted this CDROM badly. As she walked from the front door to her bedroom, tearing away at the packaging, she felt the same old thrill that she felt as a child, opening a birthday present - that same wild, excited sense of anticipation.

Within minutes her computer was switched on, the disk inserted in the drive and the program running. She searched for Rose Crowne and came up with a long list. She narrowed it down to the boroughs of Barnet and Hampstead, the boroughs that met near to the spot where Rose Crowne was killed. Only one Rose Crowne showed up. The address was in Camden Town.

'I just wanted to say a couple of things about the attack on Rose Crowne.'

He was a man and he sounded uneducated and a touch bitter.

'What about it?'

'Well, if she 'adn't been out alone at that time of night, it wouldn't 'ave 'appened?'

112

'Well, that's an intelligent comment, Graham. If she hadn't been out at night she wouldn't have been stabbed at night. And, of course, in the case of Leah Irons, if she hadn't been out during the day, she wouldn't have been murdered during the day. So, what's your solution, Graham? Would it be better if women stayed at home all day or weren't allowed out except when accompanied by a father, brother or husband, like in Afghanistan?'

'Now you're just taking the mickey. All I'm saying is if women go out at night alone, what do they expect?'

'Well, what do men expect when *they* go out at night, Graham? To be killed by bigger, stronger men?'

'No, I'm not saying that.'

'Then, what are you saying?'

'I'm just saying . . . look I'm not clever like you.'

'You're not clever like my four-year-old either. I mean, my four-year-old doesn't know as much as an adult but he's got an excuse, he's only four. What's *your* excuse? And by the time he's your age, he'll have learned a lot more than you'll ever know. You let your life go by without ever learning to use that peanut brain of yours. That's why you're a moron. Goodbye Graham. And could I just say that we're trying to hear from people who *know* something about the case, or at least who have something intelligent to say? So don't phone in unless you can shed some light on the case. We'll take one more caller who's been waiting in the meantime and then we'll take a break for some advertisements. Rupert in Harpenden on line eleven.'

'Good evening, Beth.'

'Good evening, Rupert.'

'I just wanted to say a couple of things about Martin Roebuck's behaviour. Two things really. First of all, someone called up earlier and spoke about Roebuck's sex fantasies and his letters to Annie Jacobs and then at their face-to-face meetings. But what they don't seem to know, and this was in the more detailed reports - i.e. not in the tabloids - is that in his earlier fantasies he wrote about things like having her dress up as a schoolgirl and spanking her. Now, with all due respect to that caller earlier, that's quite a common male fantasy.'

'But I think they would say that he also mentioned things like knives and blood, which the psychologist, Peter Eckland, said were what he would expect from the killer.'

'Yes, but he only started describing those fantasies after Annie Jacobs had contemptuously dismissed the earlier spanking fantasies. I mean, Eckland said he was offering Roebuck a series of ascending steps, which he was free to climb or not as he chose. But, first of all, he was offering explicit sexual bait at the top of those steps. The second point is that for all his talk and fantasies, there was nothing in the reports to suggest that Roebuck ever touched Annie Jacobs - not even once.'

'But then again they only met in public places, surrounded by loads of plain clothes police officers.'

'Yes, but Roebuck didn't know that. As far as he was concerned, they were just other members of the public. And the real killer didn't worry about it being in a public place when he did the killing.'

'Yes, but maybe there were always other people in their line of sight. He wouldn't do anything in front of witnesses.'

Beth was teasing him now. Testing the strength of his argument by playing devil's advocate.

'Yes, but he didn't touch her *at all*. I don't just mean serious violence. I mean, like grab her arm or wrist or shove her back aggressively or something like that. I've seen men do that to their girlfriends in public and even got into a few fights with them on occasion over that sort of behaviour. But Roebuck never touched her. And you know why. Because he was a talker. A talker, not a doer. I mean that Eckland may call himself a psychologist but I think that instead of all that pseudo-science he needs a good dose of old-fashioned common sense.'

'OK, thanks for those forceful comments Rupert. Well now, this is interesting. Most of the callers tonight seem to be sympathetic to Roebuck. Could it be that the tide of public opinion is changing and that as the press start to rehash the facts and stimulate the debate, people are beginning to realize that it wasn't quite what they thought it was? Or is it just that people who always thought Roebuck got a raw deal now have more courage to phone in? Let's talk to Keith on line one.'

'Hallo, Beth,' he sounded angry.

'Hallo, Keith.'

'I just wanted to talk about this moon landing business.'

'What moon landing business.'

'You know. You were saying last week that the moon landing never took place.'

'Keith, that was last week!'

'Yeah, but I couldn't get through then.'

'Keith, for God's sake! Don't you listen to the show! That was a wind-up! I just wanted to see how gullible you listeners are. And I'm sorry to say that in your case that's *very* gullible!OK. Let's go over to Conrad on line fifteen.'

'Good evening, Beth.'

'Good evening, Conrad. I understand you know something about Rose Crowne.'

'Yes,'

The voice sounded deep, like he was trying to disguise it.

'Well, go on.'

'I just wanted to say that Rose Crowne brought it on herself.'

'What, are you like the last caller? You think any woman who goes out of her home at night is a slag?'

'I mean, she had it coming.'

The voice sounded bitter. Beth sensed that there was more to this than male hypocrisy.

'How did she do that, Conrad?'

'She was a bitch.'

'A bitch? Not a slut?'

'What?'

'Well, you know, Conrad, there's an old saying about the difference between a bitch and a slut. A slut sleeps with everyone. A bitch sleeps with everyone except you. Is that what this is about, Conrad? Rose Crowne knocked you back? And it was more than your male ego could take?'

'You're a fuckin' bitch too!'

Beth knew that Jane would take advantage of the time delay to bleep the entire line off the air. But she signalled frantically to make sure that they didn't cut him off.

'Let me get this straight, Conrad. Do you know something about her death? Did she say "no" to some other man too?'

'You still haven't figured it out, have you? *I* killed the bitch.'

Beth looked down at the screen. There was no return number. Usually they didn't take such calls, but Beth had persuaded the station to make an exception while she ran the Rose Crowne/Leah Irons phone-ins.

'Because she turned you down?'

'She never turned me down. We had great sex together, the best sex I've ever had.'

'Then why did you kill her?'

'Because she had so much and I had so little.'

'How do you mean?'

'She had everything I wanted.'

Beth wasn't sure whether or not to believe him. But she sensed that if he was telling the truth now was the time to glean some useful information.

'Like what?'

'That's for you to figure out.'

Beth thought that he was about to ring off.

'OK, well, you test me. I'll guess and you see how close I come to the truth.'

She was careful not to say 'you tell me how close'. Either he would or he wouldn't. But if she told him to it would make it obvious that she was fishing.

'She had a family and you didn't?'

'Yes.'

'She had friends and you didn't?'

'Actually, she had very few friends. I mean, she stayed at home too much. That's why we got on together. I was like her in that respect and she needed me.'

'Are you telling me that you were her *friend* as well as her lover?'

'The penny has finally dropped.'

'But you said she had things that you *didn't* have.'

'That's also true.'

'Like what?'

'Like good looks. At least she *still* had hers.'

There was something mildly mysterious in the way that Conrad said this. And something highly suggestive.

116

'Do you mean you had yours once and then lost them? Or that she was losing hers? Or that by killing her in the way that you did, you *deprived* her of hers and reduced her to your level?'

'Maybe I mean I *all* of those things.'

'Could you elaborate?'

'I *could.*'

'*Would* you?'

'Hell no, Beth! That would spoil all the fun!'

The line went dead.

'Damn!' said Beth, hoping that Jane would have the presence of mind to cut it.

There was something very special about a motorway at night, a long uncoiled snake, stretching out into the distance. The sight of the lights gliding by, illuminating the way to another world, gave her a strange sense of warmth as she drove home from Heathrow Airport. Of course it wasn't really a new world. Amsterdam was not all that different from London. The people all spoke good English and were quite anglophilic.

What pleased her particularly was that the symposium had gone so well. 'Male attitudes to women,' had caused quite astir. Some of her older male colleagues from England had expected it to be a feminist's rock festival and had travelled there intending to mock and ridicule, or at least to make notes and mock the event later when they got back home. Instead, it had been a dignified conference, discussing such issues as 'Fear of women', the 'Transition to rapist', 'Men who kill women' and 'Bridging the gap between Mars and Venus'. Ruth Hoffman's lecture on 'Men whose fantasies *don't* turn to violence' had gone down particularly well. She had argued that with all the emphasis on men who cross the line into violence there is a tendency to forget that there is a large group of sexually frustrated men who do *not* turn to violence. She argued that these men should be identified and helped, not merely because this would reduce the likelihood of such men becoming rapists or killers, but also in the spirit of social equity. It had been such a breath of fresh air from the negative thrust of most of the papers that it had been singled out for favourable comment, not only by her fellow academics but also by the popular press, in Holland and Britain.

117

Ruth Hoffman savoured the sense of victory and accomplishment and the flickering lights in the distance as she drove along. The only thing missing was the radio.

Her hand reached out to the dashboard.

'That was *Diary* by David Gates and Bread.'

Beth Porter's voice came through a quarter of a million radios.

'OK to those of you who have just tuned in, we're discussing whatever you want to talk about but especially the Rose Crowne and Leah Irons cases. Yes, I know we've talked about it before and I can hear some of you saying "what?Not again!". But this time, I'm trying to find out something very specific. We've just heard a man called Conrad telling us that he murdered Rose Crowne. He said that he did it because she had things that he didn't, like a family and good looks. Although he also said that she didn't have many friends and that's why she needed him. He implied that he once had good looks but had now lost them. He also hinted that he killed Rose Crowne in that way because he wanted to destroy her looks. Perhaps her good looks were a reproach to him. Perhaps people saw them together in the street and made remarks about why a beautiful woman should go out with such an ugly man.

'Personally, I find this quite unlikely, because we often hear of cases of beautiful women going out with not so handsome or even ugly men for a whole variety of reasons. He'd've had to have been particularly sensitive if he took these comments to heart - especially as he did have Rose Crowne. After all, that was surely what mattered. I mean if an ugly man has a beautiful woman *he's* the one who has the last laugh - until she breaks it off with him.

"Maybe that was it. Maybe Rose Crowne was going out with Conrad and then she broke it off. Maybe she heard all these people saying"why do you go out with such an ugly creep?" until finally it took its toll on her. Maybe she decided that she could do better. Or maybe she got bored with him. Or maybe he kept getting angry about it and his anger frightened her and drove her away. Whatever the reason, if she broke it off with him, maybe that's the point when he came to resent her good looks. The beauty that was once such an ego-booster for him when she was at his side suddenly became a reproach to him when she left him.

'Does anyone know who this man could be? Does anyone out there know Rose Crowne?'

In the dimly lit radio broadcasting studio, Beth was leaning forward into the microphone. Jane and Mick had been with her long enough to know what this meant: she was excited and thoroughly enjoying herself. There seemed to have been a change in her over the past few weeks, a change they'd both noticed. She appeared to have developed a new sense of purpose. And if their memories served them right, they could trace it back to the murder of Rose Crowne and the assault on Martin Roebuck. It was as if something had snapped inside her when the incident on Hampstead Heath had taken place, like a hand reaching out and shaking her. Indeed, it was almost as if a commanding but distant voice had warned Beth to put some meaning into her life. To Jane, it was a bit like born-again religion. Except that in the case of Beth, the religion she seemed to have discovered and embraced was unlike any of the more conventional theologies Jane knew of. The religion, in fact, appeared to be a new-found secular philosophy of ethical journalism - something far removed from the path that Beth had followed until now. She was no longer trying to stir things up, she was trying to find the truth.

This had been clear for some days now. At first they had thought that it was just a temporary aberration but now they were beginning to realize that it represented genuine change in character. Beth was no longer the cold, calculating manipulative bitch of the airwaves. She was now the crusader for noble causes, determined that a murderer should be brought to justice.

'So if you have any information on this,' Beth was saying, 'call us on 020 7946 0909.'

In her car on the M4, Ruth Hoffman felt a buzz of excitement. This was right up her street. She wished that she had switched-on earlier and heard this 'Conrad' but judging by Beth's summary this was a case to which she could contribute, at least from the safety of anonymity via the telephone.

She didn't like using the mobile phone at all when she was driving, especially at night. Even a minor distraction could be fatal. But the road was not crowded and she had a hands-free system connected.

She reached out and keyed in the number.

In the glowing green digits on the phosphor screen, Beth saw the name 'Ruth Hoffman'. Next to it, under the word 'subject', it said: 'Knows about psychology of sex attackers.' It was like the killer left hook of a powerful heavyweight boxer. The flood of adrenalin sent Beth's heart into a frenzy of rapid thumping. For the first time, a contribution from an expert instead of an amateur.

'We'll go to Ruth on line twelve. Hallo, Ruth.'

'Hallo, Beth. I know a bit about men who attack women.' There was a strange blend of stridency and nervousness in the caller's voice - as if this woman was self-confident in her daily life, but new to radio. Some people announce nervously that they are first-time callers, in the hope that the presenter will go easy on them. But this woman didn't do that. She just gritted her teeth and plunged straight in.

'I just wanted to say that the attacks on both Leah Irons and Rose Crowne were calculated to destroy their good looks. That suggests that it wasn't merely frustration but also jealousy.'

'Well, we had a caller just now who said he did it and effectively gave that as his reason.'

'OK, well I didn't hear the caller. I only just switched on. All I can say is that usually sex killers don't call phone-ins but judging from the way you described it, I'd say that such a call might well be genuine.'

'OK, thank you very much, Ruth. Well now, that's interesting. You've heard the voice of the alleged killer and you've heard a psychological analysis. But does anyone out there have any idea who this man is? Can you good people out there help me catch him? The number is 020 7946 0909. Let's take a break. I'll be back with you shortly.'

She leaned back and pushed away the microphone as the advertisements started running. Jane was signalling her excitedly.

'What is it?'

'It's Neil Douglas.'

'Put him on.'

Jane transferred the call.

'Hi, Neil.'

'Yes. Are we off the air?'

120

'Yes.'

'OK, look I know this is going to sound silly, but I just wanted to thank you for what you were doing.'

'How do you mean?'

'Well, you're no longer lampooning me like you were before.'

'I'm more concerned with catching the killer than with blaming you for a careless mistake that you now regret.'

'Me too. I mean, I also want to catch the killer - I mean *really* catch him.'

'This sounds heavy.'

'Well, I'm not supposed to be investigating, but I have a certain amount of latitude in looking for witnesses to support me in the disciplinary proceedings.'

'Have you found anyone'

There was a pause.

'No, not yet. But I'm still looking. And maybe with your show getting the listeners involved, we might find something.'

'That's what I'm hoping.' There was an embarrassed silence. 'Hey, listen Neil. How would you like to come up here?'

'How do you mean?'

'Well, you could come up here one night when I'm doing the show and see how things work. Maybe you could even talk to people on the air.'

'Oh, I don't know about that.'

'OK, look, you don't have to talk to anyone if you don't want. I won't even tell the listeners you're here, if you prefer. But why don't you just come up here and I'll show you the ropes? You can see how a radio station works and then you can tell me how a police station works. That's a fair exchange, isn't it?'

She couldn't see him smiling. But then again he couldn't see her holding her breath.

'All right,' he said casually.

She breathed out.

'You pick the day when it's most convenient,' she added.

Chapter 10

Neil's car pulled up a short way past Peter Eckland's house, at the end of a gravel road on the outskirts of the village. A bungalow with a stucco façade, built against a ridge on a, sprawling hill, it looked out onto a stretch of freshly mown lawn, which, in turn, overlooked the wild grass and spreading trees on the untended floor of a valley. It was as if the house had been thrown violently into the air by a flood tide and now stood there frozen in time, held poised to keep vigil over the green sea that surrounded it. Apart from the excess of green, the village had a strangely Middle-Eastern feel to it. Built against the slopes of a series of adjoining hills, it had a kind of rough and rugged texture, giving it the aura of something that had remained unchanged since the industrial revolution, or even the dawn of time.

In some ways he felt in awe of the man he was about to meet. This was, he remembered, a man who had fulfilled the dream that Neil himself had abandoned.

As he climbed out of the car, Neil looked ahead at the road as it snaked away from the house, down a gently sloping ridge and then rising up again, ascending to the adjacent hill. For a few seconds he looked out onto the point where the road vanished from view, feeling that breathless sense of wondering that he always felt when he tried to look beyond the horizon.

With butterflies in his stomach, he walked along a dirt path that branched off from the road and curved down towards the house. For the first few steps he held his hand above his eyes to shield them from the sun. But he lowered it when the path dipped to where it was protected from sunlight by a procession of trees, flanking it on either side. Approaching the house was like walking down a tunnel of shaded pink light.

He felt a tremor of hesitancy as he reached out to the brass button of the doorbell.

What do I really want to ask? he wondered.

The truth of the matter was that there was quite a lot he wanted to ask. At one level he wanted the reassurance that the man whom he had put in a coma was really a murderer, whatever the courts had said -- and therefore deserved what he got. At another level he wanted some guidance in tracking down the man who had murdered Rose Crowne. He didn't know how the police investigation was proceeding but it didn't matter to Neil even if it was proceeding well. It wasn't enough that the murderer be caught. Neil had to do it himself. He had to catch the murderer with his own hands. There was nothing he could do for Martin Roebuck. His fate was in the hands of his doctors and God. But there was something he could do for Rose Crowne.

At yet another more personal level he wanted some counselling for himself. Peter Eckland was not strictly speaking a criminal psychologist, rather he was a clinical psychologist who was frequently called in by the police to help them with their inquiries. Neil Douglas, who had once harboured similar ambitions, hoped that Eckland might be able to help him with his personal guilt and self-torment.

He jumped back startled as he heard the doorbell ring, and he felt his finger on the cold brass button. He realized that while he had been daydreaming, he had pressed the button, his subconscious taking over from him - or was it his autonomic nervous system? He smiled wryly at how much of this basic material he had forgotten. Police work on the streets had bred whole chunks of his academic knowledge out of him. Or perhaps it was not the police work itself, but a defence mechanism for burying the past and avoiding having to face the fact that he had given up his ambition to live out his father's dreams.

The door swung open to reveal a portly man with a beaming smile.

'PC Neil Douglas, I assume.'
'That's right,' said Neil, reassured by the smile.

'Come in,' said Eckland, stepping aside and sweeping back with his left arm in a demonstratively welcoming gesture. Neil entered, feeling the warmth of having been befriended by one who was, when all was said and done, a complete stranger to him.

'Go straight in to the study, the second on the right.'

Neil ambled along the corridor, pausing briefly to admire the David Roberts lithographs of nineteenth century Palestine landscapes. They hung at regular intervals on the olive green walls.

Behind him, Peter Eckland's footsteps trailed off as he took a detour to the kitchen.

'I'll just bring in some refreshments,' the psychologist called out. 'Do you like fresh orange juice?'

'Fine,' Neil replied, stepping down the four steps of a short staircase leading into the study.

The study was a room of about 12 by 16, set into the side of the hill so that one side formed a wall of glass looking out onto the terraced lawn and the floor of the valley beyond, while the opposite wall was for the most part below ground level. Neil's eyes swept the room as he turned his head this way and that. The room was lined with bookcases, and panelling of mahogany or Rosewood, and seemed to be built to specifications, fitting the bevelled corners of the room as if custom designed for precisely the space it was intended to occupy. Neil noticed that the desk was positioned just to the side of the wall of glass, so that by turning his head to the left slightly, Eckland could see the lawn.

A boy and a girl in their sub-teens were playing in the garden, kicking a ball around and shouting. Eckland's children, Neil presumed.

But the most conspicuous feature of the room, was the mountain of books. Not only did they line the shelves, but they were piled up high on every available surface: the desk, the two chairs and the filing cabinet. The furnishings may have been tailored to fit the room, but the room most decidedly did not fit its purpose. Peter Eckland was a man of ample intellectual as well as physical girth and it was clear that his book collection had outgrown this room a long time ago.

Neil shifted some of the books on the desk to make room for those from one of the chairs. He was still shifting books when Eckland returned to the room with a tray of orange juice and two glasses.

'Oh, let me help you,' said Eckland.

The psychologist balanced the tray precariously on the corner of the desk while he dumped some of the books from the chairs directly onto the floor.

'I understand that you want some advice on the Leah Irons and Rose Crowne cases.'

Neil nodded.

'May I ask how much you know about the Rose Crowne case?'

Neil wondered why Eckland didn't also ask him how much he knew about the Leah Irons case, especially as it had been Eckland who had devised the undercover operation in that case to find out if Martin Roebuck was guilty. But then again, perhaps that was why he didn't mention it. The undercover operation had been a monumental flop and Eckland was probably embarrassed by it - although he still insisted that the operation had been conducted properly and the results were valid.

Neil shook his head, waiting for Eckland to continue.

'The two cases are not identical, of course,' said the psychologist. 'Rose Crowne was killed at night. Leah Irons was attacked in broad daylight.'

Neil leaned forward keenly.

'You think it was two different people?'

'It's certainly a possibility. I mean, the difference I pointed out is a fairly obvious one.'

'So you're saying it could be that Roebuck did the first but not the second.'

'Exactly.'

'But - forgive me for putting it this way - isn't it possible that your judgement is clouded by your interest in the original case? I mean, you stuck your neck out by saying that Roebuck belonged to a small subcategory of sexual deviants to which the murderer of Leah Irons also belonged.'

'True.'

'And you also said that it was extremely unlikely that two such persons were on Hampstead Heath that same day.'

'That's right. Although, in retrospect, I have to concede that there were over a hundred convicted sex offenders of various types living within easy walking distance of that part of the Heath.'

'Nevertheless,' Neil pressed on. 'You came as close to saying that Roebuck was guilty as you dared from a legal point of view.'

'That would be a layman's characterization of my words,' said Eckland, a faint patronizing tone straying into his voice.

'Well, how would you put it?' Neil challenged.

'I would say I phrased my position within the bounds of professional, rather than legal, constraints. From a professional point of view, I couldn't say that Roebuck was the murderer, only that he has some fairly precise features in common with the murderer.'

'Be that as it may,' Neil pressed on, sensing that Eckland respected a man who challenged him, 'the general thrust of your evidence was that Roebuck was probably guilty. At least that's how a layman would see it.'

'I accept that such would be the likely interpretation – by a layman.'

'So, that to admit now that Roebuck *wasn't* the murderer, would be professionally embarrassing.'

'I suppose it would be. Although, of course, that's precisely why people in my line of work qualify what we say in the way that I did.'

'Covering one's arse,' Neil shot out in jest, regretting it immediately.

'In layman's terms,' Eckland replied, still weighing in gently with the patronizing tone.

Neil sensed that the flavour of the argument had now turned hostile, and he regretted not only his untimely interjection but his whole approach. He spoke again.

'Can you think of any reason why Roebuck would have been in the same vicinity as Rose Crowne at the time she was attacked?'

Neil hadn't been paying any particular attention to Eckland's reaction. But he sensed an element of fear in the silence that followed, as if there was more to the psychologist's hesitation than a mere gathering of intellectual resources to give a measured response. Could it be professional embarrassment? Or guilt? If Eckland was wrong - if Martin Roebuck had been innocent and if Rose Crowne was murdered by the same man as Leah Irons - then it would mean that Eckland had diverted police attention onto an innocent man and not only ruined his life but discouraged the police from pursuing other lines of inquiry that might have exposed the real murderer.

That would be a pretty awful thing to live with. And both Eckland and Neil knew all about that Freudian phenomenon known as *denial*.

Eckland spoke up at last.

'If my assessment of Roebuck's character was correct, then Roebuck had a fascination with making women feel vulnerable . . . making them feel afraid.'

'So you think he was *following* Rose Crowne? And that he was doing it to frighten her?'

'It's a possibility.'

Neil took a sip of orange juice, feeling his throat drying up with the tension of the moment but he was thirsty for information too.

'And then when someone else attacked her, he went to her aid.'

He had said it neutrally. But it was unavoidable to inject a note of scepticism towards Eckland's assessment, even if it offended the psychologist.

'It's all part of the same general power lust. Wanting to make women feel afraid of him and rescuing them from danger so they appreciate his manliness.'

'But a lot of men probably fantasize about rescuing women in danger. Or at least a lot of boys.'

'It's all part of the general male power sex fantasy.'

'But not many men fantasize about committing extreme violence against women. You said so yourself, Dr Eckland.'

'Again, perfectly true.'

'But according to your interpretation from the Annie Jacobs operation, Martin Roebuck did.'

'Well, he certainly described such fantasies both in his letters and in his face-to-face meetings.'

'But are you really saying, doctor, that the sort of men who fantasize about attacking women also fantasize about rescuing them from danger?'

'Not usually. But then again Roebuck didn't necessarily fantasize about rescuing women from danger. All we know is that when it came to the crunch, he apparently did so.'

Neil considered reminding Eckland that it was he who had spoken about fantasizing about such rescues. But he didn't want to aggravate the residual hostility that still lingered.

'Doesn't--'

Neil broke off, embarrassed.

'What?' Eckland prompted.

'I know this is going to sound terribly naive, but doesn't the fact that he rescued her suggest an element of benevolence or goodwill on Roebuck's part - an element of goodwill which is inconsistent with Roebuck being a murderer.'

'It's not at all naive,' replied Eckland smiling graciously. 'It's a perfectly reasonable laymen's opinion.'

'But it's wrong?' Neil prompted, trying to anticipate the patronizing put-down.

Eckland leaned forward, enthusiastically.

'It's not wrong. It's just incomplete. First of all, I need hardly remind you that in cases of genuine multiple personality disorder, it would be quite possible for someone to demonstrate precisely that sort of diversity of inner nature.'

'But you never said before that Roebuck--'

'I know I didn't,' Eckland cut in, brushing off the interruption. 'And I'm not saying it now.' He leaned back and took a deep breath. 'I merely mentioned it for the sake of academic completeness. In Roebuck's case, there could be other explanations. He might have feared that he would be blamed for the attack on Rose Crowne if he didn't act to stop it. Don't forget, it's highly suspicious that he was thereat all. Secondly, whether or not he fantasized about rescuing women in danger, the fact is that when the opportunity presented itself, he might well have seen it as a chance to show himself as a real man and thus to have a woman in his power, not out of fear but out of gratitude.'

'Like a normal man,' said Neil.

'Like a normal adolescent,' Eckland replied, looking Neil in the eyes and smiling.

Neil looked away, sampling the view out of the window, but savouring the escape from Eckland's penetrating stare.

'But you still don't know why Roebuck was following Rose Crowne.'

It was a statement. Neil felt it was the only way he could recover from the disadvantage at which Eckland had put him.

'Possibly curiosity.'

'Curiosity? About what?'

Eckland flushed. Neil noticed a kind of awkwardness in his reaction. Not embarrassment . . . more like fear.

'Oh, I don't know. What she was wearing. Who she was. Where she lived. That's how obsessions often get started. A man sees an attractive woman and wants more than he can have. That's probably how it started with Leah Irons.'

'So you think Rose Crowne was all set to become his next victim? But a chance event - like an attack by another man- led to him trying to save her instead.'

'The only man who knows that is lying on a hospital bed in a coma,' said the psychologist. He didn't have to add 'thanks to you.' The words hung in the air as an unstated postscript.

'It just seems so unlikely that another woman should be attacked on the Heath in the same way as Leah Irons - even if it was night rather than day. I mean, don't serial killer soften refine their techniques as they go along?'

'They do. Usually one would expect them to start off using the safety of the night and then progress to day. But that's not conclusive.'

Neil was now grasping at Eckland's words.

'So it is at least possible that the man who attacked Rose Crowne was also the man who attacked Leah Irons?'

'It's possible.'

'And we know that serial sex killers usually commit other sex crimes before.'

'Well, Roebuck had a couple of minor convictions from before.'

'But one of them came about as a result of an incriminating admission he made while under interrogation in the Leah Irons case.'

'Well, we don't know what else he did.'

'We can only go by what we know.'

'That doesn't prove he's innocent.'

'No, but we know he's not guilty of the Rose Crowne murder, and if both murders--'

'Do we?'

It was like driving one's car at full speed only to crash into a barrier that materialized out of nowhere.

'Well, we know that from the witnesses.'

'You mean this Meredith de Mur?'

'Amongst others,' said Neil.

'How much do you really know about her?'

'What are you getting at?'

'A sick old woman. Probably lonely and sexually frustrated herself. She sees a young man like Martin Roebuck, a young, not altogether unattractive man. And she decides she like shim. She doesn't know that he's a psychopathic sex killer who's already murdered once. All she knows is that he's young and reasonably attractive. And she wishes she could have him, but knows she can't. So she stays in the shadows and watches him, wishing for the unattainable and dreaming the impossible dream. The next thing you know, he's murdering a woman in her presence. She's shocked and horrified. But this woman -the victim - is a stranger to her and means nothing to her. Meredith de Mur doesn't give a damn about her. But she's developed a fixation on this man - and the fact that he's a murderer makes him all the more vulnerable and brings out her latent maternal instinct. She now sees him both as a son to be protected and a strong lover to protect her. She wants both but has never had either. All she knows is that she must protect him. That is now her destiny. And so she invents another man and says that this other man attacked Rose Crowne.'

'Au-- but that's ridiculous!' Neil stuttered. 'There were loads of other witnesses. All those people watching from their windows.'

'They don't know what they saw,' Eckland declared flatly. 'It was the dead of night. They were drawn to the window by distant screams. They were watching from the distance. And what they saw probably lasted for a few seconds.'

'You're not serious.'

'You've said yourself, Neil, it was a pretty big coincidence that Roebuck was there at all. If someone else murdered both Leah Irons and Rose Crowne, what is the likelihood that Roebuck, who was suspected in the first case, would-be at the scene when the murderer struck again?'

Martin Roebuck's private room was ahead of the patient. It had been easy to dress up in the toilet and then emerge looking just like any other patient. There were so many people in a hospital, it was impossible to check up on every one. But the problem was that Roebuck was too well guarded. There was a policeman outside his room at all times and it was the room at the end. Also, the fact that it was in a private section meant that the staff might be more

130

familiar with who the patients were. But it was just after the changeover of shifts in the evening and new patients were being admitted all the time.

It was easy to walk up and down the corridor at a slow shuffling pace. It was after the doctors had made their afternoon rounds and they would look like any other postoperative patient trying to get back into shape. Of course, they were supposed to think that this was a new patient. But as long as they didn't ask any questions it would be all right.

It was on the fifth shuffle that the patient turned to the policeman.

'Do you know where the coffee machine is?'

'I think it's one floor down.'

'Thanks. Do you want one?'

'Oh, no thanks.'

Damn.

'OK.'

He sounded disappointed. The policeman felt guilty.

'Actually, could you get me coffee please. White, no sugar.'

The policeman fished in his pocket and handed over money to the patient. The patient took it gratefully and shuffled off to the lift, went downstairs and got the two coffees. Into one of the polystyrene cups went a small purple pill, 'Hypnotherapy so-called 'date rape pill', a sedative ten times stronger than valium.

Five minutes later, the policeman and the patient were sipping coffee in the corridor, bitching about the government and the lack of adequate funding for the National Health Service. Seven minutes later, the patient was reaching out quickly so as to snatch the cup of coffee from the policeman's hand as he keeled over unconscious. Then the patient emptied both cups into the nearby flower pot and dragged the policeman into Martin Roebuck's room.

It had all been done with military precision.

There was just one last job to be done: cutting off Roebuck's life-support system in a way that wouldn't alert the nursing station. That would be easy enough. The sensors could be quickly detached from Roebuck and attached to the unconscious policeman. There was just one problem, as the patient found upon turning round to the bed: Martin Roebuck wasn't there. The bed was empty.

Eckland's words were still ringing in Neil's ears when he walked past the soaring column on which stood the great statue of Frederick, Duke of York, the second son of King George the Third. The passage led to a succession of extremely wide steps, broken into three ledges, that led down to the Mall, the wide red asphalt road that stretched from Admiralty Arch in Trafalgar Square to Buckingham Palace.

The day was dulled by the haze of cloud filling the sky. It seemed to match the sense of depression that had haunted him since the incident on the Heath and the mood of lethargy that he found himself forced to overcome after a couple of days of sick leave. As he crossed the Mall to the pedestrian island in the middle, Neil looked back for signs of anyone following him. There were no familiar faces in the small group of tourists who were drifting in the same direction towards St James's Park. He was struck by the sight of the impressive cream-coloured Georgian façades lining the road opposite the park and he wondered why the past seemed so magnificent and the present so dreary. The myth of the Halcyon Age was just that-- an illusion -- but while it was a placebo to older people, it was a mocking put-down to the young. And yet he couldn't break its credibility in his mind. He knew it was a myth and yet he believed it.

He crossed the other half of the road and walked to the impressive statue of a winged horse, a memorial to the members of the Royal Artillery who lost their lives in the Boer War. It wasn't long before he saw Horace Tadditt, MP approaching.

'Mr Douglas, I presume,' said Tadditt, extending his hand.

Neil nodded and shook Tadditt's hand.

'Let's take a walk,' said Tadditt.

They set off into the lunchtime crowds in St James's Park. Neil spoke again.

'It was good of you to agree to see me at such short notice.'

'After what you told me about the Roebuck incident, it was the least I could do for you.'

'Thank you.'

'I want you to know that if there's anything I can do to support you, I'll do it. They expect you to work with your hands tied and then when one of you slips up, the press comes down on you and tries to make an example of you.'

'I know,' said Neil. Horace Tadditt sounded rather stuffy but Neil was grateful all the same.

'If they gave you greater strip-searched powers and allowed you to carry guns you wouldn't have to take your lives in your hands every time you step out onto the street sand you'd be able to catch more of the criminals which the public are clamouring for.'

'Thank you,' Neil said again.

Neil remembered that this was the man who also wanted to introduce compulsory, show-on-demand, identity cards. He sensed that a word of agreement was due, as if this man wanted to hear a note of approval or confirmation from one of those for whom he was showing support. But Neil didn't feel free to give that approval - not when his own hands had innocent blood on them. He could express gratitude but not agreement, so that pale 'thank you,' was all the approval that he could muster.

They were crossing a patch of grass leading towards the lake, that lay ahead of them. Neil noticed that some of the tree trunks had a green, rotten look about them. He wondered if it was a passing malady or the first stage of an encroaching disease that would eventually kill the trees that had stood here for so long.

'I understand that my colleagues have already asked you where you were on the night Rose Crowne was murdered.'

'Oh yes. I told the SO10 people everything.'

'SO10?' Neil stuttered.

'Oh yes,' said Tadditt. 'They've taken over the investigation. Didn't you know?'

Neil hadn't known. SO10 was one of the elite undercover units of the police. They usually investigated drug rackets and neo-Nazi groups, very often sending in people with deep covers and requiring them to immerse themselves in the roles they were playing. It was from SO10 that Annie Jacobs had been recruited for the sting operation that had unsuccessfully attempted to entrap Martin Roebuck.

They had almost reached the lake. It was still bright beneath the cloudy haze, the edge taken off the warmth by the breeze.

'If it's not too personal,' said Neil, 'where were you on the night in question.'

Tadditt smiled stiffly, as if to say 'you don't waste much time on idle chit chat.'

'I was having dinner with some business associates.'

'Business associates?'

'Yes.' Neil remained silent, as if the question hadn't really been answered. 'You see, Neil, it's very hard to live on a Member of Parliament's salary.'

'Even after the 43 per cent increase?'

'If it's any comfort,' said Tadditt, 'I'd gladly support asimilar pay increase for the police but I don't think my colleagues would go along with me.'

'I suppose as long as it's legal, it's none of my business,'said Neil, not wanting to alienate a man who had presented himself as a friend.

'I wish I could get the press to see it that way. If you think the tabloids are bad, you should see the broadsheets when they go on a crusade - especially the *Guardian*. They seem to forget that I could get a whole lot more in the private sector. I'm doing my country a service, working for low pay as an MP, and they begrudge me a little bit extra from a couple of consultancies that I hold in my spare time. If they knew how lowly a position it is to be a backbench MP, they'd realize that consultancy work doesn't even interfere with my parliamentary time. As long as I turn up for a division and recite a few hearty "hear hears" at the PM's question time, I've pretty much nothing to do in the house. I run a biweekly surgery in my constituency and the rest of my time is my own to devote to my consultancy work for the private sector, where I make my real money.'

'I guess the thing they're afraid of is that an MP with outside interests might use his parliamentary powers to advance those outside interests instead of keeping them separate.'

'Well, that's not necessarily such a bad thing. Sometimes it's only because of an outside consultancy that you get to hear about things that you wouldn't know about otherwise. I mean, you hear some sanctimonious git on the radio saying we shouldn't supply arms to some country in the Middle East or South East Asia because the government over there is a dictatorship. What he doesn't tell you is that if we don't get that arms contract then seven thousand jobs in the Midlands will be lost and the Middle Eastern government will just go elsewhere to get the weapons, making our noble gesture quite pointless.'

He was waxing passionate and Neil didn't want to offend him, but he couldn't help but feel that one could use the same argument to justify selling weapons to political terrorists.

The lake seemed green as they walked past it. The path took them past a glass encased restaurant to their right, while a fountain to the left, in the middle of the lake, close to the wildlife island, filled the air around with a gentle rushing sound. They almost tripped over the pigeons that had gathered at their feet. An elderly, foreign couple nearby had been feeding the pigeons, and the birds had assembled there, lured by that most basic of instincts.

'But what happens when conflicts of interest arise?'

'How do you mean?'

'Well like, when you want to ask a question in the house that happens to be in the interests of your . . . er. . . employers?'

'Well, one way is to get a colleague to ask it. That's usually the best way to avoid misunderstandings. But it doesn't happen often.'

'But when you have a consultancy, don't the interests that you represent expect you to work on their behalf in the House?'

Tadditt was watching Neil carefully now, realizing for the first time that the young policeman was somewhat hostile. The MP's lips tightened with indignation as he realized that his smoothing had fallen on deaf ears.

'That may be. But there's nothing wrong with that. We have to think of ourselves too. An MP's career can be a short one - even if we toe the party line religiously. We have to plan for the future. An MP's main value to a private company is precisely *because* of his parliamentary powers. I'm sure you're not naive enough to think that we're chosen for our business acumen.'

From the wildlife sanctuary island came the sound of geese trumpeting their presence to the gaping tourists. It brought a smile to Neil's lips.

'But then surely, when your political career ends, so does your business career.'

'Not quite. You see, Neil, in addition to our parliamentary *powers*, there are also our parliamentary *connections*. If we can

135

build up enough of those then we have assets to trade when we *leave* office too.'

'You make it sound all very cynical.'

'It's called reality, Neil. Most members of your profession play the game by the same rules - at least when they grow up. It's not what's right or wrong that counts. It's what you can get away with. If you had known that, you wouldn't be in the mess you're in now. If it makes any easier, don't think of it as corruption. Think of it as a new slant on the concept of performance related pay.'

Neil was thinking about his father, the rock of courage and high moral standards who had not been ready to compromise for anyone - not even his own son. This man who walked beside him now was not a source of comfort but a source of reproach. He was an enemy of everything that his father stood for, everything that his father had taught him to believe in. It left him feeling angry and exhausted.

He would have loved to sit down, but all the benches facing the lake on the long path ahead of them were filled.

'Would I be right in thinking that the kind of discussions you were having with these business associates were not the kind of discussions that you'd want discussed in or with the press.'

'Is that a threat?' asked Tadditt

'No,' said Neil. 'Just wondering.

'Let's just say,' said Tadditt, his jaw stiffening. 'That if any of this gets out, I'll hang you out to dry.'

Chapter 11

He's talking nonsense, of course,' said Jonathan Trotter.

'That's what I figured,' Neil replied. 'I just wanted to hear it from a professional.'

They were in Trotter's office in Chelmsford, a tidy office, with walnut panelling and art reproductions on the wall. Neil noticed, that in contrast to Eckland's Robert's lithographs, these were by Turner, Gainsborough and - he noted with wry amusement - Constable. The joke brought a smile to his lips.

Still the academic at heart, Neil had read up on the literature on psychological profiling. He knew that although Eckland was the most famous practitioner of psychological profiling in Britain, Jonathan Trotter was the most knowledgeable. Trotter was the pioneer who had brought the art to England and was still the country's foremost expert - even if he wasn't as quick to blow his own trumpet, or as loud.

'The truth of the matter is that it's very hard to get meaningful evidence from the scene of a single crime. There are no patterns to study and so you have nothing with which to compare it. You don't know who the murderer is so you can't compare it to his other behaviour and you can't compare it to other crimes in the sequence because there is no sequence.'

Trotter was in his fifties, leaner than Eckland, but by no means of slim build. His brown mousy hair was thick on top, but the hairline was high on the head.

'But why would you want to compare it with his other behaviour?'

'Because that's how you learn about criminal psychology. You see you can only use criminal psychology once you've got some valid postulates to work with. And the only way you can get valid postulates is by looking at the murderer after you've got him, and comparing him to others and comparing his murderous activities, his various other activities and other phases of his life. That's why it's so much more interesting to us if psychopathic killers are caught alive - even if the public is crying out for their blood.'

'But surely you must have some valid postulates by now,' said Neil, put off by Trotter's intellectual modesty and its contrast to the certainty with which Eckland had spoken.

'Oh we do. But not to the extent that the public seems to think. We can sometimes put the police on the right track or tell them that A is more likely than B, but no more than that. And we always have to be aware of exceptions. For example, received wisdom tells us that children sometimes kill other children but never kill adults outside their own family. But shortly before Leah Irons was killed, a seventeen-year-old girl was stabbed to death in a frenzied attack and it turned out that the killer was a *twelve*-year-old girl.'

'How was she caught?'

'She'd made some incriminating statements while in detention for another offence. It wasn't until four years later that she was caught, though. It could very easily have slipped through the net as an unsolved crime.'

'OK, but you said it's hard to get meaningful evidence from a single crime. But here we're talking about two crimes, so surely you can find some common features.'

'Yes, there are common features all right. But there are also distinguishing features. So we have to be careful about saying that it was the same killer.'

'You mean it wasn't?' asked Neil, a twisting pain in his stomach.

'I mean, we can't be sure. A frenzied knife attack doesn't necessarily have to be the work of the same killer or even a carbon-copy killer. Otherwise we could be looking to lay a whole lot of other crimes at this killer's door.'

'But they both took place on Hampstead Heath.'

'Yes, that's true. But the first took place in broad daylight, the second took place at night.'

'Don't killers sometimes vary their style?'

'Not like this. You sometimes see a progression in which the killer gets bolder. But in this case it was the *first* attack which took place in broad daylight, while the second took place at night, under cover of darkness. That doesn't suggest a killer becoming bolder.'

Neil thought about this in silence for almost half a minute, while Trotter said nothing. The psychologist had agreed to this meeting without hesitation but he was prepared to let Neil set the agenda.

'Aren't you making an unwarranted assumption there?' asked Neil.

'How do you mean?' asked Trotter, wide-eyed and amused at Neil's own sudden display of courage.

'Well . . . let's say this killer is . . . afraid of the dark. Then committing the second crime at night would be a sign not of a loss of boldness but of overcoming his fear.'

It was a full twenty seconds - Neil could feel them ticking by - before Trotter could respond to this unexpected layman's insight. But it only took five seconds for Neil to realize that Trotter was amused rather than angry. He could see, in the suppressed twitchings of a smile on Trotter's face that the psychologist wanted to come back with an inoffensive witty rejoinder. Eventually, when he spoke, what he came up with was quite lame.

'A killer who's afraid of the dark. Maybe he should have asked a policeman to hold his hand.'

'But seriously-'

'Yes, I'm sorry, Neil. I shouldn't joke about it. As a matter of fact, it's quite a clever idea. And not without merit.'

Again Trotter paused to consider the suggestion.

'I suppose it could be a case of the killer overcoming his own fears. Or it could be simply that he had reason to commit the first attack during the day and the second during the night.'

'So it is at least possible that it was the same attacker,' said Neil, still groping in the dark for reassurance.

'It's possible.'

'And what about Eckland's hypothesis that Meredith de Mur was covering for Roebuck in this case, out of some sexual obsession?'

'I think he's going off the rails there. You have to remember that he stuck his neck out quite a bit over Roebuck. He came as close as he dared to saying that Roebuck was guilty. So he's desperately clinging to that view. The trouble with Peter is, he has an exaggerated opinion of the power of offender profiling. Personally, I think it can do very little to help the police. It might move a few names up or down a suspect list, but it's no substitute for solid police work. And it can be misleading too.'

'How do you mean?'

'Well, in the Leah Irons case, he told the police that the killer was probably someone who didn't know her, because the killing was done in such a public place and someone who knew her would be able to find her at home or place of work. It didn't occur to him that if the killer knew her, then he might have been known by others where she lived or worked and might have therefore chosen to kill her somewhere that he wasn't known - even at the risk of doing it in a public place.'

'And if the police accepted what he said,' Neil added enthusiastically, 'then they would have focused on a suspect who was a stranger to Leah Irons.'

'And been correspondingly quicker to reject a suspect who knew her, because that would clash with what Eckland had told them,' Trotter added.

'But still,' said Neil. 'If we have two murders by the same person, then we do have some grounds for looking for patterns surely, even if it's hard to find patterns in only two cases?'

Trotter thought about this again.

'Yes, but it's important to remember that it's still not definite that it was the same killer.'

'But I thought you said it was,' said Neil, feeling the frustration of no longer knowing where he stood with this expert.

'No, I conceded that it was possible. I acknowledged that the differences do not necessarily mean that it was a different killer and that the progression from murdering in daylight to murdering in darkness could be a symptom of emboldening on the killer's part. Also, I would point out that a killer *can* become more cautious. We had a case once of a rapist who initially used to let his victims live and even showed a certain amount of concern for them afterwards, giving them money to get home for example. Then one day he switched his tactics and started murdering them after raping them. At the time we were baffled as to why he should have changed his M.O. so radically. It was only after he was caught that we found out -- and then only because he told us. It seems that one time, after he'd raped a woman, he came face-to-face with her in another context. She didn't recognize him at the time, but *he* recognized *her* and he realized how close he'd come to getting caught. So he decided that from then on he'd kill his victims. The point is that although it was an escalation in the level of *violence*, it was also a sign that he was becoming not bolder but rather more *cautious*. Unfortunately, the sign wasn't recognized at the time.'

'So if it wasn't the same attacker this time, what can be said about the attacker of Rose Crowne?'

If there were two murderers, and if he had to find just one of them, Neil was determined that it should be the one who murdered Rose Crowne.

'I can tell you that in both cases it doesn't have to be a sex murderer - contrary to what you may have heard from others.'

Neil sat bolt upright. Through all the vicissitudes of this case, he had assumed that the one constant was that these were sex attacks. And now even that certainty had fallen.

'If not sex then what?' he asked.

'One possibility is revenge.'

'Revenge?' Neil echoed, surprised. 'Revenge,' he repeated, rolling around the sound on his tongue to try it out for credibility. Words always exposed their absurdity or inappropriateness when spoken out loud.

'It's consistent with the nature and severity of the attack,'said Trotter.

'Consistent with,' said Neil, noting the cautious wording. 'That sounds like an Ecklandism - designed to avoid committing oneself.'

'While at the same time projecting a particular thought in others,' said Trotter, adding the words that Neil had thought too tactless to utter.

'That too.'

'Well, it obviously isn't the only explanation,' Trotter continued. 'That's why I said "consistent with".'

'But why would the murderer want revenge on Rose Crowne? Or Leah Irons?'

'I'm not saying he did. There is such a thing as transferred anger.'

'Is that anything like transferred malice?' asked Neil.

'Not exactly. Transferred malice is a legal concept which makes a person guilty of murder even if he accidentally kills the wrong victim. The murderer doesn't actually bear any malice towards the wrong victim, but the law holds him just as culpable as if he had. Transferred anger works differently. With transferred anger, the perpetrator of the act really does transfer his hatred from the actual object of hatred to the present victim and gains psychological gratification or at least release from tension by committing the act, even if only momentarily.'

'Any other possible motives?' asked Neil. 'Besides sexual perversion and revenge.'

'Well, another possibility, though less likely, is a more conventional murder, with added violence to camouflage the real motive.'

'How do you mean . . . conventional murder?'

'It could be robbery. It could be to silence someone. It could be to eliminate a rival to get that promotion.'

'You're not serious, are you?'

'I'm saying that it cannot definitely be ruled out. Like I said before, five weeks before Leah Irons was killed, there was the murder of that teenage girl in a frenzied attack. That attack might still have been fresh in the attacker's mind when he attacked Leah Irons. He probably decided at fairly short notice to kill her in the same way - a frenzied knife attack. That way the police would be looking for a crazed sex attacker.'

'But Leah Irons wasn't robbed.'

'I never said it was robbery.'

'You offered it as a possibility,' said Neil, almost accusingly.

'Along with several others,' Trotter replied.

'So which is it?'

'That's something I can't tell you.'

'Beyond possibilities, you haven't really told me much.'

'That's what I've been trying to tell you all along, Neil. There's a limit to what I *can* tell you. That's the limitation on offender profiling - especially when it comes to only one or two crimes. The only thing I can say for certain is that the killer probably lives near Hampstead Heath.'

'If you qualify it with the word "probably" then it isn't for certain,' Neil mocked, irritated by Trotter's manner.

'*Touché*,' Trotter acknowledged. 'But then again, at least I've helped you to see past Eckland's appraisal. My best advice is that if you concentrate on the assumption that Rose Crowne was not killed by the same person who killed Leah Irons, then you're more likely to make progress with your unofficial investigation. They *may* turn out to be the work of the same person. But if you rely on evidence from the Leah Irons case you may be led astray. Concentrate on the evidence from the Rose Crowne case and you're more likely to come up with the right answer.'

'OK, thank you very much,' said Neil, anxious to wrap up the discussion quickly. He was already thinking about the other two names on the list Nick had given him.

Pierre Chandler was lying in bed, listening to *The Bitching Hour.* Someone had told him about Beth Porter giving the Leah Irons case extensive coverage but he had tried to ignore it. It had been several years since the woman he loved had been snatched from him by a vicious murderer. He didn't want to reopen the old wounds but he had heard about her from more than one source and he had to know if she was still going on about it. So he'd switched on the radio and fiddled about with the dial until he found the right station.

'OK, so who was this man William Isaacs?' Beth Porter was saying.

'He was a friend of Leah Irons, the one that a neighbour saw walking on the Heath that day.'

The woman sounded like a village gossip. The sort of woman who likes to spread rumours from one end of the high street to the other. She was classic tabloid source material. Pierre didn't know who she was but he took an instant dislike to her from her tone of voice alone.

'But what about him?' Beth repeated.

'Well, I'm sure he was a friend of Pierre Chandler too,' said the woman.

'Why do you think that,' Beth nudged.

'Well, I'm sure I saw them together,' the woman replied, deflated by Beth's negative tone. 'And I don't think Leah approved.'

Pierre was seething with anger. He had heard these stories before. *Why are they spreading these vicious rumours?* He thought. *Haven't I been through enough?*

'How do you know?' Beth's voice came through the radio.

143

'I heard them arguing about it.'

'In the street?' asked Beth, the smile on her face creeping into her voice.

'Through the walls. They have thin walls in these places. You can hear every word of what's going on in the flat next door if you put your ear up against the wall.'

'Yes, I'm sure you can,' Beth replied, fearing that her risibility would lead her to burst out laughing over the air. 'Let's listen to a song by Clout. This one's called *Substitute*.'

As the music began, she pushed the microphone away and burst out laughing. Neil smiled.

'I'm sorry, that was very unprofessional,' she said to Neil still smiling.

'You don't have to apologize to me,' said Neil. 'I'm not keeping a scoring card. I was just wondering how the setup works.'

'I know, it's just that I should control my emotions better. I'm supposed to be the Ice Lady, the Mr Spock of the airwaves.'

'Well, you're certainly not the *Doctor* Spock.'

'*Doctor who*?' she asked and burst out laughing again.

'Gotcha,' he said, as their heads fell together in childish laughter.

She didn't know why it was happening, but she was acting like a schoolgirl around him. She was five years his senior and yet that age gap barely seemed to matter.

'So what do you think?' she said, looking around the studio.

'I'm glad I offered you a lift,' said Neil, looking around. Beth's car needed repairs, and Neil's phone call, to take her up on her offer to visit the radio station, couldn't have been timed better.

'It's an interesting setup,' Neil continued. 'Now that I see how you operate, I kind of like it.'

He was smiling. To Beth and the others, he seemed happy to be there. Or perhaps he was happy to be with her. It was strange, in a way, she thought. Only a week ago they had been bitter enemies and now they were almost friends. Was it just because she had stopped sniping at him and started to dig for the truth? Or was it just that he liked her?

She wondered why it mattered to her whether he liked her or not, and was surprised at the answer.

'I was just wondering why you're talking about Leah Irons instead of focusing on Rose Crowne.'

'I've tried to cover both. But I let the listeners call the tune. I have to admit I am rather curious about Rose Crowne. We don't really know very much about her. And it's strange that her parents haven't come forward and spoken out in your defence the way the Irons family defended the police over their handling of the Roebuck case.'

Neil shifted uncomfortably. Having raised the subject, he realized it was not one on which he wanted to dwell.

'How do you know if they're telling the truth?' he asked.

'Who?' she replied, realizing she had been daydreaming.

'The callers.'

'Oh . . . well. A lot of them aren't.'

'So what's your policy?' 'Well, I let them talk as long as they aren't saying something racist, offensive or potentially slanderous. When people phone-in with consumer complaints we tell them before they come on the air not to mention the name of the company. Mind you, sometimes people call in and talk *real* bullshit.'

He chuckled and she responded with another girlish giggle.

'So, when did he leave you?' asked Neil.

'He didn't leave me, I threw the bastard out.'

Neil winced. His own home had been rocked by tragedy, but had never lacked love.

'That was four years ago,' she continued. 'Two months after Stevie was born, in fact.'

They were in Neil's car, moving along through the dark, empty streets. He was giving her a lift home, thoroughly invigorated by the sharp verbal exchanges of her programme. He had refused to speak on the air, or even to be drawn into discussion with her afterwards about the rights and wrongs of what was said but it had certainly been an enjoyable spectacle

'Was he that bad?'

'Let me put it this way, he didn't have Stanley Kowalski's charm.'

'Stanley Kowalski?'

'A Streetcar Named Desirer.'

'Oh sorry. We don't study Tennessee Williams over here. It's all Shakespeare and Dickens.'

'How parochial!' she replied, this time managing not to giggle.

'You probably think I'm a philistine.'

'Not at all. You just needed your memory jogging. I only remember it 'cause I played the title role in High School.'

'I can't imagine you playing a streetcar.'

He delivered it straight-faced, in time-honoured British tradition. This time, the urge to laugh got the better of her. When the laughter subsided she spoke again.

'The truth of the matter is, I rushed into it. I was twenty seven and all my friends were married, and I started to worry about the old biological clock. What about you?How did you get into the police.'

'It was a case of the "following in my father's footsteps"routine.'

'You told me about that. He died in the line of duty didn't he?'

'Yes, but I was already in police training. Only his death gave me the incentive to go on. I have a feeling I wouldn't have stuck with it, if it hadn't been for that.'

It was still a painful subject for him. He felt, even now, as if he had never really faced up to it but he didn't know if he could. Beth was understanding, far more understanding than he had thought at first. But before she could understand him, he had to understand himself - and he wasn't sure if he was ready for that either.

'So what would you have become if you hadn't become a cop?'

'Well, I guess I'd've gone in for some sort of academic career My degree was in psychology but I don't know if I'd've been very good at treating people. I think I probably have too many hangups of my own.'

'Don't most psychologists?'

She was smiling, a warm, pleasant girlish smile that put him at ease.

She should be the psychologist, he thought.

'That's just the image we have.'

'*We?*'

'I mean, they.'

There was an awkward silence as they both remembered that archetypal principle in psychology known as the 'Freudian slip.'

'So what did you do after you got your degree?'

'I travelled for three years. Then I came back intending to do a master's and my father started working on me. He said if I really wanted to understand the human mind at its best and its worst I should join the force.'

'Why would that show you the best and the worst?'

'That's exactly what I asked him.'

'And his answer?' 'He said the criminals were the worst and the police were the best.'

'And you believed him?'

They both burst out laughing at the absurdity of it.

'That wasn't what convinced me,' he said.

'Then what did?'

He hesitated for a moment.

'I guess it was seeing how much the old man wanted it.'

'You mean, he was living vicariously.'

'No, but . . . after my mother died, it was like a piece of his life was taken out of him, a piece of happiness that he'd always had and that still belonged there. I remembered him as the happy, smiling father who used to take us to the park and play games with us. Who used to make up stories for us at bedtime. He used to sing his own funny lyrics to pop songs to make us laugh. Then, when my mother died and my sister got married and moved up north, it was just him and me. And that piece of happiness that he shared with others just seemed to have disappeared. But I couldn't believe it had gone for good. I couldn't let it. He'd shared that happiness with me and I felt like I owed it to him to put that happiness back. I thought that if I followed in his footsteps I could somehow put it back and make him whole again.'

He felt a lump in his throat as he finished speaking.

It was two thirty in the morning when Neil and Beth walked through the door of Beth's house. Paula, the babysitter, looked up from the TV.

'How's Stevie?' asked Beth.

'OK. He woke up right on cue at ten o'clock and wanted to listen to your show. I think he has some sort of an inbuilt clock.'

147

'How did you handle it?'

'I let him listen in bed. He fell asleep pretty soon after.'

Beth didn't really want little Stevie listening to the programme. She didn't want him to hear her being bitchy. Also, now she was discussing heavy subjects involving murder, from which she wanted to protect him. He was too young to hear about women being slashed to pieces by knife-wielding madmen.

'OK, how much do I owe you?'

Neil was standing nearby, trying to be inconspicuous. The babysitter kept looking at him and he was embarrassed to be there. Beth was handing over money and saying goodbye to the sitter. Only when they were alone together did Neil speak.

'It's a nice place you've got here.'

He realised, as this cliché fell from his lips, just how embarrassed he was. It was an average mid-sized, middle-class three-up-two-down but there was nothing special about it. It was tastefully decorated in a feminine, olive green sort of way. Perhaps the most important thing, from Neil's point of view, was that it was tidy - in contrast to his own place. For all his nineties man pretence, Neil was strictly one of the lads, without a woman in his life, and his home had deteriorated into the kind of old sock-strewn mess of a student bedsit.

His embarrassment now was not so much at being seen with Beth in her home by the babysitter as by his realization that not everyone in the world was a slob in their own home. Then again, he remembered that Beth had certain responsibilities that he didn't have.

'Mummy.'

At that moment a beautiful, golden preschool child wandered into the room in his pyjamas, rubbing his tired blue eyes with the backs of his small hands. The sound of their arrival had woken him up and the sound of voices in the other room had stopped him getting back to sleep. He staggered forward into Beth's arms as she stepped forward to meet him.

'Hi Stevie,' she said, in a little girl voice, intended to reassure him.

She scooped him up in her arms and flopped down onto the brown corduroy couch, using the thick, firm cushion in the corner for support. He held both arms around her neck, taking one hand

148

away briefly to rub his eyes again. He was still half-asleep and not to sure where he was. The important thing was that mummy was here and he was safe. Neil looked on with mixed emotions. Envy, approval, affection, regret. They were all there in varying degrees. He stood back, trying to stay out of view. This was an intimate moment between a mother and her young son and he knew that he had no right being here, at least no right to intrude on the privacy of the moment. Also, he knew that his presence could only be disruptive.

'I heard you talking,' said Stevie.

'On the radio?'

'Yes.'

'Did you like it?'

'You were laughing.'

And all of a sudden, in the space of a moment, Stevie was laughing too. Reassured by this, Neil took a step forward, but still remained silent. The boy saw him and leaned into his mother's ear, shyly.

'Who's that?' he whispered.

'That's Neil,' Beth replied, softly, but not whispering. 'He's a friend of mine.'

'Is he your boyfriend?' asked Stevie.

Beth smiled. Stevie blushed and hid his face in Beth's shoulder.

'Would you like to meet him?'

The boy shook his head, his face still buried and out of view.

Beth signalled Neil over. He walked forward, and she realized, looking at him, that she now had two embarrassed little boys to contend with. She tapped the seat of the couch next to her, indicating to Neil that he should sit down. He obeyed meekly.

'Neil, I'd like you to meet my son Stevie.'

'Steven!' came the muffled yet aggressive shout, although the face remained hidden.

'I beg your pardon, Steven.'

She stroked his hair. 'Steven, this is Neil.'

'Hi there, little fella,' said Neil, taking Steven's little hand in his and shaking it gently.

Steven pulled his hand away, but looked up, scowling pugnaciously. The boy sensed that Neil was somewhat meek, if not downright timid, and he saw the possibility of gaining an immediate advantage over him, by a show of aggression.

'Sorry,' said Neil. 'I just wanted to see what you looked like. Your mummy told me she had a handsome son. But I wanted to see for myself.'

Stevie, or Steven as he preferred, said nothing.

'I bet I know how old you are?' said Neil.

Beth stayed silent, gritting her teeth. She didn't want to interfere, but the thought going through her head was: *you'd better err on the high side*. She had told Neil that her son was four but Steven had a tendency to ask when his birthday was at odd intervals all year round and so Beth had got into the habit of telling his age in fractions. He had recently gone from being four and a bit to four and a quarter, and if Neil put his age at anything less than this, it would sour their. . . she suddenly realised that the word she was thinking had been 'relationship'.

She wanted to say something, to issue a quick word of warning, or even just make a warning gesture with her hand or face but even that was out of the question. Stevie was now wide awake and looking at each of them alternately with that quick, switching eye movement of which only a child is capable.

'I think you're five,' said Neil.

Beth breathed a sigh of relief. Steven was shaking his head vigorously, the expression on his face quite serious.

'No?' said Neil earnestly, feigning surprise. 'You mean you're *older*?'

Steven was shaking his head again in that consciously, demonstrative way.

'Younger?'

The boy nodded, with similarly exaggerated head movements.

'Four and three-quarters?'

The head shook again, the lips tightened into even greater seriousness.

'Four and a half?'

Again the head shook, but by now the boy was smiling at Neil's poor guesswork.

'Four and a quarter?' Neil asked smiling.

Steven giggled and nodded.

'But you look so big! I bet you're bigger than all the other boys your age.'

Steven smiled proudly as Neil looked for confirmation from Beth that he had done all right. He was quick toasters his proprietorial rights to his mother, and pulled himself back onto her shoulder, whispering in her ear.

'Why don't you ask him?' she whispered back.

Again, he buried his face in her shoulder.

'Do you want me to ask him?' she said gently.

'Yes,' said Steven quietly into her ear.

'He wants to know if he can show you his room.'

'I'd love to see his room,' said Neil, enthusiastically.

Steven looked up. Beth gently lifted him and put him down in a standing position. Neil stood up and held out his hand. Steven took it nervously and led him away.

The room was more or less as Neil had expected it: toys scattered liberally across the floor, a few of the boy's own artistic efforts on the wall, a low plastic table covered with papers and crayons, where the masterpieces were created, and a small low bed with a night light by it.

'Do you want to see my computer?'

'Yes,' said Neil.

Steven opened a drawer and took out a bright, colourful, plastic, battery operated contraption called 'My first computer.' He switched it on and showed Neil how good he was at identifying animals and adding numbers, pressing the right buttons on his first attempt with most of the animals, and the second with the arithmetic.

'Do you want to try?'

'Yes,' said Neil crouching down. He tried the addition, making sure to make a few deliberate mistakes so Steven wouldn't be put to shame. They spent the next few minute splaying various games and trying out the whole collection of Steven's toys. Somewhere along the line Neil noticed that Beth was leaning against the door-post watching them. After a while he looked at her with a plea in his eyes.

'Steven . . .' He appeared not to notice. She faked a cough. 'Steven. Neil has to go to bed now.'

Neil stifled a laugh.

151

'Can't he stay a bit longer?' the boy said, pleadingly.

'No. He worked hard today and he's very tired. And anyway, you've got to go to bed too.'

'But *I'm* not tired,' he said assertively, with the child's logic that defies an adult's attempt to talk around an issue.

'No, but you will be tomorrow morning.'

'OK, one more game.'

'OK, one more,' she relented. Children are very good at bargaining. He played another game, this time with one of his Power Ranger toys, trying to draw it out as long as possible. After a couple of minutes, Beth spoke again.

'OK, Steven. You've had enough now.'

'But I'm not finished the game.'

'Yes, you have.'

'But you *said*.'

He still didn't always speak in complete sentences.

'I'll tell you what. If you get into bed right away, I'll let Neil tuck you in and tell you a story.'

Steven paused, smiling an impish smile.

'*Two* stories.'

'OK, two stories.'

Steven leapt up and practically jumped into bed, while Neil looked at Beth as if to say 'thanks a lot.' He stood up and turned round, to see Steven still smiling. He knelt down and tucked in the sheet and blanket around him.

'Now the story,' said the boy, insistently.

Neil looked round at Beth, his eyes pleading for support, although not without humour. She gave him a tight-lipped smile that seemed to extend to her eyes and shrugged her shoulders as if to say 'you've signed on for it.' He flopped into a seated position on the floor and tried to remember a story from his childhood while Beth disappeared from the doorway. What came into his mind, strangely was not a story from his childhood, but one from his adolescence, a Russian play he had read in his early teens. But he couldn't tell it in that form, so he decided to adapt it.

'OK,' he said nervously. 'Once upon a time there was a young handsome prince called . . . what shall we call him. . . ?'

Steven smiled and pursed his lips.

'I know,' said Neil. 'He was called Steven.'

Steven squeezed his lips together, suppressing his impish smile, but only just.

'And this prince went off out of his kingdom on a long series of travels.'

'Why?' asked Steven, making it clear that this wasn't going to be easy.

'Well . . . because he wanted to learn about the world. He'd been sheltered from problems all his life by his father, the king, and he wanted to learn what life was all about for himself.'

'So he ran away from home,' asked Steven.

Neil smiled. Even in the life of a normal average child there are always a few islands of precociousness, when the child says something unexpectedly mature. His father told him he'd been like that himself, when he once described a woman on TV as 'false' when he was only six, although he'd probably heard the word used in a similar context before by his mother.

'That's right. But the king didn't mind him going. He knew that sooner or later his son had to see the world for himself so that he'd be a better king when he came back.'

'But I thought he was a prince,' said Steven.

'Yes, but one day he'd be the king,' said Neil. 'When his father . . .' He trailed off. One doesn't talk about dying to a four-year-old kid at bedtime.

'Anyway,' said Neil. 'He travelled far and wide and arrived in another country far away, where the people were being menaced by a dragon.'

'What does "menaced" mean?'

'Well . . . it means that the dragon was attacking people and frightening them. You know how a dragon attacks people don't you?'

Steven shook his head.

'He breathes *fire* at them.'

He tickled Steven under the arm as he said this, and the boy responded appropriately by giggling. Neil hadn't been able to think of a completely innocuous story, so he was determined to take the sting out of this one that he was making up on the fly.

'Anyway. When the prince arrived in the city, he found the people afraid and frightened, especially at night. So he asked one of them why and they said "we're afraid of the dragon". So he said "where is this dragon? I'll fight it and kill it. " But they said "no you can't do that. He's much too big and powerful for you. He'll breathe fire all over you before you get the chance to kill him. " But the prince wasn't afraid. So they told him where to find the cave where the dragon slept during the day. And guess what the prince did?'

'I don't know,' said Steven.

'He went to the cave and he called out to the dragon to come out and fight! Now the dragon was tired, because he used to sleep during the day and come out at night. But he came out in response to the challenge and blew smoke through his nose and fire through his mouth at the prince. But the prince was too quick for the dragon and each time it breathed fire, the prince moved this way or that way, so the fire missed him. And each time he moved, he stabbed the dragon in his soft underbelly, using the mighty sword that his father had given him. He kept this up for two hours until finally he drew the dragon's blood yet again, with an almighty thrust of his sword all the way up to the hilt. And the dragon breathed his last breath and then keeled over on his side.'

'Was the dragon dead?'

'Yes,' said Neil. 'Quite dead.'

'Is that the end of the story?'

'Oh no,' said Neil. 'Not by any means. You see, when the prince rode back to the city on his white horse and told the people that he'd killed the dragon, they called him a liar and spat at him.'

'Why?' asked Steven confused.

'Well, because, as the mayor of the city told him, while he'd been away, supposedly fighting and killing the dragon, the dragon had been in the town breathing fire and smoke over the people and frightening them.'

'Maybe it was *two* dragons,' said Steven.

'That's what he thought at first. But then suddenly, someone shouted: "The dragon's coming back!" and they all scattered and ran and hid. But not the prince.'

'He was brave.'

'Yes, Steven. He was very brave. But also he was curious. He wanted to see what was happening. You see, he *knew* he'd killed the dragon. But the people said the dragon was here all the time, frightening them, so he wanted to find out. And if there were two dragons he wanted to kill the second one as well. He waited for twenty minutes and nothing happened. And then the people came out and they asked why the dragon hadn't hurt him. And he said "what dragon?" And they said "what, are you blind or something? Didn't you seethe dragon?" And then he realized what was happening.'

'What?' asked Steven, his curiosity aroused.

'The dragon wasn't on the outside. It was on the inside.'

'Inside of what?' asked Steven.

'Inside the people.'

'You mean they'd eaten him?' asked Steven, yawning.

'No, I mean, it was in their minds. In their imaginations. Each one of them was imagining a dragon, including the prince. So when the prince killed the dragon, he only killed the dragon in his own mind. But he couldn't kill the dragon in anyone else's mind. They had to do it for themselves. And, so in all his travels throughout the kingdoms of the world he learned his first lesson: each person carries around with him the dragon of his own fears. And only when he slays that dragon, will he be free. But no one can kill anyone else's dragon; each person must kill their own dragon. And if they don't do it, then the dragon doesn't kill them, it just keeps them a prisoner of their fears.'

He looked down at Steven, wondering if the boy had understood the adult symbolism. But little Steven was fast asleep.

So much for my storytelling, he thought.

He dragged his feet slowly into the living room, where Beth was waiting for him on the couch with a cup of tea.

'So how's Hans Christian Andersen?' she asked.
'Tired,' he replied, flopping into the seat next to her.

'I think Stevie likes you.'

She was smiling.

'I guess boys need a father figure.'

'That's true. But I think there's more than that. My little Stevie has good instincts.'

'You mean, he's not like that with other men you've brought round here?'

'I don't often bring men round here.'

'I'm sorry,' said Neil, referring to his lack of tact rather than Beth's lifestyle.

155

'Is the tea OK?' asked Beth.

'Sure,' said Neil. He was looking at the television through barely focused eyes

'It's probably cold,' said Beth, standing up. 'I'll make you another.'

'No, really. It's OK.'

But she was already across the room and into the kitchen. She pushed in the button of the automatic kettle, took down two clean cups and started making a fresh cup of tea for herself and for Neil. Three minutes later, when she returned to the living room with the tea, Neil had fallen asleep on the couch. She returned the tea to the kitchen, took a blanket from the linen cupboard and draped it across Neil to keep him warm when the temperature dropped. Then she switched off the television and the light and went upstairs.

Neil was afraid. It was cold and dark and his uniform offered little protection against the wind. He was standing on grass, surrounded by trees. All around were reporters, and photographers taking pictures with flashlights, and asking him 'what you gonna do, Neil?' He tried to answer them, but even when he moved his lips, no sound came out. He wanted to explain that he was doing his job, but they couldn't hear him. He saw the figure in the dark standing over the woman. He felt Nick grabbing his arm, pulling him towards the man, whose face was still in shadow.

'It's your call, Neil,' Nick was saying. 'You've got to do it.' Neil was looking at Nick, asking him what to do. But again no sound came from his mouth.

'It's no good, Neil. *You've* got to decide.'

'But I don't know,' Neil was pleading, silently.

The man standing over the woman was turning and Neil knew that when he completed the turn, the man would be able to hit him. Neil panicked in the face of the danger that he felt and in a moment of frenzied terror he struck out with his baton. He heard the sound of cracking bone and heard the man cry as the man completed the turn. But when the face came into view, it wasn't Martin Roebuck. It was Neil's father.

He woke up in a cold sweat.

It was about four in the morning when Beth heard a stirring in the corridor downstairs. Someone was opening and closing the toilet door. A minute later she heard the toilet flushing. It was Neil.

Now it was her turn to drag herself out of bed.

She almost picked up the dressing gown to drape around her. But then she decided not to, realizing that it wouldn't be so terrible if he saw her in her baby dolls. By the time she opened the door, he was already in the corridor. When she had got halfway down the stairs, he was taking down his jacket from the rack by the front door, apparently having found it in the dark.

'What are you doing?' she asked, staggering quickly down the last few steps.

'I'm sorry, I must have fallen asleep.'

'You did. I put a blanket over you. But where are you going?'

'I was going home.'

'Why?'

'Well . . . I would have gone last . . . I mean I only came for. . .'

She had closed the last of the distance between them and was now putting her arms around him drawing him towards her. A tingling of longing swept over him. He'd been attracted to her when he first saw her. But he hadn't known how she felt about him, and he'd simply assumed he meant nothing to her. Until . . . well, until yesterday.

His arms encircled her and they kissed for several seconds. They staggered up the stairs, still locked in their tight embrace, edging their way down the corridor into Beth's waiting bedroom. The light was off, but there was light from the street lamps beyond the window. He was kissing her all over, exploring her body with his tongue, while she tore at his clothes. He tried to reach out for the switch of the bedside lamp, but she pushed his hand away, preferring the tactile intimacy of the near darkness. His hands were sliding thin silk straps down her soft arms, his fingertips were tracing lines down her thighs. His hands were caressing her body, exploring her most intimate areas.

He felt a high voltage charge of power as he took possession of her by touch, in a way that left no doubt as to his feelings of ownership. Not a word was spoken, but he was taking control of her body with every movement while she gave him permission by her silence and by her plaint cooperation. His right hand shifted from her breast to her thigh to her crotch, while his other hand pinioned her wrists to the pillow. She had always enjoyed role-playing in the bedroom, especially playing the victim. That was one of the few things that she had enjoyed about her relationship with her husband. The only problem was that he had never known where the game ended and reality began. With Neil it seemed different. He could play the game of being Mr Macho, taking control of her and making her his plaything to do his bidding and respond to his command, while never going too far - pushing her up to the threshold of pain but not beyond it. She had seen him at his weakest - seen him crying - and knew that what he was doing now was an act that he could not maintain in the face of her objections. She could call time-out whenever she liked, knowing that he would obey.

He was preparing to enter her, she knew that. Now was the time to insist that he use precautions. Neither had reason to think the other had long been celibate and they weren't horny teenagers. But to attempt ogive him any sort of order would be to destroy the fantasy. If he went ahead, she would just hold her breath and hope.

He shifted his weight upon her to the other side, exploring her with his other hand, preoccupied with symmetry and determined to cover every area with his possessive touch. He had yet to enter her, but she was already writhing with the ecstasy of anticipation, gasping for breath while feigning reluctance and even outright objection.

'Stop hurting mummy!'

Their hearts went into their mouths, and they turned, she to the left, he to the right. Little Steven was standing there, a picture of indignation. He was half-asleep, but still capable of setting his jaw in his own unique pugnacious style, projecting the image of the toughest kid on the block.

Neil rolled off Beth to the far side, as if trying to hide his naked body from the boy by interposing Beth between them. Beth sat up and took the initiative.

'Were you frightened?' she asked gently, holding out her hands to her son.

'Yes,' he said rushing into her waiting arms and breaking down in tears as she lifted him up and held him close to her.

'It's all right, Stevie. Mummy and the man were only playing a game.'

Chapter 12

In a poky little flat in south London, Anita Stone was listening to the radio. She liked Martin Roebuck. Her friend Alice said that it was just a case of feeling sorry for him. But Anita knew that it was more than that. She genuinely liked him. Not that she saw him as a replacement for her husband -she was happily married and had two lovely children - but she had always felt that Martin Roebuck had got a raw deal all round from both the police and the press. He was a decent man and a good neighbour and she didn't like the idea of remaining silent now that people were finally listening. She decided to speak out on Roebuck's behalf.

'The thing is, quite a lot of us thought that William Isaacs fancied Leah Irons.'

Beth was trying to find out why Isaacs was dropped from the investigation. But all she was getting was more of the same.

'But isn't that just neighbours' gossip?'

'It may sound like that to you but don't forget someone did see William Isaacs walking off in the direction Leah had taken on the morning of the murder.'

Anita Stone sounded confident, as if she knew what she was talking about.

'But do you know, in that case, why the police dropped him from their investigation?' asked Beth.

'I don't know. At first we all thought it was because his wife had given him an alibi. But that didn't make sense. I mean, you can hardly let a man off the hook just because his wife says he was in bed with her.'

Beth realized that once again, to maintain the balance of the programme, she would have to play devil's advocate.
'Well, the police evidently thought her story was convincing, otherwise they wouldn't have bought it.'

'That's what I thought. But it turns out, according to Pierre Chandler's book, that the police didn't buy his story and searched his place quite thoroughly.'

'And what did they find?' asked Beth, sensing that something was missing from the caller's words - something intensely significant.

There was a long, drawn-out pause.

'Well, I talked to Martin about this, and he told me that they found trainers with bloodstains on them.'

'And who did the blood belong to? Or perhaps I should say, who did Martin tell you they belonged to?'

'They couldn't say, because there wasn't enough of it.'

'But that's ridiculous. They can tell with a high degree of accuracy using a technique that involves artificially increasing a small amount of DNA with heating and enzymes. It's not as accurate as some of the other DNA tests, but it would be enough to say if it might have come from Leah Irons, or from Isaacs himself. Aside from that, let me ask you is this--'

But she heard the deep solid whining tone that told her that the caller had rung off.

'I don't know what happened there. I wanted to ask the caller if she knew anything about the blood on the trainers or why the police eliminated William from their inquiries.'

'I'm also a neighbour of Martin Roebuck and I helped him draft some letters to the press at the time when the papers were hounding him. He's an intelligent man but he's been hounded so much and he sometimes gets angry and doesn't express himself very well. The thing is, I helped Martin so I know a bit about this case too.'

'OK, Pearl,' said Beth. 'Let's hear what you know, especially about William Isaacs.'

'I can tell you, first of all, that William Isaacs has moved and no longer lives in the area.'

'So where does he live now?' asked Beth.

'No one knows. That's the whole point. He didn't leave a 'Interesting Anything else?

'I know a bit about the blood on the trainers.'

'Let's hear it,' said Beth warily. She had had several false alarms and calls from time wasters today, and she was alert to the possibility that this one too might be taking the piss.

'First of all, the blood sample was quite small and it was no longer fresh. Now there are various different tests they can do depending on the age of the sample and the quantity. With this sample, it was so old and small that the only thing they could say for certain was that it was human blood but they couldn't say where or who it was from.'

'Did Isaacs offer any explanation of it?'

'He said the trainers were new and that he banged his head on a garage door, you know, the sort that lifts upwards. He said that the blood dripped onto the trainers.'

'OK,' said Beth. 'Anything else?'

'Well, the thing is, the blood was mixed with mud, even though the trainers were supposedly new.'

'Did they ask him about that?'

'Not as far as I know. And also they made no effort to compare the mud to the mud samples taken from the crime scene at Hampstead Heath.'

'Are you sure about that?'

'Quite positive. And that's the strangest thing of all. Even if they couldn't DNA type the blood, they could have compared the mud. It wouldn't have been conclusive but it could at least have excluded William if the samples didn't match or increased the probability that he was guilty if they did.'

Beth felt a flutter of excitement.

'That's incredible. Had they already decided that Roebuck was a more likely suspect at that stage?'

'I'm not sure.'

'The reason I ask,' said Beth, 'is because there were several witnesses who saw a man on the Heath. After Bridget Vanderbilt identified Martin Roebuck, they decided not to investigate anyone else as matching the photofit that she gave them. But I'm wondering if they gave her a chance to identify this William character before that.'

'I don't know about that,' said Pearl, deflated.

'OK, well maybe if someone else knows they could call in. The number as ever is. . .'

She had got the address from the CDROM but she couldn't phone the flat because she didn't have the number. Even according

162

to the Irish CD database, this Rose Crowne was ex-directory. She knew that already from the official British Telecom CD database. In any case, telephoning would not have been a smart move. Rose Crowne - at least the Rose Crowne that she was looking for - was dead. So if she lived alone, then the flat would be empty.

Of course, she might have been married, or sharing a flat. But she didn't want to telegraph her intentions. It was better to visit in person.

Getting there wasn't easy. The roads were always congested around Camden Town and parking was virtually impossible in this busy commercial and residential centre, close to central London but not quite in it. She had to drive around for some minutes before she found a parking place and then it was a fair way from the flat. Still it would have to do.

As she walked past the shops and the entrances to the flats above them, across uneven paving stones, she wondered whether the area was dying or being resurrected. Certainly, it was crowded and people were not moving out but there seemed like no sign of renewal. While the Pacific tigers were throwing up towers into the sky, while areas of London's East End were being revived with steel and glass office buildings and refurbished old houses, this area seemed like it was going nowhere. The buildings were getting older, but they had neither the beauty of antiquity nor the brightness that goes with modernization.

It was depressing. It brought to mind a line that could almost have been from a poem.

Those who die slowly.

She filed it away for later.

It lingered with her as she took a turn from a side street into a main road as she continued to track her way back to Rose Crowne's flat.

She tried to think of how the line might continue.

Those who die slowly, die without being noticed, even though they die right before our eyes.

But not Rose Crowne. She had died quickly and only two men had seen it: Martin Roebuck and the murderer. No one seemed to have missed her. No one spoke out for her, to remind the world who she was or what she was.

Beth stood at the entrance, an old blue wooden door that didn't lock. No security for these people, thought Beth, wondering how they could live in these conditions with so little protection. The thought lingered with her as she walked up the two flights to Rose Crowne's flat until she brushed it aside in time to the sweeping of her hand through her hair as she stood before the door and took a deep breath.

Here goes.

She pressed the buzzer and waited. There was no sound from inside. No sign of movement. From the crack under the door she saw light, which suggested that the curtains were open. There was light in the flat but that didn't mean there were other occupants. Of course, even if there was no answer, that didn't mean that no one else lived there. She might have come at the wrong time. She might have to come back later. She might have to loiter in the area atone of the café or fish and chip shops and come back two or three times.

She buzzed again and then, without waiting, knocked several times with her knuckles against the wood. Some of the other doors had old flaky paintwork but this one was a new beige. Rose Crowne evidently took the trouble to look after the place where she lived. Unless it had been repainted afterwards.

She buzzed and knocked again. Suddenly, there was a sound but it was not from the direction she expected. The door of the flat opposite, on the same landing, was being unlocked and opened. Evidently, she had aroused the curiosity of a neighbour. The door opened and an elderly woman wearing a hairnet poked her head out.

'Oh, are you looking for Rose Crowne?' asked the woman.
'Yes,' Beth replied, after a moment of hesitation.

'Are you a friend of hers?'

The neighbour's tone was grave. Beth knew that she had to be careful. She already knew what this woman had to tell her and she wanted to get past that stage and find out as much as she could.

'The friend of a friend . . . from America. My friend Jane told me to look her up when I got here. I tried phoning a few times, but there was no answer.'

'I'm afraid there won't be. She's dead.'

'Dead?' Beth repeated, struggling to inject the right amount of surprise in her tone.

'It was in the news. She was stabbed to death. On Hampstead Heath.'

'How horrible. I thought things like that only happened in America.'

Careful, Beth told herself. *Don't overdo it.*

'It was horrible. And the police arrived and beat up the wrong man.'

'Gee, how awful. It must have been terrible for her family.'

'I suppose it must have been,' said the woman. She sounded well educated and had a certain poise that suggested that she was of a higher class than her neighbours, a woman of a good background who was down on her luck.

Beth took a cautious step towards her before speaking again.

'Did they talk about it on TV?'

'On TV?'

The neighbour sounded puzzled.

'Oh, I'm sorry,' said Beth. 'I'm thinking like an American. I guess they wanted to grieve in private.'

'Well, I don't really know. I mean, we didn't see them on television.'

'But I mean, they must have sent someone round to pick up her stuff.'

Beth was gambling on Rose Crowne not being married. She assumed that must be the case, because the neighbour had asked 'Are you looking for Rose Crowne?' not 'Are you looking for *Mister* Crowne?'

'That's the funny thing. A couple of men in suits came round along with a group of workmen and took everything away.'

Beth leaned forward keenly.

'Men in suits? Do you have any idea who they were?'

'No idea at all. I expect they must have been solicitors.'

'Why do you say that?'

'Well, I assume they were the executors of her estate.'

'Do you know who she left everything to?'

'I haven't a clue. She kept herself very much to herself.'

'Do you know what she did for a living?'

'She said she worked in an office in the city but I don't know where. Also, she had loose morals.'

'How do you mean?'

'Well, sometimes I heard her going out at night.'

'That doesn't necessarily mean she had loose morals. I mean, even good girls go out on dates.'

The neighbour looked dubious.

'Not dressed up like that, they don't.'

'Like what?'

'Well, not to put too fine a point on it, like a tart.'

'Maybe that was just her way of making herself look attractive.'

'A skirt up to her bottom, too much make-up and chewing gum. I even heard her practising an East End or South London accent. It's almost as if she *wanted* to sound cheap.'

'Maybe she had a split personality,' suggested Beth with a conspiratorial smile.

'Oh, you can joke about it all you like,' said the neighbour. 'But I'm telling you there was something very strange about Rose Crowne . . . very strange.'

Neil was asleep when the phone rang. It was four in the afternoon, but he was tired after last night with Beth, even though it had ended more with a whimper than a bang. He had spent the day looking through his notes on the discussions he had had with Justice Fortescue and Horace Tadditt, trying to find out if there had been anything in them that might suggest they were lying about where they were.

Tadditt had been brazen about the way in which he gave new meaning to the words 'performance related pay.' Fortescue had been rather more reticent about the whole thing. Perhaps because he still had a spark of ethics. Perhaps because he was more vulnerable, inasmuch as he had more to lose than his partner in 'crime'. But perhaps also because he was hiding something more sinister.

By three in the afternoon, the tiredness from yesterday had finally overtaken him.

It was always like that when he had late nights. It wasn't the mornings that took it out of him. He could usually drag himself up in the morning. But in the afternoon the fatigue always caught up with him, and by three o'clock he found himself falling asleep at the kitchen table with a pen in his hand and a notebook in front of him. So he went to lie down, telling himself it was only for a few minutes but it was an hour later when the phone rang - and had it not been for the phone, he could easily have slept for another hour.

'Hallo,' he said, groggily, as he picked up the receiver. 'Hallo,' he repeated, realizing he hadn't spoken into the mouthpiece.

'Hallo,' said a muffled voice. 'Is that Neil Douglas?'

'Yes.' He was cautious, but also curious. 'Who's this?'

The voice was so distorted he couldn't tell if it was a man or a woman.

'I'm calling from the Royal Free Hospital. I wanted to tell you that Martin Roebuck has come out of his coma and has been asking to speak to you.'

'To me?' asked Neil, deeply puzzled.

'Well, he didn't use your name, but he referred to the incident on the Heath and it's taken us a while to track down your number.'

'Did he say what he wanted? I mean, is he angry with me or he just wants to tell me what happened there or not?'

'I don't know the whole situation. I just got a message from the doctor. If you could just come here, he'll explain when you arrive. If it's any reassurance, I can tell you that he didn't seem angry - Roebuck I mean.'

'OK, I'll come right away.'

'Thank you.'

'Who is this?'

But the caller had already rung off. He pressed 1471 to recover the number, and then without waiting for the end of the message pressed 3 to redial. He heard the three notes that warned of a problem and then the message:

'This telephone does not receive incoming calls,' followed by a clicking sound and the phone ringing off. Normally, when a phone didn't receive incoming calls, it was a payphone but he guessed it could also be a special phone in a hospital, reserved for outgoing calls to contact members of staff or other hospitals. At any rate, there was no time to dwell on it. Roebuck had come out of the coma and wanted to see him. There were so many things he

167

wanted to ask. Like what the killer looked like. What he was trying to do. Why was he there in the first place?

So many questions, and now finally he could get some answers.

He grabbed his jacket and raced to the door.

'I'm here to see Martin Roebuck,' said Neil, flashing his warrant card at the girl on the nurses station on the ward in the Royal Free Hospital where Roebuck had initially been brought.

'Martin Roebuck?' the girl stuttered.

'Yes. He's been asking to see me.'

'Asking to see you?'

'Yes. I'm a policeman.' He took a deep breath. 'I was the policeman involved in the incident that put him here.'

It was visiting time and there were lots of patients walking about and guests visiting them.

'Well, as far as I know, Martin Roebuck is still in a coma.'

'Then your information is out of date. I had a call from the hospital less than a quarter of an hour ago. They said he'd come out of the coma and wanted to see me.'

'Are you sure it was from here and not UCH?'

'She said the Royal Free. Why should it be from UCH?'

'Just a minute,' said the nurse.

She called the ward sister over and they talked for a half a minute. Neil caught brief snippets of the conversation, like 'his ID seemed genuine.' He tried to ignore it, but the first traces of fear were rising up into his throat, that kind of warm dryness when one begins to realize that things are not all as they should be.

The sister came over and introduced herself.

'I understand you received a call and were told that Martin Roebuck had come out of his coma, is that right?'

'Yes,' said Neil stiffly. 'Look, would you mind telling me what's going on?'

He felt himself flushing, as if any moment now she was going to tell him that Roebuck was dead. If so, he could be looking at a murder charge. And even if he could beat the rap, he would see the face of a murderer every time he looked in the mirror.

'Are you sure that it wasn't some sort of a practical joke. I mean people don't usually come out of a coma abruptly. It's a gradual process.'

'Look, all I know is I got a brief message to come here. I tried to trace the number with 1471 and got a number, but it wouldn't take incoming calls.'

'Then it couldn't be a hospital number,' said the sister flatly.

'Could you just tell me one thing. Is Roebuck out of the coma or not?'

'I can't tell you that. If you're a policeman, then you may be able to find out through the proper channels.'

'You asked if I was sure the call came from here and not UCH. . .'

The Sister looked at the nurse angrily and the nurse turned a bright shade of red.

'Was Roebuck here?'

'I can tell you nothing about him.' The sister's tone was authoritative. She was certainly not one to be intimidated by a policeman, especially a young one. 'I suggest that you ask the officer in charge of the case.'

'OK, thank you,' replied Neil meekly.

He was flustered and confused. He had been tricked, but it was not clear by whom, or even why. He thought of rushing home to see if his flat had been burgled. But that made no sense. If someone wanted to burgle his flat they could watch from the street until he left and then break in. He had been lured here, and had done something that might potentially be seen as incriminating. But coming here didn't actually prove him guilty of anything other than concern. It made no sense.

As he turned to leave, the ward sister spoke again.

'Oh, just one other thing.'

'Yes?' he said.

'May I see your warrant card?'

He pulled it out and held it up for her to see the details.

'It's nothing personal, you understand. It's just that we were told that if there were any more attempts to see Mr Roebuck, we should make a note of the visitor's identity.'

'You mean there's already been an attempt to see him?' asked Neil, his curiosity rising to fever pitch.

This time it was the sister who blushed, while the nurse bother lip, not to avoid crying but to refrain from laughing.

'Who was it?' he demanded frantically.

'I can tell you nothing about it,' the sister replied stiffly. 'If you have any questions, I suggest you ask them of your own superiors.'

He nodded calmly, realizing that no further headway was possible.

'For the hundredth time, I don't know!' Neil pleaded. 'I got a call at four o'clock.'

'From whom!' barked the SO10 officer.

'I don't know.'

He had been here for two hours now, sitting in this chair while a pair of officers from the Set's most secretive and elite units grilled him mercilessly. It had all started when he arrived at University College Hospital. He had picked up on the ward sister's reference to UCH and gone there. He had made the rounds of the various departments and wards until he found the unit where Roebuck was being guarded. He hadn't noticed anything untoward and was even surprised at the absence of uniformed officers. He had got past the uniformed hospital guard merely by showing his police ID. But it was only when he inquired about Roebuck at the nursing station that the trap closed in on him.

For within a second of mentioning the name of Martin Roebuck, two men in plain clothes were at his shoulders, challenging him to identify himself, followed a few seconds later by two more. In spite of his police ID he was bundled roughly into a windowless back room and asked a series of brusque questions before a lull in the questioning while they called for a superior officer at the scene. With the officers outside on the alert in case he had accomplices, the interrogation continued for fifteen minutes, until it was decided to continue it at Albany Street police station.

One of the SO10 communications operators radioed ahead to the boys in Albany Street requesting an interview room and found them most accommodating. Ten minutes later, Neil was sitting on one side of a desk in a back room at the Albany Street 'nick', facing three grim, determined-looking plain-clothes officers.

'So let's get this straight. You get an anonymous call telling you that Roebuck's out of his coma and wants to see you at the Royal Free.'

'Yes.'

'And so you go there and find out that he isn't there and that doesn't make you suspicious? pull the other one!r'

'Of course it made me suspicious. That's why I came here. After she mentioned UCH I wanted to know what the hell was going on.'

'Oh, so you didn't think to tell your superiors? To confide in your colleagues perhaps? Like a sensible, professional copper?'

'I'm sorry. Look, I know it was stupid, but I wasn't really supposed to be investigating at all.'

'We know that, Neil. You're in trouble enough already.'

'Well then, you know why I didn't share it with my colleagues.'

'Assuming, of course, that's the only reason,' said the officer who had previously been almost silent.'

'Look. All I can tell you is that I got this call. You might be able to check it out with BT--'

'We know all that!' the leading interrogator barked. 'But that still doesn't explain your actions.'

'Or justify them,' said the second.

'What I don't understand,' said the third, 'is why it never occurred to you that we had a reason for moving Roebuck here?'

'Well, I thought it was because he could get better treatment here.'

'Bullshit!'

Neil jumped back at the interjection and then looked puzzled at each of the three faces in turn.

'Then why?'

'Security. Everyone still thinks he's at the Royal Free, except us, a small number of staff at each hospital . . . and now you.'

'If security is such an important consideration,' said Neil, 'then that nurse shouldn't have shot her mouth off to me. If she hadn't done that, I wouldn't have known he was here.'

'Don't you worry about that. She's going to get a right bollocking from her Senior Nursing Officer. But that still doesn't

171

alter the fact that you shouldn't have come here. You should have called your superiors right away.'

'Well, that's exactly what I would have done if she hadn't mentioned UCH so if--'

'All right, all right,' said the third SO10 officer. 'We've been here, done that and bought the T-shirt. Now let's be clear about where things stand. I'm going to have to pass a report on this to your regional DCS, with a copy to the"rubber heels" boys.'

Neil nodded passively.

'Apart from that, let me make one thing clear to you, PC Douglas: under no circumstances are you to disclose where Martin Roebuck is being held to anyone.'

'OK.'

'And one final thing. No more private investigation. This is *our* turf.'

Neil nodded. Then he spoke again.

'Just one question. Is Roebuck out of his coma?'

He held his breath in hope.

'That's none of your business.'

Chapter 13

There was a chill in the air as Beth stepped out of her house on her way to the radio station. She regretted not having brought a warmer jacket for when she went home. But she didn't want to go back in now. Stevie was settled, with the baby-sitter telling him a story, and she didn't want to disturb him.

Her car was parked just opposite under the street lamp, where she could see it from the living room window. That was where she always parked it when the spot was free. The parking space directly in front of her own house was obscured from view by the front hedge. The man who lived in the house opposite got annoyed, but he didn't own the spot. Besides, she explained to him, he could always park his car outside her place where he would have an equally good view of *his* car.

She had parked it with the driver's seat on the side of the pavement and it was as she was walking round the back of the car that a dark figure stepped out of the shadows.

'Beth Porter?' said the figure. It was a deep voice, a man's voice. And there was a hint of reassurance about it.

'Who wants to know?'

The voice wasn't threatening, but the circumstances were.

'My name is Pierre . . . Pierre Chandler.

She looked into his eyes. They were sad. It was almost as if he had been crying.

'Leah's husb--'

'We lived together.'

She was careful not to open the door of the car. Still cautious, she was afraid that he might try to bundle her inside. There was silence between them but she sensed that he was holding something back.

'Did you want to tell me something?'

'I just wanted to tell you that all these rumours . . . all these stories on your programme that people are calling into say. They're all false.'

She tried to remember what he was talking about.

'What sort of rumours?'

'Like the stories about me knowing William Isaacs. Like the stories about William Isaacs being up to something sinister and Leah knowing about it. It was all a load of rubbish.'

'So where is William Isaacs now?'

'I don't know. He moved on and vanished without a trace'

'Do you think he killed her?'

'I don't know.'

'The neighbours thought he was obsessed with Leah.'

'The neighbours are a load of gossips.'

Beth took a deep breath and decided to be bold.

'It sounds like you're defending him.'

'I'm not. At first I thought he was guilty. Then I believed the Roebuck theory. Now I don't know.'

Beth was still puzzled.

'So what do you want me to do?'

'Call off the dogs.'

'What?'

'The callers who keep attacking me.'

'No one's attacking you.'

'They're hinting at it.'

'I can't stop them. The programme is led by the callers. Like I say in the programme, I call the topic but they call the tune.'

'You can screen them better.'

She stuck out her jaw truculently.

'And if I don't?'

'I'm not threatening you. I'm-'

'You're *what*?'

She met his eyes with her hardest stare.

'I'm pleading with you.'

He looked away. She melted.

'I'll try.'

She was surprised to find that her voice had turned gentle.

Neil had a lot on his mind as he drove towards Manchester. He couldn't understand what had happened yesterday. Someone had phoned him and lured him to the Royal Free Hospital. But what for? To set him up? For what purpose?

It was interesting that he had been lured to the Royal Free and not University College Hospital. That meant that it couldn't have been an inside job. Whoever sent him on that wild goose chase didn't know that Martin Roebuck had been moved to UCH. But that still didn't explain the ploy. It served no purpose other than to make Neil look bad -and come under suspicion.

Was it a practical joke? If so, by whom? A stranger perhaps? Someone who blamed him for hitting Roebuck?Unlikely. Roebuck didn't have any friends. And besides, if it was just some kid with a warped sense of humour, how had they got his phone number?

He remembered Horace Taddit's threatening parting shot and wondered if this was the implementation of the threat. It didn't make sense, though. The threat had been conditional. Neil hadn't done anything against Taddit's interests.

He tried to put it out of his mind but it stayed with him all the way to Manchester.

'Basically, I don't have an alibi.'

'Well, that's fair enough,' said Neil. 'You don't have to have an alibi to be innocent.'

He was talking to Jerry Saville, the third suspect on the list of owners of cars matching Meredith de Mur's description.

'You don't believe me?' said Saville.

'I believe you. I was just wondering what you were doing at the time. I mean, you must have been doing something, even if you were doing it alone.'

Saville smiled.
'Oh, I was. Like I told your colleagues, I was watching TV at the time.'

Neil tried not to smile back.

'What time was that?'

The smile broadened into a childish grin.

'About eleven fifteen.'

Jerry Saville was in his late thirties and lived alone. Of the three suspects he had talked to so far, Neil thought him by far the most credible. He had copies of men's magazines lying around and seemed to be an over-the-hill 'lad'.

'And, of course, you were a couple of hundred miles away.'

'Exactly.'

'Did anyone see you in, say, the three hours before or three hours afterwards?'

'Yes. I was with a few mates at the King's Head until nine-thirty.'

'You didn't stay till closing?'

'There was a film I wanted to catch.'

'And presumably you hadn't pulled.'

'It was a Monday. Not much action, if you know what I mean.'

'Did they confirm your alibi to the police?'

'Why don't you ask them?'

'Like I said, I'm not supposed to be doing this.'

Saville smiled.

'Well, don't worry. I won't squeal on you. We've all got our skeletons in the cupboard.'

'What's yours?' asked Neil.

Saville smiled and then blushed. Neil thought he wasn't going to answer but suddenly he spoke.

'Rape.'

'Rape?'

Neil sounded incredulous.

'It was a long time ago. Twenty years, in fact. When I was in the army.'

'Who did you rape?'

'I can't even remember her name now. Just some girl I went out with. It was date rape.'

'The kind you're not likely to get caught for.'

'Oh, I was caught.'

'You were caught?'

'Yes.'

'And convicted?'

Neil hoped he wasn't looking smug.

'Yes.'

'And how long did you get?'

'Three months suspended.'

'That's all?'

'Originally it was six months. But that would have meant that I couldn't rejoin my regiment.'

'Your regiment?'

'In the army. If I got more than three months I'd have to be discharged. So my lawyer got the Appeal Court to reduce the sentence to three months suspended.'

'And you rejoined you regiment?'

'Not exactly.'

'But I thought you said-'

'They didn't want me.'

'But then why did the court reduce your sentence?'

Jerry smiled smugly.

'My lawyer pointed out that if I got a stiffer sentence, I couldn't rejoin the regiment. The court must've misconstrued her argument.'

'*Her* argument.'

'I had a lady barrister - always helps when you're being defended on a rape charge.'

'You make it sound like it's a habit.'

'Oh no, that's the only time.'

'So the bottom line is your lawyer tricked the appeal court.'

'That's the long and short of it.'

'You don't seem too bothered by that.'

Neil's tone was hostile.

'Why should I? I made a mistake. Why should I pay for it?Sorry, that came out wrong but you know what I mean.'

'Oh, I know what you mean. You're a man who likes to get his way.'

'I did something wrong. I was a young man, I didn't know the rules of the game and I overplayed my hand. I got brought up for it and I nearly paid for it. In the end, I got a slap on the wrist. I never did it again.'

'But what sort of a message did it send out to others?'

'I don't know. But that wasn't for me to think about. I just wanted to stay out of prison.'

'And you weren't averse to tricking the appeal court to do it.'

'It was trickery or jail.'

'And what about the girl?'

'She was quite bitter about it.'

'You can hardly blame her.'

'Oh, I don't. She suffered internal injuries-'

'Internal injuries?'

'Oh, she recovered. But at the time it looked pretty bad. There was a bit of an outcry at the Appeal Court when the judge said that she wouldn't have suffered the injuries if she hadn't resisted so vigorously.'

'He said *that*?'

'He meant that he was acknowledging his awareness of the severity of the injuries but it came over as if he was criticizing the girl for resisting.'

'It sounds to me like you don't really care about what you did.'

'It ruined my career. It's not as if I didn't suffer. I paid for it. I don't see any reason to have regrets.'

'Maybe because the girl suffered because of what you did to her?'

'I regret that. But people are resilient. They recover. At any rate, I paid the price that the law demanded of me at the time. I see no reason to blame myself now.'

'No,' said Neil, shaking his head as he slowly Rose to his feet. 'I guess you don't.'

Chapter 14

It was 1:45 in the morning and *The Bitching Hour* was winding down. Through the window of the dimly lit studio, Beth could see the glittering lights of Knightsbridge in the heart of London. At this time, central London was wide awake as people spilled out onto the streets from the nightclubs.

'I can tell you that Bridget Vanderbilt was quite definitely not given the chance to identify William,' said the woman with the forceful voice.

'Is that because she'd already identified Roebuck?' asked Beth.

'No, William was the prime suspect before Roebuck was even considered.'

'And why didn't they give her a chance to ID him?'

'I don't know. And contrary to press reports, her identification of Roebuck wasn't so unequivocal. At the identity parade, she walked up and down the line and at first didn't identify anyone. Then she was asked, "Are you sure?" and she picked Roebuck and said "This *might* be the man. "'

'But two days later, when she saw him on TV, leaving the magistrates court after he was convicted of a minor offence, she said that she was more certain because of his distinctive walk.'

'Yes, but if she was *more* sure, then it means she *wasn't* sure when she identified him at the identity parade, doesn't it?'

'Yes, I see what you mean,' said Beth.

'Also, they never gave three of Bridget Vanderbilt's children the chance to identify William. Remember, they were with her at the time. Nor did they give Carol Lawless a chance to ID him.'

'Who was Carol Lawless?' asked Beth.
'She was the woman who saw a man bending down by the sewage pipe, washing his hands.'

'Oh yes, that's right. Well that's incredible. They didn't ask her if she could ID him. OK, thank you, Mary. Let's take a break. This is *In the Winter* by Janis Ian.'

Beth looked round to her right. Jane was signalling her.
'What is it?'

'A man on the line, doesn't want to give his name.'

'Tell him to make up a name,' replied Beth irritably. 'I can't take a call from some one who has no name.'

'He's afraid to be identified.'

'Is he disguising his voice?'

'No.'

'Then how's he going conceal his identity from people who know him?'

'He doesn't want to talk to you on the air. He wants to tell you something in private.'

'OK, put him on. If the song comes to an end before I'm finished, run the adverts.'

'OK.'

Jane pressed a button and the call came through to Beth's headset.

'Hallo,' said Beth.

'Who's that?' asked a man's voice - a deep, rasping intensely suspicious voice.

'It's Beth Porter. Are you William?'

There was a split-second nervous hesitation. Then the voice came back smoothly.

'Yes.'

Beth tensed up

'And what do you want to say?'

'I just wanted to say that I didn't kill Leah Irons, or Rose Crowne.'

'Why should we believe you?' said Beth.

'You had someone phone in a few days ago who confessed. It wasn't me. You can tell that it wasn't me.'

'You might have disguised your voice. It sounded like he was disguising his voice.'

'Why would I do that? If I wanted to confess, why would I deny it? If I didn't want to confess, why would I do so?'

'You might have been setting me up. Confessing with one voice, then phoning in as yourself with another.'

'Look, I can't prove I'm innocent. All I can say is that it wasn't me. Surely you can get an expert to compare the voices, you know the way they look at the wave patterns or whatever.'

'That isn't always conclusive, William. And even if it is, you might have got someone else to call.'

'So I can't prove anything to you, can I? I might as well be talking to a brick wall.'

'You may be able to prove it, William, but not like that. I mean, even if the person who called in had nothing to do with you, we don't know if that caller was the killer. It could've been some joker. We get a lot of those on radio phone-ins. For all I know, you could be a joker. How do I know you're really William Isaacs?'

'What do you want me to say?'

'I want you to say, I'll come in to your show with some ID and prove that I'm William Isaacs. I want you to say that you'll submit to a polygraph test like Roebuck did. I want you to submit to agree to be interviewed and questioned like Roebuck did, and face a rigorous inquisition at the hands of the press as Roebuck did, and see if you stand up to it any better. I want to lay the evidence against you and against him side by side and see who looks the guiltier of the two. Now if you're ready to do that, then maybe I'll believe you.'

'I can't do that, Beth.'

'Why not?'

'Officially, I'm still a suspect. When the case against Roebuck collapsed, the file was left wide open. That meant in theory I could become a suspect again. That's why I moved on.'

Beth lowered her voice to a deeper pitch. A more masculine tone, she knew, sounded more businesslike and carried more credibility. This man didn't need feminine reassurance, he needed masculine bullying.

'If you're afraid to be found, is there any reason why the public should trust you?'

'I can't take a chance on that. To be honest, I don't trust the public. The public are fickle. One minute they're baying for Roebuck's blood, the next minute it's mine. I can't submit to that kind of mob. I'd rather stay out of it and let people think what they like.'

'OK, well in that case, let me ask you something else? Do you think Roebuck did it?'

'I don't think my opinion counts for much, but the truth is, I don't.'

'Do you have any idea who may have done it?'

'Not really.'

'But you don't mind if Roebuck takes the rap?'

'He can't take the rap. He was acquitted.'

'But you didn't know he would be, did you?'

'I didn't know if he was guilty or not. What I said before is just an opinion. All I know is that I'm innocent.'

'Only you're not prepared to expose yourself to the criminal investigative process?'

'I was exposed to it once. I don't want to go through it again.'

'So how did it feel having the whole press on your back for two days?'

'I wish it had only been for two days,' replied Neil.

He was sitting at a corner table of the café with Robert Vilayet, an ex-football player of no mean repute on the pitch, and considerable notoriety off it. He had once been a walking symbol of success but an expensive divorce and bum investments had separated him from most of the wealth he had once flaunted. Rumour had it that he also had to spend a sizeable chunk of his former fortune extricating himself from legal wrangles resulting from his own hot temper.

'At least you can stay out of the limelight now.'

The ex-footballer sounded bitter.

'For a while I was finding it pretty difficult. I had this bitchy radio reporter on my back.'

'She was probably a frustrated spinster.'

Neil smiled.

'Oh, she isn't that. She's quite sexy actually.'

'Wait a minute . . . you didn't. . .'

'Let me put it this way: we're friends now . . . or perhaps I should say . . . more than friends.'

'You must have French blood in you,' said Vilayet.

They laughed heartily, like a pair of lads.

'The thing I'm feeling really bad about,' said Neil delicately, 'is that the murderer got away.'

'I don't blame you. I mean, the man in the hospital will probably get over it but that poor woman's family doesn't even have the comfort of knowing that the murderer paid for it.'

Neil winced at the reminder about Martin Roebuck. He wished he could forget about that aspect of the case but it wouldn't go away. He wondered if perhaps he was using his personal search for the murderer as a distraction from what he did to Roebuck. Then again, he suspected that his lack of ease at what had happened went back to another event, before the tragedy on the Heath.

'I believe my colleagues came here asking where you were on the night in question.'

'Yes. I was apparently on a long list. Someone saw a car speeding away and got part of the number.'

Neil thought it better not to tell him that he was on the original short-list of those whose cars matched in colour and type as well as registration number.

'I was wondering if I could just ask you a couple of questions about it?'

'I don't understand why you don't just ask your colleagues.'

Neil thought it might not be a good idea to confess the truth to this man any more than he had to the others. He wasn't supposed to be investigating the case at all but he still had his fall-back excuse.

'I'm facing disciplinary proceedings, and so I'd rather gather as much evidence as I can in my own defence and then put it to them at the hearing.'

'I'll answer what I can, but I don't see that I can help you. I mean, I wasn't there and so I wasn't a witness . . . except in this funny English way of yours.'

'I was wondering what you were doing on the night Rose Crowne was killed?'

Robert Vilayet smiled.

'If this was an Agatha Christie story, you'd be waiting to see if I asked "when was that. "'

Neil shrugged.

'However, as your colleagues have already interviewed me and told me when, I can answer you as I answered them. I had a late night meeting with a friend at his flat, to make arrangements for dealing with the assault charge that was recently brought against me by a disgruntled photographer.'

'A friend? Don't you mean a lawyer?'

'No, I mean my friend. There are some things British lawyers aren't prepared to do.'

'I don't understand. How can your friend get you off a criminal charge?'

'Let me put it this way. Lawyers have professional ethics. My friend doesn't.'

'You mean, a pay-off?'

'Call it what you like.'

'But why can't you just offer an out-of-court settlement?Through your lawyer?'

'The alleged victim of the assault wants too much. Witnesses come cheaper.'

'Is this what you told my colleagues.'

'I told them I was with a friend. I didn't tell them why.'

'Then why are you telling me?'

'I figure that as we've both fallen foul of the law, I can afford to let my hair down. It's always fun to talk to a fellow criminal.'

He was smiling smugly. Neil wanted to punch him in the face - except that he knew this man could probably beat the crap out of him.

'One last question. Why were you meeting your friend so late?' 'I'm a bit of a night-owl,' said Vilayet. 'Especially since I retired.'

'So you've got four suspects: two in London, two in Manchester.'

'That's right.'

Beth was sitting by the outside rail looking out onto the Thames, keeping a watchful eye on Stevie who was clambering about all over the place. Neil was sitting near the aisle, squinting against the bright warm sun.

'And which of them do you suspect?'

Neil squirmed. They were all loathsome characters in one way or another, but none took the trouble to hide their nature. They were unashamedly bastards, and none seemed anxious to hide his light under a bushel.

'None of them.'

Neil wondered whether perhaps there was some significance in the fact that they had been so open with him. It was as if they had identified him as a kindred spirit. He had always thought of himself as one of the good guys. Yet four suspects - not one or two or three, but *four* suspects - had spoken to him freely as if he were not merely no threat to them, but one of them.

Is that what I am, he wondered. *A fallen angel A junior member of some corrupt fraternity?*

'*That's how corruption begins,*' a voice from his past was chiding him. '*That's what begins the slippery slide into dishonesty. It all starts with a little white lie, uttered with the best of intentions.*'

'How do you figure that?'

'Well, the soldier and the footballer were out of their territory. Why come all the way to London to commit a murder?'

Beth threw her head back in contemplation.

'Perhaps *because* they were in danger of being recognized in Manchester.'

'Robert Vilayet's in danger of being recognized everywhere.'

'I wouldn't recognize him if he was sitting *opposite* me.'

Neil grinned.

'That's because you're a woman.'

'And you can cut the sexism,' she snapped, but was smiling when she said it.

'And over on your right as we complete the turn to start our journey you'll see Westminster. That's where our wise leaders meet to make the decisions that make our country so prosperous.'

The voice over the public address system uttered these words with a working-class cynicism that drew howls of laughter from the foreign tourists on the pleasure boat, and wide grins from the British.

It was the weekend and they were on their way to Greenwich by river. Beth had promised Stevie some time ago that they would make this trip. She realized that she had to spend more time with him, not just being at home when he was at home, but actually paying attention to him and doing things that he wanted to do. And when she finally got round to it, she'd asked if he minded if Neil came along. Not knowing what the verb 'to mind' meant he'd said 'yes', thinking that it meant that he wanted Neil to come along. Beth had been on the phone to tell Neil that Saturday was off when Stevie picked up the phone in the corridor and said, 'Are you coming to Greenwich with us?' After the misunderstanding had been cleared up it was all plain sailing, at least so far.

'I still don't think it was Vilayet or Saville. If it was any of the suspects, it was Tadditt or Fortescue.'

'Just because they're London based?'

She had sounded sceptical. But the truth of the matter was that even *he* wasn't sure why he suspected them, or even *if* he did.

'I guess it might just be because they're pillocks of the establishment.'

'They're *what* of the establishment.'

He was grinning now.

'I'm sorry, that was Freudian. I mean *pillars* of the establishment.'

His arm rested on her lap, the palm open and face up. She put her hand in his comfortingly.

'Is that a scientific theory or just personal resentment?'

'It's personal resentment.'

It was no use pretending. She knew him well enough by now.

'So maybe your colleagues are right to go outside the scope of the original shortlist.'

'They probably are. It was dark. It's hard to tell the colour of a car in the dark. And when it's going fast it's hard to tell the make.'

'You're upset, aren't you?'

He hadn't realized that his voice betrayed it. But with Beth locked onto his wavelength it was hard for him to keep *any* secrets from her.

'Of course I'm upset.'

'And we both know why.'

He looked at her puzzled, daring her to theorize.

'It means you won't catch him. It means there are too many names to check out. It means it'll take good old-fashioned police work to catch the killer and you won't be able to deliver the killer's head on a plate to an outraged society and lay your own demons to rest.'

'What do *you* know about my demons?' he snapped.

She jumped back, startled.

'I know it's not easy carrying the burden on your own.' Her voice was gentle. 'I know that you still blame yourself for what happened to Roebuck. I know that you blamed yourself even

186

before I got on your case. I know that you're a human decent man who wants to make society a better place for--'

'Stop it!' he said, brushing her hand off. He was in no mood for sympathy.

'I'm sorry,' she said. She knew when to back off. He felt guilty about his reaction, but it was too soon to apologize. He was still hurting but he couldn't tell her why. It wasn't Roebuck. What he did to Roebuck was wrong, he knew that, but that wasn't what was tormenting him.

There was a tense silence between them, filled by the humorous voice that came over the PA system.

'And if you look to your left now, ladies and gentlemen you see the all-glass building that I was talking about. They call it modern architecture. Personally, I call it something else. It was probably designed by an unemployed window cleaner.'

A group of Japanese tourists laughed, belatedly, as their interpreter translated the joke for them.

'So how's it going with you then?' asked Neil, after half a minute.

'How do you mean?'

'Well, you seem to have almost dropped the Leah Irons case from your phone-in.'

'Actually, I've been doing a little digging of my own.'

'What? You're turning into a gumshoe?'

'Stop teasing.'

They were holding hands again.

'So what do you mean, "doing a little digging of my own"?I mean, I've heard you conducting your inquiry over the air. But if you start going into the field looking for clues, you could be getting out of your depth.'

'I can't help it, Neil. I'm a woman. Remember women?The gender noted for its incessant curiosity?'

'OK, OK. But what exactly are you trying to find out?'

'One thing's been bothering me about this Rose Crowne:we haven't heard much about her.'

Neil was startled.

'Hold on a minute. You mean you're looking into the Rose Crowne case?'

'I mean, I'm trying to find out who Rose Crowne was.'

187

'I don't understand.'

'We know nothing about Rose Crowne. We don't know who she was, what she was, where she was. Well, the last one I do know, because I found out. And that's another thing.'

'Wait a minute. You've been checking up on Rose Crowne.'

'Yes, Neil. I just said so.'

'Mummy, look at me!'

Stevie was clambering up on the railings.

'Get down from there at once!'

Not waiting for Stevie to respond, she dragged him back. 'Now sit down or I won't buy you an ice cream.'

He started to cry. She gave him a hug and told him that she loved him but he mustn't climb up on the seat unless he was between the two of them.

When things had quietened down, Neil spoke again.

'What did you mean when you said we don't know about Rose Crowne.'

'Well. Did you see her parents on TV?'

'No.'

'Did you see her boyfriend on TV?'

'No.'

'Did you see her husband on TV?'

'No.'

'Do you know where she worked?'

'No.'

'Do you know what she did for a living?'

'No.'

'Well, neither do I. And as far as I've been able to establish neither does anyone.'

'But didn't you just say something about finding out where he was.'

'Yes. I found out where she lived.'

'Where?'

'In Camden Town.'

'So maybe we could go along and talk to the neighbours.'

'I already did.'

'And?'

'I was told something very interesting.'

'What?'

'After she was murdered, some men came along and took everything away.'

'What sort of men?'

'Workmen. You know, men in boiler suits. But they were apparently acting under the orders of two men in pinstripe suits.'

'Presumably the men in pinstripes were the solicitors in charge of the estate.'

'Presumably,' Beth echoed. 'But on whose behalf were they acting?'

'And who would that be?' asked Beth.

'I don't know,' said Neil, wondering where all this was leading.

'Exactly.'

'Hold on a minute. Just because you haven't been able to find out about Rose Crowne, doesn't mean there's anything suspicious in her death. I mean, maybe she was a private person who didn't have many friends.'

'Yes, Neil, but even if she just had one or two . . . Nobody's spoken up about her. Usually, when there's a victim in a crime like this, you get friends or relatives going on TV and appealing to witnesses to come forward. Also, the fact that her things were taken away like that seems very suspicious. We didn't hear anything about a funeral. There were no appeals for witnesses and the whole thing looks damn suspicious.'

'So what are you going to do about it?'

'How do you mean?'

'Well, if they moved her things out and if she doesn't have any relatives then how are you going to find her? Did they leave a notice on the door?'

'No.'

Neil thought for a moment.

'Well, I guess you could try the landlord - if it was rented. Or check out the ownership.'

'Thank you, but I have another way of going about it.'

'What's that?'

'She was reported as being in her late twenties. I'll treat that as 24-32.'

'Birth certificates?'

'The registrar of births, marriages and deaths. I'll check-up the name Rose Crowne at the Family Records Centre.'

'It'll take a lot of time.'

'That may be. But sooner or later I'll find all the Rose Crownes in that age range, and their parents.'

'And then what?'

'Once I've got her parents' names I can look them up on my database.'

'They might be ex-directory.'

'Not that one. I got a new one. It's based on voting registries as well as phone books.'

'But voting registries are listed by address not by name.'

'Yes, but this one has a reverse search feature.'

'That's an invasion of privacy.'

'I'm the news media,' said Beth with an almost guilty smile. 'Why should I care.

Chapter 15

Beth had driven to the Angel, Islington and then asked for directions. But they had been confused, given by pedestrians who weren't familiar with the traffic system in place at the moment, so she had had to pull up in a side street and take a look in the A-Z. Eventually, she found the old Finsbury Town Hall and then had to drive round the back to Myddleton Street where she parked and walked back to the Family Records Centre.

The interior was bright and modern, amply lit by fluorescent strip lights. She had expected an old-fashioned interior, the kind of Victorian library reading room in which bearded scholars like Bertrand Russell and Karl Marx had done their research. Then she remembered that even the British Library was now housed in new ultra-modern quarters.

She walked across the reception area into the main room where the huge volumes were housed and after looking around briefly to orient herself, she proceeded to the right, deep into the far side of the room where the large red volumes containing records of births were kept. She had noticed that to her left was the desk where birth certificates could be ordered. However she didn't need a birth certificate, she just needed the names.

She looked at the volumes stacked on metal shelves and at the people who were struggling to take them down and place them on the large white Formica topped tables that filled the spaces between each unit of shelves. The people, each for their own purpose, were opening the books, flicking through their pages and making notes on the sheets of paper generously available from racks on the tables.

Beth looked at the books on their shelves, trying to figure out where to begin. She quickly figured out that the books were divided according to quarter years and alphabetic groups. Each year was divided into quarters and each quarter had four books for different groups of letters.

She had settled on an age range of twenty-four to thirty-two, so she had to go back to the oldest eligible date first. The name she was looking for was Rose Crowne and there was a faint chance that it was not her real name - or at least not her original name. But it was the name on her door and for lack of anything better, Beth had to assume that it was the right name.

Beth did a quick calculation, deducting thirty-two from the current year, and worked out the earliest year in which Rose Crowne could have been born. She made her way to the shelf with the books for that year and pulled down the book that covered the letter C for the first quarter of that year. She hoisted it down and turned round to put it on the table behind her. Spurred on by a sense of purpose, she opened it and began flicking through the old pages with their faded blue ink. Within the book the names were arranged alphabetically rather than chronologically, making it easy to home in directly on 'Crowne'. There were a few, but no Rose. Next volume.

Five volumes later, she found her first Rose Crowne. She made a note of the names of the parents. But that wasn't the end of the matter. It wasn't enough to find a Rose Crowne, she had to find *the* Rose Crowne. That meant that she had to build up a comprehensive list of all the Rose Crownes in the relevant period and then check out the parents of all of them. A few volumes later, she found another.

It went on like that for several hours. Her game plan called for inspection of only thirty-two volumes. But finding the volumes, taking them down from the shelves, flicking through to the right page and then carefully scanning the page, all took its toll in terms of the passage of time. Eventually, she built up a list of fewer than a dozen names, including a couple of Rosemary Crownes just to be on the safe side.

But then a thought struck her. What if she's as old as thirty three or as young as *twenty*-three?

She decided to broaden the scope of her search. It was only an extra two years, and that translated into an extra eight volumes. She worked her way through them. All she got for her trouble was two extra names, both twenty three years old but at least she felt safer for having covered the extra ground.

The registry of births did not give the parents' first names-only the surname and the mother's maiden surname. She had to make her way to another section of the large room to go through the volumes with green spines - the records of marriages - to get the first names of the parents. This was even more difficult because she didn't know the date of the marriage, so she had to cover a large period of time, matching men called Crowne and women with one of the maiden names on her list. Through this arduous effort she found marriages in which the partner's names matched her list and gradually built up a list of first names of possible parents.

Many hours later, her arms aching from lugging the heavy volumes off the shelves and heaving them back on again, she had a list of all the prospective pairs of parents - first names and surnames. Now came the hard part. She had the names of the prospective parents, but she had to check them out. Getting the phone numbers or addresses would be easy, she thought, because of the CDROM but she would have to phone them and ask them. Ask them what? You can't just phone someone up and ask: 'Are you the parents of the Rose Crowne who was murdered a week and a half ago?

What then could she say? She could phone all the 'Rose Crownes' on the database. But that wouldn't work. She had already done so. And there was no way to link those names with the Rose Crownes on her birth records list. So much for that.

There was only one thing to do. She'd have to take the bull by the horns and phone the parents, one by one.

Two hours later she was at home, trying to match the names of possible parents from the Family Records Centre with names on the CDROM. It was harder than she expected, because there were, in many cases, several people with the same first names. Thus each pair of Crownes on her list from the Family Records Centre translated into several sets of possible parents on the CDROM. She couldn't even eliminate those names in the CDROM where only one of the names lived at a given address, because the parents could have divorced since. Or one could have died and the other re-married. She regretted not having checked remarriages too. Then again that would have covered far more ground and taken far more time than it would save by eliminating other names now.

'Hallo, Mr Crowne?'

'Yes?'

'My name is Beth, I'm an old friend of Rose and I've lost her number.'

'Who's Rose?'

'Your daughter.'

'Sorry, I think you've got the wrong number.'

'Wait, is that Roger Crowne?'

'No, Robert.'

'Oh, I'm sorry.'

Next.

'Hallo, Mrs Crowne?'

'Yes?'

'My name is Beth, I'm an old friend of Rose and I've lost her number.'

'If you're an old friend of Rose, how come you don't have her number?'

'Well, I lost my address book.'

'Then how come you have my number.'

'I got it from BT.'

'But why didn't you ask for Rose's number.'

'I tried. But I guess it must be unlisted - I mean ex-directory.'

'No, it isn't.'

'Well, I didn't have enough information for them to find the number. I mean I don't have her current address. I tried Hampstead and Camden Town but they didn't have it listed.

'Then how did you found us. I mean there must dozens of Crownes. How did you know that we have a daughter called Rose?'

Click. Next.

'Hallo, Mr Crowne?'

'Yes?'

'My name is Beth, I'm an old friend of Rose and I've lost her number.'

'How did you get *my* number?'

'I have it in my address book, below hers. It's just that it's a bit tattered and I can't read her details. They seem to have got smudged a bit. I haven't looked at it since I went back to the States.'

'When was that?'

'Two years ago.

'But we only moved in here earlier this year.'

Click.

'Hallo, Mrs Crowne?'

'Yes?'

'My name is Beth, I'm an old friend of Rose and I've lost her number.'

'What did you say your name was?'

'Beth. Beth Mitchell.'

'I don't know any Beth Mitchell. She's never told me anything about you.'

'Well, look, I can understand you not wanting to give out her number, but maybe I could leave my number with you. Then you could give it to her. It's just such a long time since we've spoken.'

'OK, I'll just get a pen.'

Click.

'Hallo, Mrs Crowne?'

'Yes?'

'My name is Beth, I'm an old friend of Rose and I've lost her number.'

'Is this some kind of a joke.'

The voice was indignant.

'No . . . why?'

'Rose is dead.'

Beth's heart leapt into her mouth.

'Dead? God I'm sorry. I've been in America these past two years.'

'Are you sick or something?' Now the voice was angry. 'Rose died when she was five.'

Beth hung up quickly. Not waiting for the woman to hangup or shout at her any further.

Beth felt her heart fluttering. She knew that these calls might cause some discomfort, but now she had caused real distress to someone who was probably racking her brain trying to figure out what was going on. She realized, with a painful stab of guilt, that once again she had caused pain in the selfish pursuit of one of her goals. She picked up the phone and called back.

'Mrs Crowne. It's the woman you spoke to a minute ago.'

'What do you want?' she said bitterly. It was obvious that she had been crying.

'I just wanted to say that I got the wrong number. I got your number from BT, but I guess it was the wrong number. I mean it's another Rose Crowne I'm looking for.'

'But how did they know that I was the mother of someone called Rose Crowne?'

'I looked up the records at the Family Records Centre. I guess I got the wrong Rose Crowne.'

'This is getting ridiculous! It's bad enough that someone with the same name was killed a few weeks ago.'

'Look, I'm sorry. I didn't mean to bother you. Sorry.'

She hung up, not entirely relieved of the guilt but she realized that she would be causing just as much pain when she contacted the parents of the real Rose Crowne.

But it had to be done. . .

'Hallo, Mr Crowne?'

'Yes?'

'My name is Beth, I'm an old friend of Rose and I've lost her number.'

'Who is this?'

The voice sounded gentle.'

'My name is Beth. Beth Mi . . . Beth Porter.'

Something in the man's tone had prompted her to use her real name.

'My daughter was killed just over three weeks ago.'

'Oh, I'm sorry.'

'Wait a minute, did you say your name was Beth Porter?'

'Yes,' said Beth, nervously.

'Aren't you the radio talk show hostess who's been probing into the Leah Irons case recently?'

Beth held her breath.

'Is this some sort of a wind-up for your show?'

By now Rose Crowne's father was as angry as the woman she had spoken to earlier.

'No . . . look . . . I'm sorry. Perhaps I shouldn't have approached you like that. It's just that I've been trying very hard to find you. I mean I have been taking an interest in the Leah Irons case. But we've heard nothing about Rose Crowne.'

'We?'

The tone was chiding.

'The public.'

It sounded arrogant, even though she had tried to mute the tone of her voice as she said it.

'Don't you think that people in a state of grief are entitled to privacy?'

This time, the tone was more beseeching than angry, and it twisted inside Beth even more painfully.

'I'm sorry . . . you're right. I shouldn't have done this.'

'Well, what did you want, anyway?'

'I wanted to know who she was? What she was? I mean, she was a human being. She died before her time. She deserves to be remembered. It just seems sad that she should be forgotten.'

'She hasn't been forgotten by those who loved her.'

'I'm sorry, I didn't mean it like that. It's just that usually when someone dies like that, we learn a bit about them. I guess it's part ghoulishness and part sincere concern. She was a victim of a crime and the criminal is still out there. If we can't bring the criminal to justice, the least we can do is honour the victim.'

'OK, what do you want to know about her?'

'Do we have to do this over the phone? I mean, maybe we could meet somewhere?'

'You can come down to see us in Essex. It's three miles from Billericay. I'll give you our address.'

'So how long was she in the police?'

'Nearly nine years. She started her training at eighteen.'

They were drinking tea in the garden, almost half an acre of well-tended lawn. Roger Crowne was a keen gardener and it showed in the pride he took in his work. The size of the house and the grounds surrounding it suggested that the Crownes senior were well-to-do if not actually wealthy by nineties standards.

'How did you feel about it?'

'Well, like all parents, we worried. But at the end of the day, it was a case of sooner or later the bird has to leave the nest.'

'And is that how you thought of it? Leaving the nest?'

'She was at home for the first year. Then she moved out and shared for a few months with a couple of friends. Then she moved out and got a place of her own.'

'Couldn't get on with her flatmates?'

'Oh no, nothing like that. She just needed her independence. You know, when she was a youngster she hated to go away on school trips. She didn't go out much in the evenings either. Then suddenly, after a few months in the force, she became very independent.'

'Was that here in Essex or in London?'

'Oh, that was in London. We didn't move out here until a couple of years ago,'

Beth looked around, admiring the luxury.

'I'm not an Essex Man if that's what you mean. I used to be a geological and seismological engineer. I worked in the oil industry. They pay good money in the Middle East.'

'Did you say Beth didn't go out much in the evenings?'

'Yes.'

'In the early days, I mean?'

'I don't understand.'

'You said she changed after a couple of years. Started to want her independence more.'

'Yes, but even then, she was never one for going out. I mean, she was the one who always answered the phone when I phoned the flat she was sharing. Her flatmates were out at the local or clubbing at the weekend and she was at home, curled up with a cup of tea and a book, or watching TV.'

'And what about when she moved out on her own?'

'Same thing. I sometimes wished she would go out more. Then she might have found a husband and left that awful job.'

'You didn't like it?'

He looked away at the large oak tree in the distance.

'Like I said, I was worried. I mean, anyway you look at it, it's dangerous work.'

'Yes, I suppose it is.'

There was a subject Beth wanted to raise, but she had to do it delicately.

'You said, she didn't go out much. But is it possible that later on she started to go out a bit more?'

'How do you mean?'

'Well, I mean like, putting on her glad-rags and going out for a night on the town. That sort of thing.'

'Only in her undercover work.'

'Undercover work?'

Beth realized that she had blurted this out rather too forcefully.

'Yes. I thought you knew.'

'I'm sorry I didn't. I mean I didn't even know she was a policewoman until you told me.'

'I'm sorry, I'm getting a bit ahead of myself, aren't I? I thought I'd told you. You see, Rose wasn't just an achiever, she was an overachiever. She didn't just want to be a policewoman, she wanted to be in a special unit. And she trained like a pack mule to get into one.'

'Which unit?'

'SO10.'

'I'm sorry, I don't know much about the police. What do they do?'

'They're an undercover unit. Most of what they do is drug-related undercover operations. But they do other operations as well.'

'Do you mean to say that your daughter Rose was an under-cover policewoman?'

'Yes.'

Beth thought for a moment, remembering the neighbour's words.

'In the course of that work, would dress up . . . like. . .'

'Like a tart?'

Beth nodded, swallowing nervously.

'Quite possibly.'

'Is it possible that Rose's death has anything to do with her undercover work?'

'Judging by the circumstances in which she died, I shouldn't be at all surprised.'

'You know something, don't you?'

He looked at her bitterly.

'I have my suspicions.'

She realized that she would have to broach the subject gently.

'Are you ready to share them?'

'I'll tell you what I know. I don't know if I should share my suspicions as well.'

'I'll settle for what you know,' said Beth.

199

'My Rose was part of the original operation to expose Martin Roebuck as the man who murdered Leah Irons.'

Beth's jaw dropped.

'Your Rose was Annie Jacobs?'

Roger Crowne's jaw was set hard.

'Yes.'

'And she was the one who tried to get Martin Roebuck to confess?'

'That's right.'

'But what was she . . . I mean what was she doing on Hampstead Heath that night . . . when Roebuck was there.'' That's what I've been racking my brains trying to figure out.'

'You mean that's where the speculation comes in.'

'That's right.'

'But you have an idea.'

'I know that she was never satisfied with the outcome of the case.'

'She thought Roebuck was guilty.'

'As did most of the people associated with the case.'

'Go on.'

'But unlike the others, she couldn't take the result philosophically. She couldn't accept Roebuck's acquittal with equanimity.'

'There are some who say the whole investigative team had something of a vendetta against him.'

'Oh, that was just Roebuck's paranoia. I mean, sure they hated his guts and thought a guilty man had got away with it. But they were content to leave him alone. Certainly there was no police harassment. The later convictions he got were something he brought on himself. But you're right about Rose. She had a vendetta against him. She was sure it was him. I mean, sure that he'd murdered Leah Irons.'

'Because of what he said to her? His demeanour?'

'No, nothing like that. Her belief was based on the same evidence that the rest of the world saw. Yes, I know you're rather sceptical. But can you think of any other explanation?'

'For the evidence?'

'No, for the murder. I mean if Roebuck didn't do it then who did?'

'This William Isaacs perhaps.'

'The police checked every aspect of his lifestyle. They found nothing in his background that suggested he could be the murderer.'

'Is that all it's about? Personality? Was that why they suspected Roebuck over Isaacs?'

'There was the other evidence too.'

Beth thought about this for as moment.

'But there was evidence against William Isaacs too.'

'They couldn't break his alibi. Roebuck's they could.'

'But the evidence against Roebuck's alibi was tenuous to say the least.'

Roger Crowne poured Beth another cup of tea, and then one for himself.

'Personally, I agree with you. But it was better than nothing. You can't convict a man if he has an alibi.'

'But how reliable was William Isaacs' alibi to begin with?It was only supported by his wife. I mean, I can understand them deciding that they didn't have enough to convict him but that's a far cry from deciding that he was probably innocent.'

'Their reasoning was that if they could break Roebuck's alibi, even tentatively, but not Isaacs', then Roebuck was the more likely suspect. Don't forget, Roebuck was a bit of an outsider.'

'That hardly makes him a murderer,' snapped Beth.

'No, but Isaacs was a happily married man and quite respectable. There were rumours that he was a Freemason.'

'A Freemason?' Beth echoed. She remembered all those stories about policemen and criminals in the same masonic lodges.

'There was nothing sinister in it. At least Rose didn't think so. She really believed that Roebuck was the murderer.'

'And what was she trying to do about it?'

'On the day she was killed, you mean? Like I said, that's where I have to speculate. You see, it seems to me pretty unlikely that Roebuck was there by chance on the day she happened to get killed.'

'But we know he didn't kill her,' Beth insisted.

'Yes, but the fact is that it's suspicious that they were in the same place at all.'

'You think he was following her?'

'I think she was following him. Or rather, I think she set herself up to get him to follow her.'

'But why?'

'I think she was hoping to entrap him. That is, I think that she was trying to give him one last chance to incriminate himself. Either by what he said or by what he did.'

'But even if he did, they couldn't prosecute him after the acquittal.'

'That's why I say, by what he did. You see I think she was setting herself to be attacked by him so that if they couldn't get him for murder, at least they'd get him for attempted murder.'

'That was a bit risky.'

'It was extremely risky. Only it doesn't seem to have gone to plan.'

'How do you mean?'

'Well, like you said, Roebuck didn't kill her. She was attacked by someone else and Roebuck, by all accounts, tried to save her.'

'Do you have any idea who attacked her?'

'No.'

'Do you think it could have been the man who killed Leah Irons?'

'It might have been. Assuming that it wasn't Roebuck who killed Leah Irons.'

@L1Ap'Any other possible motives? Jealousy? Financial? Any¤thing.'@L0A

'I don't know about jealousy. As far as I know, she didn't have a boyfriend. As for financial, she didn't have much. What little she had, she left to my wife and me.'

'Is that what those men were doing at her flat? Boxing things up and taking them away?'

'That was the police. SO10, to be precise. Because of the nature of her work they had to cover every angle. So they took her stuff away and sifted through it before bringing it to us. That's also why they did everything on a hush-hush basis. They figured that her death might be related to her work and they figured the best way to catch the killer would be to keep everything under wraps. That's why we didn't goon TV either. They thought it wouldn't do us any good and might even put us in danger.'

'But you're not afraid of talking to me?'

202

'I'll trust you to be discreet. You can use whatever you like. I'm not afraid. She didn't tell us anything of value. If she had, I'd have already told the police.'

Beth thought for a moment.

'Did you say she left her possessions to you?'

'Yes.'

'Do you mean she died intestate and you inherited or that she actually left a will?'

'She left a will. She drew it up a few months before she died.'

'Was there any change in her behaviour at that time?'

'Not that I recall. I mean, it was hard to tell. We only saw her at weekends, and not all weekends either.'

'Do you have any idea how she tracked Roebuck down?'

'As far as I know he still lived in the same place he lived five years ago. It wouldn't have been difficult for her to find him.'

'Did she say at the time that she was writing a will?'

'Oh yes. I mean, there was nothing sinister in it.'

'Did she give a reason?'

'Just the usual one, about how it's always good to put one's affairs in order, just in case.'

'But in retrospect could it have been more than that?'

'How do you mean?'

'I was wondering why you think Rose took it into her head to try and reopen the case now, five years later?'

'That's what's been troubling me most. She'd been talking about the case more and more lately. She kept saying that she couldn't bear the thought of Roebuck getting away with it. She seemed to be taking a very fatalistic view of the whole thing. It's almost as if she knew she was going to die. I can still remember our final conversation that Sunday afternoon, the day before she was killed. She said, "I have to do it now, even if it's the last thing I do. "'

Chapter 16

Beth's pulse was racing when she got back home. The veil of mystery had been abruptly torn away and it now became perfectly clear why everything about Rose Crowne had been kept under wraps. She had to share the news with Neil. He had waited for so long for something to break in this case and now at least he would have the reassurance that something was being done. She looked at her watch. She would have to pick up Stevie from the nursery school in half an hour. That left her enough time to tell Neil, have a cup of tea and rest for a few minutes before being thrown into the maelstrom.

She slumped onto the couch, took out her mobile from her handbag, pressing the single button that called Neil.

'Hallo.'

'Hi, Neil.'

'Oh hi, Beth.'

'Guess what?'

He heard the excitement in her voice.

'What?'

'I found out who Rose Crowne is.'

'Who?'

The excitement was contagious.

'Annie Jacobs.'

'Nor!'

'Yes. I spoke to her father in the garden. Her mother was there too but she stayed inside. I think she didn't want to talk about it.'

'So what did he tell you.'

'Oh, all sorts of things. Wait a minute, what's that clicking?'

'What clicking?

'I'm sorry. I thought I heard something. Anyway, he told me all sorts of things.'

'Like what?'

'Well, for example, she was a bit of a loner herself. She didn't have many friends. No boyfriend or anything like that. The other thing was she was frustrated by the outcome of the Martin Roebuck case.'

'That comes as no surprise. So were a lot of the people involved in it, especially the police.'

'Yes, but the others accepted it with a sense of resignation. Rose Crowne was apparently deeply frustrated by it. And her frustration was apparently growing. She told her father that she was determined to bring Roebuck to justice if it was the last thing she did.'

'In a manner of speaking she did . . . if you can call what I did to him justice.'

She felt the tension in Neil's words. Only this time it was he who had been tactless, he who had stuck the knife into himself.

'So what exactly was she doing that night?'

'We don't know for sure but Roger Crowne, that's Rose's father, thinks that she was trying to entrap Roebuck in some way.'

'*Entrap* him?'

'No, not exactly entrap. I mean, get him to make some hostile move. Maybe even get him to attack her.'

'That sounds like entrapment.'

'Not legally, surely? If he attacks her that's assault, isn't it?'

'Yes, I'm sure it would have stood up in court if it had happened. But didn't she have any backup?'

'Apparently not. The police wouldn't sanction an operation like that, not after the débâcle of the original undercover operation.'

'Wait a minute. She was following Roebuck in the hope of getting him to attack her?'

'Her father thinks that she deliberately allowed Roebuck to see her, to get him to follow her. He thinks that she was hoping that he would attack her so that she could arrest him and at least get him for assault or indecent assault.'

'But how did she hope to arrest him? I know Annie Jacobs was in SO10 but I don't think she'd have been tough enough to arrest Roebuck.'

'She had a canister of CS spray in her pocket and apparently it had a clear set of fingerprints on it, as if she'd held it recently. She probably reached for it just before the attack, or maybe even as soon as she knew he was following her.'

'This all sounds very strange.'

'Only at one level, Neil. At another level, it all makes perfect sense: Roebuck being there, the two of them together. The only thing that doesn't make sense is Roebuck playing the Good Samaritan.'

'There's something else that doesn't make sense: the fact that he had something to play Good Samaritan about.'

'I don't understand,' said Beth.

'The fact that Rose was attacked at all. From what you said, she was expecting Roebuck to attack her, or at least hoping he would. But he didn't. There's nothing strange about that. Even if he had been the man who attacked Leah Irons, he might not necessarily have attacked her. He might have been suspicious. He might have smelt a trap. But the fact is someone else did attack her. So we have three people together in one place on a dark night. Rose Crowne, a. k. a. Annie Jacobs, deliberately allows Martin Roebuck to see her, in order to tempt him into making an incriminating move and while he's following her, along comes *someone else* and murders her

'None of this makes any sense. Until now the question was what was the likelihood of Martin Roebuck being at the scene of a murder so similar to the one that he was accused of doing, even though we knew he wasn't guilty of this one. Now *that* mystery is cleared up, at least to the extent that we know that it was Rose Crowne who sought *him* out and not the other way round. But there's still the mystery of who killed Rose Crowne - and why?'

In her living room, Beth nodded slowly.

'The obvious answer is, the same person who killed Leah Irons. Now that we know that Rose Crowne was Annie Jacobs, maybe this was someone who also knew. Maybe the killer knew who she was and decided to kill her too.'

Neil thought about this theory.

'No, that doesn't make sense. How could the killer have known that she was Annie Jacobs? They kept it secret even after the murder. Only the police knew. And then only the ones involved in the undercover operation.'

'And her parents,' Beth added.

'I'm sure her parents didn't tell anyone.'

'Don't be too sure. It only takes an unguarded word. A boastful remark by a proud mother or father.'

Neil was gripped by a sudden surge of excitement.

'Hey, you're right. Maybe that's it!'

Beth was puzzled.

'What?'

'You said her mother stayed inside. Maybe that's because she felt guilty. Maybe she's the one who let the cat out of the bag.'

'That's a possibility,' Beth acknowledged. 'But there was someone else who knew.'

'Who's that?'

'Rose Crowne herself.'

'If she was in SO10 then she would have known to keep her mouth shut.'

'Yes, but you forget, Neil, she was a bit of a loner. Ordinarily she wouldn't have anyone to talk to outside of work. But maybe she met a man who swept her off her feet and she told him everything.'

Neil snorted down the phone.

'Yes, and this man happened to be the man who killed Leah Irons.'

'He might have said something to someone else, who said something to someone else.'

'It all seems like too much of a coincidence.'

'You're too sceptical, Neil. Remember what that guy said in *Pulp Fiction*: "shit happens".'

'Yes, but as you said, that was fiction.'

'OK, but if it did happen. Let's just say it did. Let's say she met a man whom she really liked and he really did sweep her off her feet. In the heat of passion, she told him all about herself and one of the things she told him was that she was an undercover cop, who tried to get Martin Roebuck to confess. Now let's say that this man, by some incredible coincidence, was the man who really killed Leah Irons. He's amazed when he hears her story. He can't believe his luck. For whatever sick motive drove him to kill Leah Irons, he decides to do the same with Rose Crowne. So he deliberately puts into her head the idea of trapping Roebuck. She's frustrated by the outcome of the earlier case and so she readily goes along with it. He sets her up and then he kills her, making it look like Roebuck, or at least trying to.'

Neil laughed.

'What's so funny?' asked Beth defensively, although she half saw the humour in the absurdity.

'First of all, she wouldn't have taken the risk of an operation like that unless he agreed to be there to help her.'

'But he *was* there! That's why he was able to kill her. He hid in the shadows, killed her and then left the scene, whether by car or on foot.'

'OK, but there are other problems.'

'Like what?'

Neil took a deep breath and started rattling off his objections.

'Like what drives this man in the first place? The kind of man who did these killings is likely to be a man who has trouble forming normal relationships with women. That's one thing that Eckland and Trotter both agree on. Yet here we have a man who somehow manages to sweep a beautiful womanlike Rose Crowne off her feet and get her to fall madly in love with him - to the point of trusting him to cover her back on a dark night as she prepares to confront a killer. And this is a beautiful woman who's been impervious to the charms of other men. So whatever this Romeo looks like, he's sure got a secret I wish I had. And whatever he's got, it's not the sort of thing you'd associate with a dysfunctional man who can't strike up a relationship with women.'

'You could just as easily say that a beautiful woman like Rose Crowne shouldn't have had any trouble catching a man. Yet according to what her father said, that was the case. If an attractive woman could have such problems landing a man then why is it so hard to believe that this otherwise dysfunctional man managed to sweep Rose Crowne off her feet.'

'Because Beth, shit might sometimes happen, but not bullshit.'

'That's uncalled for!'

'I'm sorry, but this theory really doesn't hang together.'

'Have you got a better one?'

'I think my theory about her mother letting the cat out of the bag is more plausible.'

'But that doesn't explain why the killer was there on the night that Roebuck was.'

'Maybe the killer had been stalking her for some time. And now when she went out at night to trap Roebuck into attacking her, that was when the killer finally got his chance.'

'There are holes in that theory too, Neil.'

'Such as?' he asked defensively.

'Let's say her mother said something to the killer, not realizing who he was. First of all, that's also a big coincidence. And if he then said something to someone else, that's an even bigger coincidence.'

'OK, but up to a point, coincidence is possible. As long as it doesn't involve people acting contrary to the norms of human nature.'

'All right, but then how did he track her down?'

'How do you mean?'

'Well . . .' Beth was struggling to express herself clearly. The excitement of these theories and counter theories was getting to her. 'Let's say that a proud mother makes an idle remark to a stranger in a supermarket or something like that. Or maybe even to someone she sees regularly. How does this person get hold of her address or find out where she is in order to follow her? I mean, hell, it took me a long time.'

'Yes, but you did find her, Beth.'

'I had all the wonders of modern technology at my disposal.'

'Wonders of technology that are available for *anyone* with a few pounds at their disposal.'

'All right. You know what, Neil? You may be right. So what do we do now? Go back and try and talk to Mrs Crowne.'

'I don't think that's a good idea Beth.'

'But if she knows something that might help with the investigation maybe we should find out, if only to get her to tell it to the police.'

'That's what I'm saying Beth, she may well have told the police. Just because she didn't speak to you didn't mean she didn't speak to them. If she didn't speak to you it's probably because she already realizes that she may have inadvertently caused her daughter's death. It probably came out when she was being interviewed by the police. These SO10 people aren't stupid. They know to cover every possibility. And that's another thing. I've already had one brush with SO10 and I don't want another. If they find out that I'm looking into this case in any way that goes beyond the requirements of my defence before the "rubber heels" boys, they'll crucify me.'

'I could speak to her on my own. I spoke to Mr Crowne alone.'

'I don't think you'd enjoy being the subject of an SO10 interrogation either.'

'You forget, I have the power of the press behind me.'

'You don't know SO10. They have as much respect for the freedom of the press as the KGB did.'

At Neil's end, the phone clicked and went dead.

What was that?r he wondered. He waited for her to phone back. After two minutes, he phoned her mobile. The phone rang interminably until finally it was answered.

'Hallo--'

'Hi Beth. What happened?

'. . . I am unavailable at the moment. Please leave a message including your name and number and I will return your callas soon as possible.'

Damn thought Neil. Her calls were being diverted to the answering service. What the hell was going on? Why had she cut the phone off like that? Or had it been cut off by some one else? Why hadn't she called back? And why wasn't she answering her calls? Why were they being redirected?The phone must be switched off, he realized. But why had she switched it off? Maybe it was the batteries. But then the sound would have faded gradually. Maybe a fuse had blown or a chip burnt out in the phone. Maybe it was a technical problem with the network. Maybe the relay station had developed a technical fault. But that made no sense. If one relay station broke down, the others were supposed to take over automatically.

He felt a churning heat inside him and a hot flush rushing to his cheeks. Something was wrong. Could she have been surprised by a burglar? Surely not. Burglars didn't usually look for confrontation. They took the line of least resistance. If they heard the sound of a human voice they went away and looked for another place to burgle.

But he knew that this wasn't always true. While the old-fashioned burglar used to steer clear of even the mildest opposition there was a new breed of burglar :the macho burglar. Also known as the burglar rapist. The burglar who liked to lie in wait until the owner returned and then committed acts of gratuitous violence, sometimes including sexual violence.

He remembered Beth saying something about hearing something while they were on the phone. Maybe that's what Beth heard. Maybe the burglar was already in the house?

He felt the gnawing of desperation within him and beads of perspiration on his forehead. He had to do something.

In Beth's flat, a wiry figure clad in black, with a black balaclava covering his face, was holding a knife to Beth's throat. He looked like a Marine except that he was too thin and short. More like a ninja, in fact, especially bearing in mind the stealth with which he had crept up on her. Over his black sweater, he was wearing a photographer's sleeveless jacket, packed with various pieces of equipment.

When she felt the knife at her throat and looked up to seethe figure in black she realized what the clicking had been, the intruder working the latch of the door to get in, probably using the same knife that he now held to her throat. When she saw the figure she had been about to scream but a firm hand had clutched at her mouth, stifling the cry. She had expected to die instantly. Instead the figure had whispered 'turn it off' in her ear in a quiet, almost seductive voice. In a way, the voice had sounded gentle, like the sex attacker who wants his victims to like him and thinks that he is actually giving them what they really want.

She had switched off the phone as ordered and looked at the intruder with terror in her eyes. She couldn't tell what he really looked like but this was no Romeo or Adonis who had swept Rose Crowne off her feet. He looked thin and gangly, and it was hard to imagine this man charming the pants off any woman, let alone a beautiful one. But he was strong - strong enough to hold Beth in an iron grip.

'What do you want?' Beth asked, through her tears of terror.

'I want *him*.'

The voice was deep and rasping, almost a whisper, the sort of voice one might expect from one who has lost their voice from a cold, or some one who didn't want to be heard. Except that he was making no effort to make her talk more quietly.

'Who?'

'Your friend. The one you were talking to.'

'How do you know who I was talking too?' she asked confused and frightened.

He pulled a hand-held scanner from the largest pocket of the photographer's jacket.

'I had all the wonders of modern technology at my disposal.'

The voice was mocking in its confidence.

'If you want *him*, why did you come here?'

She was thinking about Stevie. At least he was safe. But she was wondering if she would ever see him again.

'He'll come here. Now that he knows that you're in danger.'

'How do you know he won't call the police?'

'That's not his style. He likes to do things on his own. Like he's been investigating the Rose Crowne murder on his own. Besides, he doesn't know for certain that anything's happened to you. He's not going to phone the police just to tell them that your call got disconnected and he's worried about you. They'd tell him not to waste their time.'

'You're very sure of yourself.'

'I haven't put a foot wrong yet. Well, almost not.'

'What do you mean?'

'I slipped up once when I tried to get at Roebuck. But I made up for it by sending Neil on a wild goose chase and landing him in it.'

'Was it you. . .'

The mouth of the figure seemed to trace the shape of a smile.'

'Who called your show a few days ago?' the intruder completed the sentence. 'Yes. That was me?'

'And you killed Leah Irons?'

'And Rose Crowne.'

'But you're *not* William Isaacs.'

'No. He spoke to you, too. Surely you compared our voices.'

'How could we? You called at different times.'

'From the tapes. You record everything.'

'Who says?'

'Oh, come on. You don't think I was born yesterday, do you?'

I'm just worrying over nothing, Neil told himself. *It's probably a general problem with the network. Or maybe she just thought the conversation was over.*

Without saying goodbye? No way!

He had to do something. But what? The simple thing was to call the police and let them deal with it. But what could he tell them? That he got cut off while talking to a woman and couldn't get through afterwards? That was hardly grounds for a police visit. He could tell them that he was a policeman himself. But that would only make it worse. They'd tell him he ought to know better. It's not like he'd heard her scream or anything like that. Or heard her being threatened.

He could lie. He could tell them that she *had* screamed. But that would make it worse. What if they went round there and nothing was wrong? Then he'd *really* have some explaining to do.

There was only one thing for it. He'd have to go there himself. But what if it took too long? There was still the danger that it might be a burglar. Then a thought occurred to Neil. If it had been a burglar and he had called back, the burglar would surely try to force her to take the call and say that she was all right. And why would the burglar force her to break the call?

Then another thought occurred to him. Maybe she had broken the call in fear. Maybe the burglar realized that he was now in danger. Maybe she wasn't answering because the burglar had killed her immediately.

No, that couldn't be. He couldn't remember how these things worked. Were the calls switched over to voicemail automatically after a certain number of rings or only if the phone was switched off?

There was only one thing for it. Whether she was alive or not he had to try. He couldn't just sit around doing nothing. And he couldn't in all seriousness ask his colleagues to go there. He'd just have to go there himself.

The intruder had forced her over to a chair and then used nylon tights to tie her up. He seemed to know how to use the tights effectively and Beth wondered if he was a fetishist or into bondage. Under other circumstances the conjecture would have been amusing but in her present predicament Beth knew only one emotion: terror.

'What are you going to do?'

'To *you* nothing.'

'And to Neil?'

'I intend to kill him of course.'

She had sensed this for a while now but she had held onto some faint hope that 'I want him' didn't mean the same thing as 'I want him dead.' Only the realist in her had told her all along that there was no difference in what the intruder wanted. That was why she had put off asking until now: to insulate herself from the knowledge that Neil was probably walking into an ambush. Before the intruder had mentioned Neil, Beth had been concerned for herself, and for what life would have been like for little Stevie without her. But strangely, she felt no better now. There had been no relief when the intruder had told her that her own life was to be spared. And as the tears rolled down her cheeks, she knew what this meant.

Neil turned his car into the street where Beth lived. He had taken the corner in third gear and was about to drive flat-out to the other end of the street to get as near as possible as quickly as possible. But a thought suddenly struck him. He remembered the hospital. He remembered how he had been set up. Someone had played him like a musical instrument and he had rung out at top volume with someone else's notes. It wasn't just a case of dancing to someone else's tune. He had actually played the tune for them.

But he wasn't going to be played a second time. This time around, *he* would call the tune.

He parked the car near the corner and raced down the street on foot. As he got closer to Beth's house he slowed down again. He could probably be seen from the window of the house. If he was being manipulated again, the chances were that the intruder was looking out for him.

I'm being paranoid, he told himself. *There's no reason to suppose that there's anyone in there with her. I'm going to look like a right prat if I storm in there like Batman and tell her that I was worried about her.*

He realized that even if there was something wrong it might not have anything to do with this case. And even the call that got him to go to the hospital might have been a practical joke. It didn't seem likely but it *might* have been. As he got as close to the house as he dared, he took a decision. The houses were semi-detached. He slipped down the side of one of the houses into the back garden. Then he clambered over a tree to jump over the fence into the next garden and then into the next.

'Hey!'

A feisty old woman, sitting in her garden, challenged him from a distance of a few yards. He whipped out his warrant card and identified himself as a policeman, covering his lips with the index finger of his right hand to indicate what he desired. The woman couldn't see the card clearly from where she sat, but she sensed who he was and what he was, and complied with his request. Another leap over another fence took him into the next garden and a few quick strides followed by another leap took him to the next.

He was beginning to get disoriented, not quite sure what number he was at. He tried to remember where he had been when he slipped round the back. Then he counted backwards to regain his bearings. *Three more to go*, the quick calculation told him.

One of the wooden fences didn't have a tree nearby and was too high to leap over. He made a flying kick and knocked a section of it down. There was no alternative. Thirty seconds later, he was in Beth's back garden. He looked in through the lounge windows. They were covered by thin lace curtains and with the bright light outside it was hard to make out anything inside. He thought he saw Beth on a chair, not an armchair but the chair at the writing bureau. Her arms were behind the chair and she appeared to be tied up, and gagged. But there was no one else in the room. Presumably the place had been burgled and she had been left like this but the room seemed too tidy. He had been at the scene of a few burglaries and the places had always been ransacked.

He must have come for something very specific, thought Neil. *Like jewellery.* Jewellery is almost always kept in the bedroom and a clever burglar would know to make his way straight there and look for it in the dressing table or a small box in the bottom of the wardrobe.

There was a small but definite possibility that the burglar was still there. There was also a chance that there was more than one but there was no sign of anyone else in the room. It was safe to act. At any rate, he was not inclined to wait for backup. With a swift kick he forced open the French doors and entered the room.

Beth's head turned and, for a split second, the look in her eyes was one of relief. A second later, it turned to terror as she jerked her head frantically in the direction of the door, trying to signal to him that there was someone else in the house.

The intruder had been standing in the vestibule by the front door, waiting for Neil to arrive, the knife strategically held in his right hand so that he could secrete it behind his back while opening the door with his left. When he heard the crashing sound from the lounge, he knew that he had been outsmarted. He rushed into the living room, knife at the ready, now transferred to his right hand.

Neil saw the black-clad figure charge into the room. This was no burglar he realized. It was the knife that gave it away. This was an assassin. Burglars sometimes carry knives to intimidate people but the coincidence of a knife like this and the case he was involved in were too much. This, he realized, was the same man as the one who had confronted Rose Crowne on a dark night and murdered her... probably the same man who had murdered Leah Irons. This was the man whom the unfairly maligned Martin Roebuck had confronted in the darkness, in defence of the woman who had betrayed him. The intruder held the knife in an underhand grip not the overhand grip for the downward thrust that one saw so often on television and that was relatively easy to defend against. This was the grip of a cool street fighter, holding the knife close to his side so it would be hard for the defender to make a grab at it and all the time ready for that lightening-fast thrust to the abdomen, chest or even face of the intended victim.

There are ways of disarming such an attacker, and Neil had learned them in his police training. Step 'inside the circle', slam the heel of the right hand into the inside forearm of the attacker. Do the same against the attacker's wrist with the left hand then press hard on his bent thumb, squeezing it in until it was bent as far as it would go. The fingers would open. The knife would drop and then with the left hand one grabs the two smaller fingers of the right hand while the right hand grabs the other two. Then a sharp twist and the wrist of the attacker is broken.

It was fine in slow motion. And it looked easy when the instructor did it, always making sure not to twist hard enough to break the wrist. But it was another thing when you had to apply that knowledge on the street. He had been in this kind of situation once before. And he had got it wrong. On that occasion he had left an innocent man in hospital. This time he could be killed, as could the woman he loved.

He froze. He was nearer to Beth than the intruder, but only just. If the attacker took it into his head to leap at Beth and kill her, he could do so with the greatest of ease. Neil knew that he had, at best, a sporting chance of disarming the attacker but he had to do it. He had no backup upon which to call. As in his dream, when his father's face intruded, he had to do it alone.

He reached into his pocket and pulled out his CS spray canister, holding it up behind him in his right hand while holding his left arm extended, fingers upward, palm towards the intruder.

'Drop the knife!' he shouted.

The intruder's eyes narrowed. This was fear, Neil realized. He had re-taken the initiative. The intruder had been caught napping twice now. He had not expected Neil to come in through the back. And he had not realized that Neil had the CS spray canister with him.

'I know your weak spot, Douglas,' the intruder rasped. 'And I can go for it any time I like.'

For a few seconds, the intruder appeared to be dithering, trying to make up his mind whether or not to chance it. All the while, Neil was inching towards Beth, making her safer by closing the gap and forcing the intruder to edge cautiously back. Then, as suddenly as he had charged into the room, the intruder's nerve broke.

'Another time, Douglas. We'll settle this another time.'

And with that he turned and ran from the room. Neil sprinted after him, making sure that he had left the flat. He considered chasing him up the street, but decided not to. A considerable gap had opened up and the attacker was fas ton his feet. Chasing a man with a knife through the streets could endanger others. Better to let him go for now.

217

He went back to untie Beth.

Chapter 17

'He said he killed both Rose Crowne *and* Leah Irons.'

'Did he give any of the details of the murders?'

'No.'

'Did you ask him?'

'No.'

The male SO10 officer was in his late thirties, the female probably a few years younger. They were questioning Beth in her own home, a common tactic for taking witness statements. People often found easier to remember events *in situ* rather than in the foreign atmosphere of a police station. They might take her down to the station later to look at pictures of suspects, but initially they wanted to question her here, amid the surroundings where she had confronted the intruder, in the hope of extracting from her every last detail of recollection. They also had a laptop computer to do a photofit, but as she hadn't seen the suspect's face, they wouldn't be using it.

'You didn't ask him *anything*?'

'Look, I'm sorry! I was frightened. I thought he was going to kill me.'

'But I thought you said you didn't think he was going to kill you.'

The SO10 detective was staring at her with uncompromising eyes that radiated scepticism. He was more used to interrogating suspects than witnesses, and the scepticism was part of his manner. He knew that real life witnesses were often confused even about physical events, let alone about their thoughts at the time of the events.

'I thought he was going to kill. . .'

She trailed off, reluctant to continue the sentence. '*Who* did you think he was going to kill?'

It was as if he already knew.

'Neil,' she almost mouthed.

'Neil Douglas?'

'Yes.'

'You thought he was going to kill Neil Douglas.'

'Yes!' she shrieked.

'Why do you think he was going to kill Neil?'

'He said so.'

'He *said* he was going to kill Neil?'

'Not in so many words. I mean yes. He did eventually.'

'What exactly did he say.'

'I want *him*.'

'Why did you understand it that way, rather than . . . say, sexually.'

'You think he had some homosexual fixation on Neil?'

'Such things are not unknown,' said the interrogator.

'He was holding a knife. He confronted me with a knife and *threatened* me. I asked him what he wanted. In context, that meant I was asking him what he was going to do with me. He replied; "I want *him*. " In context that meant he was saying "I don't intend kill you; I intend to kill *him*. "'

'You seem to be reading quite a lot into one brief statement.'

'The subsequent statements and actions bore it out.'

'What statements? What actions?'

'I told him that Neil wouldn't come. He said he would, now that he knew I was in danger.'

'How did he know that?'

'Because of the call being cut off. At least that's what he thought. I wasn't so sure. But he turned out to be right. Eventually he did say he was going to kill Neil.'

'And the actions?'

'What?'

'What did you mean about it being borne out by his actions.'

'He tied me up, to a chair, and then went to the front door with the knife. He was waiting to ambush Neil.'

'That didn't mean it was to kill him.'

'What do you think he was planning to do? Rape him at knife point?'

'He might have been planning to kill you and make it look like Neil. He could have been waiting to time your death to coincide with Neil's arrival.'

Beth opened her mouth to speak, but then stopped. This could have been precisely what he was planning. Maybe he meant not to kill Neil but to frame him for murder. This whole saga was a series of errors in which people had got blamed for the actions of others. Roebuck had been accused falsely of murdering Leah Irons. Then Neil had mistaken him for the man who attacked Rose Crowne. Maybe the next stage of the real murderer's plan was to kill Beth and then make it look as though Neil had. If the killer had killed Beth just as Neil arrived and then slipped out at the back, anything Neil had done might have incriminated him. If he'd called the police, he would have had to explain why she was killed just before his arrival. If he'd run, then people in the street might have seen him and identified him. If the medical officer arrived on the scene quickly, they could probably determine the time of death with a high degree of accuracy by body temperature, lividity and lack of rigor mortis. Then Neil would have had to explain why the killer didn't kill her when he first cut off the call. Why wait for Neil to arrive? They would have a record of the call and they might conclude that the subject of the call had Keenan argument. Neil had come storming round - as he was supposed to do - and then Beth was killed. He might beat the rap, but it would be an uncomfortable situation and he would certainly be the prime suspect until the charges were either pressed or dropped.

'I suppose that could have been his game. But I thought at the time he was planning to kill Neil. At any rate, Neil pre-empted him by coming round the back. And if he'd wanted to kill me he could have done. It would have been a risk with Neil's CS gas canister at the ready, but he had a sporting chance.'

'Then I guess it's lucky for you that he didn't take it.'

'So you carried on investigating this case behind our backs?'

'Yes.'

They were questioning Neil in the kitchen. There were two of them. The older one, about fortyish, was seated opposite him at the kitchen table. The younger one, in his late twenties, was standing by the fridge.

'You know the "rubber heels" boys could get you for that? Conducting an unauthorized investigation is almost as big a no-no as getting photographed beating up a scrote. You could get kicked off the force for it.'

'I know.'

'You told them that you were just looking for evidence to clear your name before the disciplinary hearing didn't you?'

'How did you know that?'

'Tadditt told us.'

'Horace Tadditt?'

'Yes, Neil! *Horace* Tadditt. Did you really think he wouldn't? He's quite in with the Home Secretary and he's been most co-operative with us.'

'Has he now?'

'You really do like playing with fire, don't you, Neil?'

'I had to know. I had to find out.'

'This isn't your investigation. Hell Neil, you're not even CID.'

'I had to find out,' he mumbled.

'Why? What's it to you? Rose Crowne isn't the first victim you've come across in the course of your police work. And if you manage to avoid getting yourself kicked off the force, she won't be the last.'

'It's not Rose Crowne, it's. . .'

'It's who?'

He breathed deeply in, out, in, out.

'It's Martin Roebuck.'

'Oh yes, the man you left lying in the gutter. The man who's got you feeling so guilty you're no longer thinking like a copper anymore.'

'*Yes, Martin fuckin' Roebuck!* The man I put in hospital because I couldn't keep my temper.'

'I didn't hear that, Neil.'

'I said, because I could keep my-'

'I said, I didn't hear that Neil!'

The anger silenced Neil and a tense hush descended on them as he realized that in spite of the harshness of the interrogation, they were still on his side. It was a while before he spoke again.

'Why are you so sure that Horace Tadditt was being cooperative with you?'

The interrogators exchanged quick glances, as if surprised by Neil taking the initiative.

'What do you mean?'

'Just because he told you about me doesn't mean he's cooperative, does it? I mean, it sounds more like he's trying to direct attention away from himself. I wouldn't be surprised if *he* was the man who drove away that night.'

A voice came from the other side.

'He *was*.'

Neil looked round at the second interrogator, stunned by the revelation.

'How . . . how do you know?'

By now Neil was gasping.

'He told us,' said the first interrogator.

'He... he killed her?'

'*No*, Neil, he didn't kill her. But he was there. He was attending to some . . . parliamentary business, or maybe I should say extra-parliamentary business. At any rate, he was just leaving when it happened.'

'He saw it?'

'No, Neil, he didn't see it. But he saw a police car arriving. Saw *you* in fact - *probably* saw you at any rate. And he thought it imprudent to remain there. He didn't witness the attack on Rose Crowne. He'd been meeting with someone at the Old Bull and Bush. The details needn't concern you, but suffice it to say that he was just stepping out of the pub when you arrived. He saw people at their windows shouting to you and Nick Lloyd, saw you running onto the Heath and knew that something was up. The events didn't concern him as far as he knew and he was afraid that if you started taking names and addresses of witnesses he'd have to explain what he was doing in that area and it would all end up in the tabloids. So he buggered off while he could.'

'And yet he told you everything.'

'Once we confronted him, he knew that it was better not to lie to us. He knew that we'd be discreet.'

'But you're telling *me*.'

The interrogator smiled at this amusingly compromising statement.

'Yes, Neil. We're telling you. And *you're* going to be discreet too. We're telling you because you seem impervious to normal threats like loss of your career and public disgrace. So we're telling you: *stay the fuck away from our investigation!* We don't need cowboys going blue on blue with us when we're trying to catch a murderer.'

223

'But if it was Tadditt in the car and if it wasn't Tadditt who killed Rose Crowne and if he didn't see who did, then you haven't got any leads to follow.'

'Maybe yes, maybe no. But it isn't your business.'

Neil lowered his head and looked down at the kitchen table regretfully.

'I just want to see the bastard caught. I just want to see that scum-bag who slashed Rose Crowne to pieces banged up for life.'

The interrogator's tone dropped an octave and became warmer, more comforting.

'So do we all, Neil. But there's nothing you can do. You're a good copper and you've still got ideals, which is more than some of us cynical old-timers have. But leave this one to us. It's our case and we're in a better position to solve it than you.'

'Is that why Martin Roebuck's so important?'

'What?' asked the main interrogator.

'Is that why you're guarding Roebuck so tightly? Why you shifted him from the Royal Free to University College? Why you still have uniformed guards at the Royal Free and only plain clothes people at UCH? Because he's the only lead you've got? Because he's the only witness who might be able to ID the killer?'

'Well, now we've got you and Beth, haven't we?'

'Yes. But he was wearing a mask.'

'You might still be able to finger him by height and build.'

'I don't think so.'

'Maybe Beth might. Women are usually more perceptive than men.'

'Maybe. But until now Roebuck *was* your only lead, wasn't he?'

The SO10 man nodded.

'So that's why you had to guard him so carefully. In case the killer made a move to silence him.'

'The killer *did* make a move. At least, we think so.'

'You mean, getting me to go to the hospital that day?'

'It might have been?'

'I thought that was someone's idea of a practical joke.'

'We haven't ruled that out either, Neil. But it *could* have been a trick to get you to go there to find the trail back to where Roebuck was being kept.'

224

'I don't understand. How would the killer know that Roebuck wasn't at the Royal Free.'

'Because there was an earlier attempt.'

'Earlier attempt? What? To kill Roebuck?'

'We don't know.'

'Then how do you know there was an earlier attempt?'

'Someone went to the hospital, disguised as a patient and managed to slip a mickey to our uniformed man on the door to the private room.'

'So what happened then?' asked Neil.

The SO10 officers said nothing.

'Did he get him?' Roebuck persisted.

The SO10 officers exchanged a quick glance. By now Neil was frantic.

'Is Roebuck dead?'

He had always held out the hope that Roebuck would recover, that the damage done by Neil's brief moment of anger would not be irrevocable. But now the thing that he dreaded most had happened.

'He's still alive,' said the chief interrogator. 'We'd already moved him to UCH by then. He's even showing the first signs of coming out of the coma.'

Neil breathed again.

'So they had you scared shitless and then they calmed you down.'

'That's what they do, Beth. That's the way they operate.'

They were sitting together in the living room, drinking coffee. They hadn't had much time to talk about it until now. As soon as the SO10 people left, they had picked up Stevie together and Neil had had to play Power Rangers with him the whole evening. 'It's called singing for your supper,' said Beth as she left them together and made her way to the kitchen.

It had been like an ordinary family evening together. To Stevie, Neil was already like a daddy. He had taken to him quite naturally, and Neil felt as if he had known them all his life. It surprised him to realize how comfortable he felt in Beth's home, pretending to be a kid again as he played with Stevie, helping Beth clear the table and wash up the plates after the meal. Only a couple of weeks earlier he had been a pariah in the minds of her listeners and Beth had been the bitch who was leading the sniping at him. Now he was part of her household.

He had been adopted by Stevie and forgiven by Beth. It was a warm, comforting feeling. And he needed all the comfort he could get. Tomorrow was the inquest for Rose Crowne and he was still agonizing over what he was going to do. He had received a subpoena and he had to attend, but no one could force him to speak. He could avail himself of the right to remain silent, but then he'd only become a pariah once again. Or he could testify.

If he testified, he faced another choice: should he tell the truth or should he lie? He had thought about this before and it was no easier now as he considered who might be hurt by each course of action. Did it make a difference to Roebuck? Everyone knew he was innocent. At most, it might affect the amount he could get in damages. A truthful admission from Neil that he had been motivated by anger rather than fear for his safety would land the police with a bill for punitive damages. If he lied, and said that he really thought he was in danger, Roebuck might still get compensatory damages but nothing more. So a lie would hurt Roebuck more. And Neil had already hurt him more than enough.

But the dilemma hadn't changed since three weeks ago. The truth would hurt others too. Nick had already said at the 'rubber heels' hearing that it looked as if Roebuck was about to hit him with the branch of the tree. If Neil now contradicted this it would amount to accusing Nick of lying, which could have a seriously damaging effect on Nick's career. It would be easy enough to go all pious and pompous and say that Nick shouldn't have lied and that he deserved it. But that would be a pretty ungrateful response for what he had done. Nick had stuck his neck out to save Neil's career, and if Neil told the truth now he would be threatening Nick's career as well as jeopardizing his own. This was the dilemma that he had faced before the internal disciplinary review hearing and it was the same problem now.

To hurt Roebuck or to hurt Nick. He owed nothing to Roebuck; he owed a lot to his partner. On the other hand Roebuck was already a victim. Nick was not. And Roebuck had done no wrong. Both he and Nick had. He for not controlling his temper and Nick for lying about it afterwards. Could he penalize Roebuck further for his misdeeds and the lesser misdeeds of his partner? Could he afford not to? Perhaps that's why it would be better to remain silent. Then the stark choice between telling the truth and lying could be avoided. The choice only presented itself if he chose to speak. If he chose not to, it would be other people who bore responsibility for the outcome.

'Earth to Neil. Earth to Neil. Come in, Neil.'

He became aware of Beth's voice. He looked round to see her smiling at him comfortingly.

'I'm sorry,' he said, embarrassed. 'I was just thinking about something.'

'Welcome back to civilization. I was beginning to wonder if you were Neil Douglas or Neil Armstrong.'

'Cute,' he said, imitating her American accent mockingly.

'Let's go to bed.'

'I'm not tired.'

'Who said anything about being tired?'

He lay in the bed awake, looking at the ceiling and thinking about tomorrow. It had been good, the feel of Beth's body under him. But now he was alone in the darkness. He could hear her breathing and he knew she was still with him. And yet he was alone. He looked down at her. She looked so peaceful, so happy. There was a smile on her face as she turned and her hand reached down to touch him. Even in her sleep she was aware of him, and she too wanted the reassurance of his presence.

He turned his back on her, not out of disinterest but just to get more comfortable. A second or two later he felt her stirring as she wriggled closer and fitted around him, like two spoons in a kitchen drawer.

'Mmmm. How was it for you?' she said in a long drawn-out yawn. She was still asleep . . . half asleep. But she wanted him as badly as he wanted her.

'What?' asked Neil.

'Was it good for you too?'

She was smiling in her twilight sleep, as if aware of the humour in the question.

'Yes.'

'Get to sleep,' she said softly.

That was the mother in her speaking, thought Neil. *Even in her sleep, she was alert to the problems of others around her. Even in her sleep, she felt the pain of others and offered comfort and sympathy. Just as a mother can often hear her baby stirring before it cries, so she could feel Neil's tension and discomfort even though he thought he had kept it to himself.*

And she was offering him a mother's shoulder to cry on.

It was ironic. She had just been through the shock of her life - the shock of being held at knife-point by a killer and looking death in the eye - and yet she was offering him support and he was the one who was agonizing.

Who says women are the weaker sex, he thought. He remembered his mother's exemplary courage as she wasted away, years ago. Not that his father had lacked courage when he faced danger on the streets, but his mother's capacity to look death in the face and offer comfort and support to those around her had stayed with him ever since. And Beth, whom he had once thought of as nothing but a selfish bitch, had now shown herself to be a warm, loving person blessed with both a woman's gentleness and a woman's strength.

He knew in that moment that this was the woman with whom he would spend the rest of his life . . . if she would have him.

But there was something else nagging at his mind, apart from the inquest hearing tomorrow - something that theSO10 people had said. He couldn't remember what it was but it had something to do with the killer . . . or with Roebuck.

They told him that they thought the killer had already tried to get Roebuck once, but that he had gone to the wrong hospital. Neil had managed to find the right hospital, thanks to a careless slip-up by one of the nurses at the Royal Free. Could it be that someone had also made an unguarded statement to the killer too?

No, that wasn't the problem. According to what the SO10people had told him, the killer didn't speak to anyone apart from the policeman at the door to the private room.

But Neil had gone from the Royal Free to University College. He had been sent there on a wild-goose chase Maybe he had been followed. If so, then Roebuck was still in danger.

He tried to dismiss the thought. Roebuck was well-guarded. Those SO10 people knew what they were doing. They probably had security pictures from the Royal Free and maybe even knew already what the killer looked like. They wouldn't tell him that. And anyway, if the killer was going to make a move on Roebuck, he would have done it by now. But he hadn't. Instead he had gone after Beth and him.

That made no sense. Why would the killer go after either of them? *They* couldn't identify the killer.

But that assumed that the killer was acting rationally. There was nothing rational in the murders of Leah Irons and Rose Crowne. They were the actions of someone with a sick mind, motivated by anger or revenge or sexual perversion. The man who committed such murders could not be expected to act rationally. Neil could easily imagine the murderer killing him just for the sheer sick fun of it. Or killing Beth and fitting him up as the SO10 people had suggested to Beth.

But now that his immediate plan was thwarted, how would he act? He still had his murderous desires. What would be more natural for such a person than to kill someone else?And why seek out a new victim when he already had one?He had tried to kill Roebuck once. The SO10 people were clear about that. And he had been poised to kill today. How would he take the frustration?

Neil was not a criminal psychologist. He was no Peter Eckland, let alone a Jonathan Trotter, and couldn't compete with the PhDs in specialist knowledge or credibility. But he knew that when people were thwarted in one endeavour, they often go on to indulge in another similar one. The boy who gets blown out by a girl, ending up going out alone to see the movie he was going to take her to, or - if he has less control of his anti-social impulses - raping or indecently assaulting another girl to make up for his frustration. The girl who gets blown out by a guy indulging in an evening of gluttony to make-up for unrequited lust. Cliche's perhaps. But *in cliché veritas*, to coin a phrase.

He tried to get inside the killer's mind. The adrenalin was flowing, the heart was pumping. The smell of death and the taste of blood were there. It was just begging for an outlet. It could be another woman on another dark road. But there was an obvious victim staring him in the face.

Beth had told him the SO10 people's theory about the killer planning to kill her and put him in the frame. That sounded

229

plausible enough. It was consistent with what the killer himself had said: 'I know your weak spot, Douglas and I can go for it any time I like.'

At first he thought that this simply meant his predictability, his almost Pavlovian responses to the killer's stimuli. Then he thought it meant his feelings towards Beth. But now he realized there was another thing the killer might have meant: his guilt over what he had done to Roebuck, and his passionate desire that Roebuck should survive.

That was his weak spot. Neil was a man with a conscience and he would never forgive himself if Roebuck died as a result of his actions. But there was no way that the killer could know this. It was something that he barely confided to anyone, and certainly to no one other than Beth and a handful of police colleagues. Yet the killer *did* seem to know a lot about him. Certainly he knew how Neil would act when Beth appeared to be in danger.

And he knew enough to know that Neil would go running to the hospital at the first sign that Roebuck was coming out of the coma.

If he knew that, then he knew that the best way to get at Neil, apart from killing Beth, was to kill Roebuck.

And if he still had the murderous desire, unrequited and unfulfilled then there was only one place for him to go to fulfil it . . . only one person for him to kill.

Neil leapt out of bed and grabbed his trousers from the chair.

'What's the matter?' asked Beth. She sat bold upright. Neil was getting dressed with frenetic haste.

'I have to get to the hospital.'

'What hospital?'

'University College.'

'Why?' she asked, rubbing her bleary eyes.

'It's Roebuck. I think he's in danger!'

Chapter 18

Like at the Royal Free, it had been easy enough to pose as a patient. You put on a hospital robe, put your street clothes in an opaque carrier bag and looked as if you belong there and you could walk around without any questions being asked. If you looked like a visitor you were liable to be challenged at certain times or in certain circumstances. As a patient you just blended in.

Of course, they normally gave night sedation at ten-thirty. And that meant that any patient wandering around at midnight would attract attention. But that would only be attention from the nursing staff. The police probably wouldn't realize. So they wouldn't think anything of it.

But the man who sat outside the private room had gone to the toilet and had left the room unguarded. Presumably he thought that it was safe to do so as members of the public were not admitted to this part of the hospital at this time but he had overlooked the possibility that the source of danger was already inside the portals. One could get in at any time up to the end of visiting time and then hide in a toilet. People wouldn't be suspicious because no one ordinarily would stay long enough in the toilet to realize that another person had been in there a long time. And it was easy enough to read a book to pass the time. Of course, muscle cramp could be a bit of a problem, as could pins and needles. But a few seconds' standing after every line break and a few minutes at the end of every chapter dealt with these problems easily enough.

The method of killing Roebuck was crucial because it had to be done without alerting the nursing station. As Roebuck was still on a life-support system any interruption in his vital signs would automatically sound an alert and this was a problem. In the original attempt, the plan had been to connect the EEG, ECG and blood pressure sensors to the policeman, relying on the fact that a brief break in any one on its own would not trigger an alarm.

However, it had never been a very good scheme, even at the time and contained too many risks. Sooner or later, it would become obvious that Roebuck was dead. The important thing was to guard against two dangers. The first was being caught if the staff rushed in upon hearing the alarm. The other was that they would realize what was going wrong in time to take remedial action, which meant that by the time the alarm went off Roebuck would have to be well on his way to death and the cause would have to be not too obvious.

The obvious idea was poison or an overdose of a sleeping drug and the best method of administration was in his saline drip.

So now the killer was snapping off the cap from a syringe and plunging it into the plastic bag containing the saline drip. They probably wouldn't notice the puncture mark, even when the bag was changed. The plunger was pressed and the liquid from the syringe began flowing through the hollow needle into the saline fluid.

'You can't go in there!' said a man's voice from beyond the door, in a firm, authoritative tone.

On hearing these words, the killer froze in panic.

'Look, I think that Martin Roebuck's life is in danger. I'm a policeman too. Some of your colleagues know me. My name is Neil Douglas.'

'Oh yes. They told me about you. You're the guy who came here once before?'

The guard outside was confrontational

'That's right. I suppose they told you that I'm harmless.'

'Actually, they told me you were stupid. Anyway, you should know the procedure by now. I'll have to radio through to my supervisor.'

'Are you the only one here?'

'No. We've got people around. I'll call them.'

'In the meantime, do you mind if I check up on Roebuck.'

'I can't let you go in there. It's doctors, nurses and SO10people only.'

'Then you go and check!'

'What makes you so sure he's in danger?'

'The killer told me.'

'What are you talking about.'

'Look, I haven't got time to explain,' said Neil, pushing past the SO10 officer and charging into the room.

The officer turned and dived in after him, prepared to tackle him to the ground and hold him there until back-up arrived. But he froze at what he saw.

The slide-up window was open. It wasn't supposed to be. *And it could only be opened from the inside.* The cop was about to react. But Neil was quicker. In a fraction of a second Neil was at the window leaning out. They were only one floor up and a fit person could easily make the jump. . . or a *desperate* person. Still leaning out, he turned one way and then the other, craning his neck. He saw a figure in a patient's robe, holding a plastic carrier bag, disappear just beyond view.

Realizing that it was his 'call,' as Nick had told him in the dream, he clambered onto the window ledge and jumped out. He too was a desperate man, and a fit one. He sprinted after the fleeting figure. For a second he considered calling out, in the hope of frightening the figure into looking back and slowing down or even freezing altogether, but he realized that this would merely alert his quarry to the fact that he was in hot pursuit and undermine his advantage. At the moment, there was the prospect that the killer would get tired and slow down when he thought he was out of the woods. If he knew that there was a policeman on his tail then he would get that extra adrenalin rush.

He watched while the killer took a turn and ran into University Street. Seconds later, he was in the same street, but saw no sign of the killer. It was impossible for the killer to have traversed the entire street in this time and he couldn't have gone into the pub because it was closing and the entire flow of people through its doors was in the outward direction.

'Did you see anyone run this way?' he asked the punters.

'You mean that Nick in the hospital thingie?' asked a man with red hair, apparently slightly intoxicated.

'Yes.'

'He ran in there.'

He pointed to a back entrance to a building just ahead of them. Neil ran the twenty or so yards up to the entrance and dived in. It was the emergency exit of a block of service flats on the corner of University Street and Tottenham Court Road. Once inside, Neil ran down a dank, dark corridor and up the stone stairs to the ground floor. But from here he didn't know where to go?

Had the killer gone out the front entrance and left, or was he still in the building?

He could not have gone out the front, Neil reasoned, because then he would have been visible to Neil as he ran up the street. So he must have entered the building. But where had he gone? Did he live there? Did he have access to a flat there? Or was he simply hiding? If he was hiding, how did he propose to leave?

What Neil didn't know was that the killer had ducked into the building for one reason, and one reason only: to change back into street clothes that would attract less attention. And while Neil agonized over where the killer might be hiding or what the killer might be doing, the killer was six flights up, changing into a pair of jeans, and a baggy shirt. The cold stone staircase by the lift was hardly ever used and although easily accessible was in practice designed mainly for emergencies. Hardly anyone ever went there. It was rather eerie and frightening, not at all inviting for the residents, although not actually unsafe.

There was one other item in the bag: a hunting knife and leather sheath with a shoulder holster. This went under the shirt, under the left armpit, easily accessible should it be needed.

The hospital robe went into the bag, the bag was left on the stairs and the killer swung open the door that led to the corridor between the flats, by the lifts. The building was old, carpeted and smelly, like a relic from the past, but the killer had no time to think about this. There was just one thing to do. Get the hell out of there. A single pair of up-down buttons would call whichever lift was moving in the right direction.

While this was going on, Neil was opening the door that led into the main entrance area. The commissionaire's office was to his left and the two small lifts to the right. He took three steps to the commissionaire's office, where the door was open.

'Excuse me,' he said, flashing his warrant card.

'Yes?'

'Did you see anyone run out this way in a hospital robe just now.'

'No.'

The commissionaire did not seem altogether surprised by this question. Neil assumed he knew why. The hospital was nearby and it did house patients certified under the Mental Health Act. There were presumably occasional incidents in the street nearby and as such it was not a completely off-the-wall question.

'How many exits are there here?'

'Just two. The front one here and the emergency exit where you came in.'

'How do you know I came in the back?'

'I saw you.'

He pointed to the small closed circuit TV monitor on which he could see the back entrance.

'Did you call the police?'

'Not yet. I was just about to. I assumed you were someone from the hospital.'

'Call them now. In fact, call this number.' He scribbled down a number that the SO10 officer had given him at the hospital. Tell them that PC Neil Douglas requests backup at Paramount Court.'

'OK.'

'There's something else you can do.'

'Yes.'

'Keep an eye open for a man trying to leave the building in a hospital robe. He might use the lift.'

'Where are you going?'

'I'm going up by the stairs. I'll just keep going and checking out the corridors of each floor. If he tries to make a runner, can you lock those doors over there electronically?'

'I can switch off the power to them. But that wouldn't stop him opening them manually.'

'Do you think you're up to a rough-house scrap?'

'How big is this chap?'

'Shorter than me,' said Neil. 'And he's thin and wiry.'

'I think I can give it a go,' said the commissionaire. He looked about sixty, but was quite tall and broad-shouldered and by his upright posture and self-confident look could well have been ex-military.

'There's a possibility that he might have a knife,' Neil added.

'I'll use my discretion, sir,' he said.

Neil nodded and ran off up the stairs.

Less than a minute later, the lift doors opened and three people got out: a man and woman elegantly dressed for an evening out and a man on his own in a pair of jeans and a baggy shirt. None of them had a carrier bag. The commissionaire didn't recognize the man in jeans, but he could have been a guest of one of the residents in this complex of over a hundred flats. He might be able to challenge someone on the way in, if they were trying to slip in behind others instead of entering with the key or being buzzed in from one of the flats, but he couldn't very well challenge someone on his way out just because he didn't know him. Besides, he was looking for a man in a hospital robe, not a man in a shirt and jeans.

He watched with idle curiosity as the threesome left the building and turned right. They didn't appear to be together, but they all walked towards Tottenham Court Road, only a few yards away.

Neil was taking the steps two at a time and checking each floor but it wasn't enough just to poke his head out at each floor. He also had to go round the lifts and look down the length of a long corridor, because the flats were arranged on either side of two corridors forming an L intersection by the lifts. He also had to remain alert to the possibility of being ambushed as he pushed open the doors from the stairs and stepped out into the corridor intersection. He knew that this was a killer who used a knife and although there was no sign of a knife wound on Roebuck at the hospital, it could simply have been that the killer was disturbed before he had had the chance to make his move. At any rate, the danger was there and Neil had already seen how dangerous the killer could be. He knew that he had to exercise caution- all the more so as his backup hadn't yet arrived.

By the time he arrived at the fifth floor, Neil was exhausted but he had to press on. It was as he reached the landing of the sixth floor that he got the shock of his life. There was the carrier bag. He pulled out its contents and saw the hospital robe.

Damn!

He realized immediately what had happened. Once changed, the killer must have gone down again. There was virtually no possibility that he had stayed in the building or lived here. If so, he would not have left the bag on the landing.

Then Neil thought again. There *was* the possibility that he *did* live here and that he left the bag deliberately to make it look as if he has then left the building. But Neil dismissed this immediately. Roebuck had been moved to University College Hospital for security reasons. What was the likelihood that the killer just happened to live near the hospital that he was transferred to? The killings of both Leah Irons and Rose Crowne had taken place on Hampstead Heath. The killer obviously lived in that area. No, the only reason the killer had come here had been to change quickly. That was clear now. That was why he had entered via the emergency exit which by law had to remain open. He couldn't get in via the front because he didn't have the key and didn't know anyone in the building who would let him in. People in buildings like this tended to be very security-conscious. Many of them were old and all of them had been warned not to let people into the building unless they knew them.

So the killer had given him the slip. Neil couldn't bring himself to admit it. Still, Neil wondered, *how much of ahead start did he have?* It couldn't have been much. He had covered the stairs and the commissionaire had covered the lifts. The commissionaire might not recognize him in street clothes but no one left either by lift or by the stairs while they were talking. He could not have left until Neil started up the stairs. That meant only a few minutes.

Neil knew what he had to do. He ran in and pressed the button to call the lift. It seemed like an eternity. He considered running down the stairs instead, but he realized that these were fast lifts and once this one arrived it would be a very rapid descent, as long as no one called it on the way.

He leapt in when it arrived and slammed his fist against the button for the ground floor. He almost cursed the old man who entered on the third floor, stopping the lift's rapid descent to the ground. But he held back. It wasn't the fault of someone else if he had made the wrong decision about waiting for the lift. When the doors opened, Neil leaped out, not giving any signal to the old man who had almost cowered in a corner of the lift in response to the implacable look on his face.

'He changed clothes,' said Neil frantically. 'Did you see anyone?'

'Three people. A couple and a man on his own.'

237

'How long ago?'

'About three or four minutes.'

Damn! Neil thought. He'd never catch him now.

'What did the man look like?'

'He was wearing blue jeans and a dark shirt.'

'Can you remember the colour?'

'I think it was a darkish blue - and it might have had white stripes. And it was kind of baggy. He was wearing it over his jeans. I mean, it wasn't tucked in.'

'Which way did he go?'

'Right. Tottenham Court Road.'

That would be a nightmare, thought Neil. This was the heart of the West End and the street would be crowded at this time. At the intersection, he could have gone left towards Euston Road or right up the length of the road. Neil ran out to the intersection. He looked both ways but there was no sign of anyone matching the commissionaire's description. Then again, he didn't expect there to be. It was too long. He'd be lost in the crowds by now. And he couldn't even be sure which way. Then he had an idea. He walked a few steps in the direction of Hampstead Road and saw, on his right, a 'gentleman's' club. There was a door attendant at the front.

Neil flashed his warrant card as he walked up to him.

'Excuse me, did you see a man in jeans and a blue baggy shirt with white stripes walking this way?'

'Not walking. Running.'

'Which way.'

'That way,' said the door attendant, pointing towards Euston Road. 'He seemed like he was afraid of something, kept looking back.'

'Did you see where he went?'

'Yes, I was watching him. He crossed the road. At first I thought he was going to McDonald's but I think he could have been heading for the station.'

The station in question was Warren Street underground station on the Northern and Victoria lines.

'Thanks,' said Neil, sprinting off in that direction.

He didn't wait for the traffic lights. As soon as he saw a break in the traffic he sprinted diagonally across the road. The food shops on either side of the road were closed, but although this was the northern end of Tottenham Court Road, it was still crowded. There were people at bus stops, people begging, people going in and out of the Grafton Hotel. Even the Euston Tower still had a few lights on, although he assumed that it was the cleaners as the building had been abandoned by Capital Radio and the government offices wouldn't have been working this late. He sprinted past McDonald's and into Warren Street station.

Now what? he wondered. There were ticket machines and the ticket office was open but who could tell him where he had gone? There was the Northern line and the Victoria line, and each had both northbound and southbound routes.

He turned right and strode quickly to the ticket office, flashing his warrant card at the irate customers as he pushed to the front of the queue.

'I'm a policeman,' he said to the man behind the counter. 'Did you see a man in a baggy blue shirt with white stripes come this way?'

The man behind the counter smiled blankly.

'I see so many people here, I don't remember their faces as long as they behave themselves.'

'It would have been only about three or four minutes ago. He might have been a bit agitated.'

'Maybe he bought a ticket from one of the machines.'

'They're not giving change at the moment,' said Neil. 'He would probably have come here.'

'There was someone who looked like he was in a bit of a hurry. I remember now. He asked if the last train to Edgware had gone yet.'

'So he went to Edgware?'

'No, he bought a ticket to Golders Green.'

'OK, thanks.'

And with that Neil vaulted over one of the barrier machines and sprinted down the long down escalator, pushing people aside if they stood on the left side instead of walking down as they were supposed to on that side. At the foot of the escalator she ran round to the right, ignoring the Victoria line entrance ahead of him, and down a second, shorter escalator. Then he came to staircase to the left and a straight path to the right. A quick glance at the map showed him that the steps led down to the northbound branch, and a rumbling sound told him that a train was arriving. He sprinted down the steps, just in time to avoid coming up against the wall of customers who insisted on using the entrance as an exit.

He looked left and right, searching desperately for a sign of the killer. Not seeing him, he looked up at the dot-matrix indicator. It said High Barnet, the wrong destination. If he wanted Golders Green he needed the Edgware branch. But if this was the last train, then it meant that the customers would have to take it and change at Camden Town. A couple of people remained on the platform, suggesting that this was *not* the last train, but no one matching the commissionaire's description was among them. That in turn suggested that the killer was already on the train, or that he had caught the train in front. Neil looked around frantically, desperate for any sign of the killer.

Suddenly, just as the pumping pneumatic sound of the doors closing Rose audibly, a man emerged from the exit passage, barged past the customers and jumped onto the train. The doors closed, and Neil knew that the killer was on the train. He was not about to give up now. He pushed past the last of the departing customers and banged on the doors, one carriage down from the one where the killer had taken refuge. The Northern Line still had two-person operated trains, but the noise failed to attract the attention of the guard at the rear, whose job it was to operate the doors. Neil waved at him, but the guard merely looked at him intolerantly as if he were at best a troublesome customer and at worst a maniac.

The train started to move and Neil's desperate and frantic gesticulating to the guard as he looked out through his open door left the guard cold and implacable. Neil realized as the rear carriage drew close that he couldn't blame the guard. There was no way he could have known that Neil was a policeman. Nor could he have known that there was a dangerous murderer on the train but Neil knew that having come this close, he couldn't let the murderer slip through his grasp. He had a score to settle.

The rear car came running by and Neil saw the guard leaning in to close his door as the last carriage was about to leave the station. In the fury of desperation, he realized what he had to do. Stooping low in preparation he lurched forward and leapt through the guard's door just before it closed, knocking the guard back as he did so. The guard, a big black man, was about to take defensive action when Neil whipped out his warrant card and held it out in front of him.

'Metropolitan Police,' he gasped through failing breath.

'What's the problem?' said the guard, holding out a hand to steady Neil as passengers murmured in fear and confusion.

'There's a murderer on the train.'

'Do you want me to stop it? We can hold the doors closed until the transport police get here.'

'No, that would only alert him.'

'Is he dangerous?'

They both smiled at the absurdity of the question.

'He may have a knife.'

'I can alert them at Euston via the track telephone. They can call the transport police from there, but they won't have time to get there before we arrive and it would mean keeping the doors closed.'

Neil reasoned that if the killer realized that they were onto him he might turn on others or grab a hostage. He thought about it for a few seconds but decided that he couldn't take a chance on anyone else getting hurt because of him. On the other hand, having come this far, he couldn't delegate the decision-making process. It was his call.

'No, just carry on normally. Alert them, but don't keep the doors closed.'

'If I alert them, they'll order me to keep the doors closed until they arrive.'

Neil knew that this was the standard procedure and that they followed it religiously, even if it meant risking hostages being taken. Neil reckoned that he knew the killer better than they did. This was a killer who was brave to the point of recklessness on the one hand, but who tended to panic when things went wrong. Neil had seen that at Beth's place, and at the hospital. And it probably explained what happened on the Heath. He couldn't take a chance on anyone else's safety, even if someone else took the responsibility.

He'd stuck his neck out several times now, with his career and his life. If he had to, he would stick it out one more time.

'No, in that case don't alert them. Not yet. I'll try and get him myself. Just carry on normally. If I haven't contacted you again by Camden Town, call them then.

'With that Neil opened the inter-carriage door in this carriage and the one of the next and crossed over into the adjacent carriage. He looked around and was met by curious stares. The carriage was crowded, the last few trains at night usually were, but he had to get through to the end. The killer had got into the carriage just after the front. Like every member of the Metropolitan Police, Neil had done a one-day training and acclimatization course with London Underground and he remembered that the Northern Line trains had seven carriages, except for the very old stock, which had eight. By Neil's reckoning, that meant that he would have to walk through four or five intervening carriages to get to the killer. He started pushing his way past the numerous standing passengers, occasionally flashing his warrant card at them when greeted with a New York-style 'hey what's your problem?' from the younger male passengers.

It took him almost a minute to get to the inter-carriage door to the fifth carriage, and even longer to get to the fourth.

Two or three more, he realized, as they arrived at Euston. He looked out through the single door at the rear to see if anyone got off. Lots of people did but, as far as he could tell, no one matching the man who had got on at Warren Street. Of course, he couldn't be sure. So many people were getting on the train he couldn't really say for certain. Euston, although not as busy at this time as Tottenham Court Road or Leicester Square in the heart of the West End, was still relatively busy. He had to make his mind up quickly. The doors were about to close.

No, he told himself. *He bought a ticket to Golders Green. That must be where he's going.*

As the train started moving forward he edged along the central passage of the fourth carriage. Unfortunately, this one was even more crowded and it was almost two minutes before he got to the end of it. Also the end of it was somewhat problematical because it was a driving motor car with a driving cab at the end, and he knew that it looked out onto another similar carriage, positioned in reverse so that the two driving cabs faced each other. That meant it would be harder to cross over. He'd have to break the emergency glass to get into it.

By this time the train was slowing down to five miles an hour. They were about to enter Mornington Crescent, a station which had been closed down for several years for refurbishment that had got delayed due to funding shortages and a government refusal to ante up for capital investment. Although the station was not in use, safety requirements necessitated slowing all trains passing through it to five miles per hour.

As he was about to open it he got the shock of his life. Through the window, on the platform, he saw the killer having apparently just leapt from the train. He realized what must have happened. He must have entered the driving cab at the back of the third carriage and opened the door on the platform side. As the train drifted past the killer, towards the end of the platform, Neil realized that he must do the same thing.

He used his elbow to smash the glass that shielded the door handle from improper use. Then he lowered the handle and entered the empty driver's cab, By this stage the train was starting to speed up as the driver cleared the end of the station. Neil realized that he had to act quickly now. He opened the door on the platform side and leapt out onto the platform, practically spinning round in a complete circle in order to maintain his balance. In a state of total disorientation he looked to the other end of the platform and saw the killer dash through the passage to the southbound platform.

At this end of the platform, there was no such passage and he had to run back about fifty feet to get to another passage where he could run through. By the time he got to the other platform he could see the killer at the far end of the platform. But he couldn't see the face. In addition to the shirt and jeans, the killer was wearing a knitted balaclava face mask just as he had when he held Beth captive in her own home. Neil started walking slowly towards him. As he drew near, he saw the killer reach inside his shirt, under the armpit, and produce a large hunting knife.

'Don't do anything stupid,' said Neil. 'We can talk about this.' He started to edge closer.

Meanwhile, in Coburg Street, close to Euston Station, in the dimly lit control room of the Northern Line, an urgent call came through from the guard of the train. He had seen the killer and Neil on the platform of Mornington Crescent and had decided that to wait any longer before telling them what was happening was more than his job was worth. He had told the driver over the train's intercom and the driver had in turn called through to the control room.

In the lower part of the control room a single signal operator was monitoring the final trains as they completed their runs for the night. He had control over the signals which could be left on various levels of automatic mode but had to be monitored and supervised. But he had no control over such matters as power to the lines or general security. That was dealt with by another man from a second, higher section, looking out onto the room like a judge sitting on the bench in a courtroom. He was the line controller and it was he who had ultimate responsibility for the entire line when he was on duty.

When the call came through, he picked up the phone from the panel pressed a red switch and answered.

'Control room, Ali speaking.'

'Euston, we have a problem.'

Ali chuckled.

'I bet you've been waiting a long time for a chance to say that, Charlie.'

Of all the drivers on the Northern Line, Charlie was widely known as the joker. He was recognized as the clown prince even by the passengers, who were always cheered up by his levity as he drawled on humorously to explain why they were stuck in a tunnel outside a station. On this occasion, however, he quickly switched to a serious tone and was at pains to emphasize that he was not joking as he told the controller what the guard had told him.

'OK, carry on as normal. I'll notify the transport police.'

Ali flicked another red switch and got through immediately to the transport police.

'Hallo, this is Ali from the Northern Line. We have a problem at Mornington Crescent. A couple of passengers apparently got off the train there?'

'How did they do that?'

'We think it was through the cabs in the mid-section driving cars.'

244

'Oh, the idiots! It would serve 'em right if we let them sweat it out there for a couple of hours. I suppose they phoned through on the emergency phones.'

'No, the guard saw them.'

'Well, why the hell didn't he stop the train?'

'It's a bit more complicated than that. You see, one of the people is a policeman - at least he had a warrant card- and the other, according to the copper, is a killer. He said something about him having a knife. The guard didn't want to endanger the other passengers.'

'It sounds like a load of bollocks . . . oh no, hold on a minute . . . I've got them now.'

'Are you picking it up on the monitor?'

'Yes. There's a man with a knife wearing a balaclava face-mask and another man, also in plain clothes.

From their headquarters, the transport police could tap into the closed circuit TV cameras at all the stations, including the security cameras at Mornington Crescent. Through the monitor they could see Neil edging slowly towards the killer, apparently talking. But the killer was backing away, brandishing the knife.

'I hope that idiot doesn't try and tackle him alone,' said the policeman.

Ali tapped in to the Mornington Crescent platform and saw what the policeman was seeing. From the control room he couldn't see through all the CCTV cameras at the ticket hall level, as the police could. But he could see all the views from all the *platform* cameras. Suddenly, as Neil got close, the killer spun round, jumped onto the track and disappeared into the darkness of the tunnel that ran towards the Charing Cross branch at Euston station.

'Oh my God,' said Ali.

'Is the traction current down there yet?' asked the policeman.

'I don't think the last train has cleared yet. That's why the emergency lights aren't on. I'll take it down now.'

Ali picked up a second phone, flicked another red switch and told the power supply controllers at Leicester Square to cut the traction current to that subsection, explaining the entire situation in barely more than a dozen words.

'Just for the seven minutes or for the night?'

In emergency situations the power could be shut off for seven minutes to give a train driver time to take remedial action or to contact the control room.

'Seven minutes. I'm not sure if the last south bound is clear.'

The signal operator, who had been following the situation with one ear, half-turned and called back to the controller.

'It's clear.'

'OK, shut it down for the night.'

'Northbound too?'

'No, just the southbound. We don't want to hold up the customers at Camden.'

Ali switched back to the transport police.

'OK, that section's isolated southbound. At least, the idiot won't get fried. How are you going to handle it?'

'We'll have people waiting for him at Euston. And we'll pick up the other chap from Mornington.'

At Mornington Crescent, Neil saw the emergency lights come on in the southbound tunnel that led to Euston. They were not very bright, but bright enough to run by. These were the lights that track maintenance people relied upon to check the track for cracked rails and loose 'keys'. And he knew that these lights only came on when the traction current went off. That meant that it was now safe to walk the line. There would be no more trains that night and even if he touched both the positive and negative rails he would not get electrocuted.

He didn't know what action the guard had taken or if anyone else knew they were there but he knew that he had to act.

He clambered awkwardly onto the track and strode off in pursuit of the killer.

Chapter 19

Neil tried to run down the track, stepping quickly between the wooden sleepers. The sleepers were about a yard or so apart separated by troughs of so-called ballast, basically nothing more than shingle and pebbles like those scattered across all too many British beaches except that this shingle was black with soot and dust, caked in over many decades and in some cases a hundred years.

It was hard to run on this surface. He was wearing shoes rather than boots and although the ballast provided friction to stop him slipping, it seemed to give way under him and he found it hard to plant his feet evenly. He shifted to walking fast rather than running, placing his feet on the sleepers rather than the ballast. Fortunately it was summer and the sleepers were dry but still they were slippery, especially as the soles of his shoes were almost new.

He still couldn't see his adversary but he fancied that he could hear him in the distance. His pace slowed down, as exhaustion set in. The burning on his cheeks and the wrenching in his gut warned him of his limitations and he wondered if the killer was feeling the same way. He remembered his cross-country racing days in school. Back then, he had always felt tired after the first two minutes and he usually wondered how he was ever going to find the strength to finish the race, wondering too how the others kept going. But as the race wore on it always seemed to grow easier rather than harder and he had very often overtaken most of the rest of the field by the halfway stage. On one occasion he had even come fourth in the final dash on the home straight across a flat field, and was convinced he would have come second if he had known before that how close he was to the finishing line and hadn't slackened. He had asked the sports master about this and been told that it had to do with the muscles functioning more efficiently when they warmed up. The result was that you could feel tired after two minutes and yet be running well after twenty. He hoped it would be the same now, for it was on the same reserves that he had to draw.

At any rate, he had to keep going. This wasn't just schoolboy pride at stake, it was justice . . . and possibly even human lives.

Nothing, not even school, had prepared him for the gloom of these dimly lit tunnels. They were illuminated - if one could use the word - by emergency lighting, but it was still darker than a corner of a wine bar, and less relaxing. Now and again he had to change his pacing as the distances between the sleepers changed at the join between the rails.

At one point he tripped over a piece of metal, a loose or spare key in the ballast. He fell against the right side of the tunnel, putting out his hand and catching onto a metallic-looking signal control box. He steadied himself and started running again. It was hard. His muscles had not yet warmed up, and his vision was blurry from the dust in the tunnel. The dust encrusted the signal cables that ran along the length of the tunnels, suspended on blackened metal brackets, and seemed to form wavy lines that danced up and down ahead of him. In fact, they didn't droop from the brackets. It was his blurred vision and unsteady running that gave the impression of undulating waves.

As he slowed down, he heard something in the distance. It sounded like heavy, footsteps on the ballast. The killer wasn't far ahead of him and he was rapidly catching up. Ironically, it was the slowing down that had made him aware of how much he had closed down the gap. He wondered if the killer could hear him. There was a sound of crunching ballast, as if the killer was speeding up, and Neil realized that the killer must have heard him too. But now that he was so close, he had to make his move. He started sprinting down the tunnel. It was like that home straight across the field on that cross-country run, except that there was no sunlight to illuminate his effort, and no fresh air to breathe along the way.

As he rounded the curve and entered a straight segment of tunnel, he caught sight of the killer. And the killer looked back at him, as if sensing that he was now in his pursuer's line of sight but as Neil felt the gap closing, the killer did something unexpected. He dived into a side passage.

Neil realized what had happened. The killer had crossed over to the other side through a bolt-hole. Now he had to think quickly. Once in the other tunnel the killer could go in either direction. Neil had to make a decision. Should he run back to an earlier bolt-hole and cross over there in the hope of heading him off? Or would the killer simply carry on in the same direction thereby building up a bigger lead and possibly throwing Neil off his tail altogether?

There was another problem too. Was it safe to run along the northbound track? Neil knew that the northbound trains ran later in this section than the southbound. Was the power off in that section yet? The traction current subsections were longer than the signal sections and so the controllers would have to wait until the last train had left that entire subsection before switching off the traction current.

As he reached the bolt-hole, Neil saw that there were lights on the northbound track which meant that the traction current had been switched off there too so it was safe to run there, for both of them. But where was the killer? Was he waiting on the other side, knife at the ready, poised to kill Neil? There was only one way to find out.

He crossed through, looking quickly this way and that as he stuck his head through and then pulled back. He had been expecting a knife to come at him from one side or the other, and his hands had been ready to deflect or parry it. But no attack came. And he saw in that brief moment that the killer had indeed doubled back and was now heading north to Mornington Crescent. He stepped into the northbound tunnel and started walking briskly after the killer. He knew that it was futile to run, as he would only tire himself out but he was determined to keep the killer in view. Even on these straight tracks there were opportunities for evasion: bolt holes, shunting points, etc. This was especially true at Camden Town where the Charing Cross and Bank branches met up and led into the Edgware and High Barnet branches in the north.

'Well, where the devil are they?'

'I don't know sir.'

The transport police had staked out the northbound and southbound branches of the Charing Cross branch of the Northern Line at Euston. There was no need to stakeout the Bank branch, as the tunnels from Mornington Crescent didn't lead to it. On the other hand, they had also staked out the Victoria Line, as there were shunting points leading to it from the Charing Cross branch.

'Could he have caught him?'

'It's possible. He said he was a copper.'

'Do we have any idea who he is?'

'No sir.'

'Could they have doubled back?'

'Anything is possible, sir.'

'All right. Send a squad to Mornington Crescent.'

'They won't have the keys.'

'Well, get them, man.'

'Where from?'

'I don't know. Try the bloody station supervisor here. If that doesn't work, try Camden Town.'

'Yes, sir.'

Another stride, then another. It hadn't been a hot day and Neil wasn't overdressed yet he felt himself sweating. The tunnels were not heated yet they could get exceedingly hot. When the trains were running during the day, the flow of air generated by the movement of the trains had a cooling effect but at night, when the tunnels were deserted, the heat tended to build up, even after the evening drop in temperature. And the fast walking and running accentuated this effect, as did the fear.

He could see the killer ahead of him, struggling to open up a distance between them. And he was equally determined to keep the killer in his sights.

They had hit the great spaghetti junction of intersection sat Camden Town. By the time the police had arrived at Mornington Crescent and got down to the platform, they had already gone past it. And now, at Camden Town, the killer had gone off to the left, following the shunting points to the Edgware branch. Neil followed, slowing down his pace as he stepped carefully between the mass of rails that almost intertwined at these points. He was aware of running downward, crossing under the High Barnet Branch then he sprinted past the Edgware branch platform and out the other end.

They were now running towards Chalk Farm, and Neil knew that from here the tunnels would get longer as they moved progressively closer to the suburbs.

The killer looked back. Neil was still there, relentless in his pursuit. The gap between them was less than fifty yards and closing. Suddenly, there was a rumbling sound ahead.

It was a train!

But that was impossible! The traction current was off

Then Neil realized what was happening. There were battery-operated 'ballast' or engineering trains used to bring supplies into the tunnel. The tunnels had to have spare rails left at strategic intervals in case cracked or worn-out rails needed to be replaced. These rails were left on the tracks usually lying flat between the negative rail and the leftmost running rail, where they wouldn't interfere with the running of the train. If they were needed for a quick replacement they were already there in the tunnels and didn't need to be brought in specially each time a rail got cracked or wore out. There were also boxes on the side, with electrical power sockets, so that if the rail needed to be trimmed it could be done with power tools plugged into the socket.

What was happening now was that a battery-operated engineering train was being driven down to bring rails to some place on the line. But why was it going south along the northbound track.

Of course, he realized. *They know-we're here! They assumed we were still on the southbound track but they didn't want to delay the rail delivery so they sent the engineering train on the northbound track.*

It made sense when looked at like that, but it didn't bring him any comfort. His life was now in deadly danger and he was gasping for breath and for the faintest idea of what to do about it.

Ahead of him, Neil saw the killer disappear down a passage. It was clearly down and Neil realized that there must be a concrete staircase there. Either that or a ladder. They were now at a point where the northbound and southbound tracks were not at the same level. The problem for Neil was that there was no way he could get to that passage or bolt-hole before he came smack up against the engineering train. And he felt his heart leap into his mouth as his mind pressed the panic button.

He remembered that, a couple of hundred yards back, was another passage, accessible by a metal ladder. It was further back than the passage that the killer had taken. But at least he would be moving away from the train instead of towards it as it closed in towards him.

Realizing that it was his only chance, Neil sprinted back the way he came, remembering that home straight in the cross-country race. He made it to the hole several yards ahead of the train and practically slid down the ladder like a fireman. He was surprised that the driver hadn't seen him, but then again he wasn't wearing a Hi-Vi, the regulation high-visibility jacket that is obligatory for anyone walking the track, day or night. These bright orange or green jackets - also worn by policemen on traffic duty - had reflective stripes that would be picked up in the headlamps of oncoming cars or trains. But dressed as he was in dark blue jeans and a dark grey shirt, it was hardly surprising that the driver hadn't spotted him as he ran away, with not even the brightness of his face to reflect the light.

Once down on the southbound track he began the slow steady walk back north after the killer, who by now must have had a considerable lead over him.

'We've just had a really strange report, sir.'
'What is it?'
The transport police were controlling the operation from the Coburg Street control centre, near Euston.
'The driver of the engineering train carrying rails for the Angel said he thought he saw a man on the track. He knows about what's going on because the controller told him when he diverted him to the northbound track. Anyway he said the man wasn't wearing a Hi-Vi.'
'Did he say *one* man or two?'
'No, just the one, sir.'
'I see. I dare say that could mean that the other is underneath his wheels by now.'
'I don't think so, sir. He'd have noticed that.'
'Maybe the one in behind ducked for cover before he got to see him.'
'That could be,' the controller interrupted. 'There are plenty of bolt-holes and side-passages. Some of them lead through to the other side. Others are just closed ended inlets looking a bit like

chapels. We use them to store supplies that might be needed on the track for later work.'

'I see,' said the inspector heading the operation.

'Where did Neil go?' said a child's voice

Beth had been pacing the living room, smoking her first cigarette in over five years. She had given up when she became pregnant with Stevie and not even her ex-husband had be enable to drive her back to it. Now, as she waited desperately-for news of Neil, she had been unable to resist the urge.

Little Stevie was looking at her with one eye while rubbing the other. She knew that her pacing couldn't have woken him up. He wasn't such a light sleeper. And the sound on the television was turned right down. She wondered if it washer nervousness that had somehow permeated the walls and alerted him.

'He had to go out,' she said gently, stubbing out the cigarette on a saucer. 'But don't worry. He'll be back.'

She had tried to sound reassuring, but even in the dim light of a room illuminated only by the television set in the corner, he could see the tears in her eyes. He rushed up to her and threw his arms round her as she knelt down. This time it wasn't she who was comforting him but rather the other way round.

They flopped onto the couch together and she sobbed in his arms, while he stroked her head and said, 'It'll be all right, mummy.'

She had tried to phone the hospital but they had told her nothing. They merely took her number and said that they would call her back. She couldn't understand this. If they were guarding Roebuck so tightly, surely they would want to interview her right away. Then again this was a bureaucracy. And the wheels of bureaucracy grind slowly. Any minute now, they would probably burst down her door and send in a team of armed officers to search the place.

She dismissed the thought. *They don't work like that,* she told herself. She realized now that she probably hadn't got through to the right people. She had phoned the hospital general switchboard, where the night operator probably just wanted to get her off the line so that she could get back to her knitting. The operator probably didn't know what was going on with Roebuck and had neither the initiative nor the inclination to find out who did. She had probably just made a note of her phone number and done nothing. She would probably give the note to one of her superiors in the morning. Or maybe she'd just file it in the 'round filing cabinet' under the desk.

Beth thought about phoning back. But what good would that do? She would only end up speaking to the same person. It would be impossible to get past that barrier of ineptitude until the morning.

Perhaps this was unfair. The night operator would surely know the extensions for all the emergency departments but Beth had to admit that from the point of view of an ordinary member of hospital staff this wasn't an emergency. A woman phoning up to inquire about her boyfriend who was a policeman and who had gone to the hospital at night to check up about the security of a patient whose life was allegedly in danger was more a matter for the psychiatric department. She could hardly blame the operator for not being too helpful. It was hardly an everyday sort of call, and there probably wasn't any contingency procedure for dealing with such an odd inquiry, especially at night when there were few superiors available to ask for help.

But it was Neil she was really angry with. What made him think that it was his responsibility? Why didn't he just phone his police colleagues and confide his fears and concerns to them? Why did he have to go off half-cocked, like a gun-toting sheriff in the wild west.

'Don't cry, mummy,' said Stevie as he hugged her and stroked her hair the way she so often did to him when he was crying.

But she couldn't stop herself.

'Why do men have to be so stupid?' she asked, forgetting that she was talking to a child. 'Why do men have to have such fuckin' big egos?'

They had trudged on past Chalk Farm and were now on their way to Belsize Park. This tunnel was slightly longer than the last and they were both feeling it. But it had one advantage for Neil and that was that it had a long straight stretch that enabled him to see the killer in the distance. That gave him the assurance that at least he hadn't doubled back again. Furthermore, the killer hadn't

254

looked back yet and this meant that Neil had an advantage. He could gain ground on the killer, now that he knew that he was back on track. And when the tunnel curved he could gain even more.

He had told the platform cleaners at Chalk Farm to call the police and try to arrange an interception at Belsize Park, but he didn't know if they would do it. Nor did he know if the police would even listen to them or take them seriously. They-probably would, but he couldn't be sure. And he couldn't be sure they'd get there on time. Although this was a Sunday night, when they weren't so stretched, they would have more policemen on leave and so be short of staff. To young people, and especially the least law-abiding among them, the weekend started on Friday night and ended on Sunday morning. To the police therefore, the weekend *began* on Sunday morning, at least in practice, and ended on Tuesday morning. At least that was how it felt in terms of the intensity of their law enforcement activities.

So Neil had to keep going.

They had made their way back to the northbound track, Neil once again following the killer's lead. Suddenly he heard another rumbling but this time it was on the southbound branch. It sounded much louder than the previous rumbling- louder and slower. But it was on the other side and Neil had no time to wonder where it was.

Little Stevie was asleep in her arms but Beth held him close to her heart as if he were still a baby. She was afraid to put him down, in case he woke up. Also it was comforting to her to hold him. The doorbell rang. Beth's face lit up, and then she froze. Neil wouldn't ring. He had a key. And who would come round at this time? She gently put the sleeping Stevie down on the sofa, hoping that neither the movement nor the doorbell would wake him up, and went to the front door.

Through the translucent glass on either side of the door she saw a flashing blue light and could make out the shape of two or three figures. But she couldn't be sure.

'Who's there?' she said.

'It's the police. SO10. Is Neil Douglas there?'

'No, he isn't?'

'Can we come in?'

She felt a wave of relief, followed by a second wave of fear. She had thought that something had happened to Neil. That they were here to tell her. But it seemed that they didn't know where he was. So she was still in limbo.

She opened the door and saw four people, a uniformed man and woman and two men in plain-clothes.

'Can we come in?'

'My son's asleep. I don't want to wake him.'

'We'll be quiet.'

'All right. Let's go into the kitchen. He's asleep downstairs on the sofa.'

She let them in and led them to the kitchen, but didn't offer them tea.

'Do you know where Neil is?'

One of the plainclothes men had taken the lead in asking the questions. The policewoman was filling the kettle after looking at Beth for confirmation that it was all right.

'He went to the hospital. He said he thought Roebuck was in danger.'

'Did he say why?'

'No, but I think it may have been something the man with the knife said. You know, the man who tied me up.'

'Do you have any idea why he didn't mention it when we questioned him?'

'I don't think he remembered at the time. He woke up in the night and got into a panic. I think he just remembered something. It might even have been a dream.'

'What, you think he dreamt that the knife man said something?'

'No, but it might have been a dream that triggered it. Look, I don't know. I'm not even sure if he fell asleep at all. He might have been awake the whole time. It might have been troubling him at the back of his mind. I'm not a fuckin' psychologist.'

She was under stress. As a trained radio presenter she-wouldn't normally use such language. She wanted to light another cigarette, but she was determined not to give in to the urge. She had felt embarrassed enough that Stevie had seen her smoking.

'When did he go to the hospital?'

'I don't know. I think it was after midnight.'

'And he hasn't been in touch since?'

'No.'

The policewoman put a mug of tea down in front of her. She hadn't made any for herself or for any of the others.

'Does he have a mobile phone?'

'I don't think so.'

It was three-thirty in the morning. They had passed Belsize Park. Once again Neil had asked the platform cleaners to contact the transport police and to get them to contactSO10. This time he had given them his name and the name of the man in SO10 to ask for, but he feared that they would get the names mixed up. In the meantime he had to press on. The sweat on his clothes was now beginning to make him feel uncomfortable, and as the temperature began to drop slightly it felt somehow wetter, as if he had been caught in the rain.

The cleaners had confirmed that a man in a knitted mask had raced through the station and that he had brandished a knife when they tried to challenge him.

He felt a surge of energy when he heard this. It was no longer a case of merely *wanting* to stop the killer. He knew now that he *had* to. He had to do it before anyone else was killed. He strode briskly into the tunnel at the other end of the station, being careful not to run. Running would merely tire him out and not be the most efficient use of his energy.

This tunnel he realized would be longer than the last one, although not as long as the one from Hampstead to Solders Green if he couldn't stop the killer before he got there. It seemed like only a few minutes later when he walked past a curve into a long straight and again saw the killer more than a hundred yards ahead of him but almost as soon as he saw him, the killer walked past the next curve and disappeared from his line of sight.

Got you bastard! Neil thought as he quickened his pace.

He felt the flood of adrenalin as he sensed victory in his clutches. Not that he had any grounds for over-confidence. The killer still had a knife. But the killer had been afraid to make a move against him before and he had no reason to assume that it would be any different now. So far all the killer's victims had been women. And although he had also tried to kill Roebuck, he hadn't stabbed him. Neil wondered, in fact, if he had tried to kill Roebuck. He didn't really know what had happened in the room just before he arrived. Certainly, the killer must have been in there seconds earlier. The open window suggested a hasty retreat. The killer's proximity suggested that he had been there only seconds before.

But what had he done? As he strode on, as fast as his legs could carry him, in a desperate effort to catch up with his adversary, Neil wondered what the killer had done to Roebuck. Had he cut off his life support system? Poisoned him? Or simply been about to stab him?

He didn't really know.

He wondered if *they* would know. Would the SO10 people be able to figure it out? Or the doctors?

Of course they would. That was their job. They would check for anything and everything that an intruder could do.

Neil wondered if he could even be sure that the intruder was the killer. He hadn't seen him in the hospital. He had picked up his trail afterwards. Even then, how would he recognize him? The only give-away feature was the knitted mask . . . and the general size and build.

Yes, of course it was the killer. It was the same man who had held Beth at knife-point and told her that he was the killer. The same man who had phoned Beth on the air and told her that he had killed both Leah Irons and Rose Crowne.

And now Neil could see him ahead once again as he entered another straight stretch of track.

He knew that the killer had no way out until Solders Green. All the stations up till then were underground. But just before Golders Green the tunnels ended and the track came out into the open and at that point the killer could leap over a fence and walk away, a free man. Until then, he was like a desperate animal being tracked by a determined hunter.

Suddenly the tunnel lights went out, plunging him into total darkness.

Neil froze with terror. It was not that he was afraid of the dark. Even in this pitch black tunnel he could still stagger forwards and feel his way along. And he knew that the killer must be feeling the same terror. It was just that he knew what this meant. His one-day course with London Underground during his training for the Met had told him that when the tunnel's lights went out, it meant that the traction current had come back on. That meant, 420 volts in the positive rail on the outside and 210 in the negative rail in the middle, the differential due to electrical resistance in the rails themselves. Stepping on the middle rail would give one a nasty jolt, but stepping on the outside rail would be fatal.

But the real danger lay not so much in the fact that the traction rails now carried live current as in the reason *why*. Neil knew, from the time, that it was too early to restart the current, It couldn't be an engineers' train, because they used battery power. It could mean only one thing.

He remembered the very loud rumbling that he had heard before. That had been the tunnel-cleaning train, a special train with engines at both ends and special vacuum equipment in the middle to suck dust, bottles, cans, newspapers and debris out of the tunnels. As he heard a faint rumbling behind him, his worst fear was confirmed. It must have made its way down to Camden Town and then crossed over at the points there, for a return run.

But surely they must know by now, at the control room, what was going on here? Surely they must have people out preparing to enter the tunnels at various stations to trap the killer. Perhaps the staff shortages and coordination problems had slowed them down, but at least they should keep the tunnels clear.

Or maybe this was part of their plan. After all, the tunnel-cleaning train operated at one-and-a-half miles an hour when performing its cleaning function within the 150yards on either side of the platform. Of course, the driver could manually override the traction current resisters for the journey between the stations but he didn't have to. Maybe that was what they were doing. Maybe they were sending out the tunnel-cleaning train to act as a sort of hunter vehicle, or to flush out the intruders in the tunnel. Travelling at one-and-a-half miles per hour and with a powerful set of headlights it could easily stop well before hitting someone. And even if they weren't wearing Hi-Vi's, they'd be clearly visible in the beam of the headlights.

So maybe that was it. But the problem was still that traction current. As long as he didn't step on the positive rail on the far left, he wouldn't be killed but he'd get a painful zap from the negative rail, even if it wasn't fatal. Perhaps he should remain stationary, stand here at the beginning of a bend rather than the end of one, and wait for the tunnel-cleaning train to arrive. The driver would see him and stop and he could get into the cabin with the driver. Then they could go off together and try and catch up with the killer.

But that might not work. Maybe the killer wouldn't stick around to be caught. Maybe he'd cross over and carry on running on the other side. Or maybe he'd even double back. It wouldn't take him to immediate freedom but he was playing a cat-and-mouse game of survival and had already proved himself to be unpredictable.

Neil couldn't afford to take the safe way either. He started striding forward, carefully placing one foot directly in front of the other. He kept to the space between the negative rail and the rightmost running rail. But he took the steps as briskly as he could, keeping his hand on the right hand wall for guidance. His heart was beating more frantically than ever as the terror grew to new heights within him. He was desperate, not only to catch up with the killer, but to outrun the tunnel-cleaning train that was creeping up behind him, its rumble growing steadily into a deep growl and then a mighty roar. Ahead of him, to his right, was a shaft of light and he knew with a sigh of relief that he had arrived at a bolt-hole through which he could cross to the other side. He took the last few steps quickly, as he could hear the tunnel-cleaning train looming up only tens of yards away from him and as soon as he reached it he dived through to the southbound track. He turned left and carried on, rounding another bend and catching sight of the killer yet again.

So his adversary had made it too. But then again, he had been further away and was probably nearer to a bolt hole when he heard the train approaching.

'OK, look, what we'll do is have our squad cars keep their eyes open for him and--' The SO10 officer's mobile phone rang. Everyone in the room jumped, except the man himself who whipped it out and flipped it open. 'Hallo. DCI Ford speaking.'

'Hallo. This is Inspector Cassel of the Transport Police. We've just had a message to call you. We have a situation here in which a policeman is in pursuit of a suspect on the Northern Line.'

'I thought it'd stopped running by now.'

'Oh, it has. But he's chasing him on foot.'

'One of *my* men?'

'I'm not sure. His name is PC Douglas and he-'

'*Neil* Douglas?'

Everyone in the kitchen paid attention, Beth most of all.

'That's right.'

'Where the devil is he?'

He was walking in a northward direction in the southbound tunnel at Hampstead Station, less than a minute after the killer had walked the same stretch. This was the longest tunnel of all, some two thousand metres. A train travelling at fairly high speed took four minutes to cover this route. Hampstead Station was the lowest Station on the underground and they were now entering the deepest place in the tunnels at some two hundred and twenty feet beneath the ground. They were walking upwards, but the ground above them was also getting higher and so they were still walking through the lowest place on the underground, relative to the surface, although not the lowest place below sea level.

Neil arrived at the shunting points between Hampstead and Golders Green. It was here that a train could be turned around and sent back to patch up a gap in the running schedule. It meant that some passengers would have to wait at Hampstead or Golders Green, but the alternative was for the trains to run behind schedule all day. He noticed that the lights were now back on along the northbound track which meant that the traction current was off again. The tunnel-cleaning train had cleared this section and was probably now asleep for the night at the Golders Green depot.

He knew that he had to be careful at these points, because they sometimes tested them at night. Put a foot between two shunting rails when it's about to be tested and you could lose that foot. At least that was what they had told him at his London Underground course.

He strained for sounds ahead of him. The killer was closer than he had previously thought and he realized why. The network of shunting rails was so tight and the rails so closely packed together that it was very tricky to walk through them. The killer had crossed over back to the northbound track. He could hear the sound of footsteps in the ballast and he knew that his quarry was nearer than he had thought. Now he had to be careful. If he could hear the killer, then it was quite possible that the killer could hear him.

As he stepped gingerly across this network of rails, Neil realized that its complexity reflected the complexity of the underground train service as a whole. He sympathized with the people who worked for it. People expected them to make it work perfectly and abused them when things went wrong. In some ways, it was like the police.

He was now back on the northbound track, walking north. The killer was nearby, and they had a long way to go before the tunnels came out into the open just before Golders Green. And before that was North End, or the Old Bull and Bush, the station that had been excavated at platform level but never opened.

'OK, we'll go down by the stairs.'

SO10 had sent an Armed Response Team to Hampstead Station. They knew that they were too late to catch Neil and the killer there, but they were sending another squad to Golders Green to cut them off at that end. Their plan was to enter the tunnels from both ends and trap them in the middle.

They would also try to get the key for the Old Bull and Bush from the station supervisor at Golders Green, but that was a long shot. Until they got the key, until they got to the surface entrance behind Manor House Hospital, until they got down there on foot, single-file, it would probably be too late - even though the Old Bull and Bush was nearer to Golders Green than Hampstead.

The main thing was to close off all four ends of the tunnels: Golders Green and Hampstead, northbound and southbound. The problem was Murphy's Law. Everything was going wrong that *could* go wrong. There was power to the lifts at Hampstead, but there were no maintenance crews at hand which meant that the lifts could not legally be used. They could chance it but if half a dozen coppers from the Armed Response Unit got stuck in the lift and left a killer loose there'd be hell to pay. The tabloids would have a field day and the Home Secretary would want the field commander's head on a plate, to serve up as a scapegoat to his colleagues in the House of Commons.

So they had to take the stairs, all three hundred-plus of them.

It was not beyond their physical capacity, these were fit and well-trained men but it slowed down their operation at the worst possible time.

Neil saw the lights of the Old Bull and Bush ahead of him. Although they were brighter than the tunnel lights, the atmosphere was still gloomy. Neil saw the killer make a dash for the right. This could mean one of two things: either he was simply crossing over to the southbound platform or he was going to try to get out at the station's emergency exit.

By now the exhaustion was almost unbearable. He was drenched in sweat and his cheeks were flushed to the point of conflagration. He had always thought of spontaneous human combustion as one of those superstitious myths that gullible people believed because they hadn't got a life. Right now, he felt that if it were possible at all, then he would surely be its next victim. He comforted himself with the knowledge that the killer must be feeling the same way.

Neil tried to orient himself in relation to the ground. This was the Old Bull and Bush station. Strictly speaking, the entrance to the station was quite a few yards from the famous pub, closer in fact to a small private hospital. But it was near enough to where the events of this sorry saga had started. As he staggered into the station, he realized that he- and presumably the killer - were virtually under the very spot where Rose Crowne had been murdered, and where he had struck Martin Roebuck on the head with his baton.

After changes upon changes we are more or less the same, the old song went. And here they were now, back where it all started. Full circle.

There wasn't a full platform at the station, just a large area to the side of the track where the tunnel opened out and where the platform had been intended to be built. The area was stacked with boxes of supply materials for use by track maintenance staff. There was, in fact, a small concrete platform, somewhat lower than full height, with a short staircase that led to a crossover passage to the southbound track. It also led to a network of split-level corridors, and locked rooms intended for use by the station staff, separated by short flights of stairs.

Neil heard a sound coming from it and he knew that the killer was nearby.

The killer had, in fact, come to the conclusion that escape from this station via the surface route would be impossible. The door at the top would almost certainly be locked - possibly with a chain and padlock on the outside - so there was no point struggling to ascend the tight, winding turns of the long spiral staircase to the surface, with a view to walking out there.

However, in addition to the staircase, there was also a lift shaft and a one-man lift. The lift was not operational, but the shaft extended below it, and there was a trap door and a ladder leading about ten feet down below the lift. It offered a perfect place to hide...

'I know you're there,' said Neil, as he walked carefully around the corridors, straining to hear any sound, alert to any sudden moves from the corridors that branched to either side. 'You know the game is up. You can't get away from here.'

No answer.

He realized that he was only giving away his own position. He checked very carefully everywhere that he thought the killer could be.

Nowhere. He checked the southbound track: *not there.*

That could mean only one thing. The killer was climbing the stairs in the hope of getting out at the top. Neil smiled. This meant that he had him trapped but he didn't feel like gloating. Gloating meant issuing a provocation. And he had no wish to compare testosterone levels with a double-murderer who was armed with a knife. The killer was trapped yet common sense told Neil that *he* was the one who was in danger.

He began climbing the spiral staircase slowly, being careful not to touch the railing, which was covered with thick black dust going back as far as the days when this station was first excavated, in 1907. It was a long way up by the spiral staircase and his knees were already aching. He was dripping with sweat, not only from the pursuit but also from fear, but he couldn't let up now. He had come this far and he had to see it through to the end. He didn't know how far ahead of him the killer was but it didn't matter. The door would be locked at the top. There was no way out. Once they got to the top they would have to confront each other. Neil knew that this was the end of the line for one of them.

He was afraid. He knew that his adversary had a knife while he had no weapon. And he couldn't be sure that his unarmed combat training would be sufficient to counter the threat. He still had his CS spray canister but it might not be enough to stop such a frenzied attack as the one that had ended the life of Rose Crowne.

'Listen,' he said nervously into the darkness. 'I want to talk with you . . . All right I won't ask you to answer. I know you're afraid. I mean, I am too. We're both afraid. But at least let's talk . . . I'll tell you what . . . how about, if you don't want to talk, I'll talk and you listen. And any time you want to say something you just shout and I'll shut-up and let you have your say . . . OK?'

He was playing it by ear now, trying to reach out and build a bridge between himself and the killer. Whatever this man had done, he tried to tell himself, he was still a human being, and he still had the same frailties and failings as the rest of us. He still had the capacity to feel pain, even if he-had erected his own walls to protect himself from it. Neil knew that, if there was a chance in a million that he could open up a line of communication with his adversary, then it was worth a try.

'I know how you must feel . . . all the frustration and rage-that goes with whatever personal sorrow you've had in life. But you know, you're not the only one who's had sorrow. I've had more than my share of pain too. My mother died when I was in my early teens and my father . . . well, that's a long story.'

He fell silent and strained his ears for any sign of a reply, even a faint murmur of breathing would have been sufficient, just to assure him that he wasn't alone in this hole under the ground.

'My father wasn't like me. He was a stickler for rules and regulations. He was a copper too but he'd have made a good military man. He believed in doing everything by the book. He didn't believe in taking short-cuts and he didn't believe in bending the rules. Was your father like that? A bit of a disciplinarian?'

Two more steps . . . then three.

'But he was always fair. You know he used to report the heavy-handed interrogation methods of some of his colleagues. And on one occasion he encouraged a suspect to report the way he'd been interrogated to the Police Complaints Commission.'

Three . . . four . . . five more steps.

Neil was trying to encourage the killer to identify with him. He suspected that this man had had brushes with the law before and didn't take too kindly to any sort of-authority. By painting his father as a rebel, he was trying to break down the stereotypes in this man's way of thinking and get him to think of this policeman who pursued him now not as authority but as a friend. He also had to show his weak side. This killer had been wounded by life and had lashed out at those who seemed complete and whole. By presenting himself as a victim too, Neil was making it harder for this killer to hate him. The killer did not sympathize with the weak or vulnerable - if he did, he wouldn't have attacked women - but he might sympathize with someone whom he thought had already been hurt too much, someone who was a victim of life's harshness too.

'Yes, my father rocked the boat quite a lot. Not because he resented the rules, but because he insisted that they apply to everyone . . . even coppers. But they still loved him. And you know why. Because they always knew where they stood with him, because he was so straight. He was the straightest man I know. That's why even villains knew they couldn't count on him for mercy when they were in the wrong, but they could count on him for justice when they were in the right. He wasn't the sort of copper to look the other way when a colleague used excessive force on a suspect.

'It was just after that time with the suspect's complaint that he got himself . . . killed.'

There had been a break in Neil's voice. It still hurt him to talk about it.

'I can still remember that day. You see, that morning my father and I had argued. I was in police training by then. That's a twenty week course with continual assessment. One Friday, I missed my weekly assessment test. I came in late that day with a hangover. That's because I went out drinking on a Thursday night instead of a Friday. That was with some of my friends from university, not

266

from the police training centre. They had enough sense not to go drinking the night before an assessment test. But I thought I was impervious to harm. I was the only one in the class with a university degree, but I wasn't all that streetwise. I guess what I needed was a good cold dose of reality.'

One . . . two . . . three more steps. He was getting closer to the top, but it was getting harder. And he was making it harder for himself by talking but he had to keep trying. He had to open up the lines of communication and try and solve this problem the peaceful way. His father had always taught him that force should only be used as a last resort. It's just that it was so hard for Neil. And he didn't even have the comfort of knowing exactly how close the killer-was. He strained his ears again, but couldn't hear a thing.

'The trouble was, I was insulated from reality by my father. He didn't consciously set out to do it, but that's the effect-that it had. You see, they knew at the training centre that I was the son of Inspector Douglas so they gave me special treatment. They let me sit the exam in the afternoon. He didn't ask them to let me do that, you understand. He didn't-even know about it till afterwards. But they knew who he was and so they quietly rescheduled the exam for me. That-meant I could also take it on my own when I didn't have the-others around to make me nervous . . . I even got a warning-from a couple of the other chaps about one or two of the-questions.'

Neil thought he heard a sound, but he couldn't place it in space. It was just a brief echoing sound and could even have been his own voice reverberating off the concrete walls.

'It was when I told him that evening about getting the exam rescheduled that the shit really hit the fan. When I told him what had happened, he got angry. He told me that corruption was like a poisonous plant that grows from a single seed. He said that I'd swallowed the seed of corruption and let it take root inside me. Then I told him about the exam and getting a preview of the answers, just to wind him up, and he blew his top. He yelled at me that he wouldn't tolerate a stranger breaking the rules and so how could he tolerate it when it was his own son. I told him that it wasn't his business and that he didn't run the police training centre and that made him even madder. He said that I had used his name to get them to bend the rules and then I compounded the offence by cheating in the exam. I wanted to argue more with him but I couldn't 'cause I . . . I knew he was right.'

Neil felt himself choking on his words. This was the first time he had admitted this to a living human being. He struggled on, finding it almost as hard to climb the steps as to voice the truth that he had held locked away for so long within him.

'But I couldn't bring myself to admit it at the time, so I just got angry with him. I told him that the reason he was still an Inspector at his age was because he didn't know how to use his initiative, because he was straight-jacketed by the rules and didn't know how to live in the real world. Then I stormed out and got drunk again. That was on a Friday night. And we all know what Friday nights are? Time for boozing and fighting and drunken brawls. And my father was on duty that night.'

He felt himself getting nearer to the top of the stairs. But as he leaned over and looked up he saw that he still had along way to go.

'Usually the constables and sergeants are on the front line, but when it's a Friday night they need every spare hand they can get. So when they had one call-out about a disturbance at a pub, he had to go along too. And being the kind of man he was, he insisted on being the point man. That was Dad. When it came to confronting the gang of rowdy youths who had congregated outside the pub, *he* had to be the one who walked up to them first. And because he didn't believe in using force except as a last resort, he didn't even have his baton at the ready, or his CS spray. He tried to reason with the ringleader first. But reason doesn't work with some people.'

Neil wondered if he was making a similar mistake with this man. But he had to try. The fact that his father had failed in his goal didn't mean that he had been wrong to *try*. And the only way to honour his father now was to do things the way he would have done.

Or was it trying to follow in my father's footsteps that has been my mistake?

'The ringleader of the yobbos had been holding something behind his back. My father probably couldn't see what it was. Apparently none of his colleagues could, either. They thought it was a knife. Presumably he felt that if he stayed out of range he'd have enough time to step back or pull out his CS spray or baton if the yobbo made a move on him. But it turned out to be a piece of lead piping which was a bit longer than a knife. And while my father was still trying to reason with him, the scum bag whipped it out and smashed it across my father's head.'

There were tears running down Neil's cheeks. It was all coming back to him in a flood of pain and self-loathing and anger. Anger at the yobbo for the wasted life of such a good man and at himself for arguing with his father before that.

'He was rushed to hospital and when I got home I found a message on my machine from the hospital. I phoned the hospital and they told me what had happened. He'd been operated on to remove a blood clot from his brain and he was still alive, but he hadn't come out from under the anaesthetic. I raced to the hospital, but when I got there they told me that he'd died a few minutes before.'

Neil was sobbing now - sobbing harder than on the day when he'd hit Roebuck and put him in a coma. Because he now realized *consciously* what he'd only been affected by *unconsciously* on that night on Hampstead Heath. Through his choked-up throat, he spoke again.

'And I never had the chance to tell him I was sorry. I never had the chance to tell him that he was right. I never had the chance to tell him that I loved him.'

Now, finally, Neil understood why he was taking this case so personally. It wasn't that he had hit an innocent man as such. It wasn't even that he had injured him in a way that was similar to the way his father was killed. It was just that by acting as he did he had *dishonoured* his father. He had gone against everything that his father had taught him: to obey the rules, to use force only as a last resort and most important of all: to accept responsibility for his mistakes.

He was at the top of the stairs now, and he knew that the killer had to be nearby, possibly even just round the corner, on the concrete path leading to the exit door.

'You're the first person I've told this to. I've never been able to say it to anyone - not even my - '

He suddenly realized how he thought of Beth.

'I've never even faced up to it myself... until now. You've really held up a mirror tome, you know? You've forced me to look at myself. And I have to admit that I don't like what I see.'

He remembered that play about the dragon that he had reshaped for little Stevie.

Each person carries around with him the dragon of his own fears. And only when he slays that dragon will he be free. But one can kill anyone else's dragon, each person must kill their own dragon. And if they don't do it, then the dragon doesn't kill them, it just keeps them a prisoner of their fears.

Suddenly, he heard a sound behind him. He spun round to see the killer sprinting up the last few stairs, the knife raised high. The face was hidden by the knitted mask but Neil could still see the killer's rage by the fire in the eyes and the violent contortion of the mouth. Realizing that there was no time to reach for the CS spray canister, he adopted a defensive posture as the knife came down.

This was an amateur's way of using a knife.

It was probably what saved him. He blocked the arm with the knife using his forearm and punched the killer in the face. The killer let out a cry of pain and dropped the knife. It fell down the central well of the stair-shaft, clinking heavily against the metal railing a few times until it hit the concrete at platform level, over two hundred feet below.

The look of anger in the killer's eyes gave way to one of fear and, in that instant, a wave of sympathy swept over Neil. He still couldn't think of this person as having no redeeming features, perhaps only because he knew he was so far from perfect himself. He had wanted to hate this man, and he still held in his memory the lifeless body of Rose Crowne, reminding him of the coldly implacable evil of which this monster was capable. But now, as he confronted the depths of his own soul, his capacity to hurt the innocent and his inability to face up to it until forced to by a stranger, he could no longer feel unadulterated hate for this murderer. If there was hatred and anger towards him, Neil realized, then it was anger tempered by pity. If this man was an animal then perhaps he was a *wounded* animal, lashing out at anyone who got too close - as wounded animals tend to do.

While Neil was paralyzed by indecision, the wounded-animal saw its chance. The killer turned and sprinted down the stairs three

270

at a time, building up a huge lead before Neil could respond. When he did respond, Neil realized that the tide was shifting against him once again.

Going down was easier than going up. But as he was already tired from going up, he barely felt 'ease' in the task. Nevertheless the descent was rapid and it made him dizzy as the platform level loomed up closer.

As he got to the bottom of the staircase, he noticed that everything had gone silent. The killer had got to the ground and had presumably run off in the direction of Solders Green. And he had probably left the knife behind. Neil was determined not to lose him. Once he got out at the end of the tunnel it would be too late to catch him. He could get out into the open and onto the streets where he would be home free. Neil knew that he had to throw caution to the wind.

Spinning like a whirling dervish, he took the last dozen steps three at a time. Then he ran off the shallow concrete platform and onto the tracks and sprinted off towards the other end of the tunnel when, out of the blue, the killer stepped out from the shadows just beyond the shallow platform and looked him in the eyes. He froze. Held flush against the killer's side was the knife, the razor-sharp hunting knife that Neil had confronted before at the top of the stairs: the knife that had claimed the life of Leah Irons and Rose Crowne.

He looked the killer in the eyes yet again, wondering what was going on in that head, behind the knitted mask. The killer had already made it clear that he was no longer prepared to flee. He had tried to kill Neil at the top of the stairs and now he was confronting him again - no longer running.

'If you're going to kill me, perhaps you'll let me see your face first,' said Neil.

'Why do you want to see my face?' rasped the killer in that irritatingly low, whispering voice.

'Because I want to see the face of my executioner. I want to see the face of the man who killed Leah Irons and Rose Crowne. And I want to understand how anyone can be so wounded and so damaged that they can do what you did to a fellow human being.'

'You might not like what you see.'

271

'I don't like it already. Seeing it in full focus won't make it any harder to bear.'

'You might not understand it.'

'I don't understand it now. I know you get some sexual thrill out of hurting women.'

The killer smiled and with his free hand reached up to the base of the mask. He slid it up and whipped it off in a flourish. Neil stared at the face in amazement. The features were masculine and the hair was short but even in this dim light he could make out the face that he had seen once before.

It was Meredith de Mur.

'I said you wouldn't understand it.'

'Why?' he asked, his voice straining in bewilderment.

'Like I told Beth Porter on the radio, because Rose Crowne had everything that I no longer hand. Beauty, friendship.'

You mean, you killed her because you were jealous of her beauty?'

'If you care to put it that way. I had beauty once. But it was taken away from me. I had breast cancer. I had a double mastectomy and then chemotherapy that made my hair fall out. I've been in remission several times, but it keeps recurring and I know that sooner or later the Grim Reaper's going to get me. He's already robbed me of my beauty. He robbed me of my looks! We're judged by our looks you know. After decades of emancipation, we're still judged by our looks. And every beautiful woman I saw on the street became a reproach to me. I had to dress in feminine clothes and wear padded bras just to be recognized as a woman. And even then some people thought I was a transvestite. I suppose you think that sounds funny.'

'I'm not laughing,' said Neil, quietly.

'No, but you want to.'

And you want to, as well, thought Neil. *Or rather, you wish you could find something in life to laugh at.*

'Was it just her beauty that you resented? Or was it the fact that she had the gift of life?'

'That was the one thing she didn't have. At least she had it, but she was in danger of losing it.'

'I don't understand,' Neil stuttered.

'She had cancer, too. That's where we met. In the cancer support group.'

'She was dying?'

'She had liver cancer. We don't know if she was dying. Medicine is an inexact science. I mean, hell, they got *my* prognosis all wrong. Maybe they got hers wrong too. At least they would have done if I hadn't given a helping hand to fate.'

'That's why she was so anxious to close the file on Martin Roebuck.'

'You got that one right. It was me who put the idea in her head.'

Neil took a step forward, not to try to disarm her but because he was now fascinated by what she was saying as the truth began to unravel.

'How did you do that?'

'I befriended her at a cancer support group. I became her best friend. That's because I was the longest surviving member. She was desperately afraid - having to look her own mortality in the face. She knew all about risk-taking from her job but looking at the prospect of a long, drawn-out painful death was something different. So I took charge. I befriended her and I gained gradual control of her life. It got to the point that she wouldn't do anything without asking me first. And she'd always do everything I said.'

'And you got her to set herself up as a decoy for Roebuck?'

Meredith smiled.

'I convinced her that this might be her last chance to bring him to justice. Although her prognosis was good, she realized that her police career would soon be over. I told her that I'd be there to protect her. We both had CS spray canisters, although of course I had no intention of using mine. The plan was that she'd let Roebuck see her and then follow her and I'd be on his tail. He'd be looking ahead at her so he wouldn't see me. She agreed that we couldn't tell her superiors in SO10 because they wouldn't sanction the operation - especially as Roebuck couldn't be charged with the Leah Irons murder now. All we could do was get him to try and make a move on her and then arrest him for that.'

'But you never really planned to catch him.'

'No. I was just setting her up. My real plan was to kill her. I half-thought that Roebuck might actually do the job for me.'

'But he didn't.'

'He was following her. But there was no reason to suppose that he had a knife with him. Remember, he didn't kill Leah Irons either. The only reason he was angry with her was because she'd set him up before - the same as I set her up, in fact, by befriending the intended target. That's probably why he was following her: a mixture of curiosity and anger.

'And you were following him.'

'I wasn't actually following Roebuck. I took a different path across the Heath. I knew that area like the back of my hand and I could find my way about there in the dark. I crept up on her and stabbed her. But then Roebuck turned up. I hadn't finished her off yet and I wanted to make sure, just in case she could identify me. I would have killed him too. There was always the danger that he might have realized I was a woman. But then you showed up. I saw the lights of a police car and ran. I ran back onto the Heath and ran back a safe distance to where I could cross the road. Then I walked over to the other side. That was when I saw the car speed off. I knew it had nothing to do with the case because it wasn't Roebuck and *I'd* killed Rose Crowne but it gave me the perfect opportunity to set up a false trail for your colleagues to follow. Who did the car belong to, by the way?'

'Some corrupt politician.'

Meredith smiled.

'I bet that really set the cat among the pigeons.'

'You could say that. How come the police never found out that you and Rose Crowne knew each other?'

'Because I told her not to tell them. She told me that if they knew she had cancer they'd relieve her of her duties in SO10. So I told her not to tell them anything about me. That way they'd never need to know where we met.'

'But wasn't there a danger that she'd tell her parents about you?'

'She didn't tell them about the cancer either. She was in denial. She thought that if she didn't tell other people about it she wouldn't be committed to it and then she wouldn't have to believe it.'

'But she might still have told them about you.'

'I told her not to. You forget that I had extraordinary influence over her because of the way she was leaning on me for support. And don't forget we weren't only friends, we were lovers. The reason she'd never had a boyfriend was because she was a lesbian. She'd never admitted it to herself, so she just stayed single. I told her that our relationship was too special to share with anyone else, even her parents. And she bought it. Part of the reason was, I suppose, because she was afraid of losing me. That's how I got her to become my lover. One night she came round in despair and that's when I made my move. I held her close to me and told her everything was going to be all right and started feeling her up. I guess, by then, my own sexual preference was changing. She pushed my hand away and looked shocked. She was in denial about her sexual preference too. I told her that if she didn't believe in giving our love a physical expression then she was insincere. I stormed out and stayed away. I let her sweat it out, not taking her calls and then two days later she called me and left a message on my machine saying she wanted me back on my terms. That's when I knew I had her. From then on, she did what I told her.'

'So you were the dominant one.'

'Oh, that's just a stupid stereotype. But I suppose that to an outsider that's how it would have seemed.'

'Didn't people see the two of you together?'

'They might have done, but that doesn't mean anything. London may not be swinging any more but that's only because the rest of the world has caught up. It's still a free city and anything goes here.'

'But I mean, didn't any of her friends see you together. Anyone of them might have told the police.'

'She didn't have any friends. And I destroyed the one-piece of evidence that might have linked us.'

'What was that?'

'Photographs. She had quite a few photographs. After I killed her I went round to her place in Camden Town and used my key to get in and retrieve them. Then I destroyed them. There was no trace left of our relationship apart from a few vague memories of a few neighbours she hardly knew- and we all know how unreliable neighbours are.'

'What about Leah Irons?'

'She was my first killing. And like Rose Crowne, I sodomized her - with the handle of the knife.'

'Did you know her too?'

'No. She was just someone I saw walking on the Heath. She was beautiful, too. I hated her. It was just after my operation, when I was on my first course of chemotherapy. My hair had all fallen out and I was feeling really self-conscious. I used to see her walking about on the Heath, without a care in the world. And I saw the way men looked at her. It was the way they used to look at me. One day I saw her and something snapped.'

'You mean it was spontaneous?'

'Oh no, I planned it out carefully. It's just that one day it was all too much for me - seeing the way men looked at her. I couldn't take it any more. Couldn't bear the thought of men looking at her like that after I'd been robbed of my looks. Something just snapped inside me and I decided to kill her.'

'How come no one was able to identify you? You did it in broad daylight.'

'My hair was even shorter then remember. And it was after the double mastectomy. A few people must have seen me in the area, but as far as they were concerned I was a man. And of course no one would suspect a woman of committing a murder with multiple stabbing in a public place, even though there have been other cases like that.'

'I can understand something snapping and you deciding to kill her. But you said you planned it carefully. That means you went away and thought about it.'

'Once I put my mind to something I usually go through with it. That's why I'm going to kill Beth too.'

'You're what?'

Meredith smiled.

'After I kill you. I'm going to kill Beth. I might even do-it in front of her son.'

On hearing these words, Neil knew that he had to act. It-was no longer his life at stake. She had had the chance to kill Beth once before, but his spur-of-the-moment decision to enter the house via the back had probably saved the day. Now he had to settle the issue once and for all. He charged-at Meredith.

She lunged at him with the knife in her right hand in an upward motion, but he stepped to his right and used the heel of his hand on her inside forearm to deflect the knife. Then he caught her wrist. He was about to lock his other arm around her head and spin her round when – with her free hand – he clawed at his face. While he was still stunned she brought her knee up between his legs, catching him in the groin.

They fell to the ground together in a huddle. He was in agony and she had landed almost on top of him. She clawed at his face again forcing him to release her wrist with his other hand but now the underhand position that was so efficient for stabbing a standing opponent became inefficient as her supine opponent offered a smaller target, covered as he was by her.

She pulled back the knife and lunged at his face with it again, but he caught her hand at the wrist and used his fingers to press on her thumb bending it in, forcing her to spread her fingers and drop the knife. If he had been thinking straight, he would have followed it up by catching the open fingers and twisting them round far enough to break the wrist. But he was still in agony from the kick to the groin and much of his training deserted him. Instead, he gave a mighty push to force her off him and they rolled over on the side and then continued with him ending up on top. Fighting with the ferocity of one who has lost touch with reality, she grabbed the knife again and lunged at him with an overhand blow. Again he blocked it with his left hand, but this time the blade caught his wrist and he let out a cry of pain.

He retracted his hand for a split-second and she lunged again, but he leapt off her and rolled aside. She dived on him for one final thrust but he caught the wrist of the hand with the knife, using both of his hands, and they rolled over again. They must have rolled three or four times before they came to a halt and there were cries of pain or terror from both of them.

Then they lay there unmoving for a few minutes.

When he finally regained enough strength to stand up, Neil saw Meredith lying on her back, bleeding from the stomach. Her eyes were open, but they were not blinking.

For a split-second the thought that came to mind was that Rose Crowne and Leah Irons had been avenged. But then he remembered that it was these thoughts that had led him to strike

277

Roebuck without just cause. It was these thoughts that dishonoured his father. And it was these thoughts that he had to drive out and banish from his mind. The dragon inside him wasn't the dragon of fear, or even of guilt - it was the dragon of hatred.

Only when he slays that dragon will he be free, he had told little Stevie.

That was really what he had learned from his father.

He turned from the dead figure of Meredith de Mur and staggered slowly, in tired, painful steps towards Solders Green. After four hundred yards he saw light at the end of the tunnel. A few more pain-ridden steps and he found himself standing at the mouth of the tunnel, just two hundred yards from the station.

When he stepped out of the tunnel, he saw the dawn breaking.

Chapter 20

'This inquest is now in session,' said the coroner.

It was Monday afternoon. The morning had been taken up with testimony from Nick Lloyd and the doctor who had performed the post-mortem on Rose Crowne. The testimony had been gory but delivered in that dry, unemotional style of a professional who was numb to the emotions that went with the gruesome details that he had described. The press benches were packed and a lot of people were wondering if any of the findings were going to leave a spillover into the Martin Roebuck incident. Strictly speaking, the verdict was a foregone conclusion. There was only one verdict that the coroner's jury could reach in a case like this and that was unlawful killing.

It was not like in the old days where there were verdicts like 'murder by persons known' or 'murder by persons unknown.' It was not for the jury to attribute blame to any one individual but merely to make a finding of fact in the abstract as to whether this was a case of unlawful homicide, an accident or a suicide. There was also the possibility of an open verdict – the legal equivalent of a 'don't know' in an opinion poll. But there was no chance of the verdict being anything other than unlawful killing. On the other hand, the coroner might ask for a narrative verdict and ask the jury to decide on various other related questions.

The question was, would the events concerning Martin Roebuck filter through into the evidence. The coroner had made it clear that he wanted no extraneous comments from any of the witnesses and that the subject of the inquest was the death-of Rose Crowne and *not* the injuring of Martin Roebuck, or the death of Meredith de Mur. And she had stuck rigidly to this line through both the factual testimony of Nick Lloyd and the macabre medical testimony of the pathologist.

Now, after a lunch that no one really enjoyed eating, it was Neil's turn to testify.

'Call Neil Douglas.'

The bailiff went out to summon him.

'Neil Douglas,' he said into the witness room.

There was a long drawn-out silence as people held their breath in the courtroom. It had been widely reported in the press that he had been injured. There had even been speculation that he wouldn't show up, although the summons meant that he must either appear in person or notify the inquest of a valid reason for not attending.

Finally, after what seemed like an eternity, Neil Douglas entered the courtroom.

'What is your religion?' asked the clerk.

'I'm an agnostic,' he replied. He had been tempted to say atheist. But the truth of the matter was that he wasn't sure- wasn't sure of anything.

'Take the card and read out the words.'

'I do solemnly, sincerely and truly declare and affirm that the evidence I give shall be the truth, the whole truth and nothing but the truth.'

The clerk took back the card.

'Your name is Neil Douglas?' asked the coroner.

Neil swallowed nervously.

'Yes.'

'Do you recall the events of the night of May the twenty-fourth of this year?'

There was a long drawn out silence. Neil looked at Beth, then at Nick. Then at Beth again. Nick tried to give him an encouraging look, as if to say: 'You just have to bite the bullet and say it the way I told you.' Nick had in fact told him not to mention what he did to Roebuck at all, but only to describe the state of the body. Nick had explained to him that he could refuse to answer specific questions if they were liable to incriminate him, while at the same time answering others.

Beth, on the other hand, was offering a coldly implacable face. She had shown him sympathy at the hospital. But now she looked at him coldly, so as to tell him that he was on his own, just as he had chosen to go off on his own in pursuit of the killer. He realized why she was doing it. He had shown her that, at the end of the day, he was a man who acted on his own judgement. So now, and when he had to live up to that boast, she could only stand by as a spectator and watch.

280

'Yes,' he said finally. 'That was the day I hit at an innocent man with my baton in cold blood.'

A gasp went through the courtroom and Nick Lloyd lowered his head into his hands as if to say 'Oh my God, he's going to do it!'

But Neil didn't look at their faces. He looked only at Beth. It was all too much for her. She got up abruptly and left the courtroom.

'Are you afraid they might prosecute you?' a journalist shouted to Neil as he left the courtroom forty minutes later.

Neil lowered his head and kept his eyes on the ground. He wasn't going to talk to the press. He had said what he had to say in the courtroom.

'What do you think about what your partner said?'

He didn't know what Nick's testimony had been or whether he had effectively contradicted it and landed Nick in trouble. At one time he would have cared. Now he didn't. He had told the truth. That was all that mattered.

'Do you think your testimony has ended your career?'

This was something that he had thought about. It almost certainly would end his career but he no longer cared about that either. He had become a policeman only to please his father but now he realized that pleasing his father and honouring his father were two different things. He could honour his father by being truthful but he could only fulfil his potential by being true to himself. He had always aspired to an academic career and now he would go away to some obscure university or college and pursue one. Or maybe he would work in the community and try to help people before their problems became unmanageable.

He pushed his way through the throng of journalists on the steps of the court building and found himself looking at Beth who was standing in front of him. She wasn't smiling but, in some way that he couldn't define, she looked happy.

'I was wrong about you,' she said, ignoring the cameras and microphones that were being thrust into Neil's face. 'I called you a gung ho pseudo-hero.' He noticed tears of regret forming in her eyes and felt similar tears in his own. 'But you know what? You *are* a hero.'

'Come on,' he said. 'There's something I still have to do.'

'I'll see if he can see you,' said the doctor.

They were in the waiting area, outside Martin Roebuck's private room. He was out of the coma and off the life-support system. The nursing staff had changed his saline drip bag and the doctors had checked the contents of the old one. They had found the sedative and realized how close he had come to death.

Now he was out of danger, in every sense of the word. He was slowly regaining his consciousness and the murderer who had wanted to silence him was dead. He had actually surprised the doctors by saying 'did they catch her?' Meredith de Mur had been right to fear him. He had known that it was a woman and could probably have set the police on the right track.

The doctor was walking towards them, a relaxed easy look on his face.

'He's ready to see you now, but he's still very weak. I think I'm going to have to limit it to a few minutes.'

'Thank you,' said Neil. He looked at Beth beseechingly. 'Well . . . wish me luck.'

Beth smiled encouragingly, holding his hand gently for a moment longer before releasing it. She watched him walk away slowly and disappear into the private room, closing the door behind him. She knew that what he was doing took courage - more courage in fact than confronting the killer or telling the truth at the inquest - but as with those other courageous actions, it was something that Neil had to do alone. She would always be close at hand to give him moral support. But just as he had faced the darkness alone, he would also have to face the light of day alone - even if he didn't like what he saw.

THE END

Afterword

If you liked this book, please go to Amazon and share your opinions with others by giving it a good review and clicking on the **LIKE** button. If you've got time, you can also give it some relevant *subject tags* or agree with other people's tags about the subject matter, to spread the word and get it out there.

Oh and also don't forget to tell all your friends how good it was and spread the word on Facebook, MySpace, Twitter etc. And if you're a member of Goodreads, Library Thing, Shelfari or any of those reader sites, don't forget to give it a good review there too.

Also, don't forget to check out my website: http://www.davidkesslerauthor.com. It contains not only the latest information about my books, but also my ranting and raving blog about the many subjects that I feel strongly about.

Finally if you haven't read it yet, don't forget to check out the first two Alex Sedaka thrillers as well as my many other titles, including those written under the names Adam Palmer, Dan Ryan, Nigel Farringdon and even Karen Dee!

www.ingramcontent.com/pod-product-compliance
Lightning Source LLC
Chambersburg PA
CBHW070854180626
46817CB00003B/774